MEDUSA'S MASTER
BY
CINDY DEES

AND

HIS WOMAN
IN COMMAND
BY
LINDSAY McKENNA

MEDUSA'S MASTER

BY
CINDY DEES

All the characters in this book have no existence outside the imagination of the author, and have no relation whatsoever to anyone bearing the same name or names. They are not even distantly inspired by any individual known or unknown to the author, and all the incidents are pure invention.

First published in Great Britain 2011
by Mills & Boon, an imprint of Harlequin (UK) Limited,
Eton House, 18-24 Paradise Road, Richmond, Surrey TW9 1SR

© Cynthia Dees 2009

ISBN: 978 0 263 88526 2

46-0511

Harlequin (UK) policy is to use papers that are natural, renewable and recyclable products and made from wood grown in sustainable forests. The logging and manufacturing processes conform to the legal environmental regulations of the country of origin.

Printed and bound in Spain
by Blackprint CPI, Barcelona

Cindy Dees started flying aeroplanes while sitting in her dad's lap at the age of three and got a pilot's license before she got a driver's license. At the age of fifteen, she dropped out of high school and left the horse farm where she grew up to attend the University of Michigan.

After earning a degree in Russian and East European Studies, she joined the US Air Force and became the youngest female pilot in its history. She flew supersonic jets, VIP airlift and the C-5 Galaxy, the world's largest airplane. She also worked part-time gathering intelligence. During her military career, she traveled to forty countries on five continents, was detained by the KGB and East German secret police, got shot at, flew in the first Gulf War, met her husband and amassed a lifetime's worth of war stories.

Her hobbies include professional Middle Eastern dancing, Japanese gardening and medieval re-enacting. She started writing on a one-dollar bet with her mother and was thrilled to win that bet with the publication of her first book in 2001. She loves to hear from readers and can be contacted at www.cindydees.com.

This book is dedicated to you. Yes, you. Without you and all of the other wonderful and loyal readers who have supported the Medusas over the past five years, this series would have died off long ago. But because of you, the snake ladies live on, we all get to keep playing in their awesome world. Thanks from the bottom of my heart. To all of the wonderful readers who have supported the Medusas over the past five years and kept them going strong through thick and thin.

Chapter 1

Katrina Kim stepped out into the cavernous H.O.T. Watch headquarters, gazing around in shock as much at the banks of computers and analysts as at the domed enormity of the cave enclosing it all in perpetual night. And she'd thought the mini-submarine ride to get to the inside of this hollowed-out volcano had been wild. This place was *incredible*.

"Ahh, there you are, Captain Kim." An attractive woman wearing khaki shorts and a dark polo shirt strode toward her, holding out her hand. "I'm Jennifer Blackfoot."

Katrina studied the offered hand impassively. A grab and twist at the base of the thumb would put the woman down on the ground. Or, there was the pressure point in the wrist, which would bring a grown man in a full battle rage to a screeching halt. Or there was always the tried-and-true bend-and-snap to break fingers and generally maim the sensitive instrument that was the human hand.

Gently, she clasped the woman's proffered hand. "Please.

Call me Kat." Standard protocol to ask civilians to use her first name. It put them at ease around Special Forces operatives like her.

Kat was one of the founding members of the Medusas, the first all-female Special Forces team the U.S. military had fielded a couple of years earlier. The Medusas had long since earned their battle stripes and were well respected within the Special Forces community. At the moment, the Medusas were in North Carolina on call, waiting for a crisis to blow up somewhere that required their particular brand of attention. In another month, all the Medusas were scheduled to stand down and go into a training cycle. In the meantime, she'd been sent to this classified facility in the Caribbean on a special assignment.

She didn't know anything about the mission. She'd been awakened by a phone call early this morning, telling her to be at the airfield in an hour in civilian clothes with warm-weather gear for immediate deployment. And here she was, none the wiser as to what would be expected of her, knowing only that it would be extremely high risk. Otherwise, they wouldn't have called her.

God, she loved this job.

Suppressing an actual smile of enjoyment at the low-level hum of adrenaline coursing through her veins, she glanced over at the civilian woman walking beside her and asked, "When will I receive my mission briefing?"

Her guide looked over, surprised. "General Wittenauer didn't fill you in?"

"No, ma'am."

The woman laughed. "Don't 'ma'am' me. I'm just a civilian. My friends call me Jennifer or Jenn."

Kat pursed her lips. She rarely stuck around anywhere long enough to make actual friends. "The way I hear it, you run this outfit."

Jennifer shrugged. "I run the civilian side of the house.

Commander Hathaway runs the military side. Frankly, being in charge around here mostly consists of sprinting like crazy to stay at the front of the stampede."

Kat nodded knowingly. Although they all tried to impose as much order as possible on their world, Special Ops was often a chaotic enterprise.

Jennifer ushered her through a thick, steel door and into a low, long corridor hewn out of rough rock. "You'll be working with Jeff Steiger. His handle's Maverick. He'll bring you up to speed on his little project."

A little project, huh? An odd choice of words for a Special Ops mission.

Jennifer pulled out a cell phone and made a call. "This is Raven. Where's Maverick?" A short pause. "Thanks."

Raven? A good handle for the woman. She had long, black hair that formed a shimmering, silken fall almost to her hips.

"Captain Steiger is in the gym."

"There's a gym down here?" Kat asked, surprised.

"We've got it all. Cafeteria, sleeping quarters, long-term food supplies…there's even a small infirmary."

Impressive. She followed Jennifer-Raven through a labyrinth of hallways to yet another anonymous door. If this place were ever invaded, she wished the intruders luck finding anything. Nothing was marked in this maze, and every hall, every door, looked exactly the same.

As they stepped into a well-outfitted gym, her companion announced, "Ladies' locker room is behind the weight machines. You'll probably find Maverick on the fighting mats pummeling some poor sod. I saw on the training schedule that he and his Ops team were going to be practicing unarmed combat this afternoon."

"Is he good?" Kat murmured.

"He's unofficial champ of the entire bunker. And we've got upwards of sixty operators attached to this outfit."

Interesting. It had been a long time since anyone had given

her a real challenge in unarmed combat. Oh, she faked having to struggle against most guys, but she usually held back. It was for the best that way.

Jennifer made her farewells, and Kat looked around. It smelled like every other gym in creation, of sweat and disinfectant, burnt rubber and iron. Weights clanked on the far side of a currently empty basketball court, and off to her right, a group of men made the distinctive shouted grunts of martial artists in training. Hidoshi-san, the man who'd adopted her and had been father, teacher and sensei to her from infancy, had called the shouts *kiais,* but each martial school had its own name for them.

She strolled across the hardwood basketball floor, observing a half-dozen pairs of men wrestling around on the mat, practicing ground-fighting techniques. It looked like a Brazilian jiujitsu variant they were doing, with some of the usual rules suspended to modify it for urban combat.

BJJ was a twentieth-century variant on a much older form of judo. Mentally she turned her nose up at it. Her training had been in the original, classical traditions from one of the great modern masters: judo—the way of grappling, karate-do—the way of the open hand, kendo—the way of the sword, iai-do—the way of the fast sword, even aikido—the way of harmony.

The men's movements looked jerky and forced as they moved through joint locking and choking exercises. However, in a real fight, it wasn't about beauty. It was all about putting the other guy down before he put you down.

She set down her gear bags and rifle case to watch. The men finished the sequence and climbed to their feet, breathing hard. They began to spar in a standing position, trading kicks and punches.

One of the men, a good-looking guy with blond-streaked hair and a surfer's tan, glanced over at her, then did a double take. His partner took the opportunity to clock him with a fast kick to the side of the head. Surfer guy went down like a ton of bricks.

She bit back a smile at his expense. That had to have hurt. He rolled onto his back and executed a nifty back-arch and flip that landed him on his feet. Showboating for her, no doubt. The move took stomach strength and looked good in the movies, but was impractical in most actual fights. Any half-decent ground fighter would never give you a chance to get back to your feet at all, let alone in so flashy a fashion.

She studied surfer guy as he swaggered over to her. Strong. Lean. Fit. Lacking in flexibility if she had to guess. And in subtlety, for that matter. The grinning leer in his gaze was beyond obvious. According to her Eastern upbringing, it bordered on insulting. In the West, it was a mild flirtation. She sighed. Yet again, her two worlds collided. She had to admit, though, he was cute. No, strike cute. He was hot.

"Hey, baby. Y'all new in town?" he drawled with a hint of New Orleans in his voice.

"You're not talking to me, are you?" she replied smoothly. "Because I don't recall giving you permission to call me that."

"Whatchya gonna do about it…baby?" Were it not for the utterly charming grin and devastating dimples that accompanied the comment, she'd have flattened him on the spot. As it was, she stepped forward politely and held out her hand.

"My name's Katrina Kim—"

He smiled triumphantly over his shoulder at the other men, who'd all stopped sparring to stare at her. Still grinning confidently, he took her hand.

In a flash, she spun and yanked, twisting the guy's entire arm and flipping him neatly over her hip. He slammed heavily to the floor. Before his bulk had hardly finished smacking the mat face-first, she pounced, kneeling on his neck with her knee and yanking his arm up and back uncomfortably behind him.

"—and don't call me baby," she finished coolly. Inside, she churned. She *hated* being forced into having to reveal a glimpse of her martial arts skills. Hidoshi had always considered it a grave failure of *Shin,* the Mind, to be forced into using violence. But sometimes a girl had to do what a girl had to do.

The other men gaped, equal parts stunned and appalled.

Without letting the man on the floor go, she asked them pleasantly, "Is one of you Captain Steiger? I was told I might find him here."

The guy beneath her lurched, and she gave a sharp jerk on his arm, effectively and completely subduing him. Grins were beginning to spread across the other men's faces.

One of the men answered gravely, "You're standing on him, ma'am."

A thoroughly unladylike curse shot through her head. Great. She'd just taken down and humiliated the man she was supposed to work for on this mission. Why was it the Medusas always seemed to get off to a rocky start with the men they worked with? She sighed. At least she and the good captain had established that she didn't like being called baby. It was probably handy to have gotten that out of the way, at any rate.

Lying facedown on the floor, Jeff Steiger tried wiggling something small—he started with his pinkie finger. Mistake. Pain shot down his arm and exploded in his shoulder. Man. So much for impressing the hot chick in the gym. She was a little thing, not particularly heavy kneeling on his neck, but damned if she didn't have him tied up practically in a pretzel.

Thankfully, she released his arm and let him up without him actually having to cry uncle. He climbed painfully to his feet, eyeing the young woman warily.

As if it wasn't bad enough that she'd taken him down, she

was also a drop-dead eyeful. Exotic, definitely part Asian.
Maybe Korean. Her features were refined. Delicate even. But
that grip on his hand had been pure steel, and the strength
behind it that had put him on the ground had been shocking.

He smiled at her ruefully. "How 'bout we start over? My
name's Jeff Steiger. But you can call me Maverick if you
like." Putting on his best Sunday church manners, he added,
"It's a pleasure to meet you, ma'am."

She nodded briefly.

"You said you were looking for me?"

She frowned, and even that was a delicate thing, her finely
drawn eyebrows arching together over an elegant nose. Her
eyes were a clear, sweet tea brown.

"General Wittenauer sent me to work with you."

Wittenauer? The Old Man himself? He was the commander-
in-chief of the entire Joint Special Operations Command. Jeff
had sent a request up channels for a Special Forces operator
who was unusually agile and had expertise in electronics. Why
in the hell had the general sent down this girl instead?

Jeff cursed under his breath. It could only mean one thing.
Wittenauer thought his theory on the robberies was a load of
bull. He hadn't even taken Jeff's report seriously enough to
send him a real operator, let alone the one he needed.

He realized the girl was staring at him expectantly. He
mumbled, "Uh, sorry. Did the general send me a message or
something?"

"No. Just me."

What the hell? "If you'll pardon my bluntness, who are you?"

She lifted an eyebrow at that. "Captain Katrina Kim. U.S.
Army. Joint Special Operations Command, Medusa Project.
Sniper, linguist, electronics and black ops specialist."

He stared. He didn't even know where to begin reacting
to that mouthful. Her? A sniper? *No way.* Black Ops? *Get out.*
Finally, he sputtered, "What the hell is the Medusa Project?
Never heard of it."

She pursed her mouth into a Kewpie-doll pout and said mildly, "You must not have a high enough security clearance to have heard of it."

"Are you dissing my security clearances?" Indignation started low in his gut. "I'll have you know the *name* of my security clearance is classified, lady."

Somehow, even with her face completely devoid of expression and her body utterly still, she managed to convey complete disdain for him and his clearance.

"What the hell kind of clearances do you have?" he challenged.

She shrugged. "I'm allowed to carry firearms in the presence of the president of the United States."

Jeez. He was familiar with such a clearance, and they didn't come much higher than that. "And have you ever been armed in the presence of the president?"

She answered evenly. "Several times. He awarded me my first combat medal."

Who in the hell was *this lady?*

"Perhaps we can go somewhere more…private…to talk?" she suggested.

He glanced over his shoulder at their avid audience. "My guys are okay. They're all operators, complete with fancy security clearances. They won't tell tales."

One of them piped up drolly. "But we're bloody well telling everyone in the bunker that an itty bitty thing in a skirt tossed your happy butt on the floor."

Jeff scowled. Damn. There went his reputation. To the itty bitty thing in a skirt in question, he said, "Let me clean up. And then we can go to my office and talk."

She was waiting for him when he emerged from the locker room five minutes later. He'd intended to take a long, hot shower and make her wait, but inexplicable curiosity, eagerness even, to learn more about her had turned his shower into a hasty affair lasting barely two minutes.

"May I take your bags for you?" he offered, startled at how bulky and heavy they looked now that he paid attention to them. She didn't seem fazed by them, though.

"No, thank you. The Medusas make a policy of hauling their own gear."

They stepped out into the hallway and he turned toward his temporary digs in an underground warehouse space that he'd appropriated a few weeks back.

"What exactly are the Medusas?" he asked as they walked.

"'Who are they?' is the appropriate question."

Not real chatty, this self-contained woman. When she didn't continue, he said, "Okay, then. Who are they?"

"Special Forces team. All-female."

"All—*what?*" Female? No. Freaking. Way. There was *no way* women could do the job he and his buddies did. None. Not possible.

She didn't bother to reply. Apparently, she figured he'd heard her correctly the first time.

She might not let him carry her bags for her, but he did open the door for her when they arrived at his office. She nodded her thanks as she stepped inside. The true black of underground shrouded the room, and she paused in the thin shaft of light spilling weakly into the space from behind them. He reached out and flipped the wall switch beside the door. Halogen lights flashed on overhead, illuminating the cavernous space.

His companion studied the elaborate mock-ups of walls, and partial rooms scattered all over the spacious room, looking like stored television show sets. He closed the door behind them. "Welcome to my laboratory."

"What are you researching?"

"The appropriate question is 'Who is the Ghost?'"

"Okay. Who is the Ghost?"

"Our mission. Yours and mine."

"Come again?"

He smiled at the incongruousness of such a quintessentially military phrase issuing from her quintessentially feminine mouth.

"The Ghost. We'll talk more about him later if it turns out you can actually help me. My desk is over here." He led her to a glass-enclosed space tucked in one corner of the storage area.

He led her inside and moved behind his desk to sit down. He actually felt safer with the bulky piece between them. She'd taken him by surprise with that throw of hers. Next time, though, he'd be ready for the move. "I'm afraid I need you to tell me a little more about yourself before I can bring you on board this project."

"Captain Steiger, I am an experienced and decorated Special Forces operative, and General Wittenauer thinks I'm the right person to help you with whatever you're doing. This isn't a job interview. It's a done deal; I have been assigned to this mission."

He studied her, frustrated. What the hell was he supposed to do with a girl? What on God's green Earth was the Old Man up to?

He must've muttered that last question aloud, because Captain Kim replied dryly, "I don't speak for General Wittenauer. Why don't you call him and ask?"

His eyes narrowed. He could smell a bluff at a hundred paces. Fine. He picked up the phone. "Hey, Carter, get me JSOC headquarters, will ya?" He'd show her a thing or two about playing poker with a good ol' boy.

The familiar voice of Mary Norton, General Wittenauer's personal secretary, came on the line. Jeff drawled, "Well, hey there, Ms. Mary. How's my favorite lady in the whole world doing today?"

The secretary's formal tone thawed considerably. "I'm fine, Captain Steiger. And what can I do for you?"

"Is the Old—is General Wittenauer available?"

The secretary laughed. "Yes. The Old Man's here. He's only in his early fifties, you know. One moment."

A brusque voice said, "Go."

"Sir. This is Captain Steiger down at H.O.T. Watch. I'm calling about the operative I asked for to help me catch the Ghost."

"Hasn't she arrived yet? Her plane must've gotten held up."

Her. He'd said *her.* The woman sitting before him wasn't a mistake. Sonofa—

"She's a hell of an operator, Jeff. Just the ticket for what you need."

"But I need a combat operator. Someone to catch a thief—"

The general cut him off. "And that's why I sent you Cobra. If anyone can get the job done, it's her. Trust me, Steiger. She's a pro."

Cobra? She had a field handle? Great. Some chick with delusions of being one of the boys.

"Let me know how your experiment goes, son. We've got some very high-powered folks breathing down the necks of their congressmen, and that sort of crap rolls downhill fast. It's landing on me deep and still steaming over here at the Pentagon."

"Yes, sir. I will, sir." He hung up the phone, staring at it stonily.

A melodic voice interrupted his dark musings. "We're going to catch a thief, are we? What's he stealing?"

"Art."

"What kind of art?"

"Paintings. The cheapest one so far has a price tag in the two million dollar range."

"Where are these paintings being stolen from?"

He looked up at her grimly. Wittenauer wanted him to give the girl a try? Then that's just what he'd do. "Come with me."

He led her out into the larger room and over to one of the full-room mock-ups. He stopped in the doorway of the two-story-high structure. He flipped a switch, and a labyrinth of red laser beams cut across the space. He pointed to a window on his left.

"Come in through that. Don't touch the floor. Cross the room to that painting over there." He pointed at a poster-size print of a buxom blonde in a skimpy, wet bikini, hanging on the far wall.

Kat commented dryly, "The little known follow-up portrait to the Mona Lisa? The Moaning Lay-me?"

He grinned reluctantly. "That Da Vinci dude was sure 'nuff a fellow of fine taste."

Kat eyed the mock-up assessingly. "What equipment may I use?"

"Whatever you want. I've got climbing cups, rope, grappling hooks, crampons, you name it." He gestured at a pile of gear on a table just outside the door.

"I'll need to change my clothes."

"Fine."

"Where?"

He jerked a thumb over his shoulder. "My office. I won't look."

She shrugged. "My lingerie covers more than that girl's bikini."

"Too bad," he quipped. A twinge in his shoulder from his earlier fall kept him from saying more. She might not catch him by surprise again, but he didn't relish a straight-up fight with her. After all, he had a rule against hitting girls. Yup, that was why he didn't want to tangle with her, he told himself firmly.

She emerged from his office in a one-piece gray bodysuit that made him about swallow his tongue. Whoa. She was *perfect*. She had curves in all the right places, was slender in all the right places. She was a tiny little thing. No more than five foot three. Though slim, definite muscles flexed beneath her sea-land suit.

The high-tech gray fabric was waterproof when submerged, but when dry, it breathed like cloth and allowed the wearer to sweat normally, unlike the neoprene suits divers traditionally wore.

While he struggled not to stare, she moved to the pile of equipment and confidently sorted through it, slinging climbing ropes over her shoulders and strapping on a climbing harness. She clipped carabiners and belaying devices on to her waist belt and quickly strapped a knife to her thigh. She certainly handled the gear like she knew what to do with it.

She asked, "Have you got three or four handheld, signaling mirrors?"

"Coming up." He went over to an equipment locker and pulled them out.

She held out her hand without even looking over at him. The mirrors disappeared into one of her waist pouches. She walked over to the "outside" of the window.

"Does noise matter?"

"Not for today's purposes."

"Time limit?"

"Not this time."

She leaped up onto the window ledge as lightly as her feline namesake and balanced there easily. He watched with interest as she threaded a spare radio antenna through the sighting hole in the middle of one of the mirrors. She broke off the end of the antenna and poked its now sharp end into the drywall above her head. A slight adjustment, and the mirror caught one of the laser signals and reflected it away from the space above the window. She repeated the process until she'd created a gap in the net of lasers. Clever.

She ran a stud finder across the wall above the window until it flashed green and beeped. Quickly, she reached up and hammered in a crampon. She slapped on a carabiner and ran the end of her nylon webbing rope through it. With surprising upper-body strength for a woman, she pulled herself up a couple of feet and tied off her harness.

She repeated the whole process until she'd reached the ceiling. The laser beams stopped about four feet shy of the ceiling. Bemused, he watched her pull out some sort of

climbing cleats that hadn't come from his pile of gear and buckle them to her feet and hands.

His jaw dropped as she struck the ceiling hard to sink her cleats into it, and commenced crawling, spiderlike, across the surface. How she clung upside down like that and didn't fall, he had no idea. He'd never seen anything like it. In three minutes or so, she'd reached the far wall. She planted a crampon, tied off a rope and shimmied down it quickly, using her mirrors to deflect the lasers.

"You want me to take the picture, or just draw a mustache and horns on it?" she asked casually, spinning gently in her harness next to the poster.

Damn. She didn't even sound out of breath!

"Whatever you do, don't defile Bambi. She's an icon around here."

"Do you need me to retrace my route, or have you seen enough?"

"That's enough." He tried to sound unaffected, but he'd never seen anything like what she'd just done. The strength it took to cling to a ceiling like that boggled his mind. She must have a crazy strength-to-weight ratio.

Well, why not? He'd predicted that the Ghost had a similar strength-to-weight ratio. It was the only way to explain some of the climbing the guy had to have done to successfully steal the paintings he had. Jeff just hadn't expected to encounter the same sort of strength in a woman.

Kat efficiently retrieved her climbing gear and lowered herself to the floor. She walked toward him, winding her climbing rope around her left arm as she came. "Any more hoops you want me to jump through before you believe who I am?" she asked, looking him dead in the eye.

Without ever taking his eyes off hers, he reached for the holster at his right hip lightning fast and quick drew his pistol, whipping it out to point it at her.

Chapter 2

Kat had a split second to react to the weapon. She had two choices: aggression or evasion. He was a Special Forces operator—the gun *would* be loaded and the safety off. She opted for both responses. She dodged low and across his body from the gun, and then launched herself upward. Like most shooters, he'd turned his gun shoulder forward slightly, which threw him slightly off balance. She slammed her body into him to accentuate his balance problem. A quick hook with her ankle, a karate thrust with the heel of her hand to his shoulder, and he spun to the ground, his gun arm trapped underneath him.

He made a credible grab for her in the jiujitsu style, but she ducked and slipped the grappling hold. This time she rolled him swiftly to his back and straddled his chest. She wanted to look him in the eye when she told him to cut out the martial arts crap. To that end, she maintained a simple thumb hold on him. It was enough to control him if he got any crazy ideas, but it wasn't as psychologically overwhelming as the armlock she'd put on him earlier.

He relaxed beneath her legs. She glared down at him and…and her thoughts derailed completely. Wow. Now those were *blue* eyes. A bright cobalt color lifted straight from the Caribbean Sea.

His mouth curved up into a disarming smile. "I can't believe it took pulling a gun to get you to show your true feelings for me, darlin'."

She leaned back on her heels, which put most of her weight on his stomach. His abdominal muscles contracted into a hard washboard beneath her rear end, supporting her body weight easily. *Yowza.* It was a struggle to maintain her usual even expression.

"Are you done pulling stupid stunts on me, Captain Steiger, or am I out of here?"

His grinned widened. "Depends on how you define stupid."

She arched an eyebrow and replied dryly, "Are you sure you want me to respond to that remark? I'm not sure your ego could take it."

"Ouch. No wonder they call you Cobra. The lady has fangs."

She shrugged. "I thought it was because I spit so well."

Startled laughter escaped him. "How 'bout I put down the cap gun and you let me up off the playground before the other kids start calling me a sissy? As a show of good faith, I'll go first."

She watched impassively as he laid the pistol down by her left knee and slowly lifted his hand away from it. She released his other thumb, her senses on high alert.

She leaned forward, preparatory to climbing off him, when he murmured, "Where are you going? I kinda like you like this."

It wasn't his words that froze her in place. It was the low

purr of his voice, sliding roughly over her skin, no longer boyish but suddenly all man. Or perhaps it was the explosion of…something…low in her belly in response to that black velvet tone of voice.

Her gaze lifted to his in shock. Blue met brown. And to his credit, he didn't smirk at her. In fact, he looked nearly as stunned as she did. They stared deeply at one another for an eternity. Instinctive recognition flared between them. If she didn't know better, she'd say they'd met before. Been passionate lovers in some previous place and time.

"Little Kitty Kat," he crooned.

Shock exploded in her. How did he know that was what Hidoshi called her in his rare affectionate moments? He couldn't possibly… It was just coincidence…but a superstitious chill shivered through her, nonetheless.

His big hands moved slowly—smart man—and came to rest on the tops of her thighs, by her hips. Through the thin fabric of her bodysuit, his palms scalded her.

"Don't go," he murmured, half order, half plea.

"What's happening?" she breathed.

"Don't you know?"

She shook her head, wide-eyed.

"Grandmère called it Cupid's Bolt."

She frowned. Sometimes she felt at a real disadvantage with American slang. Having spent her childhood abroad, she often missed pop-culture references. "I'm sorry—what?"

The last thing she expected entered his brilliant gaze. Unmistakable tenderness. He replied softly, "Cupid's Bolt. It's when you meet someone and it feels like you've been gobsmacked by a big ol' bolt of lighting. Grandmère says it doesn't happen to many folks. But to a lucky few…"

"What happens?" Kat prompted when he didn't continue.

He shrugged. "Game over. True love. Soul mates. Till death do us part."

She was so stunned her jaw actually sagged open.

"We've been struck by Cupid's Bolt, darlin'. It's inevitable. You and me. Get used to it."

"You're telling me we shared a look, and you've declared me your future...what?...sex kitten?"

He laughed. "That doesn't begin to cover it."

Panic threatened to creep into her voice. She managed to force it down, but it was a close call. "What then? Wife? Mother of your children? Soul mate? That's absurd. I'm not even in the market for a relationship, let alone that other stuff."

"Glad to hear it because you're plumb off the market, effective now. You're mine."

"Oh, puh-lease."

He grinned up at her. "I get dibs on telling you I told you so."

He was positively out of his mind. Sure, a tiny part of her twittered like some green girl at how romantic the whole notion was. And he certainly was easy on the eye. But soul mates? Happily ever after? So not in the cards for her.

Long ago she'd dedicated her life to a principle, *junjo-do*, the way of the pure heart. She hadn't dedicated part of her life to that way. She'd dedicated her entire self to the pursuit.

He shrugged philosophically, causing movement between her thighs that drew her attention sharply and completely. His voice was dead serious. "You wait and see. That was Cupid's Bolt, or my name's not Jefferson Delacroix Steiger."

Desperate to lighten the mood and distract him, she quipped, "Delacroix? Did your parents hate you?"

He grinned. Better. Although, man, that thousand-watt smile went right through her. She became aware of his thumbs rubbing absent circles on her legs, straying disturbingly near the sensitive flesh of her inner thighs. She was torn as to whether to ignore it or call attention to it by asking him to stop.

"Delacroix is my mother's maiden name. Our firstborn can

have your maiden name, if you like. Although with a name like Kim, I sure hope it's a girl. I'd hate to stick our son with Kim for a middle name."

"Our—" She was speechless. He was already naming their children? He was certifiable!

He continued blithely, "I suppose growing up with a name like that would help a boy develop character, though."

"Or a hell of a right hook," she added wryly.

Jeff nodded gravely. "If you teach him to fight, he'll have nothing to worry about on that score."

She couldn't help it. She laughed. This was the craziest conversation she'd ever had while sitting on someone's chest. "You're nuts."

She rocked onto the balls of her feet and stood up. She stepped aside lightly and held a hand down to him to help him up. He was tall enough—and she was short enough—that he didn't have to sit all the way up to grasp her hand. He gave a swift yank, and before she knew it, she was sprawled on her stomach across his big body, her face inches from him.

"See, I knew you'd fall for me sooner or later," he murmured.

Oh, my. He smelled good. "Let me up," she demanded.

"Gotta say please. It's important to teach our kids good manners, you know. And we have to set the example for them."

She contemplated fighting him for her freedom, but in this position, his strength would work to her disadvantage. Part of being a warrior of the way was knowing when to back down, too. She sighed. "Pretty please?"

"Pretty, am I?" His voice dropped to a whisper. "You're pretty, too. Beyond pretty. Perfect, in fact."

He thought she was perfect? A rush of warmth shot through her before she knew what had hit her. Then hard, cold reality set in. It didn't matter what he thought of her. They were coworkers. Colleagues. Professional acquaintances. Nothing more. And she had neither the time nor the inclination to allow a man into her life.

His hand, splayed intimately on her lower back, began moving in small, slow circles, expertly massaging away her tension. Her entire lower body turned to jelly right there on the spot. Oh, Lord, that felt good. Coworkers, darn it!

She stiffened reluctantly.

He sighed. "Okay, baby. We can go back to work. For now. But tonight, I'm taking you out for a romantic, candlelit dinner."

He turned her loose without warning. His magic touch was gone, and she felt…bereft.

What in the *hell* was he doing to her?

Jeff climbed cautiously to his feet, watching the woman who'd not once but twice dropped him with an ease that was breathtaking. This tiny little thing—she didn't even reach his chin, for crying out loud—had absolutely manhandled him. Of course, maybe he was just so damned distracted by her he wasn't thinking straight. But, Cupid's Bolt or not, he had a hard time believing that decades of finely honed fighting skills had deserted him at the sight of a pretty face.

Although, pretty didn't quite cover it. She was mesmerizing. He couldn't take his eyes off her. Everything about her was as he'd declared. Perfect. Her skin was flawless—all shades of ivory and cherry blossom pink. Her glossy, black hair was smoothed back into a ponytail with not a single hair daring to stray out of place. And her body—in that wet-dry suit, not a whole hell of a lot was left to the imagination, and every inch of it was exquisite.

To his consternation, she took the chair across from his desk in the gray suit and seemed in no great hurry to get out of it. Maybe she knew the effect it had on him and was using it to throw him off balance. It was working, whether she intended it or not.

He opened the file sitting in the middle of his desk. He didn't actually need it; he knew every fact in it by heart. But it gave him something to look at other than her hypnotic beauty. He cleared his throat. Work. Concentrate on work. "A string of robberies have taken place over the past several months in Barbados along a stretch of real estate known as the Golden Mile. Are you familiar with it?"

"No."

Her voice reminded him of wind chimes. Work, dammit. "It's a string of mega-mansion getaways for the super-rich, lining several beachfront miles. A who's who of the world's richest people own these places. And that leads to a healthy dose of one-upmanship in the homes and their decorations."

A faint smile flickered in her eyes, but her features otherwise remained impassive. So self-contained, she was. Made him wonder what was going on behind that still façade of hers.

"Recently, it has become the vogue to cram these winter hideaways with art. But not just any art. The most expensive art the collectors can find and flaunt."

She replied, "And now this collection has attracted the finest art thieves the world has to offer. Don't these places have pretty outrageous security? The owners can afford it."

Intelligent. She'd already made the next logical leap ahead of his narrative. He nodded. "Go on. Continue your line of thought."

"The U.S. government has been asked to help catch this guy. Which means the local police have failed. I'd guess some influential Americans have been robbed, and they're raising a stink with their congressmen golfing buddies. In a smashing display of not understanding the limitations under which various government agencies operate, said congressmen have had their aides call the FBI, who threw up their hands and declared it outside their jurisdiction. Compounding their blunder, the aides called the CIA and possibly even Interpol. Eventually, their complaints ended up in the Pentagon's lap, and the whole mess has rolled downhill and landed on your desk."

He leaned back in his chair, studying her intently. "That's so accurate it's frightening."

She shrugged. "I've been in the Spec Ops community a while. I've seen a few ops get hosed from above."

He grimaced and didn't bother to reply. They both knew precisely what she was talking about. The bane of the Special Forces world—bureaucratic intervention from desk jockeys thousands of miles from the field of battle.

She looked him square in the eye. "So why am I here? What do you need from me?"

The corner of his mouth quirked up. He answered dryly, "The possible answers to that question beggar the mind. Let's start by reviewing the robberies. I have a few theories about how our thief is pulling off the jobs, but I'd like to hear your thoughts before I share mine."

They put their heads together over all the information he'd painstakingly gathered: police reports, blueprints of homes, schematics of security systems. It took them several hours to sort through all the data. Kat didn't say much. She asked occasional questions, but mostly she just absorbed it all. He dumped a ton of information on her, yet several times near the end, she asked pointed questions about details he'd mentioned briefly, hours earlier. Yup, definitely some extra chocolate chips in this smart cookie.

Finally, she leaned back, staring at nothing in particular. He could all but hear her mind humming as she processed the briefing. He didn't disturb her. Besides, it gave him a chance to study Kat more closely.

She had small ears. Her fingernails were almond shaped, done in one of those pink-and-white manicures. Her skin was satin smooth, noticeably devoid of body hair. The veins in her hands and neck, faintly visible beneath the transparency of her skin were well-defined for a woman's. Runner's veins.

After the past few hours, he was rapidly coming to the conclusion that she was exactly who and what she said she was. He didn't know whether to be dismayed, appalled, or impressed to death that a woman had managed to breach the testosterone fortress of Special Ops.

"You hungry?" he blurted.

She blinked, called back from wherever her thoughts had taken her. "Umm, yes. I guess so."

"Let's go topside. I know a little place on the beach… under the palm trees, drippy candles…the best seafood you ever tasted."

Was that alarm flickering through her gaze? She was so damn hard to read.

She said quietly, "I didn't know we could go to the surface."

"Most of the staff is assigned two-week periods yearly to go topside and act like tourists visiting the island. A few staff members get to pose as people living here, and they can go topside anytime they want."

"Which are you?"

"I'm in the first week of a two-week 'vacation' to the island. I can go up anytime I like. Because you're only here temporarily, you can go up, too."

"Well, then, I guess we're having dinner at your little place on the beach."

Hot damn. And he hadn't even had to let her take him down to get her to agree.

Chapter 3

Jeff hadn't exaggerated the romantic atmosphere of this place. Kat couldn't help but relax and enjoy the ambience of the beachside restaurant. Their table sat under a private tent on the sand. White gauze curtains fluttered around them, and the sounds of silverware on china and clinking glass blended with the rolling crash and retreat of the ocean only a few dozen yards away.

She had to admit he looked…amazing. He wore a charcoal turtleneck, its sleeves pushed up to reveal muscular, tanned forearms. He didn't appear remotely dangerous, even though she knew him to be so. He was elegant. Urbane. Some chameleon.

Of course, he was probably thinking the same thing about her. The Medusas included girly clothes and makeup in their standard operating equipment. Sometimes their best disguise during a mission was to look as feminine and harmless as possible. Hey—sex worked. Get a target thinking about maneuvering you into the sack, and a pistol in your purse or a microphone down your bra was the last thing on his mind.

Tonight she wore a plum silk dress with a high hem and a low neck. Spaghetti straps held up the whisper-soft fabric.

"This spot is beautiful." She sighed appreciatively.

Jeff smiled. "I'm glad you approve. I thought it would be a good place for a beginning between us." He picked up his wineglass. "A toast."

Was he still hung up on that Cupid's Bolt thing? Alarmed, she picked up her crystal stem.

"Here's to a long and fruitful relationship between us," he murmured.

Somehow, she didn't think he was talking about catching the Ghost. She took a sip of the crisp Chardonnay he'd ordered for them and, setting down her glass, said, "Tell me about the stolen art."

"It's an interesting assortment. All the pieces are by masters. Various schools of art, though. A Holbein, a Turner, a Cézanne, a Brecht."

"How valuable?"

He shrugged. "It's hard to place a price tag on these high-end pieces unless you actually take them to auction and see what the collectors are willing to pay. But we're talking two to ten million apiece."

"Why haven't these thefts been all over the news?"

"Shockingly enough, these aren't particularly large thefts. Pieces worth a hundred million or more have been stolen. Those make the network news shows."

"I can't imagine any painting being worth that much," she confessed.

"It's all about covetousness. Having something famous and beautiful all to yourself. You get to look at it and nobody else." He reached out to where her left hand lay on the white linen tablecloth and twined his fingertips with hers. His voice went low and husky. "It's a lot like possessing a beautiful woman.

Except a painting transcends time. People the world over, for decades or centuries, have coveted that piece, and now it's yours."

She replied wryly, "Plus, there's the added advantage that a painting won't get PMS and act bitchy or divorce you and take all your money."

He chuckled and released her hand. "There is that."

Odd. She was faintly disappointed that he'd let go. The feel of his fingers had been nice. "Personally, I'm not crazy about the notion of being possessed by some man."

His smile ran as lazy as a river on a hot summer day. "Then the right man has never possessed you, darlin'. Don't get me wrong. It's not about owning another human being, body or soul. It's about cherishing her. Savoring her, doing anything for her. Making her feel like the most special woman in the world."

Wow. She'd never imagined any man might actually want to treat a woman like that, let alone imagined finding one for herself. Uncomfortable, she retorted lightly, "I dunno. Sounds almost creepy."

He gave her a reproachful look. "There's no need to be evasive with me. If the idea of being loved that deeply scares you, you can tell me. I'll still love you even if you have a human weakness or two under your superhero skin."

She had to catch her jaw to keep it from sagging. First, she was stunned that he'd read her that well. Nobody ever saw past the impassive mask she'd been trained from earliest childhood to show the world. Second, he'd pegged her as superhero material? Granted, she'd tossed him around and employed an old ninja climbing trick, but he'd put his finger on her most closely guarded secret within a few hours of meeting her. She couldn't count the number of times Hidoshi had told her through the years never, ever, to let anyone know what she was truly capable of. He'd warned over and over, "If you show them your skill, they will insist upon testing it."

He was so right. She'd gotten distracted by Jeff's sex appeal in the gym and let down her guard for an instant. A single, simple takedown of the man, and already he'd tested her reflexes twice more—once with a gun. She'd bet the men who'd seen her drop Jeff were just waiting for their chance to have a go at her, too.

As usual, Hidoshi's advice was spot on. Too bad he'd never given her any advice on how to react to a gorgeous lunatic who was convinced she was destined to be his.

The rhythmic crash of the ocean gradually soothed her inner turmoil. As she neared the end of her scallops in cream sauce, she asked, "What do the stolen paintings have in common?"

"None of them are particularly famous, but they're all excellently executed. Perhaps most notable is the fact that all of the pieces have been held by private collectors for most or all their existences."

Kat frowned. "And that's significant why?"

"Museums publish extensive catalogs and prints, and publicly display paintings. Which is to say, museum pieces are vastly more identifiable than privately held pieces."

"Ergo, the privately held piece can be stolen and hung on a new owner's wall with less chance of being recognized as a stolen work."

"Exactly. If a shady collector wanted to flaunt his trophies, he'd need to acquire little-known pieces."

"Is the thief stealing on behalf of a specific collector, or is he stealing pieces he can fence more easily because they're less well-known?"

Jeff smiled broadly. "Well done. That is, indeed, the sixty-four-thousand-dollar question. For a newcomer to the art world, you've put your finger on the heart of the matter astoundingly quickly."

"And you're not a newcomer to it?" she asked in surprise.

"My family has owned an art gallery in New Orleans for over a hundred years."

"Did you work in the business to have learned so much about the art world?"

He winced. "Not entirely. I—" He paused, embarrassed. "—majored in art history in college."

She stared. "How in the world did you end up—" Aware of other ears nearby, she finished circumspectly, "—in our line of work?"

"Easy. Art history majors don't get the hot chicks."

She laughed, startled. "You got into the biz to pick up women? And how's that working out for you?"

His gaze took on a heat that stole her breath away. "So far so good, if I had to make an initial assessment."

"Oh, really?" she asked lightly, butterflies flitting in her stomach. "What makes you think that?"

He tipped the wineglass in his hand slightly in her direction. "The lady's wearing a sexy dress for me. I'd say that's an excellent start."

She shrugged. "It's just what happened to be in my gear bag."

"You haul around sexy little numbers like that in your work gear?" he blurted.

She nodded casually, studying the remnants of her meal. No sense telling him she had several other dresses to choose from and this one *had* been the sexiest of the bunch. His ego was already big enough. She glanced up to find him staring at her in open consternation.

"What?" she demanded.

"What exactly do you ladies *do* in your line of work?"

"The same thing you do. Why?"

"Is that all you do?"

She laid her fork down very gently. "I don't like what you're implying."

"Neither do I," he replied grimly.

She leaned forward and spoke with quietly intensity. "I'll say this once and once only. The Medusas have never been asked to nor have they done anything remotely like what you're thinking in the execution of their job. Understood?"

"Loud and clear, darlin'. And may I say, I'm relieved to hear it. I'd hate to have to ask you to choose between me and your work."

"Excuse me?"

"Well, once we're officially together, I'm not going to be a fan of sharing you with anyone else, particularly some hostile target you've been ordered to romance."

"Jeff. We are not together. Not that I'd personally be comfortable romancing a hostile anyway, but that would be my decision to make—not yours. My job. My career. My decision."

He looked pained. "I never thought I'd end up with a career woman, especially a military one. I wasn't planning on facing these sorts of issues."

"Gee. I'm sorry to have fouled up your grand plan for a nineteenth-century marriage—or did you have something more fourteenth century in mind?"

He grinned. "I have to say, now that I've found you, I'm surprisingly okay with you having a career. Even the one you have."

She rolled her eyes. "Thanks so much for giving me permission to do my job."

His grin widened unrepentantly.

Now that he'd *found* her? He said that like he'd been *looking* for her. Those pesky butterflies were knocking around her stomach again. "For what it's worth, most of the men who've gotten involved with my teammates seem to have struggled initially to accept the danger we place ourselves in."

He frowned. "What sorts of ops do you run?"

Thankfully, the wind had picked up, pushing the waves more noisily onto the beach. With one eye trained on the nearest tents, she replied, "Exactly the same kind you do. Only exception: The missions are profiled to include less heavy lifting and fewer long-distance ingresses and egresses. We're the first to admit that we can't begin to match the strength and stamina of a male team. Our job is to work around that limitation."

He blinked, looking startled at the admission.

"For example, my sniper rig is modified to weigh less than a standard model. I sacrifice some range on my shots, but it's a trade-off. Pass out of exhaustion trying to hump in the weapon to a target, or work my way in for a closer shot and actually make the kill."

"So you're a short-range specialist, then?"

She nodded. "I don't do half bad with a long-range rig. But if I'm hauling my own gear to the kill zone, I usually go short. If I were as big and strong as some of my teammates, I might consider doing more long-range work, though."

"It's daunting to consider women stronger than you. I felt you take me down this afternoon. You're no wimp, honey."

"Nah, I'm the little, quick one on the team. Python and Sidewinder are a lot stronger than I am."

"How many of you are there?"

"Six, plus one prospect in training."

"Any plans to expand the team?"

"You'd have to take that up with General Wittenauer or the president. We'd like to expand the program, though. We've been talking about how to recruit and train more women and the sorts of skills sets we'd look for."

"Like what?"

She smiled. "Well, a big, strong sniper for one. More linguists with a broader range of languages. And—" she broke off. Jeff probably wasn't ready to hear the next idea they'd been tossing around.

"And what?" he prompted.

"Nothing."

His gaze narrowed. "And a few high-priced call girls with a penchant for guns, perchance?"

She jolted. How had he picked that thought out of her brain? She schooled her face to perfect stillness. "An interesting idea. What do you think of it?"

He frowned. "My knee-jerk reaction is to hate the idea of asking women, regardless of previous experience, to use their bodies to do my job."

"And your reaction after you give it some thought?"

He shrugged. "I can see the usefulness of a…skill set…like that. It could certainly open some avenues of intelligence collection that the Special Forces have not traditionally had access to."

"But it would be controversial."

He snorted. "As if the idea of women running around in the Special Forces killing people and blowing stuff up isn't?"

"Well, there is that."

They traded smiles.

He murmured, "I gotta confess, I'm having a little trouble wrapping my brain around the whole idea of women operatives. Had I not seen you do what you did today, I'd be highly skeptical."

"And now you're only moderately skeptical?"

"My shoulder still aches from where you twisted it, my thumb is sore from when you dropped me the second time, and my ego's definitely bruised. When pain's involved, I'm a quick learner."

Hidoshi used to say she would never become a great warrior because she spent all her time trying to avoid getting hit and not attacking. But she'd learned. She could take pain with the best of them now.

She commented. "Lots of male operators get cranky when they first find out about us. They forget we're all playing for the same team. That we uphold and defend the same Constitution and fight for the same values." She looked him squarely in the eye. "You're not going to make that mistake, are you?"

He sighed. "Honestly, I had about as Neanderthal a

reaction to the idea of female operators as the next guy." He looked up at her and grinned. "But then you planted me on my butt. Twice. I guess I'd have to say I'm convinced."

"I didn't really hurt you, did I? I was trying not to."

He grinned ruefully. "I'd hate to see you go at it when you really mean someone harm. Nah, I'm not hurt. Nothing that won't recover. Except maybe my ego. Sometime I want to go one-on-one with you on a mat…when I'm prepared for you to jump me."

She grinned impishly. "It won't help. I'll still win."

He laughed. "Oh, really? Care to place a small wager on that?"

Finally. A natural response to her that he might give to one of his male counterparts. She smiled. "Anytime, any place, big guy. Name your bet."

Chapter 4

When the check came, Kat reached for her purse.

"Don't even think about it," Jeff growled. "My mother would tan my hide if she caught me inviting a woman out and then not paying for the date."

Kat started. This hadn't been a date—had it? Sure, there'd been romantic candlelight and the ocean and the sexy guy, of course. But a date? She didn't do dates. She had no time for them.

Wary, she watched as he stood up and came around behind her chair to hold it for her. His fingertips trailed lightly along her bare shoulder, sending shivers shooting through her. Oh, God. He'd given her goose bumps. She silently prayed he wouldn't notice her reaction to his touch.

"Can I tempt you into a walk along the beach?"

She hesitated to accept the offer. Whatever was happening between them was moving far too fast, slipping out of her control. Caution and control—those had been her mantras her whole life, and they'd never let her down so far.

Jeff coaxed, "I'm pretty sure it's a felony to visit a tropical paradise and not walk on the beach by moonlight."

Caution, indeed. This guy was a runaway freight train! "Jeff—" she started.

He effectively cut off her protest by pulling her seat back and cupping her elbow lightly. Caution and control fluttered away on a warm breeze that smelled of salt air and mystery. One touch from this guy and so much for a lifetime of training. She mentally shook her head in disgust at herself since Hidoshi wasn't there to do it for her.

"Why so quiet all of a sudden?" Jeff asked as they headed toward the water.

She glanced over at him, surprised. "I'm always quiet."

"You don't say much, but I can hear you thinking most of the time."

Startled, she stopped in the act of bending down to kick off her high-heeled sandals. "How?"

"I suppose I'm reading body language. Your eyes are always moving, you're always assessing everything and everyone around you."

"Like you're not? All special operators do that as a matter of habit."

He shrugged. "It's more than a habit with you. It's like you're always waiting for the next attack. You don't always have to be on duty, you know."

She stopped. Turned to face him. The moonlight sculpted his features in pale relief. The man had definitely hit the jackpot in the genetic lottery of looks. "It's not about being on duty or off. This is who I am."

If it was possible for a marble statue to convey skepticism, he did so then, staring down at her for a long time in silence. Finally, he said, "You mean to tell me you have no feelings? No desires? No personal life? Just the job?"

Frustration roiled through her. Of course she had those things. But they were private. To be kept to oneself. Never on display for others to see. "I am not, at heart, American. I am Asian. Old school."

"What does that mean?"

"I was taught not to wear my emotions on my sleeve as you Americans do. I was taught to be…" She didn't know what word to use next. *Refined?* That would insult him by implying that Americans were coarse. *Restrained?* That sounded like she hog-tied her feelings and totally denied them. *Repressed?* Probably accurate, but not exactly something she liked owning up to.

"Kiss me," he ordered abruptly.

Rattled to her core, she sputtered, "I beg your pardon?"

"You heard me. I'm not convinced you actually have any emotions at all. Prove it."

"By kissing you?"

"By kissing me." He braced his feet in the sand, his expression implacable as he stared down at her.

"This is ridiculous. I'm not letting you double-dare me into kissing you like a couple of kids in the schoolyard."

"Ahh. So you're a coward, too," he commented blandly. "I wouldn't have guessed it. I pegged you for more courage than that."

Courage? He dared to question her courage? "Is this the part where I fling myself at you and kiss your lights out to prove how brave and emotional I am?" she retorted scornfully.

"It would help. I'm beginning to have serious doubts over whether or not a heart beats inside your chest or if there's only a robot ticking in there. Which is it?"

Hurt streaked through her. After all his talk of Cupid's Bolt and destiny, how could he say something like that? She whispered, mostly to herself, "Sometimes I ask myself the same question."

He stepped forward so quickly she had no time to evade him. Or maybe something deep inside her didn't want to evade him. Either way, his arms came around her gently, wrapping her in the warmth and shelter of his body. "Ahh, baby, I've looked into your soul. You're all woman in there. You just have to learn to let her out."

Easier said than done. A lifetime of teaching said to do otherwise.

Jeff murmured, "It's not hard. Watch. Like this."

And before she knew what was happening, he'd put his finger under her chin and lifted her mouth to meet his. Shock ripped through her, followed by a melting warmth that all but buckled her legs out from under her. It was an innocent enough kiss, just his lips, warm and firm and gentle on hers. No demands, no invasions, no assertion of macho dominance. And it was all the more seductive for the lack of aggression.

His hair was silky beneath her fingers—how in bloody hell did her hands get around his neck and into his hair? As quickly as the question exploded in her brain, the answer followed, a soft sigh of surrender deep in her soul. Who cared how they got there? The fact was her arms were twined around his neck, her breasts pressed intimately against his chest, his belt buckle jabbing her belly, his muscular thigh rubbing the junction of her thighs as his right arm drew her up more tightly against him.

Oh, my. He felt so…right.

His left hand slid under the weight of her hair at her neck, cupping her head as he sipped at her, kissing and nibbling until a foreign irritation built low in her gut, a driving need for more—more of his touch, more of his mouth and hands upon her, more skin on skin, more *everything*.

She raised up on tiptoe, her mouth opening beneath his, her kisses abruptly—and wholly independent of her will— eager and demanding. Something wild within her wanted more than a hint of this unleashed man. She wanted his passion, his body; heck, his soul.

Jeff broke off the kiss, thankfully panting as hard as she

was. It was with extreme reluctance that she let him go. Only the threat of seeming obsessive and clingy unwound her arms from around his neck. But damn if her palms didn't land on his chest, measuring the bulge of his pectorals. A whole lot of push-ups had gone into those.

"See, Kat? There's a passionate woman in there, waiting to get out." He spoke lightly, but she guessed at the effort that carefree tone took.

His arms fell away and she stumbled back in the deep sand, appalled. She'd just kissed her boss. With tongue. While squirming against him like a cat in heat.

She swore long and hard at herself in every language she knew.

They stood there an embarrassingly long time, both catching their breath and staring at one another in varying degrees of shock. He looked as shaken by what had just happened as she was. Her thoughts spun frantically. Was that a good sign or a bad sign? Had she been a terrible kisser? Was he having second thoughts about his Cupid's Bolt? What if—

She broke off her panicked train of thought sharply. These sorts of thoughts were exactly why she'd sworn off relationships entirely by the time she'd graduated from college. She just didn't need the insecurity and uncertainty of it all.

"I—"

"You—"

They spoke simultaneously, and she was quickest to murmur, "You first."

He huffed in what sounded like frustration. "I ought to apologize, but the only thing I can think of is to ask you to do that again with me. That was…amazing."

The tone in his voice on that last word was almost worshipful. Abject relief turned her innards to jelly. "Really?"

He opened his mouth to answer and she waved a sharp hand to cut him off. "Strike that. I'm not sixteen and don't

need the boy to tell the girl he liked kissing her. If you liked
it, you'll do it again sometime. If not, I'll live."

He swept her up in his arms before the words had hardly
escaped her lips. His mouth swooped down on hers this time
with all the aggression—and finesse—she'd expect of a
hunky Special Forces soldier who'd had his pick of women
for most of his adult life. His body, his mouth, his hands, his
essence, surrounded her, drew her in to him until she wasn't
sure where she ended and he began. It was much more than
a kiss. It was a blending of souls. She was staggered by the
sensations, both physical and emotional, that he evoked in her
so effortlessly.

When he finally lifted his head to smile down at her, she
could only stare up at him in shock.

He remarked matter-of-factly, "All right then. I believe
we've established that I like kissing you and plan to do it
again. Thoroughly and often."

Her toes curled into the cold sand, squishing it up between
her toes pleasurably. Thoroughly and often, huh? Her pulse
leaped at the thought.

He added ruefully, "I promised you a walk on the beach,
didn't I? And I never break a promise." He gestured at the
silver strip of sand stretching away from them. "Which do
you want? The ocean side or shore side?"

"Which side would your mother tell you to take?"

He grinned. "She'd tell me to walk on the ocean side
where the water's deepest and coldest and let you dribble your
tender little toes in the foam."

"Well, let's not disappoint your mother," she replied
lightly.

He laughed warmly. "Honey, when you give her grand-
kids, she'll think you walk on water."

Kids? Them? The mere thought knocked her completely
off balance. Jeff steered her along the water's edge, mindful
of her tender little toes. Which was ridiculous, of course.

The two of them regularly swam in water much colder than this as part of their training. They both had experienced depths of hypothermia most people never imagined, let alone suffered through. With her small body mass and low body fat, cold water training was particularly miserable for her.

"What are you thinking about?" he murmured. "You're frowning."

She started. She never showed facial expressions if she didn't want to, and at the moment she wasn't going out of her way to exhibit a frown, thank you very much. "I am not frowning," she disagreed.

He stopped and turned to face her. "Are too. I can feel you frowning without even having to look at you."

If she weren't consciously focusing on her expression at the moment, her brows definitely would have slammed together in a big frown. "What? Are you psychic?" she asked lightly.

"It's Cupid's Bolt. We've got a connection, darlin'. I'm tellin' ya. We were meant for one another."

"What's my mood now?"

He grinned. "You're annoyed that I read you like an open book, but it doesn't take being psychic to know that. You're also wildly attracted to me and confused as hell over what to do about it."

"That's a pretty good pickup line. I bet you get lots of girls with the whole 'destined for each other by Cupid's arrow' bit."

One second she was walking down a starlit beach, and the next he'd spun her around to stare up into the face of fury. Although dark shadows shrouded his features, she couldn't miss the genuine anger rolling off him.

"I've never spoken of that to any woman, let alone experienced it with one. It's a long and honored tradition in my family, and I would never use it as a cheap pickup line." His gaze narrowed even more. "Trust me. I don't need a line like that to get laid. I get all the girls I want without it."

After that kiss he'd planted on her, she didn't doubt it. But then a second reaction overcame her. She struggled for a moment to identify it, and then froze in shock. She was jealous. She staggered back from him, stunned that the idea of him sleeping around with women he casually picked up bothered her so much. Something was wrong with her. Her emotions were flying all over the place. She was *never* like this! Her hormones must be out of whack. Or maybe she hadn't gotten enough sleep recently.

Formally, she said, "I apologize if I offended you or your family's honor." She made a low bow of apology with her palms pressed together before her.

She straightened, and Jeff was peering at her quizzically.

"What?" she muttered. "That's how I was taught to apologize."

"Why the bow?"

"If you wanted to strike me, I was giving you an opening to do it."

"Why in hell would I want to do that?"

"To save face, of course."

Comprehension lit his face. "You really were raised in traditional Asian fashion, weren't you?"

"You have no idea."

His hand touched her upper arm and then slid down to her hand. He turned, tucking her hand in his elbow and commenced walking. "Tell me about it."

She never talked about it. Not the grueling hours of workouts, not the secret training methods that elevated her skills beyond what most mortals dreamed of, not the traditional code of honor, passed down for centuries from warrior to warrior. Nor did she talk about the slow death of the ancient way of life that had forced Hidoshi to pass his legacy on to an orphan girl he'd picked up out of a gutter.

Jeff murmured, "I'll tell you about my life if you'll tell me about yours."

To her shock, she heard her voice say, "I was born in Seoul, Korea. My grandfather was from Japan. He raised me on a small farm in the country."

Hidoshi hadn't been her blood relative as far as she knew, but he'd adopted her in an ancient, if not legally recognized, ceremony. More to the point, he'd pulled her off the streets where she'd been wandering as a toddler and had likely saved her life. And then there was everything else. Her education, her martial arts training, the affection and respect he quietly gave her. Somehow, calling him her grandfather wasn't nearly description enough of what he'd meant to her.

"You love him a great deal, don't you?" Jeff murmured.

How *did* he do that? If she didn't know better, she'd say the guy was, indeed, psychic, the way he picked her thoughts out of thin air. "He meant everything to me."

"Past tense. He passed away?"

She nodded.

"When?"

Under normal circumstances, she'd politely change the subject about now, or if someone waxed persistent, she'd tell them outright it was none of their business. But for some reason, she found herself completely lacking in her usual reluctance to talk to Jeff about Hidoshi.

"He died when I was seventeen."

"How did you end up in the States?"

To her knowledge, she'd never answered that question to a single living soul. Only a few anonymous clerks in the American consulate in Seoul knew once and had hopefully forgotten long ago. Jeff stopped walking and turned to face her as if he knew this was something very private and personal to her. He could really stop doing that.

She ventured to look up at him and was startled at the depth of compassion glowing in his gaze. It wrapped around her, offering comfort and quiet understanding. In her own sudden flash of insight, she realized he'd lost someone very close to him, as well. He knew the pain, the loss and bewilderment of her entire world evaporating in an instant. And maybe that was why she answered his question.

"When I was going through his personal effects, I found something."

Jeff waited patiently, merely patting her hand a little in encouragement.

"My birth certificate. I'd never seen it before. I didn't know—" She hadn't even known her mother's name until then. It had never occurred to her that Hidoshi might have tracked the woman down in the opium dens of Seoul's slums and found a nameless orphan's identity for her. His quiet, unswerving love, even in death, had moved her to her first and only tears after he'd died.

Kat glanced up and realized she'd just been standing there, remembering, and Jeff was still patting her hand.

She continued, startled by the catch in her voice. "I didn't know my father was American. I took my birth certificate and went to the American consulate in Seoul. They researched it and found out he was a serviceman stationed in Korea at the time I was born and was known to keep a Korean mistress. They decided my birth certificate was legitimate and issued me a U.S. passport. All of a sudden, I was an American citizen."

"Have you ever met him?"

"I doubt he knows I exist." A spurt of shame took her by surprise. She'd thought she'd gotten over that long ago. She shrugged. "But it's okay. I had everything I needed growing up. I had no need to drop into some foreigner's life and ruin it."

"You're a remarkable woman. Any man would be proud to call you his daughter."

Suspicious heat filled her eyes. She said lightly, "I have to give your mother credit. She certainly taught you good manners."

He grabbed her roughly by the shoulders. "I didn't say that

to be polite, dammit. I mean it. You're smart and beautiful and athletic as hell. You've got it all."

That's what they all said. Hearing the same old line from Jeff disappointed her. She sighed, then replied emotionlessly. "You're doing what everyone does—judging me purely based on what you can see. You don't know me at all."

"Ahh, but that's where you're wrong. We're alike, you and I. We're soldiers. We live by a code of honor most other people scoff at, but we don't care. We can and do kill without regret. It's part of keeping our country safe, so we do it. We take our work seriously and have both made sacrifices, particularly in our personal lives, to do this job we love."

She blinked up at him as he fell silent. She supposed they did know a lot about each other after all, just by the nature of the profession they shared. It took a certain type of person to do what they did.

"Sorry," he muttered. "I don't usually climb on that soapbox. And besides, you know that chorus already." He turned and they continued down the beach in silence.

They'd walked for maybe another ten minutes when Kat noticed lights nestled in the midst of a verdant forest carpeting the mountain that rose steeply on their right. "What's that up there?"

"The Gray estate."

"It looks white to me."

Jeff chuckled. "The mansion is white. But the owners are Carson and Lucy Gray. They own about half of this island."

"Seriously?"

"Yeah. He comes from a shipping family. Owns a big fleet of container ships. He donated the caves to us, in fact. His wife is American. A geologist of some kind. Supervised the construction of the H.O.T. Watch facilities. They have three or four kids now. Nice family. I see them on the beach sometimes."

"How long has the H.O.T. Watch complex been operating?" Kat asked curiously.

"Construction started about five years ago. It's been up and running for about a year."

She nodded. "That would explain why I haven't heard of it before now."

He grinned over at her. "You have your secret Medusa Project, and I have mine."

She smiled back. "Touché."

Without warning, her purse erupted into sound, her cell phone emitting the custom ring that indicated the office was calling. Simultaneously, Jeff reached for his buzzing cell phone.

She flipped open her phone. "Go ahead." No need to identify herself. Anyone who had this number knew who she was.

"Jennifer Blackfoot here. Sorry to interrupt your evening, but we need you and Maverick back here. There's been another robbery."

Chapter 5

Jeff thought fast. They needed to get back to the Bat Cave right away. It would take them a good hour to hike from here to a road, get a taxi to the south beach, and board the minisub for the long ride back to the H.O.T. Watch complex. Or they could use the emergency entrance, which was quite a bit closer.

He looked over at Kat's filmy silk dress and asked regretfully, "Is there any chance you can run in that outfit?"

She glanced down in surprise. "Sure. I could do a marathon in this if I had to. Although I'd tear my feet up. I haven't conditioned them for long distances barefoot."

"How 'bout a couple miles on a sandy beach?"

She shrugged. "No problem."

"Let's go, then." He took off running and Kat followed suit. "You set the pace," he told her.

"How big a crisis is this?" she asked, breathing deeply but easily.

"Don't kill yourself, but we need to get there with dispatch."

"Six-minute mile okay, or do you need faster? I can do one four-thirty mile in a pinch. Although on sand…maybe five minutes would be my best time."

He stared in shock.

She loped along beside him as easily and lightly as a gazelle. "I run marathons in my spare time."

He just shook his head. "You're one of a kind."

"Actually not. One of the women on our team is a triathlete. Now *she's* tough to keep up with."

Jeez. They were all superhuman. Scary.

They settled into a hard but steady run down the beach. He tried not to notice how her silk dress fluttered back against her body, outlining it in glorious, flowing detail. She was as graceful in motion as she looked standing still. He immensely enjoyed the pounding surf, the cool night air rushing in and out of his lungs, the wet sand giving gently beneath his feet and the unison he and Kat fell into, side by side, step for step with one another.

After a good two miles at the killer pace, Kat glanced over at him. "How much farther?" she asked.

"Why? You winded?"

She chuckled. "Not at all. Just curious. Actually, I'm just getting warmed up."

He was more than "just warming up," but he could certainly hold this pace for a good long while. "We're almost there. Emergency entrance to the H.O.T. Watch. Highly classified. I'll have to kill you if you tell anyone about it."

She nodded, smiling, and kept running. At least she had the grace to be working hard enough beside him to avoid chatty conversation. But damn, she was in good shape. He'd never met another female who could keep up with him in a full-out run like this.

They rounded a point, and Pirate's Cove arced away before them. The low, ramshackle shape of Pirate Pete's Delivery Service came into view. The courier business was a cover for the H.O.T. Watch's more visible operations on the island, like airplanes and helicopters coming and going and deliveries and departures of large, unmarked crates.

"Over there." He directed her to Pirate Pete's and they stopped under the porch's shadowed overhang. As he dug keys out of his pocket, he commented, "This is the part where you breathe hard after that run and make me feel macho."

"Oh. Sorry." She commenced panting loudly.

He inserted a specially coded magnetic key in the lock and glanced up at her, grinning. "Take it easy on that heavy breathing or the guys on the other end of the surveillance cameras are gonna wonder what we're up to out here."

She glanced around sharply. "I didn't see any cameras—"

"They wouldn't be hidden if you could see them. But trust me. They're here."

The sound of voices erupted behind them and he spun to face this new threat. A group of a half-dozen tourists had staggered onto the beach. The three young couples looked drunk off their asses. Their raucous laughter drowned out the ocean behind them.

"Hey!" one of them called out. "There's some locals. Watch how frien'ly they arrre…" he slurred, weaving purposefully in their direction.

Jeff cursed under his breath. The last thing they needed was to get tangled up with a bunch of drunk kids. He needed an instant distraction. Something that would drive off the intruders—or give him an excuse to drive them off.

He turned to Kat and swept her up in his arms. She went tense, prepared to do him bodily harm.

"Roll with me on this and don't kill me," he muttered. And then he leaned down to plaster his mouth against hers.

She gasped as their lips touched…but then, so did he.

If he'd thought Cupid's Bolt had slammed into him like a brick before, this time it bowled him over like a rushing freight train. She was exactly *right* for him. Perfect. A sense of destiny washed over him. This was the woman he was meant for. He sucked in another surprised breath, and then inhaled her. She tasted like berries, tart and fresh and sweet all at once, and suddenly he was starving.

Her body hummed, as tense as a bow against his, and then all at once she gave way, melting into him, pressing into him as if a wave of need shoved her against him whether she willed it or no. Her hands clutched his shoulders for balance, and his arms tightened around her convulsively.

She sucked hard at his lower lip, pulling him down to her, seeking his tongue and finding it with hers. Her hands crept up to the back of his head while his crept down to her buttocks. They both used their not inconsiderable strength to draw closer to one another. *Good* didn't even begin to describe how she felt against him. Delicious, succulent, opulent images raced through his brain, and none were adequate to describe her or the cravings she evoked in him.

He backed her up against the wall and she wriggled in his arms, straining toward him as hard as he strained toward her, wild in her need. He drank in her desire, as greedy for her as she was for him. Avidly, he absorbed her essence, learning the delicate but iron-strong feel of her, savoring the faint floral scent that seemed to hang around her, touching her satin hair and the softer satin of her skin.

"Hoo, baby! Look'ee at 'em goin' at it! You go, guy!"

Jeff lurched as he abruptly remembered the drunks behind them. He tore his mouth away from hers to glare over his shoulder. "Can't you see we're busy? Go find your own dark corner to neck in. This one's occupied."

"Well, daa-amn, I guess so, dude. Youze two's throwin' sparks all the way to Miami. Git out the fire extinguisher, Roscoe!" one of the drunks caterwauled back.

He continued to glare at them steadily, letting overt threat infuse his body language. In his experience, it took strong signals and a few extra seconds for drunks to perceive peril.

He held his pose, a promise of violence glinting dangerously in his gaze.

Finally, sluggishly, the group registered the menace he posed. One of the girls grabbed a guy by the arm. "C'mon," she whined. "I wanna swim in the ocean."

Another girl piped up. "I wanna skinny-dip. First guy there gets to take off my bra."

With a whoop, the young men took off running, tripping and stumbling in the sand, the girls trailing behind. Their laughter faded into the roar of the waves. Jeff watched until they disappeared around the point, and then he turned back to Kat.

"Now, where were we?" he murmured.

"What's happening?" Kat whispered. "What is this between us?"

"This, my dear, is grandmama's bolt. Hits ya kinda hard, doesn't it?"

"Like lightning," she grumbled.

He laughed quietly. "Nothing to do for it but to sit back and enjoy the ride." He pushed a lock of sable hair out of her eyes. "Who'd have guessed you'd be the one? Never in a million years did I expect you."

She tensed in his arms. "What's wrong with me?"

"Not a blessed thing. You're perfect." He leaned down to show her how perfect she was, this time kissing her gently, letting his lips slide across hers, letting their tongues play lightly, sipping sweetly at each other. The pounding lust of a minute ago was less hurried now, still driving spikes of need deep into his gut, but with quiet assurance that time to explore this thing between them was near at hand.

"I've never…" She hesitated.

He prompted, murmuring against her lips, "Never what?"

"Never…felt like this before. What are you doing to me?"

"This is commonly referred to as kissing. Or necking, or canoodling, if you want to be old-fashioned. It's when a boy

and a girl mash mouths together and swap spit while fanta-
sizing about doing much messier and more intimate things
with each other."

She laughed, a breathy wisp of humor that shot straight to
his groin. "Thanks. I got that part. How is it that of all the
guys I've ever kissed, you make me feel like this? I mean, like
you said, a kiss is just mashing mouths and trading saliva."

He jerked back far enough to look down at her. "How
many guys are we talking about, here?"

She blinked up at him, startled. A slow smile spread across
her face. "Enough to know you're the best kisser I've ever
gone out with."

"Honey, I'm the last kisser you're ever going out with."

Skepticism shone in her gaze, but he ignored it. "So, you like
kissing me? I like kissing you, too. You taste like blueberries."

"Blueberries?"

He nodded, dropping light kisses across her neck to her
cheek and back to her mouth. "You never know when you bite
into a blueberry if it's going to be sweet or sour, but it tastes
uniquely like blueberry either way. When I touch you, I don't
know if you're going to toss me on my butt or kiss me till my
hair catches fire, but I know I'm gonna love it either way."

That garnered several owl blinks out of her. "You like me
tossing you?"

"Actually, it hurts. A lot. But I love the fact that the woman
I'm going to marry can plant me on my butt now and then.
Not that you'll ever need to. I'm going to spoil you so bad
you'll never need to lift a finger."

"M-marry?"

As he closed the inches between them for another lingering kiss, he murmured, "Mmm-hmm. It's fate, darlin'.
Cupid's Bolt always strikes true…."

And then all thought of bolts went right out of his head as
Kat kissed him back. They might just have enjoyed a gourmet

meal, but darned if she didn't make him hungrier than a bear in the spring. He wanted more of her. A lot more.

Both of them were breathing hard when Kat slid right, holding his hands, to draw him away from the porch.

"Ow!"

His senses went on to instant alert. Who or what had hurt her? "What's wrong?" he replied quickly.

"I banged into something sharp…" She turned in his embrace to examine the wall. "It's this knob."

Knob—oh, Christ. The H.O.T. Watch intercom. The summons to the bunker. They'd been standing out here trading lungs, and the folks downstairs were waiting for them.

A horrifying thought popped into his head. Had they been pressing on the intercom button all this time? Transmitting their steamy kiss to an audience below? He closed his eyes in despair. "Did you just bang into the button now, or have you been leaning on it?" he asked reluctantly.

"I just hit it."

Thank God. He didn't need Kat taking endless ribbing from his guys. They wouldn't bug him too much because he'd take them out on the practice floor and break them in half. Although, now that he thought about it, Kat might do the very same thing to them.

"Ready to face the lions in their den?" he sighed.

A pause. "Oh, yeah—work."

He swung open the concealed panel beside the front door to reveal a palm telemetry reader. He laid his hand on the pliable gel surface, which squished up between his fingers slightly. A click in the door lock indicated he'd been recognized. He turned the knob and stepped inside.

"Thanks," he commented to the dark interior of the store, or more precisely, to whatever duty controller downstairs at the other end of the security cameras had let them in. "This way," he said, leading Kat quickly toward the storeroom behind the counter.

A loud voice erupted without warning from the large birdcage in the corner. "*Baawk!* Pirate Pete is a dirty old bird. Repeats everything that he's heard. Especially the bits about asses and tits—"

Jeff called out sharply, "Shut up, Pete!" To Kat, he muttered, "Sorry. That's Pirate Pete. He's a parrot. With a filthy mouth, I might add."

"Shut up, Pete!" the bird squawked.

Kat giggled.

The sound was incongruous coming from her. Particularly since at the moment, her knees were deeply bent, her hands held shoulder high before her, and everything about her announced her readiness to kill something right here, right now. Apparently, when Pete had opened his big beak, she'd used those lightning-fast reflexes of hers to drop into a defensive stance.

She straightened to her full height, relaxing from the battle alert Pete's outburst had thrown her into. Jeff commented, "In case I haven't mentioned it yet, your reflexes are freaking unbelievable."

She shrugged as he opened the storeroom door, using a keypad and a retinal scanner this time.

"In here." He led the way into a cluttered storeroom littered with packing boxes, rolls of tape, and garbage bags full of packing peanuts. And dust. Lots of dust.

Using the tiny penlight on his key ring, he found his way over to what looked like a circuit breaker box in the corner. "If you'll close the door…" he instructed over his shoulder.

Throwing him a perplexed look, she did as he asked.

He pushed on one of the circuit breakers, which was actually an elevator switch, and the room lurched. Kat grabbed at the nearest shelf in surprise to steady herself.

He grinned. "The entire room is an elevator. Cool, huh?"

She grinned back. "Very cool."

They rode downward for nearly a minute, the silence between them so thick with the memory of the steamy kisses they'd just shared that he could hardly breathe. *Work, buddy. Focus on work.*

The storeroom/elevator lurched gently to a stop. "You can open the door now," he said.

She did so, and one of the familiar stone tunnels of H.O.T. Watch headquarters stretched away from them. He followed her out of the elevator, unabashedly enjoying the view of her pert little derriere.

She asked curiously, "How do people navigate around here? All the halls and doors look the same."

"They're supposed to. When you get assigned to work down here, the first job you're given is to memorize a map of the place. If any intruder were ever to get in, he'd have a hell of a time finding his way around."

She nodded. "That's what I figured."

Man, she was quick on the uptake. He'd bet she was hell on wheels when it came to gathering intelligence from live targets. She'd talk circles around ordinary mortals. But then, all she probably had to do was flash those big brown eyes of hers and her targets would sing like Pavarotti.

"This way." He headed right.

"Is this really a hollowed-out volcano?" she asked as they strode down the hall.

He matched her businesslike tone. If she had the discipline to set aside for the moment what they'd just done together, he could, too. "Yup, this is an extinct volcano. Problem with most natural caves is too much water. And with all the electronics we needed to put in this facility, we had to find a dry cave system. Volcanic remnants are often dry cave networks."

"Aren't they occasionally very hot, lava-filled places, too?" she asked.

He grinned down at her. Their gazes met and instant sparks leaped between them. Hah. So she hadn't entirely put their kiss from her mind. His ego was unaccountably gratified. Belatedly, he answered, "We've been assured this volcano is extinct. But just in case, we have seismic sensors all over the island to monitor Mount Timbalo."

She threw him a skeptical look, but then he stopped in front of another anonymous door, opening it for her. She brushed past him, and yet again, their gazes snapped to one another. Oh, yeah. She was as aware of him as he was of her. Her mouth twitched for the barest instant into a smile, and then she was back to being all business. He followed her into the Ops Center.

The sheer size of the main control room never failed to daunt him a little. Kat, in front of him, hesitated before striding toward the cluster of people at a console in the middle of the room. They were staring up at one of the Jumbotrons in the far wall.

He glanced up. Monet's study for his painting, *The Poppies near Argenteuil*, shone down at him. Jeff winced. The Ghost was moving up in the world. That had to be a twenty million dollar painting if it was worth a cent. No doubt the pressure to catch the thief was going to ratchet up commensurately. Sighing, he walked over to his boss.

Navy Commander Brady Hathaway glanced up at him. "You know the painting?"

Jeff nodded. "Where was it?"

"The Valliard estate."

Another one of the fabulous estates of the Golden Mile. The Valliard place was not the largest among them, but was touted as one of the most opulent. "Did the Ghost take any other paintings?"

"Just the one," Hathaway replied. "There are other valuable pieces in the house. Why only this one?"

Jeff shrugged. "He may have a specific buyer for this piece, or he may prefer to travel light."

Kat added, "The thief may also want to limit his risk and only take time to steal a single piece."

Jeff nodded. "Could be." To Hathaway, he said, "When did the theft happen?"

"Sometime in the past twenty-four hours. A caretaker

reported it stolen about an hour ago. Said he walked through the main house yesterday afternoon and everything was intact. But when he went through tonight, the painting was cut out of its frame."

Jeff cursed under his breath. That was an enormous window of opportunity for the thief. He kept hoping for a theft where the Ghost would have to work fast. It would tell them a lot more about the thief's M.O. But to date, all the thefts had been of unoccupied estates. The winter season didn't start for a few more months, bringing the residents of the Golden Mile to its tropical shores. Of course, at the rate he was going, the Ghost would have picked the island clean long before then.

Kat asked him, "What's the common link between all the paintings?"

He'd been over that a thousand times from every conceivable angle. "They've got no common thread except that they're excellent, if little-known, pieces by masters."

"Any chance I can make a phone call to a colleague about this?" Kat asked.

Jennifer Blackfoot glanced over at Hathaway. The two exchanged a nod and Jennifer said, "There's a phone right here. Any help would be appreciated."

Jeff listened with interest to Kat's one-sided conversation.

"Viper, it's Cobra. Sorry to call you so late. Did I wake you up? Morning sickness at night? That sucks. Hey, I have a problem. We're trying to find a link between a half-dozen paintings that have been stolen recently. Can you get a minute or two on the super array to run them and see if there's some obscure link between them? Great. I'll send you an e-mail with the information in the next few minutes. You rock."

Kat hung up the phone and looked up at him. "Do you have a detailed inventory of the paintings?"

"I'll have to add the Monet to it, but that'll only take a minute. Were you talking about the supercomputer array at the Pentagon, by any chance?"

Kat nodded.

"Your friend will have to wait for weeks to get time on that puppy. It's booked up solid."

Kat grinned. "Not for her. Besides the fact that the Medusas can usually get time on the basis of operational necessity, Viper knows a bunch of the computer techs who work on the array. A couple of them owe her favors."

Jeff nodded. Ahh. The ubiquitous favor owed. Special Forces types had a tendency to collect long lists of people who owed them one. When it was your job to save the world and help people out of impossible binds, gratitude frequently followed suit—along with offers to repay the favor.

He sat down at a computer terminal. It was an easy matter to look up an online catalog listing Monet's works and cut and paste information about the newest theft into his existing list of stolen works. He glanced over at Kat. "Where do I send this file?"

She rattled off an e-mail address, and he hit the send button. He highly doubted this Viper person and her supercomputer would have any success, but he was grateful for any help he could get.

"Incoming call for Captain Steiger," Carter Beigneaux announced from the next row of consoles over. "It's General Wittenauer. I'll patch it to your station."

Great. No doubt the Old Man was calling to breathe fire down his shorts to get cracking on catching the Ghost. Sympathetic glances came his way from the people standing nearby. Wittenauer was a great guy until he didn't get exactly what he wanted. And then, watch out.

The phone in front of Jeff buzzed and he picked it up. "Good evening, sir."

"Evening. You hear about the latest theft?"

"Yes, sir. I'm in the Ops Center right now looking at a picture of the stolen piece."

"Any idea who did it or how?"

"I assume it was the Ghost, but that has not been confirmed."

"Time to take your theories operational, Maverick. Now that you've got Cobra to help, I want the two of you to take direct action to stop this guy. I'm catching all kinds of heat over this."

Jeff grimaced. He knew the feeling.

The general continued. "I want you two to go to Barbados. Catch this guy, dammit."

"This is a police matter, sir—"

"You and Cobra are smarter than the average bear. Use your heads. Be creative. Come up with a way to bag this guy that the police haven't thought of. And do it fast."

Gee. No pressure there. Jeff stared at the receiver as the line went dead. He glanced up at Kat. Her face betrayed not a hint of expression, but he knew without question that she was as surprised at he was to get this order to go operational. How he knew that, he had no idea. Maybe a few of grandmère's psychic genes had come down to him, after all.

He commented to the gang in general, "Looks like our research project just turned into a mission. Who's the lucky dog who gets to control it from this end?"

Jennifer Blackfoot spoke up. "I'll take it. Knowing you, Maverick, you're going to piss off the local authorities and need my special touch to keep your carcass out of hot water— or, in your case, more like boiling oil." She glanced over at Kat. "If he ticks you off, you have my permission to kick his butt."

Kat nodded with an outward serenity he doubted she was actually feeling while everyone else grinned widely. But then Kat startled him by asking Jennifer, "Which one of us is in charge?"

He started. He'd assumed he'd lead the mission since it had been his baby first. But now that she mentioned it, maybe that wasn't such a straightforward assumption. He and Kat were both captains by rank. Both experienced field operators. Both capable of leading a combat team. Hathaway and Jennifer exchanged another one of those wordless looks of colleagues who've worked together for a long time and know how the other one thinks.

Hathaway looked over at Kat. "You okay with Maverick spearheading this thing?"

She shrugged. "Sure. No problem."

Jordan Yokum, one of his guys in the gym earlier, snickered. "If you pick it by who can kick whose keester, the chick ought to be running the show."

Jeff surged to his feet and had Jordy by the throat all in one move. "You wanna talk about her, you do it with respect, buster. She's a hell of fighter, and she can rip your head off in a New York second. If you call her a chick again, I'm gonna order her to do it. She's Captain Kim to you, or you can call her ma'am. Got it?"

The vignette froze in time as everyone went perfectly still around him. Theirs was a notoriously polite community because their capacity to cause violent harm to one another was so great. A confrontation like this was rare and dangerous.

Kat spoke quietly from behind him. "Thanks for the knight in shining armor bit, Jeff. But it's okay. I'll take care of what your guys call me."

He realized in shock that the fury coursing through him was completely out of proportion to the provocation. Why in hell was he already so possessive of her? He'd known her for approximately eight hours. Yeah, they'd kissed, but he'd kissed plenty of women he'd just met and never roared to their defense like this. She was right. He had no business designating himself the official defender of her honor. Especially when she could, indeed, kick her own asses.

He turned Jordy's neck loose and took a step back.

The other man mumbled, "Hey, man. I'm sorry. I didn't mean to piss you off."

Jeff shook his head. "No, I overreacted. My fault."

Hathaway said grimly, "My office, Jeff. Now."

Crap. He was gonna get a serious butt-chewing, and he deserved it, too. Even Jordy threw him a sympathetic look as he turned to follow his boss.

Kat said behind him, "If someone will show me to Captain Steiger's office, I'll pack my gear. I gather General Wittenauer wants the two of us to leave right away for Barbados. Who around here can arrange for our transportation?"

Gratitude flooded through him. Her comment, made plenty loud enough for Hathaway to hear, was a clear statement of support, an unequivocal announcement that she still wanted to work with him, despite his Neanderthal outburst of a moment before. It would go a long way toward making the upcoming conversation with his boss easier. She didn't have to do it. But she had. Publicly.

Son of a gun.

Maybe the lady liked him for more than just his magnificent kissing, after all.

Chapter 6

Kat was surprised when the guy who'd called her a chick in the Ops Center poked his head into Jeff's warehouse/office a little while later.

"Captain Kim? Captain Steiger will meet you at the boat dock in fifteen minutes. I'm supposed to take you down there."

She rose easily out of the cross-legged pose she'd been sitting in, meditating in a futile effort to relax and re-center herself. If she were being brutally honest, she'd been trying to erase the memory of Jeff's kisses and her reaction to them. And frankly…it was not happening.

In less than a day, one man had undone twenty-five years' worth of intensive training and self-discipline instilled by one of the great martial arts masters of his time. She didn't know whether to be intrigued as hell or scared to death of Jeff Steiger. Either way, she was horribly discombobulated and out of balance.

If she couldn't actually be calm, at least she could fake it. She spoke smoothly to the nervous man before her. "You can call me Cobra if you like."

He smiled gratefully, acknowledging the offer of her field handle as the gesture of forgiveness it was. "I didn't mean anything by that comment, you know. Maverick can whup all our butts. And the way you took him down today, I figure you can whup all of ours, too."

No doubt she could. But she wasn't about to comment on it. "All's forgotten," she murmured. She picked up her gear bag and rifle case. "Lead on…" She left the sentence hanging.

He obligingly filled in with his field handle. "Chain. Short for Chainsaw."

She quirked an eyebrow. "Hmm. An evocative handle."

"In BUDS, my trainers accused me of having the subtlety of a chainsaw. The name stuck."

"Well, at least it didn't have anything to do with your massacre weapon of choice."

He grinned. "Can I take one of those bags for you?"

"No, thanks. I've got them. I didn't know this place had a boat dock."

"It's left over from a smuggling operation that ran out of these caves briefly a few years back. It's at the other end of the facility, though. Bit of a hike. Sure you don't want me to get one of those?"

"I've carried these bags to hell and back. I'll be all right."

"Maverick said you're a Special Forces type. Did you do the dreaded eighty-mile march, too?"

She rolled her eyes in recollection of the Special Forces training rite of passage. "Ugh. Did you have to remind me of that?" Normally, she wouldn't be even remotely this talkative with a stranger, but the guy was trying so hard to make up to her that she felt obliged to throw him the bone.

"Yup, that was a bitch—" He broke off abruptly and started to stammer an apology.

She replied gently, "Unlike Maverick, I'm not going to bite your head off for using the B-word in front of me. I've been known to use it myself, and I'm sure I qualify to have it applied to me now and then. Captain Steiger seems to have a rather old-fashioned view of how women should be treated. But we Medusas aren't tense about such things, particularly around our colleagues."

From her, that was quite a speech. But the guy seemed sincerely sorry and also seemed badly in need of a little reassurance that he and she were square.

Chain glanced over at her curiously. "Is there really a whole team of you women operators?"

"Yes."

"I gotta say, I'd like to see you all in action sometime."

"Who knows? Maybe you will. We haven't done much training in this part of the world. We may head down this way someday."

"That'd be cool. As long as I didn't have to spar with you. You moved like lightning in that gym."

She suppressed a smile. She'd actually jumped Jeff pretty casually in the gym. Her move-now-or-die speed was quite a bit faster than that. They walked the rest of the way to the dock in silence. Chainsaw seemed satisfied that peace was restored between them, and indeed, in her mind, it was.

The Medusas had learned to have thick hides when it came to initial skepticism from their male counterparts. They'd also learned long ago to let their actions speak for them and not to rise to verbal baiting. The only thing perplexing to her about the whole "chick" incident was why Jeff had reacted so violently.

They arrived at the dock, and a burst of heat flooded her at the sight of Jeff waiting beside a sleek powerboat. Lord, he was good-looking. Head-turning handsome. Her hands itched with the memory of that muscular chest and washboard waist sliding beneath her palms. Conversing casually with the boat's driver, he oozed confidence. Charisma. Ease with command.

When he saw her coming, he climbed aboard the vessel and reached out to take her bags from her. Their gazes met, and his gleamed hotly with inappropriate thoughts…no doubt the same inappropriate thoughts streaking through her head. She looked away hastily.

She started to climb aboard and wasn't surprised when he held a hand out to help her. Normally, she'd ignore such offers. After all, her balance was superb. But she took Jeff's proffered hand anyway. Of course, it had nothing to do with her ongoing craving to touch him, to feel his energy flowing through her, yin to yang, chi to chi.

His fingers were warm and strong and steady and sent a rush of something feminine fluttering through her. And then an awful thought struck her. He was her *boss* now. First order of business was to quit touching him. Regret stabbed her. And kissing—definitely no more kissing. Darn it.

"Buckle in," Jeff murmured. "This baby can fly."

The driver nodded over his shoulder at both of them and the vessel leaped forward, skimming across the black, glassy surface of the Caribbean, circling around Timbalo Island in mere minutes and pulling up at a wooden pier. She followed Jeff to shore, where a helicopter waited for them. With the ease of long experience with the birds, she stepped under the rotors and passed her bags to Jeff inside the sleek Eurocopter EC 155 with its distinctive built-in tail rotor.

She climbed inside and wasn't surprised when Jeff took the seat directly across from her. The helicopter lifted off and she asked him, "How long to Barbados?"

"An hour and change at top speed."

She nodded. Paused. Nope, she couldn't resist. "Mind if I ask you a question?"

He flashed her those killer dimples of his. "Anything, darlin'. My life is an open book to you."

"Why'd you get so mad at Chainsaw for calling me a chick? Believe me, I've been called a lot worse and I'm still in one piece."

His eyes went a turbulent shade of sapphire. "Commander Hathaway asked me the same thing."

"What'd you tell him?"

"I told him I expect my men to act like gentlemen and didn't appreciate Chain calling you that. I mentioned the need for my guys to accept the reality of female Special Forces operatives, too, I think."

"In other words, you didn't tell him the truth. Did he buy your answer?"

Jeff's dimples flashed. "Not for a second. But he didn't press me on it."

"Why *did* you jump him?"

He gave her a reproachful look. "Do you really have to ask? Even Commander Hathaway knows the answer to that one without having to hear me say it."

An urge to gulp nearly overcame her. While it was flattering in the extreme to have a guy this charming and handsome and sexy laying claim to her like this, she wasn't at all sure how it was going to impact their mission.

"What's wrong?" he murmured.

Her frown deepened. She wasn't even sure she could put it into words. "What have you done to me?"

The corner of his mouth tipped up. "I kissed you. And given how flummoxed you seem, I'd say I made quite an impression on you."

"You don't have to look so satisfied with yourself." She grumbled.

His smile broadened, but he wisely made no reply.

"You don't understand—" she started.

"Then explain it to me. What's got your feathers so ruffled?"

She exhaled hard. "I'm…a warrior." She paused, searching for words.

"So am I. And your point?"

She glanced up, relieved to see he wasn't laughing at her. In fact, he seemed to be concentrating intently on her. Which was perhaps more unnerving. "My life is devoted to a principle. To discipline. To duty. To…honor."

He nodded encouragingly, apparently still waiting for the big reveal.

"That's it," she huffed. "That's the problem. I don't have time for…other pursuits."

"Why ever not? My life is about honor and discipline and duty, but I still have time for a personal life."

"I don't see you with a wife and two kids and a minivan."

He shrugged. "I hadn't met you yet."

"But don't you see? I'm not about having two kids and a minivan!"

He stretched his legs out until his ankles tangled with hers. "That is going to present us with some logistical issues, isn't it? I understand your desire for a career. Hell, I'm not ready to hang up the old rifle yet. I guess we can wait until we're both done with the Special Forces to start a family."

Exasperation shot through her. "Will you quit talking like I've already agreed to marry you? I'm not even sure I want to date you!"

"But you want to kiss me again, don't you?"

An urge to scream bubbled up in her throat. Damn if he wasn't exactly right. She took a deep breath, held it for a count of ten and then released it very slowly. Familiar calm flowed over her, washing away the foreign emotions cluttering her thoughts.

She would face this problem head on. Calmly. Rationally. Honestly. "Yes, I do want to kiss you again. I want to do a lot more than that with you."

He sucked in a sharp breath as she continued. "I also know it is not the right thing to do and it would interfere with the mission. Therefore, I shall set my desires aside and focus on the task at hand."

"Just like that?" He sounded surprised.

"Just like what?"

"You can turn off your feelings like a light switch? No random imaginings of getting naked with me? No speculation on what making love with me would be like? No trouble keeping your gaze from going places it shouldn't? You can just decide to set all that aside, and it's done?"

She blinked, startled. She hadn't really considered if the actual execution of her plan would be hard or not. She'd only gotten as far as it being the right thing to do.

He leaned forward abruptly, startling her. He popped her lap belt and dragged her across the space between them and onto his lap. She should've broken his wrist, but somehow she ended up sprawled across his thighs, his mouth slanting down toward hers, his hands plunging into her hair, and she let him.

Somehow she ended up arching toward him, her body taut with need. Somehow her mouth ended up plastered against his, her hands moving frantically across his chest, her entire being vibrating with uncontrollable need. Somehow the buttons of his shirt opened beneath her fingers, her palms flattened against his hot flesh. A moan escaped her throat and she all but crawled inside him. She turned in his arms until she faced him, straddling his hips with her thighs. How her own shirt fell open, she had no idea. But when his hands closed upon her throbbing breasts, she didn't think twice about pressing more deeply into his hands, about writhing on the hard bulge between her legs, about making a good-faith effort to extract his tonsils with her tongue.

Jeff murmured laughingly, "Honey, my hat's off to you if you can turn this off on command. There's not a chance I can do it."

Whether it was a sigh or a sob that escaped her lips, she

wasn't sure. But she knew she wanted him worse than she'd ever wanted anything in her life. Beneath his clever hands she danced, responding to every touch, every caress, every stroke and pluck upon her aching body. How her pants got unzipped, she had no idea, but she couldn't fail to notice when his fingers invaded her most private space, driving her half out of her mind. Pleasure completely overtook rational thought, spinning her up and out of herself, to a place of heat and light and tingling sensation that took her breath away.

And Jeff was there, all around her, between her thighs, against her breasts, kissing her neck, breathing her in. And it felt…so…good.

Eventually thought stopped altogether, and she flung herself into the drowning glory of the moment.

"Honey, you're killing me," he muttered.

She pulled back to stare at him. "I'm not hurting you, am I?"

He responded with a pained laugh. "I thought you were the one who was supposed to be able to turn off this thing between us. Don't count on me to be all noble and stop it. I'm not that strong."

What was "this thing" between them, anyway? She struggled to form intelligent thought, but the current of her lust was incredibly powerful and sweeping her wildly forward toward oblivion.

"What have you done to me?" she managed to whisper.

"Bluntly put, I believe I've turned you on. And Lord knows, you've done the same to me. Ain't it grand?"

She laughed ruefully and pressed her forehead against his. Grand didn't even scratch the surface of it. "We've got to stop, you know."

"Yeah. I know. Here I go, setting you off my lap, buttoning up our shirts and thinking serious, mission-related thoughts." He didn't move a muscle as he uttered those words, other than to run his fingers through her hair, smoothing strands of it lightly across her breasts.

How had her hair gotten out of its usual French braid?

"Okay, your turn to do something," he muttered.

"Right. I'm climbing off you. Going back to my own seat. Meditating until my mind is clear." Her fingers traced the line of his jaw, the outline of his ears, the shape of his mouth.

"We're formulating our plan of attack for Barbados now," he mumbled. "First order of business…take you to our hotel room and get you naked…"

She nodded soberly but couldn't keep the twinkle out of her eyes. "And then we talk to the police and come up with a brilliant plan to trap the Ghost while lying in bed together watching the sun rise."

He laughed. "I love the way you think."

Gradually, sanity was beginning to return to her. She sighed. "And then the Ghost gets away, we fail at our mission, and we let down General Wittenauer and American citizens who are counting on us."

The laughter in his eyes dimmed. "There is that."

She looked deep into his cobalt-blue eyes. "What are we going to do?"

He sighed. "I suppose we're going to try it your way for a while."

His big hands spanned most of her waist as he gently lifted her off his lap and placed her back in her own seat. Abruptly abashed at her earlier boldness, she fixed her clothes and re-braided her hair. She ventured a gaze over at Jeff, and he was studying her inscrutably. Had he really succeeded at shutting down his lust? What was the world coming to when a fun-loving good ols' boy had more discipline than a highly trained martial arts master?

He murmured, "Working with you is going to be a royal pain in the ass, you know."

"Why?" she blurted.

"Because we've got to set this thing between us aside for now. And I'm going to spend every waking minute wanting to put my hands on you again and hear you make those sounds again and taste you again…"

She gulped. Oh. Yeah, that.

Okay. So deciding not to have any feelings for him and not to react to him hadn't worked out so well. Time for Plan B. They might not be able to control what they thought or felt, but at least they could control what they did. And they both obviously lost all self-discipline once they touched each other. From here on out they were simply going to have to observe a strictly hands-off policy. No kissing, no handholding, no casual brushes against each other. Yup, it was going to suck rocks. But what other choice did they have?

Chapter 7

They pulled up in front of police headquarters in their rental car a little before midnight. She observed while Jeff did the talking. He was very smooth and managed to extract a few details about the latest theft, but the police held their cards close to the chest.

Kat and Jeff wandered toward the exit, and when no one was paying attention, ducked down a side hall that brought them to the evidence locker. Jeff flashed her a Special Forces hand signal to fall back. One eyebrow raised, she did so, fading into the shadows well down the hallway.

And then his tactic became clear. He bellied up to the check-in window and plied his considerable Southern charm on a female evidence officer, who in short order was hanging over the gate and flirting right back at him. Kat had to give him credit. The woman was putty in his hands in a matter of minutes.

Almost as fast as she'd succumbed to him, dammit.

Kat barely registered the additional details he coaxed out of the woman. If that woman leaned much farther forward, she was going to fall out of her uniform. Jeff must be getting an eyeful of the woman's ample cleavage. Only one painting taken last night from the Valliard place.

Oh, and now the chick was fondling her top button, toying with the idea of "accidentally" slipping it free. Hussy. The Monet was, indeed, stolen sometime in the past twenty-four hours.

If that woman licked her lips one more time, Kat was going to lick them for her—with her knuckles. The police strongly suspected the Ghost based on the complete lack of evidence left behind.

Jeff pocketed the slip of paper with the woman's phone number on it and turned to sashay down the hall. Kat fell in behind him, closing on his six like a dutiful wingman.

Not that she felt the least bit dutiful at the moment, however. Equal parts fury and humiliation swirled in her afterburners, making for an explosive mix. Had she fawned all over him like that? Had he flashed her a smile and a suggestive look or two over dinner and then watched her fall into his arms on cue? He was insufferable to behave like that! And she was a fool to have fallen for him like some gullible groupie.

Except that his desire for her had been real. She might not know much about men, but she was dead certain he hadn't been faking in the helicopter. *Desire* being the operative word, however. For all his big talk about her being his soul mate, so far he'd only actually displayed a large dose of healthy male lust for her. And he'd turned on the charm for another woman fast enough.

Hah. And he said he never used sex to help with his work. She might have hassled him about it, but she had no desire to further probe the little green monsters bouncing around in her stomach.

One thing she knew for sure. She was a mess. How Jeff

Steiger had managed to throw her this totally off balance this
fast, she had no idea. But she didn't like it. When they got to
their hotel, she was having a nice long meditation and getting
him thoroughly out of her system—regardless of her failure
to do so in the helicopter.

As for the job at hand, there wasn't much to mull over
about the theft. There was no sign of forced entry. An excellent security system had inexplicably been circumvented.
The caretaker had worked there for thirty-five years and had
an airtight alibi for last night, not to mention a sterling reputation on the island. It was the Ghost, through and through.

On their way out of the police station, they ran into the detective in charge of the art theft investigation. The guy seemed
none too pleased that they were still hanging around.

Jeff asked the detective, named Elgin D'Abeau, "Would
you mind if we went out and had a look at the Valliard place
in the morning?"

All guise of friendliness evaporated. "Sorry, mon. Dis is
a police mattuh. Stay out of it, and tell your people to stay
away, too."

Kat assumed that by "your people," the detective meant the
American government. Yikes. Lack of police cooperation would
spell big trouble for their op. Time for a quick intervention.

She spoke up smoothly. "As you know, Detective, Mr.
Steiger represents certain American interests. I, however, do
not." She caught the flash of surprise in Jeff's eyes, and also
how quickly he masked it. He was good, all right.

Time for a little flirtation of her own. After all, what was
good for the gander was good for goose. She smiled intimately at D'Abeau and let her hand drift up to the detective's
shoulder seemingly of its own accord.

"Actually, I work for Lloyd's of London—" her hand
drifted lower. Slid off his elbow and fluttered to her throat.
"I'd appreciate it if you could keep that under your hat—you
understand—the sensitive nature of this case—"

She tucked a lock of errant hair behind her ear, running her fingertip suggestively around her earlobe. She let her voice go breathy and took a small step forward, bringing her subtly but definitely into the guy's personal space. "I wouldn't dream of interfering in any way, of course—"

His nostrils flared, and his pupils expanded sharply as he nodded in agreement.

Time to go for the kill. "My employer is deeply concerned about this string of thefts and Lloyd's would like to offer any assistance we can in the matter. I'll see to it personally." Loaded emphasis on the *deeply* and the *personally,* of course.

The detective swayed forward, a slow grin unfolding on his face. He purred back, "Of course, Ms. Kim. I completely understand."

She'd bet he did. She continued in her huskiest voice, dripping with all the sex she could muster. "Of course, my firm wouldn't want to cause a fuss by advertising my presence here—perhaps even scare certain residents into leaving the island. I must ask that you exercise the utmost discretion regarding mentioning my affiliation—deeply appreciative and all. Our intent is to stay completely clear of your investigation, of course."

For good measure, she stroked his arm again. The guy about came out of his skin. He drawled, "Lloyd's, is it? Well now, little lady. I'm proper glad you're here. We'd be grateful for any help you can give us. You understand that I can only help you unofficially."

"But of course. I'd have it no other way. I'm happy to share anything I learn with you. We understand each other, then. I'll make sure my American associate behaves himself." She let a hint of disdain enter her voice as she referred to Jeff.

Thankfully, Jeff was lightning fast on the uptake and didn't react to her comment. But if she wasn't mistaken, there was a certain whiteness about his mouth—or maybe it was the clenched fists jammed deep in his pockets that gave away his tension.

She shared an overlong handshake with the eager detective, then turned to leave. She spoke to Jeff in approximately the same tone she might use to address a Great Dane. "Come along, Mr. Steiger. I need a decent cup of tea before I retire. I sincerely hope I can get one on this island."

"Along with a rousing game of cricket and some kippers," Jeff grumbled under his breath in a fake British accent.

She bit back a smile as she sailed out of the police headquarters. The car had pulled away from the curb before Jeff burst out, "Lloyd's? What if D'Abeau checks your credentials with them?"

Not going to say anything direct to her about flirting with the detective, was he? Smart man—he must realize she would call him on the little game he'd played with the woman back in the evidence locker.

"One cover story coming up." She dialed H.O.T. Watch Ops on her cell phone. "Hey, Jenn, it's Kat. I need you folks to patch a phone call through for me. Lloyd's of London. I know it doesn't open till nine London time, but they've got a twenty-four-hour number and they'll connect me to the person I need."

The H.O.T. Watch staff found the number and put the call through impressively fast. In a few moments, a woman's British-accented voice said briskly, "You're speaking to Lloyd's of London. How may I help you?"

"I need to speak to Michael Somerset. Could you ring me through to his home number straight away? Tell him it's Cobra. He'll take the call."

To the operator's credit, she didn't make any comment on the strange request. A familiar, albeit sleepy, voice came on the line.

"Cobra? What can I do for you at this lovely hour of night?"

She laughed. "I need a cover. For the next few weeks, I need to be a contract investigator for Lloyd's. Can you arrange that?"

"Sure. The boys owe me a few favors after the mess I just helped them clean up."

"You're the best."

"Anything else I can help with? Do you need any information from Lloyd's to assist in this investigation of yours?"

"Now that you mention it, I could use a list of properties in Barbados. Private homes in particular with insurable art collections."

"I assume we're talking about high-end pieces?"

"Yes."

"Do you need it now, or can I roll over and take care of it first thing in the morning?"

"Morning's soon enough."

"Is Mamba with you?" he asked hopefully.

Mamba was Medusa Aleesha Gautier's field handle. She and Michael had met and fallen in love on a mission two years ago. "Alas, no. She's still doing what she has been for the past several weeks."

"Got it."

As special operators, both of them were conditioned never to mention the specifics of any training or mission over a telephone line, secure or otherwise.

"Thanks, Michael. You're the best." She disconnected and noticed Jeff glaring over at her. "What?"

"Who in the hell is Michael Somerset?"

Amusement flashed through her. My, my. Was Mr. We've-got-to-set-this-thing-between-us-aside jealous, perchance? Apparently, after her flirting with the detective, a middle-of-the-night phone call to another man to collect a major favor was too much for Jeff to swallow.

Entertained, she shrugged. "I met Michael on a mission a couple of years back."

"And?"

She blinked innocently. "And what?"

He glared for a moment, but then, oddly, his features

smoothed out. The jealousy drained from him as quickly as it had flared. "You wouldn't be teasing me if you actually had a thing going with him."

He smiled over at her, a lopsided expression conveying chagrin. "Okay, so I deserved to have you yank my chain like that. For some inexplicable reason, I've developed a jealous streak as far as you're concerned. And no, I don't usually react this way around women. You're an anomaly. Normally, I'm the soul of nonjealousy. But then, I don't usually meet the woman I'm planning to marry, either. I plead the novelty of that event to explain my weird behavior."

He stopped babbling to shift lanes of traffic.

"Are you done yet?" she asked, now truly amused.

That earned her a baleful look.

Chuckling, she took pity and let him off the hook. "Michael helped the Medusas stop a cruise-ship hijacking. It was a dicey mission we couldn't have pulled off without him. He's British Intelligence, and he happens to be finishing up an undercover op at Lloyd's at the moment." She paused. "He's engaged to one of my teammates, if that makes you feel better."

Jeff digested that in silence for several minutes. Then he asked, "So how does it work when one of you ladies wants to get married?"

"Well, the man usually decides to pop the question, then he buys a nice engagement ring, and he thinks up some romantic and creative way to ask the Medusa in question—"

"Very funny. I'm talking about your careers."

She shrugged. "How do you guys get married and maintain your Special Forces careers?"

He frowned. "It takes a special woman to marry an operator. She has to understand the long absences, the inability to talk about our work, the psychological and emotional residue of missions…."

"It works the same for us. We have to find men with the

same qualities. Plus, they have to be okay with being around women who are a wee bit athletic and trained to do violence."

"So I gather jokes about PMS and mood swings are not recommended around y'all?"

She smiled. "Probably not at the time of the actual mood swing, no."

"Duly noted." A pause. "What about kids?"

"I'll let you know. Our team leader is pregnant right now. She's the first one of us to cross that bridge."

"Will she go back out in the field after the baby's born?"

"I don't know. The best female marathon runners in the world claim they don't reach their peak until after they've had a child. She should be able to make the physical comeback. I suppose it'll boil down to whether or not she wants to leave her baby and go back out."

"What's the military's take on it?"

"They'll work with her. They don't want to lose her."

Thankfully, the rather bizarre conversation broke off as they reached the hotel. Jeff took charge of checking them in. It was nice for a change to let someone else take the initiative and do the work. She was so used to being independent, a loner even, and to doing for herself that she almost forgot people occasionally interacted with, and even helped, each other. Her teammates aside, of course. They were family, and they all looked out for each other. It was the Medusa way.

The folks at H.O.T. Watch had arranged for a two-bedroom suite in an elegant hotel and it was ready and waiting for them. Together, she and Jeff did a routine check of the suite for bugs and cameras, and it was clean. Not that she expected otherwise. They hadn't been on the island long enough to attract that kind of attention.

When they finished, Jeff asked, "Are you up for a little field trip?"

"To the Valliard estate to figure out how the Ghost pulled off last night's heist?"

"Exactly. I thought we might indulge in a bit of breaking and entering."

She laughed up at his sparkling gaze. "How romantic. I thought you'd never ask."

"Hey, do I know how to sweep a girl off her feet or what for a second date?"

Another date? Oh, boy. They both knew it couldn't really be a date—not after their encounter in the helicopter—but even the mention of one sent her pulse racing. Meditation. She definitely needed some serious meditation. She hadn't been this jumpy and emotional since she was a kid.

She was a calm human being. Rational. In control.

And one hundred percent in lust with Jeff Steiger.

Besides kissing like a god, the man made her laugh, for crying out loud. How was she supposed to resist that?

Chapter 8

In preparation for their little field trip, Kat changed into a pair of black stretch leggings and a black turtleneck. She almost took a minute to put on a little makeup and brush her hair, until it occurred to her what she was contemplating. Disgusted with herself, she grabbed her utility belt and stuffed it into an oversize purse. Regardless of her determination not to regard this scouting mission as a date, she failed entirely to banish the thought from her mind.

They drove south from Bridgetown to the exclusive, beachfront area where the Valliard estate was located. The mansion was not visible from the road, but shielded by a thick stand of bearded ficus trees and tropical foliage. Jeff parked the car well off the road. They did a quick radio check of their headsets and mouthpieces, and then climbed out.

"I'll take point," he murmured.

They made their way swiftly through the trees. Quick electromagnetic emission scans revealed no motion sensors or cameras. The estate's security must all be concentrated up around the house. Jeff flashed her a hand signal to follow him as he made his way to the edge of the broad lawn surrounding a tall, ultramodern structure of glass and steel. Frankly, it looked like a giant, white shoebox—and was about as ugly as one.

Jeff donned a nifty set of night-vision goggles that allowed him to see infrared light, heat and even look through the home's walls. He commenced studying the estate.

"What have you got?" Kat murmured.

"Motion-sensing grid all over the lawn. A mouse couldn't get through there. I'd lay odds there are pressure sensors to match."

She gazed at the concrete walk leading up to the wide porch and its three-story-high overhang. "Is the sidewalk clean?"

Jeff studied it. "Yup. Just a sec." He adjusted his lenses. "Rotating cameras are spaced at even intervals covering the walk."

Kat looked where he pointed, and was able to pick out the small, rotating cameras. "With the right timing, those should be easy enough to slip past."

"Agreed."

"What about the house itself?"

Jeff studied the structure at some length. "I see all kinds of mechanical locks and energy sources inside the doors and windows. We're talking museum-quality security."

Her gut said the Ghost had approached the house on the sidewalk. It was certainly what she would have done. No need to take the hard way in if the easy path was wide open. As for entrance to the house itself, if the windows and doors were impenetrable, what other means could the Ghost have used to get in? She eyed the industrial-homage building. It even boasted ugly commercial air-conditioning units on the roof.

The roof. If she could get up there, she might find a way in from above. She eyed the trees on either side of the house.

Too far away to jump from one to the roof. She eyed the house itself. The Ghost might have used suction cups to scale the walls, but the rough, stucco exterior would have made using them difficult and likely would have left circular scars on the stucco. Surely Detective D'Abeau was competent enough to have spotted something that obvious.

Maybe the Ghost could've gone up one of the tall windows with the cups, but not all glass would hold an adult's weight. It would be a big risk to scale those three-story-high glass panels. How, then?

"I've got it," she announced. "I think I can get in."

"How?"

"Up the sidewalk, then up one of those porch columns. Across the roof to an air-conditioner vent and inside."

Jeff eyed the smooth concrete columns flanking the front of the house. "You couldn't climb those without damaging them. They've got no hand- or footholds. And I don't see anything at the edge of the roof that would catch and hold a grappling hook."

"I could climb one."

"Hey, I know you're a monkey, but come on. Those things are six feet across. You'd get no purchase on it. Even with a lumberjack's rig, you couldn't get enough traction with your feet to do it."

"Oh, ye of little faith. I'm telling you, I can do it."

"This I have to see."

He actually wanted her to try it? "You gonna come up on the roof with me and take a look around?"

He murmured, "I'd never ditch a lady on a date."

While she gaped at him in surprise, he added, "If you can get up there without setting off the alarms, send a rope down. I'll come up and play with you."

"Hold my gear." She stripped down to only her basic climbing equipment to reduce weight, slung a rope and cara-biners across her chest, then pulled out a small spray can.

"What's that?"

"Stickum. Athletes use it—illegally, in most cases, I might add—to make their gloves or hands sticky. Helps them make the crucial catch in the big game. Since cricket's a national obsession in Barbados and it involves catching balls, I assume this stuff's available on the island."

"Wouldn't it leave a residue on the column that the police could find?" Jeff asked.

"The good stuff that the pros sneak onto their gear evaporates quickly. Leaves practically no residue. That's how they get away with it."

Ready to leave, she paused and asked impishly, "Care to place a small wager? I say I can do it."

He grinned. "Winner gets to kiss the loser."

She laughed under her breath. No matter who won or lost, they'd get to kiss again. "You know we can't do that. Once we start, we'll never stop. How about loser pays for dinner?"

"You're on." A pause, then he added, "Chicken."

Her eyebrows shot up. "I assume you're announcing what you plan to eat, for surely you wouldn't call me that."

He grinned mischievously at her and said deliberately, "You're a chicken. Coward. Yellow belly. You're scared to kiss me again."

"And you're not scared to kiss me?"

He shrugged. "I'm willing to take my chances. I think we can be lovers and still pull off the mission. But you—you're scared of letting go. Of losing control. At the end of the day, you're more scared than I am."

Her knee-jerk reaction was to retort that she wasn't, but honesty stopped her. *Was* she that afraid to kiss him? What if she couldn't stop the next time? Then what would she do? Then she'd be in a hell of pickle, that's what. A pickle she had no intention of allowing herself to fall into, thank you very much.

Without replying to his oh-so-accurate assessment, she

took off running, skirting the edge of the lawn until she reached the sidewalk, where she crouched down. Spotting the cameras, she timed their rotation cycles and then did some quick math. In two minutes and ten seconds, they would align perfectly.

She counted down on her watch, and as the first camera swung past her, she walked quickly along behind its arc. A quick dive onto her belly as the next camera swung her way, then she was up and walking again, behind its arc. She repeated the maneuver until she stood behind one of the massive porch columns.

She pulled out a long rubber strap and passed it around the column. A quick spray of her shoes with the stickum, and she was on her way up the column. It was awkward clinging to the curving surface like a fly, but it was definitely doable. Pausing about halfway up to re-spray her shoes was tricky, but she managed.

She lunged upward with one hand to grab the edge of the roof. In the other hand, she maintained her grip on the climbing strap. For a hazardous moment, she hung precariously by her right hand, three stories above the concrete porch below. But then she flung the climbing strap around her neck and reached up with her second hand. From there, it was a piece of cake. She threw a leg up and scrambled onto the flat roof.

She ran lightly to the big air-conditioning unit, found a sturdy structural post, and attached her rope to it. Then it was back to the edge of the roof and lowering the rope until it hung a few feet above the ground. Jeff mimicked her progress up the sidewalk, then climbed the rope hand over hand quickly to join her. Dang, he'd made that look easy. Sometimes she envied the men their incredible upper-body strength.

"Now what, Spider-Woman?"

"Over here." She led him to a flat vent on the roof. "Does that caulk look fresh to you?"

Jeff knelt down beside the grate, fingering the white gel oozing out around its cracks. "Yeah. It's not entirely dry.

Smells like a liquid adhesive." He grinned up at her. "Shall we pry it up and see where it goes?"

She grinned back. Who'd have guessed breaking and entering with him would be this much fun? "After you."

"I hate to say it, but you probably ought to go first. You're so much smaller than I am; if you get stuck, we know I can't make it through. And if you do get stuck, I'll still be up here to haul you out."

"Your call, boss."

He pulled out a small crowbar and pried up the grate. The glue gave way with a moist, sucking sound. She lowered herself into the rectangular hole. After about four feet, the vertical ventilation shaft connected to a horizontal one of similar size. She eased along the low aluminum tunnel to another grate like the one above. This one showed fresh scratches in the galvanized aluminum around its screws. Yup. They'd found the Ghost's entry point.

She whispered into her microphone. "Come on down."

In a few seconds, Jeff touched her foot. "Is there room for me to slide up beside you and take a look below with my goggles before we go in?"

Kat murmured an affirmative. It was only after he'd joined her in the now very tight space, their bodies pressed against each other, rib to rib, hip to hip, with breathtaking intimacy, that it occurred to her he could've just passed the goggles forward and let her take a look around. She ought to be annoyed at him, but strangely enough, she wasn't. Such was the desperation of her craving to be near him like this. Oh, man, was she in trouble.

As they banged elbows yet again, trying to maneuver in the close confines, he whispered, "Roll on your right side."

She complied, and was stunned when he rolled onto his left side, bringing them belly to belly, chest to chest. An errant urge to ravage him right there made her freeze in shock.

"What?" he demanded. "Did you hear something?"

Yeah. Her heart about pounding out of her chest. "No, it's all clear," she replied.

"I'm going to lift the grate off and then stick my head out for a look around," he murmured.

Her nod turned into a gulp as his hard, vibrant body slid upward against hers and her nose rested somewhere in the vicinity of his zipper. Kowabunga. He made some sort of physical exertion above her head, and his body flexed unexpectedly, lurching toward the hole. She grabbed him fast, wrapping her arms around his upper thighs in case something had caused him to momentarily lose his balance.

"Give me a sec if you want more of that," he murmured. "I'll be right there."

"Are you okay?" she muttered, chagrined. "It felt like you were falling."

"I already fell for you, darlin'."

She rolled her eyes and turned his hips loose. But it wasn't like there was anywhere to retreat to. Her eyes squeezed shut in mortification, she tried to ignore the obvious view and asked in desperation, "What do you see?"

"Doesn't look like there's a stitch of security in here. Apparently, the owners relied entirely on the perimeter system."

"An expensive mistake," she replied.

"Wanna take a look around?" he asked.

"Sure. We might learn something about the Ghost."

Thankfully, his crotch finally slid past her face as he slithered through the opening and landed lightly below. She pulled herself forward with her elbows until her shoulders projected out of the opening.

"Need me to catch you?" he murmured.

By way of an answer she dived face-first through the opening, performing a neat flip in midair and landing catlike on her feet beside him. Faint moonlight from down the hall lit the startled look on his face.

She moved out silently on the balls of her feet. This was

when her traditional, soft-soled, Japanese slipper-shoes really earned their stripes. She paused before the first doorway, waiting for Jeff to join her. They fell automatically into the usual patterns of spinning low and fast past openings and leapfrogging past one another as they advanced toward the front of the house. The place was empty.

She couldn't resist showing off when they reached the stairs. A three-inch-wide stainless steel ribbon served as the handrail for the curving staircase. She leaped up onto it and ran down it, pausing only when she reached the bottom of the staircase. She stopped just short of the main floor. If the owners had any sense at all, they had pressure sensors or some sort of motion detectors down here.

Jeff looked appropriately shell-shocked when he joined her a few seconds later.

"Damn, woman. If you ever get tired of this gig, you should consider a career in the circus." He added sourly, "Please don't do that again. My heart couldn't take it."

She grinned unrepentantly at him.

Standing on the first step, he took a long look around the ground floor through the various modes of the goggles. Finally, he declared, "I can't believe it, but the ground floor's clear."

She shook her head. These people had been *asking* to be robbed. Kat looked around the expansive space. The place looked like an art gallery, with an eclectic collection of Impressionist and post-Impressionist art occupying every wall. She was no expert, but some of it looked familiar and really expensive.

"Why'd the Ghost leave all this behind?" she asked. "Why only the one painting? Once he got in here, he could've taken every last one of these works at his leisure."

Jeff frowned and moved off toward the far wall and a blue, cubist painting. Even she recognized it as a Picasso. "That's an excellent question. Particularly since I'd estimate we're looking at easily two hundred million dollars' worth of art."

She was staggered. "Really?"

Jeff nodded grimly as he examined a painting closely. "This Picasso is probably more valuable than the Monet that the Ghost took."

"Sounds like our guy's stealing on commission then. He's not going after random art to pawn. He's stealing specific pieces for a collector."

Jeff moved away from the Picasso and stood back to look at a large Impressionist scene of water and boats. "No doubt about it."

She commented lightly, "Good thing we're on the right side of the law. Between the two of us, we could make a fortune nicking this stuff."

He grunted. "This one job would set us up for life."

They traded knowing looks. Temptations like this weren't uncommon in their line of work. However, it was the rare operator who crossed the line, and neither of them were of that weak-willed ilk.

She asked, "Now what? You wanna climb back out of here, or should we make a phone call to Detective D'Abeau and give him heart failure?"

Jeff grinned. "The guy could use a good heart attack. Serve him right for flirting with you the way he did."

"He wouldn't be amused," she warned.

"Yeah, you're right," Jeff replied reluctantly.

She followed him back upstairs, using the actual steps this time. They reached the air vent and she looked up at it. "If I were the Ghost, I'd have left a rope hanging here to climb out on," she remarked as she hoisted herself back into the vent.

"Now that you mention it, there's a rounded dent in that far corner of the vent opening," Jeff commented. "Like a rope would make if a lot of weight were put on it."

"Good eye," she replied. Jeff nodded, acknowledging the compliment as she asked, "Need a hand up?"

"Nah."

He showed off a bit himself by jumping and grabbing the lip of the opening. While hanging there, he curled up in a ball and then shot his feet up and forward through the opening. As intellectually advanced as she might consider herself, a primitive part of her still thrilled at the masculine display of strength. Yup, she was officially a mess.

They crawled back out onto the roof and re-secured the vent cover before easing over to the edge of the roof. From there it was an easy matter to retrace their route down to the porch, down the sidewalk between the cameras, and back out to their car.

They reached their hotel room slightly before dawn and retired to their respective beds quickly. It felt exceedingly strange, knowing that Jeff was sleeping so nearby, enjoying the hotel's six-hundred-thread-count Egyptian cotton sheets against his skin the same way she was. Eventually, she resorted to a self-hypnosis exercise and managed to put herself to sleep, but it wasn't an easy thing. Memories of sapphire eyes and a vibrant male body pressing intimately against hers kept interrupting her best efforts to clear her mind.

A delicious smell of freshly fried bacon woke her up the next morning. She opened her eyes and jolted to see Jeff standing beside her bed, smiling down at her.

"Good morning, beautiful."

Oh, crap. Pajama check. Thank God she'd pulled on a sloppy cotton T-shirt last night and not the whisper-thin silk nightshirt she usually favored. "Uh, hi." She pushed her hair out of her face and rubbed her eyes. "What are you doing here?"

"I brought my favorite cat burglar breakfast in bed."

She sat up, propping several pillows behind her back. He set a lap tray across her legs, and she stared down at steak, fried eggs, stewed tomatoes, bacon, a stack of pancakes, and half a red grapefruit. "I couldn't eat all of this in a week of breakfasts!"

He shrugged. "I didn't know what you'd like, so I ordered a variety."

"Have you eaten yet?" She picked up a spoon and dug into the juicy grapefruit.

"Heavens, no. My grandmère taught me that a gentleman always feeds his lady first."

"You know, I think I'm starting to like your grandmère."

His eyes clouded over. "Too bad you can't meet her. She passed away a few years back. Cancer."

Quick sympathy speared through her. She knew how bad it hurt to lose a beloved anchor in one's life. "I'm sorry."

He shrugged, but there was old pain in the gesture. He changed subjects abruptly, and she went with the flow in total understanding. "Here's the morning newspaper. You and I managed to stay out of it."

"Thank goodness. That's the last thing we need." She dug into the fried eggs and pushed him the stack of pancakes.

She watched, appalled, while he drowned the flapjacks in syrup.

As he cut into them, he asked, "So where'd the Ghost get the stickum he used to climb the column? Yours came in an aerosol can. If he flew to Barbados, he couldn't have brought it with him. So where on the island did he pick it up?"

She shrugged. "A sporting goods store, probably."

"Can't be too many of those on this island. Think it's worth tracking down?"

"Our particular talents are probably better used elsewhere. Why don't I mention it to Detective D'Abeau? He's got plenty of manpower to check it out, and he'd love to hear from me again," she said lightly.

A black look flitted across Jeff's gaze, but to his credit, he made no comment.

Feeling a little guilty for the poke, she said quickly, "What are the odds that we can guess where the Ghost will strike next? I'm not fond of always being one step behind the guy like this. I'd rather be waiting for him at his next hit."

Jeff opened his mouth to reply, but a knock on the hallway door startled them just then, and he was out of the room before she could blink. She leaped out of bed and threw on pants, grabbing a pistol and sliding toward her bedroom door on bare feet.

"You can come out," Jeff called. "The hotel had some faxes to deliver."

She didn't question the fact that he knew to tell her to stand down. He'd assumed she would cover his back, and he'd assumed correctly. She stowed the pistol in the holster sewn in the back waistband of her slacks and stepped out into the sunny living room. "Who're the faxes from?"

"Lloyd's of London sent you a pile of stuff. And there's one here from Viper—unless you know anyone else who signs their notes, *V.*"

She scanned Viper's fax quickly. "The supercomputer came up with a catalog called 'Undiscovered Masterpieces of the Great Artists,' published last year. All the paintings stolen so far have been in it."

Jeff gaped. "No kidding?"

She passed him the paper. "Vanessa says she's contacted someone who's going to send a copy of the catalog to her. She'll scan it and send us the file as soon as she gets it."

He nodded slowly. "The Ghost's employer isn't an art connoisseur if he's using a catalog to identify what constitutes great art. Which means any rich bastard in the world could be our guy. I was really hoping a sophisticated trend would emerge in the collector's taste. It would narrow the suspect list considerably."

His logic sounded on target. Which meant they couldn't go through the Ghost's client to get at the thief. They'd have to catch the guy directly.

Jeff was flipping through the second sheaf of papers, the ones from Lloyd's. "If we can get a hold of that catalog, we can check it against this list of insured art on the island and see if any more of the paintings in it are here in Barbados. Your friend Michael didn't only send us Lloyd's list of insured art, here. It looks like his buddies at Lloyd's called all the other major insurers of art worldwide and compiled their lists of insured pieces in Barbados, too."

"Gotta love that British efficiency."

He grinned. "Yeah. And friends in high places."

"Amen. So. With that list in hand, do you think we can predict the next piece the Ghost might go after?"

"It's worth a shot."

Kat's PDA beeped distinctively on her nightstand. "That's the incoming e-mail signal. Maybe that's the catalog now." She dashed into the bedroom to check. "Yup, it's the file." Jeff hurried after her, and they huddled over the handheld device as the pages of the catalog scrolled across its tiny screen.

She was *not* paying attention to the fact that she and Jeff were sitting on the side of the same bed. She was *not* imagining falling backward across it, their limbs tangled in naked abandon while they made passionate love with each other. She hardly saw the paintings go scrolling by, so vividly aware was she of Jeff only inches away from her, smelling like expensive shampoo and subtle aftershave. He smelled good enough to eat. She probably smelled like the sour sweat of last night's exertions, and her hair was no doubt sticking up all over her head like broom straw.

She mumbled, "Mind if I jump in the shower while you compare this catalog to the list of pieces here on the island?"

Such was Jeff's concentration on the incoming file that he barely acknowledged her as she slipped out of the room. Or maybe he was just covering up being as flustered as she was. She hoped the latter was the case.

When she stepped out of the bathroom a half hour later,

wearing form-fitting white yoga pants and a matching tank top, lotioned, powdered, perfumed and primped within an inch of her life, Jeff looked up from the papers…and stopped cold.

"Wow. You look fantastic."

She smiled even as she mentally shook her head at her absurdly pleased reaction to the compliment. She had to admit, having him around did wonders for her ego. "Any matches?"

"Yes. Several. What say for our third date we stake out a ghost? I'll even throw in a picnic."

Another date. Complete with the close quarters and adrenaline rush of a stakeout? And food, no less? How could a girl say no to that? Her mouth curved up into a smile. "I had no idea that running a Special Ops mission could be so civilized. We Medusas have obviously been doing it all wrong."

"Obviously." His dimples flashed and her knees went weak on cue. "Stick with me, babe. I'll show you the ropes."

"Or maybe I'll show you how it's done, big guy."

His dancing gaze met hers. "We haven't even begun to have fun yet, darlin'."

Chapter 9

From the catalog, Jeff picked out the likeliest painting of the three that were still left to steal here in Barbados, and he and Kat obtained grudging permission from Detective D'Abeau to stake it out. But after Kat had advanced a plausible "theory" of how the Ghost had gained entrance to the Valliard estate, the cop had owed her one. Not to mention that she'd flirted with him some more. The memory of her casting come-hither looks at that cop continued to set Jeff's teeth on edge. It might be just business, but he still didn't like it.

Kat's buddy in London had sent them the house layouts and security plans of the likely target, along with a note that of the three properties they'd identified as being probable targets, this one had the least extensive security system. If the Ghost was going to strike again, Jeff was betting they'd pegged his next mark correctly.

He and Kat spent all afternoon poring over the house plans and wiring diagrams, planning how they'd rob the place if they were the Ghost. Anticipation at the idea of nabbing the bastard made Jeff edgy. His tension had nothing to do with the mesmerizing woman leaning over the drawings across from him, giving him tantalizingly incomplete glimpses down her shirt of small but perfect breasts that his hands itched to touch and his mouth itched to taste. He was a cad to look, but his gaze broke completely out of his control every time she leaned across the table just so.

This mansion, a sprawling one-story affair unoriginally called Shangri-La, had copious security measures inside the house as well as out. Kat suggested several outrageous methods of bypassing the system…things even an acrobat of her caliber would surely not be able to pull off.

But when he challenged her on it, she casually claimed she could do everything she was suggesting. And somehow, he believed her. He'd about passed out when she took off down that railing last night. She'd looked like a circus performer running along a tightrope. He'd never met another operator who could do some of the things she could. And damn if his imagination didn't keep straying to adventurous things he'd love to try with her in bed that took advantage of her atheleti-cism and flexibility.

After hours of brainstorming together, they arrived at the conclusion that the Ghost would have to disable the entire security system, or simply set it off and move in fast to make the hit and leave before the police arrived. And, frankly, if there was a way to turn off the security system and not have the police know about it instantly, the two of them couldn't find it.

Which was outstanding news for them. If the Ghost were operating in a two- or three-minute window to get in and get out, they reasoned he'd have to eschew fancy circus maneuvers and just make a fast grab at the painting in question. Which also meant they stood a decent chance of nabbing the guy.

Jeff was exultant. Finally, the setup he'd been waiting for to move in and catch this bastard.

Ideally, they'd be inside the mansion for this stakeout, but the Bajan police didn't trust them that much, flirting or no. And frankly, neither he nor Kat wanted the exposure to suspicion if something went wrong and the Ghost got away. In that event, they'd be left as the only people known to have been inside the house when the painting went missing.

The painting was one of Turner's smaller landscapes, a brilliant piece. If Jeff were an art collector with ten million bucks burning a hole in his pocket, he'd snap it up in a heartbeat. The art catalog Viper had sent them raved about the piece, claiming it was one of the finest privately owned landscapes in the world. Oh yeah. Their greedy collector wouldn't be able to resist this tasty morsel.

Jeff retired to take a nap before the night's festivities began. He slept restlessly, dreaming of dark eyes and ivory skin and silky black hair falling down around him. That girl was a fever in his blood. He thought about her constantly, and none of his thoughts were platonic in nature. How in hell he was going to keep his hands off her for days or weeks to come, he hadn't the faintest idea. And he suspected this torturous itch would get a whole lot worse before it got better. He wanted her worse than any woman he'd ever laid eyes on.

When he finally got up and went out into the living room, he was startled by the sight that greeted him. Kat had pushed all the furniture back to the walls, and was in the midst of performing a complex and insanely difficult martial arts routine. Oh, Lord. And now he had these images to add to his fantasies of her. The thought of what they could do with a few of her contortions plumb stole his breath away.

He didn't know whether to be grateful or dismayed when she caught sight of him and froze. He mumbled, "Don't stop on my account."

"It's okay. I just needed to clear my mind."

He nodded in understanding. "Sweat does wonders for my thought processes, too." He moved over to the sofa, which was now tucked underneath the window, and flopped down on it. "What style of martial art was that you were practicing?"

"It's a hybrid form. Part judo. Part kung fu. Part…other stuff."

"What other stuff?"

She frowned. "Just stuff Hidoshi-san showed me. I don't know where he got it from."

"Liar."

He said the word so calmly it seemed to take Kat a moment to register it. Then she whirled to face him, staring.

He explained, "You've studied your whole life, or darned near all of it, to have achieved your level of proficiency. You're not some casual hobbyist, you're a martial arts master. And every practitioner with your level of dedication knows the pedigree and sources of his art back as far as it goes."

"You overestimate my skill."

"My dear, I think not only I, but also the United States government, have grossly *under*estimated your skill. Do General Wittenauer or your teammates have any idea what you can really do?"

"Why do you ask such a thing?" she asked sharply.

"Because if anybody knew what you're capable of, you'd be famous in the Spec Ops community. Hell, you'd be a legend."

Something approaching panic flitted across her face. "Nobody must know," she choked out.

"Why not? Why not shout to the heavens about your abilities? Do you have any idea the things you could do for our country?"

Panic flashed openly in her gaze now.

"My vow—" She broke off.

"What vow?"

She shook her head quickly. "I mustn't speak of it."

"Let me guess. Hidoshi-san taught you the ancient family

fighting form. You're sworn to silence and mustn't ever reveal the family secrets."

"Close enough," she replied reluctantly.

"And it's only to be shared with blood relatives."

That caused a pained look to cross her face, but she made no reply.

"Your secret's safe with me, darlin'. After all, we're practically family already. Once we're married, will you be able to teach it to me? I'd love to learn some of what you can do."

She burst out, "Will you *stop* talking like that?"

He surged to his feet and closed the space between them quickly. "I'm serious, Kat. I want you and I'm going to have you. I've never met another woman like you. Cupid's Bolt or not, I'd still go after you full bore."

She stared up at him in wide-eyed disbelief.

Irritation flooded through him. "What's so damn hard to believe about that?"

She just shook her head.

Throwing caution to the winds, he grabbed her shoulders in both hands. Thankfully, she didn't toss him to the floor. He asked low and furiously, "Why won't you believe me?"

"I don't…I can't…"

"Can't what? Can't talk to me? Can't tell me how you feel or what you're thinking? Can't—or won't, Kat? I'm sick to death of this strong, silent act of yours."

Her mouth quirked wryly. "I thought that was usually the girl's line."

"Hah. You're the ninja in this relationship."

Kat went completely still. Horror flowed through her and into his hands. *What the—*

He burst out, "Oh, God. A *ninja?* Is that what your grandfather trained you to be?" It made perfect sense. The acrobatic things he'd seen her do…the amazing fighting skills… the crazy climbing ability… He swore again under his breath.

It was her turn to grab him by the arms. "Nobody must know, Jeff. *Nobody*."

"Why not? My God, think of the training you could give our Special Forces—"

"But that's the point. That's not how it's done. I can't pick and choose cool pieces of the Way and share them with outsiders. There's a code…consequences."

He studied her intently. "You're really worried about this. Is there some super-secret ninja society that'll come and get you if you give away their secrets?"

Momentary humor flickered in her eyes. "No, nothing like that. But I took a solemn vow. I *can't* break it. It would dishonor Hidoshi-san's memory." She threw up her hands. "I know to a Westerner that sounds completely lame. But it's a big deal to me."

He captured her restless hands and drew them against his chest. "It doesn't sound lame to me. Hey, I'm a soldier, too. Honor counts in my world. Promises matter to me. I get it."

She blinked up at him, suddenly still. "Do you mean that?"

He frowned. "Yes, I mean it. If you don't want me to tell anyone about your training, I won't."

"Just like that?"

He flung her hands away from him and turned to pace the room. "Why do you always question everything I say? Why can't you accept that I stand by my word? Are we Westerners that weak and untrustworthy in your eyes?"

"I… You… No…"

He stopped prowling and crossed his arms over his chest as she sputtered to a stop. "Darlin', that was not the most convincing denial I've ever heard."

She huffed. "Fine. I admit it. I don't generally think too highly of Western promises."

Ouch. He had to give her credit, though. She didn't flinch from speaking the truth. "What about your teammates? These Medusas you speak so highly of? Do you trust them?"

That got a rise out of her. Oh, she didn't stomp or yell or anything so crass, but abrupt anger rolled off her. Only a faint tightness in her voice betrayed her irritation. "I trust them with my life."

Such control she had. Were it not for the inexplicable, but very real, connection between the two of them, he doubted he'd have had any clue she was so pissed off at the moment.

He asked reasonably, "Why them and not me? Is it because you and I haven't come under hostile fire together yet? Do I need to take you out with my team the next time we take a stroll through hell to gain your trust?"

Her forehead twitched, but she never actually frowned. He waited her out while she mulled over his question. Finally, she replied, "You would have had to have been there when the Medusas formed to understand. The powers that be did everything they could to make us fail. The only reason we made it through our initial training is because we all—every one of us Medusas—committed everything we had to each other."

He nodded in total comprehension. An operator's team was much more than a bunch of coworkers. More than family, even. Facing death together time and again forged a bond unlike anything else. It went way beyond words.

He asked matter-of-factly, "You've worked with other special operators, haven't you? Men, yes? Do you trust them? Or is it something special about me that causes you not to trust me?"

She sighed. "I do trust you."

"But not enough to believe what I say."

Her face went expressionless, her voice flat. "Why are you pushing this argument?"

She was pulling back from him. Again. Every time they approached a truly intimate moment, physical or emotional, she backed away like a big dog. Enough was enough. He wasn't going to stand by and let it happen again.

He stepped into her personal space until she leaned away

from him uncomfortably, and spoke silkily. "Am I making you mad, Kat? Is that why you're shutting down on me? More of that stoic Eastern fatalism you're so proud of?"

"Fatalism?" she echoed ominously.

"Yeah. And it's a load of crap, by the way."

He all but saw her hackles rise at that. "Emotional control is all well and good. But there's a time and place for it. I thought balance was part of your precious Eastern philosophy. Where's the balance in never allowing yourself to feel a damn thing?"

"I feel things," she said, flaring.

Ahh. Better. "Right," he grunted skeptically. "That's why you always run and hide behind your superhuman self-control. Because you're so busy feeling stuff."

Her voice was very nearly snippy when she retorted, "Just because I choose not to wear my every thought or feeling on my sleeve doesn't make me overcontrolled. If you want to live your entire life as a wide-open book for any old passerby to see, that's your choice. But it doesn't make my choice wrong."

He allowed himself a smile at that not-so-subtle jab. Finally. He'd gotten a visible rise out of her. "Very good, Kat," he said approvingly. "You're learning. Now if we can just get you to shout now and then, you'll be on your way to a healthier balance in your life."

She stared at him, clearly surprised out of her snit.

"Honey, you're not the only one who can mask feelings and motives. Just because I choose to express mine honestly and openly to you doesn't mean I'm not capable of reining them in or disguising them outright."

"So you set out deliberately to make me angry?" she asked, dangerously softly.

Instinct screamed at him to beat a hasty retreat from this lethal woman. Instead, he shrugged with what he hoped was enough arrogance to really tick her off. "What of it?"

Even though he expected the move, when she leaped at him, it happened so fast he had no chance whatsoever to react. Even if he had managed to throw up a block in time, he wouldn't have done it today. If it took letting her knock his head off to get her to open up to him, so be it.

Her foot flew past his nose so close that he actually felt the faintest brush of it on his skin, as light as butterfly wings, but deadly in its explosive power. The edge of her hand, as stiff as a knife blade, stopped a millimeter from his neck. He dared to glance down and saw her other fist poised in front of his sternum, stopped midblow in a strike that would have crushed it like glass.

He looked up, capturing her furious gaze. He asked much more calmly than he felt, "Why didn't you hurt me?"

Frustration seeped into her eyes.

"Go ahead. Say it," he challenged.

Still the silent war within her raged, a lifetime's worth of repressing thoughts and feelings winning out over what he knew she really wanted to say and do.

"Need me to help you?"

She opened her mouth but no words came out.

He reached out and wrapped her, lethal hands and all, in his arms, dragging her up roughly against him. He kissed her then, holding nothing back. She was too angry for finesse, too wrapped up in her repressed rage for anything other than extreme measures to register. Kissing an enraged woman wasn't his first choice in self-preservation, but if it was what she needed, he'd take his chances.

There was nothing elegant about their kiss. He flattened her lips against her teeth as she fought him, flatly insisting that she acknowledge and react to him. She tried to hold out, but he tightened his grip on her, forcing her body to arch backward beneath his onslaught.

She fought, but not with real intent to harm him. She could've just as easily bitten his lip, kneed him in the groin, or executed a dozen other moves to incapacitate him. And yet, she did none of those things. As he'd thought. She wanted him to force her out of her emotional shell. And he was good and ready to have her emerge from it himself. She tested his strength, trying to pull out of his arms, and he obliged her by engaging his superior strength to hold her right there against him.

In spite of their wrestling embrace, he couldn't help but register that she tasted like plums, rich and sweet and tangy. Her mouth was ripe and juicy, and he devoured her hungrily, sucking in the taste of her, drawing her into him until she became a part of him. He'd love to gentle the kiss, to savor the rich taste of her, to enjoy her languidly and completely.

But first, he wanted all of her—no reservations. He felt the piece she was holding back. It dangled tantalizingly, just beyond his reach. But he also felt her control of that piece of herself slipping.

He schooled himself to patience, following through on the forceful embrace cautiously, making dead sure not to lose himself in the violence of the moment. He would never, ever attack a woman in anger, particularly with a strong sexual element in the mix. He might be forcing the issue, but he refused to force the woman.

Finally, she tore her mouth away from his, swearing in several languages he did recognize and a couple he didn't. "You're a beast," she hissed.

He maintained his grip on her, keeping her arms safely pinned between them. After all, he wasn't a complete fool, and she was still one very pissed off ninja at the moment.

"Passion is not bestiality, Katrina. Nor is it lack of control. If I had no control, you'd be on the floor right now beneath me while I had at you like a true beast. Like it or not, darlin', I'm bigger and stronger than you are. You might be a ninja, but I've got you in a position where I can outmuscle you. And yet, I'm not mauling you, nor am I falling upon you mindlessly. This is about *you* letting go—not me."

She still vibrated with anger, but her explosive readiness to do violence seemed to diminish slightly.

He spoke gently then, silken strands of her hair lightly caressing his lips. "Human emotions are not bad things. In fact, they can be wonderful things. Why do you deny yourself pleasure—hell, real happiness—like this? Surely, your grandfather didn't want that for you."

More of the tension drained from her, replaced by something else he recognized very well indeed. A humming sexual awareness of him, of her body, of how he made her feel. Nonetheless, he didn't loosen his grip quite yet. After all, deception was part of both their training.

"Give it a try," he murmured. "Let go. Allow yourself to really feel something. Just for a minute or two. It'll be our secret, like your ninja training."

When she still hesitated, he took a mental deep breath and made an enormous leap of faith. He turned her loose.

She stood there for a second, gazing up at him, her fists resting lightly on his chest, her body so close to his he felt her warmth radiating through their clothes.

Had he blown it? Would she turn away from him now and never look back? Or kill him, perhaps? He had no doubt she could do it with her bare hands. And he didn't have it in him to stop her if she tried. He could never hurt her that way.

Lord, he felt exposed. Like he was standing in front of a firing squad.

And then her hands moved slightly on his chest, her fingers splaying open gradually until her palms rested against him, warm through his shirt. Her hands slid so slowly, and he held his breath, not sure if he was experiencing a miracle or slow-motion murder.

She swayed slightly toward him. He could swear that was wonderment dawning in her eyes. He stood perfectly still, letting her do whatever she liked to him. Thus encouraged, her hands strayed from his shoulders to his face, her fingertips lightly tracing his cheekbones, the line of his jaw, his mouth.

"You're beautiful," she whispered.

His eyes widened. Could it be?

Slowly, she rose up on tiptoe, leaning lightly against him. Her right hand went around the back of his neck and tugged lightly. He bent his head down for her, never breaking eye contact with her as she raised her mouth by slow degrees to his.

Their lips touched.

Where before they'd met in violence, this time they came together with the lightest of touches, igniting an aching ardor in his soul that was unlike anything he'd ever experienced. This transcended lust, went beyond simple pleasure. It was as if something sacred and rare were unfolding within his soul.

All from the barest touch of her lips to his?

Maybe there was something to this Eastern control stuff after all.

Kat stepped back. "There," she murmured. "That's a proper beginning between us."

Chapter 10

Shangri-La and its tempting Turner landscape were about a mile from the Valliard place on the same stretch of mansion-strewn beach. In daylight, the house—almost a parody of island architecture—would be a tacky flamingo color, with white plantation shutters galore. Tonight it was faintly peach in the moonlight. Kat studied the gaudy architecture and had to shake her head that anyone would build, let alone live in, something so garish.

She and Jeff had chosen to approach the mansion from the beach in extreme stealth, on the off chance that the Ghost was lurking nearby, casing the place. Hence, the two of them were crammed side by side in a hollow beneath a cluster of sharp-leaved palmettos, incidentally exchanging more information about their anatomies than she'd ever imagined possible completely clothed. Who'd have guessed a guy's deltoids flexed like that when he propped a pair of binoculars in front of his nose? Or that a man's thigh went quite that hard when a girl had to drape her leg over it while reaching into her waist pouch to retrieve a lens attachment for her surveillance camera.

"Having fun yet?" Jeff murmured.

Fun? This was like having a root canal without painkillers. It was so much easier to be out in the field with a bunch of women. None of these errant thoughts and sensations distracted her from the job at hand. Except she'd worked with men before, and this had never been a problem. It was definitely Jeff who messed her up like this.

Was he right? Was her life out of balance because it lacked real emotion?

Belatedly, she responded to his question in an undertone that wouldn't carry more than a few feet. "I wouldn't go so far as to call this fun. I feel naked without my sniper rig."

He laughed under his breath. "Now there's a line I've never heard on a date before. What's the longest shot you've ever made?"

"Confirmed kill?"

"Yeah."

"About thirteen hundred yards. But I mostly do short-range work."

"Who's the most famous person you've taken out?"

She looked over at him askance. "You keep score of such things?"

He grinned. "I've never been out on a date with a sniper. I'm not exactly sure how to engage in small talk with you."

"Well, what do you talk about with the other women you date?"

"Ahh, darlin'. We don't usually get around to doing much talking."

If he'd had his night-vision goggles on at that moment, her face would have lit up bright white with embarrassed heat. And it obviously amused him. The cad.

He asked, "Don't you ever feel like blowing off steam after a mission? A little hot, meaningless sex for the hell of it?"

Sex? Her? Not so much. It was too overwhelming. Too personal. Okay, fine. Too emotional. She replied dryly, "I go to the dojo and get in a hard workout if I need to burn off adrenaline. But usually I go someplace peaceful and green to meditate for a while."

He tsked. "You don't know what you're missing out on. Adrenaline-pumped sex is incredible. You should try it sometime."

She just shook her head. She could not believe she was out on a stakeout and having this conversation.

He continued, "When I come off a tough mission, I want to do something mindless and physical to remind myself that I'm still alive. I don't know any guy who doesn't want sex right after he came off a rough op. Maybe it's a guy-girl difference." He paused, then added, "Do all the Medusas meditate after missions?"

Kat suppressed a startled sound of laughter. "Not hardly. They go out and party. Or nowadays, they go home to their guys. I'm the only bachelor left in the bunch."

"Why do you meditate instead of partying?"

"After I make a kill, I usually feel a need to re-center myself."

Sounding mildly alarmed, he asked, "You don't take kills personally, do you?"

"Not at all. If I didn't do it, someone else would. I'm just the tool that carries out a decision made way above my pay grade."

"What about when a mission goes to hell and you end up unexpectedly having to shoot your way out? Or hasn't that happened to the Medusas?"

She answered wryly, "It's happened more than once. Then it's even simpler. In that scenario, it's kill or be killed. You pull the trigger and you don't think twice. I never look back from those kills."

"I've got to say, I never thought a woman could take such a broad view of killing. I always assumed women wouldn't get it."

"You think we're all wilting lilies who wring our hands over squishing a bug and have to ask a man to do it for us?"

He laughed under his breath. "Are you kidding? I've read my history. Some of the most violent soldiers in history have been women. Did you ever hear what Russian women did to German prisoners of war in World War II? It's no wonder the Germans always saved one bullet for themselves."

Kat was familiar with the Russian women's practice of tying enemy soldiers to trees and whipping them until their innards wrapped around the trunk. Although after what the Nazis had done to the Soviet Union, she couldn't blame the women for their rage.

She murmured, "Surely you talk with women a little bit about something besides killing when you're out on a date with one. You know, normal stuff."

She hoped she didn't sound like she was fishing to find out what normal was. Even if that was exactly what she was doing. Jeff countered with, "What did you talk about on dates with boys when you were in high school or college?"

"I didn't date in high school. Hidoshi-san didn't pass away until I was seventeen. When I came to the States to go to college, I was so busy trying to bring my English up to speed and keep my grades up and adjust to the culture shock that I didn't have much time for a social life." And the few relationships she'd had with college boys had left her unimpressed with dating in general. The guys she'd gone out with didn't have a fraction of her focus or drive, and she'd found them…frivolous.

"Why didn't Hidoshi-san let you date?"

"Oh, he'd have let me date. But I was too busy training to spare the time for such silliness."

"Wow. You must have been one mega-serious teenager." He grinned over at her self-deprecatingly. "The same could not have been said about me. My high school teachers always harped at me about applying myself more. About all I applied myself to back then were sports and girls. And not necessarily in that order."

She didn't find that hard to believe. And yet, when the two of them had talked through possible plans for catching the Ghost, he was as focused as any operator she'd ever worked with. He seemed to subscribe to the theory of working hard and playing hard in about equal measure.

He asked, "Were you always so committed to your martial arts, even at a young age?"

"I started training when I could barely walk. I've done it hard-core my entire life. It's who I am."

"That's a strong statement."

"If you're so determined to pursue a relationship with me, you need to believe me. My training runs bone deep. The physical aspects, the mental aspects, the ancient code of honor—all of it."

"Why did you choose the martial arts as your framework for self-definition?"

She turned her head to stare at him.

He shrugged. "So, sue me. I was a psychology minor in college."

Great. She'd fallen for an amateur shrink. She sure could pick 'em. His question was insightful, though. She finally murmured, "I had nothing else. No one else. Hidoshi-san loved me when no one else did. Becoming like him was the least I could do to show my gratitude."

"No one else loved you? The absentee father, I understand. But what about siblings? Aunts and uncles?"

"Nada."

He shifted the weight off one elbow and reached out to touch her cheek. Just the slightest graze of his fingertips against her skin. "Are you still completely alone?"

The loneliness aching within her radiated outward in a terrible tension that froze her facial muscles beneath his brief touch. Her entire being felt stiff as she answered, "I have the Medusas now. They're my family."

He nodded as if he knew the feeling well. And, given that he had a team of his own that he ran with, he probably did know the feeling. "But what about you? Isn't there anyone in your life just for you?"

"Is all this psychoanalysis really necessary?" she asked lightly.

"You're avoiding the question. Your grandfather has passed away, and you have no one else, do you?"

He was prodding painful places in her soul that she'd just as soon have him leave alone. She retreated into the emotionless cool she always did when people tried to get too close to her. Except this time, she felt like a coward for running away. Damn him! She'd been happy the way she was before she met him…or at least at peace with herself. Why did he have to go and tear away the veil of her lonely existence like that and show it to her for what it really was?

She answered in a tone that sounded stilted, even to her. "I don't need anyone else, so your question is moot."

He nodded sagely. "The lady has built her very own fortress of solitude. And here you were, doing so well at starting to crawl out of it. I'm a pushy jerk, aren't I?"

Secretly relieved that he'd poked at her—given her an excuse to come out of her emotional cave, really—she rolled her eyes. "You got one part right. You are a jerk." But she said it without any real heat.

He grinned over at her. "And you love me anyway."

Stunned, she jerked her gaze back to the estate in front of her while she turned the concept over in her mind. Did she feel love for him? Was it possible? She'd loved Hidoshi. But that was different. She'd loved him as a child loves a parent or grandparent.

But Jeff? Could she love a man like him? As an equal? A mate? She stared fixedly through her spotter's scope, seeing a blurry morass of green and peach, vividly aware that he was studying her in the meantime.

"Dare I hope?" he breathed. "Are there really feelings for me lurking behind that inscrutable exterior of yours?"

She started to lower the fist-size telescope to glare over at him, but something caught her attention at the farthest edge of her vision, and she jerked the scope back up to her eye. "I've got movement," she announced. "I do believe our Ghost is putting in an appearance."

Jeff lurched, his attention swinging back to the mansion. "Say position," he responded tersely, abruptly back in full mission mode.

"Eleven o'clock. North end of the upper terrace. Moving in low and fast toward the shed housing the main electrical boxes."

They'd been right, then. The Ghost was simply going to knock out the alarm and make a speed run for the painting. Earlier, they'd discussed trying to nab the guy as soon as they spotted him or waiting until he'd stolen the painting and then catching him. Their concern was that if they grabbed him before the theft, the police wouldn't have enough evidence to hold the guy. He'd slip away from them, this time for good.

"Good eye," Jeff murmured. "He's practically invisible."

"I should think any respectable thief is invisible most of the time," she murmured back absently, concentrating hard on not losing sight of the elusive figure. Likewise, any half-decent sniper ought to be able to follow a figure like him at this distance. And she was more than half decent.

Jeff breathed, "Let's move in closer. Full stealth. We don't want to spook this guy."

She nodded, rising silently to a crouch and easing off through the imitation Balinese landscaping behind Jeff. She didn't hear a sound as they slipped through the night. Jeff was every bit as good as she was at this silent sneaking thing— and she'd been trained by the best. Hidoshi had been one of the last great ninja masters.

Jeff hand-signaled her to go around the house and watch the front doors while he took the oceanside doors. She nodded and Jeff hand-signaled. "First one to spot him leaving calls for backup. Then we move in on him."

She nodded and glided off into the dark, at one with the night. Adrenaline sang through her veins and her body was light and responsive. She was ready for whatever came. Moments like this, where she got to fully turn her skills loose, were rare. But in these moments she was profoundly grateful to Hidoshi, to whatever quirk of fate had led her to him, that she'd been granted the opportunity to do this. To be this.

Jeff found a carved tiki pole casting a deep shadow and had just taken up position behind it when every light in the mansion abruptly came on and a piercing noise split the night.

"Time hack," he announced. He looked down at his watch. Three-twenty a.m. on the nose. He figured they had about sixty seconds to wait, and then one of them should spot the Ghost leaving with his prize. He scanned the ground-floor doors and windows on this side of the house, watching for the slightest movement anywhere in his field of vision.

Eighty-two seconds had passed since his time hack when two things happened simultaneously. He heard the first police sirens in the far distance, and Kat radioed, "I've got him. He's coming out the front door now."

"Go get him!" Jeff ordered as he took off sprinting around the house.

And then all hell broke loose.

No less than five heavily armed men burst out of the bushes in front of Jeff, forcing him to screech to a halt and drop to the ground. "Incoming!" he whispered urgently to Kat. "Five armed men heading your way. Might be cops. Hold your fire!"

The men charged forward away from his position—toward Kat and the Ghost. A spurt of panic broadsided him. Those guys were headed straight at Kat! He briefly considered standing up and shouting at the men to draw their attention and their fire away from her. But then his brain kicked back into gear. She was a trained Special Forces operative. She knew what to do when a bunch of guys ran in her general direction.

As the men moved away, Jeff ran lightly behind them, staying well out of their line of sight and possible line of fire. Who *were* these guys? If they were police, they were certainly acting weird. Cops would have shouted for the Ghost to halt, would have fired warning shots in the air. Searchlights would flare to life, rows of police cars would shine their headlights, and the Ghost would be well and truly caught.

But these guys were sprinting grimly, pistols at the ready, silent, coordinated, and for all the world moving like a team of commandos closing in for a kill.

He careened around the side of the house and spied the front door gaping wide open. One of the men was just leaving the front porch to rejoin his buddies. Jeff ducked behind a lush hibiscus as the guy raced past him. The guy was wearing a black knit cap and black greasepaint on his face. SWAT team maybe, but no regular cop dressed like that.

Jeff risked whispering to Kat, "Where are you?"

"Running," she grunted.

As a powerful engine gunned nearby, the men dropped any attempt at stealth and took off running, yelling back and forth in what sounded like something Slavic.

"Cobra! Five targets straight at you!" Jeff called urgently. He swore violently as the team of armed men sprinted right at Kat. He was too far away to fling himself in front of her but, had he been beside her, he'd have done it in a heartbeat.

She veered off to the right, smartly separating herself from the Ghost as a target. The bad guys lurched and slowed momentarily in their surprise at spotting her. But now they had her in their sights and seemed determined to bag her, too. Three men peeled off after the Ghost; the other two went after her.

It was a no-brainer which group he was going after. No way was he leaving her alone to face down these guys on her own.

Neither he nor Kat was heavily armed. Without knowing how skilled—or unskilled—these guys were, he dared not take them on directly in any kind of a fight. Besides, for all he knew, these guys were law enforcement types.

"Take cover when you can," he ordered Kat tersely as he darted out from behind a palm tree to follow the black-clad men chasing her.

He was maybe thirty feet behind the last assailant when he spied Kat's lithe form ahead, slender and dark, sprinting through the trees. She dodged bushes and tree trunks with incredible agility, and the armed men fell back slightly. But then the lead guy raised his pistol.

"Incoming fire," Jeff bit out frantically. He was too close to the hostiles to be talking on the radio, but he had no choice. If they heard him and turned to fire on him, so be it. Unfortunately, he was too far away to tackle the guy with the gun.

He expected Kat to dive for the ground, to reduce her target profile to practically nothing, maybe even for her to roll on her back and fire back at the shooter. But instead, she picked up speed and literally ran up the trunk of a tree, momentarily going horizontal about six feet off the ground. She sling-shotted back down to the ground with an extra dose of momentum, zipped across the shooter's field of fire and took a running start at a medium-size palm tree. She ran the first eight feet or so up the trunk, then in one smooth move, slung a short rope around the tree, grabbed the free end as it whipped around the trunk, and used the rope and her feet to shimmy up the tree as fast as any chimp.

Jeff stared in disbelief. He'd never seen anything like it. Apparently, neither had the hostiles, for they both slowed to an incredulous jog, staring up into the treetops where she'd disappeared.

A moment later, a black shape hurtled out of a neighboring palm tree, swinging down and out on a long frond, landing lightly in the path well ahead of her pursuers. Then Kat was off and running again, this time with enough of a head start to duck into the deep shadows and vanish from sight.

Belatedly, the men took off running again. They slowed and peered into the area where she'd disappeared, but after thirty seconds or so of fruitless searching, gave up and turned to run for the road, where their buddies were shouting. Sounded like the other team wanted these two to join them already.

Jeff was stunned. He'd seen enough cheesy martial arts movies in his youth to know Hollywood's images of ninjas, but he'd never dreamed that any of the spectacular feats portrayed on film might actually be real. Had he not just seen that with his own eyes, he'd never have believed it possible.

A vehicle roared away, its sound disappearing into the night. Sounded like the Ghost was making his getaway on a motorcycle.

Kat panted into his earpiece. "Who are these guys?"

"No idea. They're acting military. Say status," he bit out.

"A van just pulled up. The men are getting in. I'm taking the car."

Jeff swore and veered toward the main road. He was in time to see their compact sedan peel out from behind the shrubs where he'd hidden it and take off down the road at high speed. Across the street, the last black-clad man piled into an unmarked white van, and the vehicle gunned its engine. Its tires spit gravel, and the rear end fishtailed as it pulled out onto the road, accelerating hard.

"They're giving chase," he called. "White van. Rear license plate obscured. Blacked-out windshield. You shouldn't have trouble spotting it. It'll be the only thing on the road behind you doing a hundred miles per hour."

"Thanks," Kat retorted.

"What in the hell were you thinking, leaving by yourself?" he demanded over his radio as he took off running futilely down the road behind the fleeing vehicles. Christ. She was out there by herself now, caught between the Ghost and those commandos. *And he wasn't there to protect her.* A cold fist of dread closed around his throat.

"I was thinking about not losing the Ghost," she replied tartly. "I'll let you know where he leads me. I just passed a moped rental place. It's about a quarter mile from the mansion. Hot-wire one if you can't wake up the owner. I might need backup."

"Ya think?" he snapped.

He cursed her roundly as he ran for all he was worth. His mind churned as fast as his legs. Who were those guys? He'd lay odds they weren't cops. D'Abeau knew they were staking out Shangri-La. The detective's men wouldn't have pulled weapons on him and Kat. Private mercenaries, then? Maybe hired by the homeowner to protect his art? But then why had they given chase to the Ghost and not stuck with the art collection? What private citizen bothered to or could afford to hire a half-dozen hard-core mercenaries, anyway? Such men did not come cheap.

Who, then?

They'd moved in when the Ghost came out of the house. Enemies of the thief's, perhaps? What did an art thief do to merit such enemies? Had he robbed the wrong man? Maybe stolen something besides art in a former job?

All that came into his mind were questions and more questions. He wanted some answers, dammit! He humped the quarter mile to the moped stand in about a minute. Not long in the real world, but a lifetime when his team was split up and an op was going to hell fast. After determining that the owner didn't live there, it took him another minute to break a flimsy chain lock on one of the mopeds and hot-wire it. A two-and-a-half minute head start for the

Ghost, Kat and the mystery commandos. More than a lifetime. An eternity.

Swearing under his breath, he peeled out of the stand and threw the throttle wide open. The lights of Bridgetown twinkled in the distance and a salt breeze whipped in his face, making his eyes water. He kept his mouth shut to avoid swallowing bugs and confined his cursing to silent epithets in his head.

Far ahead, a line of flashing sirens came into sight, racing down the highway toward him.

"He just turned off the main road," Kat announced. "Avoiding those cops, no doubt. Turn right after a supermarket sign—green letters on a white background. I didn't catch the name." Exertion strained her voice, and squealing tire sounds came over the radio along with her voice.

"Don't kill yourself chasing the bastard," he cautioned, his heart in his throat.

"Are you kidding? Offensive driving is a blast. I'd love to do this in the middle of a bunch of New York City cabbies sometime—show them what combat driving really looks like."

Jeff couldn't help grinning. She did sound like she was having fun. "Did the van make the turn behind you?"

A pause. "Looks like it. I see a cloud of dust behind me."

Kat continued to call out turns and mileages over the next several minutes, and he actually started to close the gap between them. Urban driving was as much about maneuverability as it was speed, and his Vespa was extremely nimble.

He spied a pair of taillights partially obscured by dust ahead and yelled into his radio, "I'm approaching the van. Where are you?"

"Just coming into Bridgetown proper. He's heading straight through the city. He knows we're back here. This could get ugly."

He snorted. Like it wasn't already? Would those men assume Kat was the Ghost's accomplice and take her out, too? He dared not risk it, no matter how bad he wanted to bag the Ghost. "Pull off the chase, Cobra. Lose the van. Make sure it's following the Ghost and leaves off you."

"This may be our only chance to catch the thief! I'm not stopping now. This island isn't that big. We'll corner him."

"And the guys behind you may kill you both. If you get in their way, they may very well shoot through you to get to him."

"I have been known to shoot back, you know. I'm not defenseless."

"One-on-six, you are."

She retorted rather sharply. "I'm a Medusa, not some average infantry grunt."

He swung wide around a corner, keeping his speed up and drawing a few more yards closer to the van. He supposed she was right. If she were a SEAL or a Ranger, he'd be a lot less worried about that van full of gunmen. She deserved the same benefit of the doubt as her male counterparts. At least that was what his head said. His heart screamed in denial. She was small and weak and female and he wanted her for his own. It was his job to protect her and keep her safe from jerks with guns.

"I stand corrected, Madam Medusa," he replied reluctantly.

"Watch the left turn in front of the school—you should hit it soon. It's a greater-than-ninety-degree turn and the road slopes away from you. Take it slower than it looks like you ought to."

"Roger."

The word was no sooner out of his mouth than the sound of screeching tires made him look up sharply. The van's grip on the road gave way as it careened around the very turn she'd just described. It teetered on two wheels and looked like it was going to settle back down onto all four when the right front fender clipped a parked car.

The van went airborne, sailing in a slow motion half roll a good thirty feet through the air. Then the front end hit the ground and the entire van snapped into a fast log roll, flying down the street sideways, flipping no less than six complete revolutions. Debris spun off in every direction. Jeff braked hard, dodging pieces of flying metal, swerving violently in and out among the litter. And then he was past the van.

He looked back over his shoulder and saw a man crawling out through the passenger's side window. As Jeff opened the throttle once more, he glimpsed the guy in his rearview mirror, limping over to the nearest parked car and smashing the butt of a rifle through the car's window. Those guys weren't done for yet. Whoever had survived the crash was going to hot-wire a car and come after them.

"The van crashed. But they'll procure another car and give chase. Where are you now?"

"Going into a residential area. A slum, actually."

"Keep calling your turns."

"Roger," she replied.

"How close are you to him?"

"I'm practically riding the back of his bike. A hundred yards, max."

She sounded distracted.

"He just took a right. First street past a crab shack. Red crab legs painted around a name on a white sign. Begins with a W or an M. Sorry I didn't see more."

He was amazed she was catching the details she was, what with driving like a bat out of hell, the darkness, and the adrenaline of the chase.

As the neighborhood deteriorated around him, Jeff cursed under his breath. Barbados, for all its wealth, had a few pretty rough areas. He didn't know whether to fear for Kat or for the locals if she got into a scrape in this neck of the woods.

Either way, he emphatically didn't want her alone. "Can you slow down a little?"

"Not if you don't want me to lose this guy. And by the way, he's small in stature. Lean. I'd estimate five foot seven at most, maybe 140 pounds. Great balance. A hell of a motor-cycle rider. Black clothes, black ski cap, black gloves. Lemme see if I can get close enough to see his face."

A pause followed.

"Left at Old Joe's General Store. Looks like a little neigh-borhood market." And then she announced, "Third right after that, maybe a hundred yards past the store. It's a dirt road. No landmarks or sign. Be careful, it's narrow."

Then she said, "He just looked back over his shoulder. Caucasian."

Even this much information was a major breakthrough for the investigation. But Jeff would rather bag the guy and be done with it.

And then the sound of a gunning engine behind Jeff made him lurch. And swear. Looked like he had the crazy comman-dos on his tail now. He risked a glance back. They were still well behind him, no more than a pair of headlights in the distance. For now. Bastards were no doubt following the giant rooster tail of dust he was throwing up. But there wasn't a damn thing he could do about it. At least there was grim relief in the fact that now they'd chase him and not her.

Jeff flew down the road, pushing sixty miles per hour, keeping an eye out for the turn ahead.

"He just went up a set of stairs on his bike. I'm going on foot."

"You can't catch him on foot!" Jeff exclaimed. "Go around."

"I can catch him if he doesn't have a back tire."

Oh, crap. "Shooting is not authorized, Kat! You're in a residential area! Chock full of civilians—"

She cut him off. "Too late. I just took his bike tire out. Our boy's on foot. I'm closing."

"Don't engage him. I repeat, don't engage!" Jeff shouted into his mike.

No answer. Damn, damn, damn!

He slowed to take the next turn, and that engine behind him got a whole lot louder all of a sudden. The gunmen were going to catch him fast at this rate.

There was the first turn. He screeched around the corner, skidding violently. He slammed a foot down on the pavement, saving himself from a nasty wipeout. He righted himself, and accelerated with a screech of tires. Old Joe's. Old Joe's. C'mon, c'mon.

There it was. He took the corner way faster than he ought to have. One street. Two streets. Brake. Skid wildly around the third corner… Up ahead he spied their car, parked at an angle across half the narrow street, its driver's side door open.

He pointed the moped up the steps beside the vehicle, banging up their bone-jarring length. He burst out into an alley. Looked left and right. There. In the distance. A familiar dark, running figure disappeared around a corner. He pointed the moped that way. His back tire was getting soft. Didn't like that flight of stairs, apparently. *Hold together just a few more seconds, baby.*

He turned the corner and looked around this new alley frantically. His heart dropped to his feet. Two figures ahead, up high, racing across a rooftop. Crap. The Ghost and Kat were climbing now. He didn't stand a chance of following them up there. He rode along below them, trying to hear them above the wounded sound of his moped. It was no good. The bike was getting too difficult to control. He ditched it and took off running.

"Talk to me." He panted into his mouthpiece.

"Heading north," she bit out. She sounded like she was exerting herself pretty hard.

He made the next turn to head north. He passed a couple of tough-looking locals smoking weed in a doorway, but he went by so fast they hardly had time to react.

"Damn, this guy's agile," Kat complained. "He's jumping gaps."

"Don't fall," Jeff retorted in alarm.

"Huh."

The alleys got darker and narrower and dingier. He dodged sleeping goats and startled the hell out of himself when he narrowly avoided drop-kicking a chicken, who proceeded to take extremely loud umbrage at being awoken.

All of a sudden, intuition washed over him, certainty as real as the dirt beneath his feet. *Kat was in trouble.* As the hen squawked behind him, Jeff put on a burst of speed.

"Where are you, darlin'?"

Nothing.

"Click if you're running silent."

He waited. And waited. Nothing. Dammit! Even if she'd gone to ground and was hiding, she should've been able to ease a hand up to her throat to give him a lousy click on the radio to let him know she was okay.

Purely following his gut now, he slowed to a walk. It was a bitch to control his breathing, but he forced himself to breathe light and quiet. He thought he heard a scuff ahead. He raced toward the sound, pausing in the shadow of a doorway and easing around the corner.

Aw, hell.

He spotted two grappling figures teetering on the edge of a rooftop.

He took off running for all he was worth. "Hey!" he shouted at the Ghost.

One of the figures glanced up, startled. And then…oh, God…the fighting pair overbalanced. And fell, plummeting toward the ground two stories below.

"Kat!" he shouted frantically.

Chapter 11

The Ghost lurched in her grip and it was just enough to throw off the razor's edge of balance they both wavered upon. Kat only had time to register dismay before the two of them launched into space. The ground rushed up from below. She twisted to take the impact on her left hip and shoulder. But then something massively heavy crushed her, and that was the last she remembered.

"Kat. Honey, wake up."

She vaguely heard the words. Vaguely registered frantic hands running quickly over her body. She managed a groan.

"Don't move," the worried voice instructed.

She exhaled, managing with great effort to form words. "Go get him."

"To hell with the Ghost," Jeff snapped. "Can you feel your feet? Move your fingers for me, sweetheart."

Obediently, she wiggled her fingers, although it hurt every bone in her body to move even that small amount. She took as deep a breath as her battered body would tolerate and released it slowly, exhaling the pain as Hidoshi had taught her, closing it off in a remote corner of her mind, far, far away.

"How many fingers am I holding up?"

She squinted up at Jeff. The poor guy looked about ready to puke. "Uh, three."

"We need to get out of here. Those commandos are still behind us somewhere."

Before she had time to be startled, he'd scooped her up in his arms and stood up. It was a patently annoying display of manly special operator strength that she could never hope to duplicate. Although, at the moment she was profoundly relieved simply to relax in his grasp and let him carry her. Her head was spinning like a top and her body announced in no uncertain terms that it had had enough.

"You okay?" he muttered.

"Uh-huh," she managed to mumble back.

"Okay if I run?"

"Maybe not."

"I'm afraid we need to, darlin'. If you're gonna get sick, lemme know and I'll set you down."

Reluctant humor tugged at the corners of her mouth. "I'll bet you say that to all the girls."

He grinned down at her. "I don't generally pick up puking-drunk women. I like them reasonably sober and alert in my bed."

"That's right. You go for all that sparkling conversation."

He laughed under his breath. "No. I just like them conscious and able to scream my name."

"Picky, picky."

He must've heard her fading, because he murmured, "Just rest. I've got you."

Normally, she'd rebel in no uncertain terms if some guy said that to her. She was beholden to no man, thank you very much, and she certainly didn't need to be patronized by one. But damn, it felt good to close her eyes and let Jeff carry her swiftly into the bowels of the neighborhood. Where he was going, she had no idea. But he seemed sure of himself. And why not? He was a far more experienced operator even than she was.

Had she really run this far? Or was it just that she felt so crappy now that it seemed to be taking forever to get back to the car?

"There's that damn chicken again," Jeff muttered balefully. "He's lucky you're hurt or I'd stop and make fryer parts out of him."

She smiled against Jeff's powerful chest. He smelled salty, but she detected a sour note of fear in his sweat, too. Had he been scared for her? He'd sounded mostly pissed off at her on the radio earlier. She hadn't meant to ditch him. It was just the only way not to lose the Ghost.

"I got a look at him," she murmured. "Not a good one, but a look. Thick, dark eyebrows. Narrow nose. Slight droop to the outer corners of his eyelids. Small mouth. Full lips."

"Could you pick him out of a lineup?"

She considered the question. "Probably. But he'll change his appearance if he doesn't leave the island."

"True."

Jeff strode on in silence for several minutes. And then all of a sudden he ducked into a dark doorway and let go of her feet so her body slid down his torso to the ground. He glided left to put himself between her and whatever threat he'd seen or heard.

She knew better than to ask what he'd seen. When he could tell her, he would. She felt the zen calm flow over him that operators were taught when they needed to hide. She mimicked the action, too groggy to know if she'd eliminated the intangible essence of her presence or not.

"Let's move out," he breathed over his shoulder. "Nice and slow. You stay behind me."

She gave one tap on his back to indicate that she understood and would comply. Assuming she didn't pass out, of course. How long they crept down dark alleys, paused before corners and ducked behind various forms of cover, she had no idea. But she did know she ached from head to foot and the adrenaline of the chase had long ago worn off, leaving her nauseous and exhausted.

These were the moments Hidoshi had prepared her for in all those grueling years of training. She called upon his legacy now, and upon the legacy of the Medusas that endured any pain for the sake of the team. It was purely mind over matter. As long as she was conscious to will her body to move, she would keep going, no matter how agonizing.

Finally, after an eternity, Jeff murmured, "Here we are."

"Is it safe to take our car?" she mumbled.

"No. That's why we're taking this one. The owner left the keys hanging from the sun visor. I'll return it tomorrow. But right now, I need to get you back to the hotel and get some painkillers in you."

How he knew she was hurting, she didn't bother to ask.

He asked quietly, "Can you climb in?"

Strangely enough, after all the running around she'd just done, the act of bending down to duck into the tiny Peugeot all but made her pass out.

"Allow me," Jeff murmured as he scooped her off her feet and placed her gently in the passenger's seat.

Maybe it was the blow to her head that she'd taken in the fall, or maybe it was just her accumulated delirium that prompted her to murmur, "You are one serious hunk, Jeff Steiger."

He scowled at her. "You picked a hell of a time to tell me that, woman. You're half conscious and bruised from head to foot, and I can't do a damn thing about what you just said."

She grinned lopsidedly at him. "I am a little loopy, aren't I?"

"Oh, yeah. Let's get you out of here." He leaned her seat

back for her and buckled the seat belt across her hips. She wasn't sure which one of them was more surprised by the faint sigh of pleasure that escaped her as his hand ran across her lower belly. Quickly he went around to the driver's side and started the engine.

"I've got to call D'Abeau," he announced as he eased away from the curb.

She closed her eyes as Jeff guided the car back toward their hotel, presumably watching their tail for any signs of the commandos. As he drove, he dug out his cell phone and dialed the detective. She'd bet D'Abeau was pretty ticked off right about now. The Ghost was making fools of them all with these repeated and successful robberies.

Jeff identified himself, and through the phone, she heard the agitated sounds of D'Abeau throwing a hissy fit.

Jeff replied calmly. "Yes, I know. The Shangri-La estate. A Turner landscape, yes? We were there. Saw the Ghost break in."

Even she heard D'Abeau squawk, "*And you let him get away?*" More shouting ensued.

Jeff managed to interrupt the tirade with, "Can't come in right now. My associate's…not feeling well. We'll come down tomorrow and make a statement, but in the meantime here's the quick and dirty update." He proceeded to give a brief summary of what they'd seen and how they'd chased the Ghost into east Bridgetown, leaving out all description of her circus high-wire act antics with the thief.

She reached up to feel for her throat mike. Gone. At one point in the fight, the Ghost had grabbed at her throat and ended up with a fistful of high-tech electronics instead. It had seemed to surprise him. Enough that it had given her an opening to slip his hold and force him to the edge of that roof.

The thought of how badly that fall could've turned out accentuated the nausea rising in her gut. She settled into a simple mantra. Don't throw up. Don't throw up. Don't…

Eventually, the interminable car ride ended and Jeff pulled up behind the hotel.

"Can you walk?" he murmured.

"I think so. It'll draw less attention if I do."

Jeff grinned. "Either that or you'll have to act drunk off your ass."

"Very funny. I don't drink. I'm allergic to alcohol."

"Man, I'm sorry to hear that. It's the surest and fastest way to get a woman into my bed—ply her with enough booze to drop her inhibitions and blur her vision."

Kat followed him into the service elevator and smiled up at him foggily. She reached a hand out and steadied herself against his chest as the enclosure lurched into motion. "You're plenty pretty, big guy. No need for the girls not to be able to see you."

"Glad to hear you think so," he murmured low. He added lightly, "Especially since you're gonna be looking at this mug for the next eighty years or so."

She started to shake her head, but stabbing pain traveled across her skull and down her neck. She settled for grousing. "You and your Cupid's Bolt. Thing is, I don't play by Cupid's rules. I play by Medusa's."

"I'm okay with that if she shoots arrows of true love at her followers."

Kat stepped out into the soft night light of their hallway and murmured, "I wouldn't know personally, but her track record with my teammates isn't half bad."

"Give it time, darlin'," he murmured, smiling. "Give it time."

By noon the next day when Kat woke up, Medusa had definitely tossed a whole bunch of arrows at her, and they'd lodged in every part of her body, radiating waves of pain. Carefully, Kat climbed out of bed and headed for the hottest shower the hotel could offer up. She stood under the steaming jets until her muscles unwound a little and the pain had subsided from excruciating to merely miserable.

She took stock of her injuries. She had a spectacular bruise on her left hip, and the one on her upper left arm wasn't far behind. Her neck hurt, and she was generally stiff and sore. Although she had a smashing headache, she'd didn't have the blurred vision and piercing pain of a concussion.

The Ghost was no doubt fine. She'd cushioned his landing to the extent that he'd walked away completely unfazed from that fall. After all, he'd fled the scene quickly enough that Jeff hadn't been able to give chase. Or maybe Jeff had chosen not to give chase. Hmm.

She dressed carefully and made her way out to the spread of fresh fruits and pastries Jeff had obviously ordered earlier.

"How're you feeling?" he asked with concern.

"I'll live."

"That was a spectacular fall you took. I'm amazed you walked away from it."

She glanced up at him over the rim of her coffee cup. "I was pretty out of it, but the way I remember it, I didn't walk away from it."

Jeff shrugged as if slightly embarrassed.

"Not used to carrying your teammates home, huh?" she asked lightly.

That put a smile on his face. "Not unless they're pretty drunk, no."

She gave voice to her curiosity. "Why didn't you go after the Ghost?"

"You were down. No way was I leaving you if you were seriously injured. That was a rough part of town, and there was no telling whether or not anyone would've come out to help you. Besides, I couldn't take a chance on those commandos finding you while I was off chasing the Ghost. Our thief can wait. We'll get him next time."

"I can't imagine there'll be a next time," she retorted. "Surely, he'll jump the first plane out of here."

Jeff shrugged. "I dunno. D'Abeau and his boys have the

airport locked down tight. Your description is enough for them to work with."

She shook her head and immediately regretted the move. "He'll change his appearance radically. They won't recognize him if he decides to leave."

Jeff sighed. "You're probably right."

"Now what? How aggressively does General Wittenauer want us to pursue this guy?"

Jeff frowned. "We'll stay on it a little while longer before we give up and go home. At a minimum, we can keep an eye on the other pieces in that catalog. If one of them turns up missing, we'll know (a) that Viper's theory on the collector wanting the paintings in that catalog is right, and (b) we'll know the Ghost has *cojones* the size of an elephant's and is still here in Barbados."

"I'm sorry I lost him."

He stared at her in shock. "You nearly died trying to catch him. You went above and beyond the call of duty."

"But I failed."

"You can't win 'em all, Kat."

She flashed him a wry smile. "But that doesn't mean I can't try."

He laughed at that. "Spoken like a true Special Forces operative."

She fiddled with a croissant, shredding it into flaky pieces on her plate. "We may have a small problem."

"What's that?"

"Not only did I get a good look at the Ghost, but he got a good look at me, too."

Jeff asked quickly, "Did he threaten you while the two of you were grappling?"

"No. He didn't speak at all."

"Did he pull a weapon on you? A knife or a gun? Brass knuckles?"

"Nope. He fought me bare-handed."

"Sounds like an old-school art thief."

She frowned. "And that's significant why?"

"Used to be that art thieves weren't violent criminals. They didn't injure anyone in taking their prizes. In turn, the police usually didn't shoot them. They might end up in jail for fifteen or twenty years, but they didn't end up dead or sentenced to life in prison."

"And now?"

He shrugged. "Times have changed. Art thieves won't hesitate to kill guards or bystanders nowadays. But if this guy's old school, I doubt he'll come after you for knowing what he looks like."

"Gee. That's reassuring."

Jeff grinned at her across the table. "Hey. I've got your back. Nobody's killing you on my watch."

She smiled back at him. She knew it already, but it was nice to hear him say it. In fact, it made her feel a little embarrassed all of a sudden. Which was ridiculous. All special operators looked out for their teammates as a matter of course. It went without saying that he had her back and that she had his. Must be the blow to the head making her go all sappy and sentimental this morning. It couldn't have a thing to do with the memory of his worried voice when he'd reached her, or his protective arms cradling her close as he'd picked her up, or his gentle consideration getting her back to the hotel.

Frustrated with her train of thought, she asked briskly, "What's on the agenda today?"

"We need to visit D'Abeau. I did promise him we'd come in and make statements. If we hang around for a few more days and the Ghost doesn't strike again, then we'll head back to the Bat Cave and wait for something more to turn up on the guy."

She made eye contact with him across the table. It clearly galled him to think of going home empty-handed. Their kind didn't suffer defeat easily or well. She smiled bravely at him. "Maybe we'll catch a lucky break."

"In the meantime, we get to spend a few days in a beautiful tropical resort on Uncle Sam's dime. Gotta love this job."

She'd spent plenty of ops in below-zero temperatures or sweltering heat, had gone for weeks without a proper bath, had crawled through slime and muck and manure and suffered about every form of misery possible for a human to experience in her work. This elegant hotel and her lethally attractive companion weren't half bad. Not half bad at all.

The interview—or thinly veiled interrogation, as it turned out to be—with D'Abeau took most of the day and was a royal pain. After four grueling hours of browbeating, only flashing the detective her massive bruises seemed to convince him that she and Jeff had not been the thieves themselves. Never mind that U.S. government officials had verified that Jeff worked for them and that she was who she claimed, also. In fact, General Wittenauer personally told D'Abeau he'd assigned Jeff to investigate the Ghost. Interestingly enough, D'Abeau never challenged her affiliation with Lloyd's. She'd have to thank Michael again the next time she saw him—hopefully at his wedding to her teammate, Aleesha, later this year.

The sun was low in the sky and Kat was tired, sore, hungry and cranky by the time she and Jeff were allowed to leave police headquarters.

Jeff grumbled. "You hungry?"

She replied, "Starved."

"Want some seafood?"

"Perfect." Heck, shoe leather and wilted lettuce sounded delicious right about now.

They veered into the first authentic-looking place they came to—a pub crammed with cricket memorabilia and advertising the "Best Fish and Chips in the Lesser Antilles."

They ordered two plates of the house specialty, which turned out to be excellent. They spoke little. Not only were they in public, there wasn't much to say about the afternoon's waste of time. They'd told the truth, stuck to their guns, and no matter how suspicious D'Abeau was, their story had held up.

Kat found herself examining every patron who walked into the bar, comparing facial features against her indistinct impressions from last night. No sign of the Ghost. Of course, if she were the guy, she'd be hiding under the darkest rock she could find and trying to figure out the fastest way off this island. Frankly, she expected he was long gone. Bankrolled by someone rich and shady as he was, surely the Ghost had access to private transportation. She grimly recalled the long row of swanky charter jets parked at Sir Grantley Adam Airport when they'd arrived.

After the meal, Jeff asked, "How about a walk on the beach—or are you too sore for that?"

"It would probably do me good to work out a few of the kinks."

And so it was they came to be down on the waterfront, reveling in the pristine white sand as the moon rose, casting a pearlescent glow across the serene ocean.

Jeff smiled at her. "Pretty romantic, huh?"

She quirked an eyebrow back at him. "Are you fishing for me to fling myself into your arms and kiss you senseless?"

He regarded her much more seriously than she'd expected. He answered slowly, "No, I don't think flinging will ever be your style. You're more subtle than that. More sophisticated. In public, at least. I confess, though, that I am hoping you like to cut loose in private."

"What if I'm the world's worst kisser and terrible in bed? It would surely suck to be saddled with me for eighty years then."

He chuckled and closed the distance between them, bringing him squarely into her personal space. "Most skills can be learned. At the end of the day, it's all about how you feel, anyway. If you really care for someone and try to express that, nothing you do in bed is wrong. But if you're worried about it, I stand ready to give you expert instruction."

"You're incorrigible." He was so close she could breathe in his intoxicating scent. Since when had sniffing some guy made her head spin like this? Maybe it was left over from the blow to her head last night. But somehow, she didn't think so.

He murmured, "I prefer to think of myself as single-minded."

"Obsessed?"

He leaned even closer. The broad silhouette of his shoulders blocked out most of the ocean behind him. "Focused."

"You are tempting," she murmured reluctantly.

"Go ahead. Try me. I dare you."

Chapter 12

Jeff held his breath as Kat gazed up at him. *C'mon, baby. Take the plunge. Let go of all that self-control for just a second.*

Moving tentatively, she reached across the yawning chasm that was the last few inches between them to lay her hands on his chest. Her fingertips settled against his shirt, every bit as subtle and evocative as he'd anticipated. His entire being contracted with need. A need for more of her touch upon him. For satin flesh sliding across his, silky hair falling around them, ruby lips sipping at him…

"You know," she murmured, "I think I ought to bed you just to get it out of the way. Then we can both stop wondering what it would be like."

Bright fireworks colored by equal parts anticipation and disbelief exploded in his brain. Had she really just said that? She didn't have to give *him* that invitation twice. He turned immediately to head back for their car and their hotel room. Or more precisely, his big, comfortable bed in their hotel room.

She said earnestly, "We need to focus on the Ghost. But I'm afraid that until we both scratch this itch, we'll be performing at less than optimal levels."

"Brilliant logic," he managed to mumble. How he held himself back from falling upon her and ravishing her right there, he didn't know. It was a close thing. No, he wanted his butterfly to come to him willingly and unfold freely beneath his touch.

She stopped and turned to face him. Rose up on tiptoe. Reached up and twined her fingers in the short hair at the back of his neck. He stared down into her dark, dark eyes, surprised as something akin to trepidation flickered through them.

"Don't you know how crazy I am for you?" he whispered. "There's nothing to fear from me."

And that seemed to do it. She tilted her chin up the last fraction of an inch and their lips met. Her mouth was luxuriously soft against his, and he inhaled appreciatively, tasting sweetness on her breath. Their kiss was languid, a warm and easy thing this time, the slow savoring of something rare and exquisite. Gradually, she pressed herself against him, bit by bit losing her inhibition. For him, it was torture. Talk about self-control! But he *had* to let her set the pace.

Her tongue traced his lips, then ventured beyond, shyly inviting him to deepen the kiss. Groaning in relief, he accepted. His tongue swirled around hers, stroking approvingly. Her hips surged against his, and he blinked down at her in surprise. Her eyes were closed, the look upon her face rapturous in the moonlight.

She was going to be one of a kind when they finally got naked together.

He slipped his hand beneath her shirt, running his fingertips lightly up her spine. She shivered beneath the caress, and her entire body undulated against his. His brain locked up on the spot.

"We've got to stop doing this in public," she mumbled against his lips.

"You'll have to pull the plug," he muttered back. "I can't do it."

"Me, neither."

Their smiles met and merged as they became more familiar with one another, found the best angles of approach and retreat, explored more freely with hands and lips and tongues.

While the surf rolled in rhythmically behind them, the moon smiled down on them approvingly and a warm breeze wrapped them in the beguiling romance of the islands. Soft sand beckoned them to stretch out upon its residual warmth and succumb to the allure of the night and the moment.

"We're in trouble," she sighed.

"Why? Seems to me like we're finally working things out the way they're supposed to be."

She laughed rucfully. "Allow me to rephrase. I'm in trouble."

He drew back far enough to look down at her, but not far enough to break the delicious contact of her lithe body against his. "How so?"

"You're distracting me from being who I am."

"What if I'm helping you discover who you really are?"

She stared up at him. "You think so?"

"I know so."

"I want to believe you."

"Why don't we go scratch that itch and then see what you think?"

She smiled widely. "Let me guess. In your mind that logic is flawless."

"And it's not in yours? Honey, I can smell the desire on you. I can taste it. Hell, your entire body's humming with it. Your control has been superhuman. And, frankly, so has mine. Now that we've proven we can resist this thing between us, don't you think it's time to see what happens when we give in to it?"

That made her laugh. "I give up. Your argument is impeccable."

Thank God. He wasted no time heading for the new car the folks at the H.O.T. Watch had arranged for that morning. The drive back to the hotel was quiet. Kat sat, lost in thought. Hopefully, she was pondering which sexy little thing she was coming to bed in. He was just grateful that the awful tension of waiting was about to be over.

They didn't have to act to race through the lobby of the hotel like a pair of impatient lovers. They tumbled into the elevator, falling into each other's arms before the doors had even finished sliding shut. Only the ding announcing their floor tore them apart, and they took off racing down the hall to their room. He unlocked the door and held it for her with an old-fashioned bow that made her laugh.

She stepped past him into the dark, and as the hall door opened fully, the white sheers billowed into the room on a soft breeze.

Kat dropped into a defensive crouch and spun right, away from the opening. What the hell? He didn't question her reaction, though. He spun low and left, scanning the living room urgently as his eyes sluggishly adjusted to the dark. She glided on silent feet toward her bedroom door, and he headed for his. What in the world was going on? The room looked deserted. Felt deserted. Not that gut feelings were always reliable. A seasoned operator could fade into the woodwork right in front of you. He proceeded with caution, operating on the assumption that there was an intruder until a thorough search proved otherwise.

A quick glance under the bed was clear. He flung the closet door open and pushed aside all his clothes. Nothing. That left only his bathroom. On the way past his backpack, he pulled out a pistol. Behind the door—clear. Shower— clear. Linen closet—too small to conceal a man, but cleared nonetheless. He'd just started to straighten to his full height when Kat called out sharply from her bedroom.

"In here!"

His heart leaped into his throat. Was she in trouble? The protective instincts of a lion roared through him, and by the time he reached her bedroom door, he was in full kill mode. Nobody was messing with his woman. He burst through the half-closed door, looking around wildly for a target to blow away.

"Easy, Rambo. It's just a note."

"A note?" His mind didn't initially make sense of the word, so frantic was he to make sure she was safe.

"Yes. You know. A piece of paper with words written on it that kids pass back and forth in school without getting caught."

"What note?"

She pointed at her bed.

He looked, and tucked partially beneath her pillow was an envelope. "Can I turn on the light?"

"I doubt we'll be able to read the note unless we do," she replied dryly.

Scowling, he hit the light switch. Bright light flooded the room, and he squinted in its glare.

Kat reached for the envelope and he bit out, "Don't touch it."

She looked up, surprised. "You want to treat this as an explosive device?"

"Let's assume the worst until we check it out."

She shrugged and moved to her closet. She pulled out a small nylon bag and unzipped it. "Stand back."

While he stepped back, using the doorframe to block him from direct line of sight of the envelope, she pulled out a handheld meter and passed it over the note.

She announced, "No electronic or magnetic emissions."

He nodded tersely.

She used a long pair of tweezers to lift the edge of the pillowcase away from the note and pointed a flashlight beneath the eiderdown pillow. "No visible wires," she called.

"Any fluid stains or visible powder?"

She took out a magnifying glass and shone her flashlight

on the envelope for extra illumination. After a minute's examination, she shook her head. "Nothing. I think it's just a note."

"Any writing on the envelope?"

"Nope. It's plain linen. Cream colored. The kind that might come with personalized stationery."

"Do you have gloves to pick it up with?"

She glanced over at him. "If this is from who I think it is, he won't have left any fingerprints on it."

Jeff stared at her for a blank moment and then his brain finally kicked into gear. The billowing curtains. An open window. And they hadn't left any open this morning. Only one person he knew of would enter a fifth-floor hotel room through the freaking window. He remarked, "Let's see what the Ghost has to say to us. This should be interesting."

Kat picked up the envelope gingerly and opened it. She unfolded a single piece of paper, and he moved to her side swiftly to read over her shoulder.

I must speak with you. I appeal to the same honor you displayed last night in not killing me. It is a matter of utmost importance. My word of honor—I mean you no harm. Welchman Hall Gully. Tomorrow. Midnight. By the old entrance to Harrison's Cave.

It wasn't signed.

She tipped the heavy envelope over and a single Polaroid picture fell out into her hand. It showed a loosely unrolled canvas, its edges frayed like a painting that had been cut out of its frame. The Turner landscape.

Kat frowned. "The Ghost wants to talk to me?"

"So it seems. How'd he find you?"

She shrugged. "He could've followed us back to the hotel last night. It wouldn't be too hard to find out which room a certain petite Asian woman and her male companion are saying in. Heck, he probably knows the names we registered under."

"Perhaps he's hoping to find a higher bidder for his prizes."

Kat shook her head. "I think not. He'd go straight to his contacts in the art world for that."

"Maybe you scared the hell out of him and he's looking to negotiate a surrender?"

Again, she shook her head. "He was confident as he jumped those roofs. He was sure of himself and his ability to defeat me until the last moment before we fell."

Stunned at what she was implying, Jeff asked, "Are you suggesting that he actually could have taken you in that fight if you two hadn't fallen?" He found the idea of anybody matching her martial skills hard to believe.

Kat shot him an offended look. "He didn't stand a chance against me. I was trying very hard not to kill him, and that's why it was taking me a while to put him down."

He gaped. "You mean you had a chance to take him out and you didn't do it?"

She drew herself up and replied defensively, "That's correct."

"And why not?"

She huffed. "He wasn't trying to kill me."

"This isn't the eighteenth century and your meeting wasn't with pistols at dawn! Gentlemen's rules don't apply to hand-to-hand combat between you and some criminal you've been ordered to catch. You're a soldier, for God's sake. You're paid to *win,* dammit."

She spoke with angry precision. "I have *never* done this job for the money. If I did, I'd be a private mercenary and make ten times what the U.S. government gives me."

"So you let our target go because it wouldn't have been sporting to use all your skills on him." It wasn't a question. It was an outraged statement of fact.

He could not believe her! He didn't even know what articles of the Uniform Code of Military Justice she'd just blasted to smithereens, but he had faith she'd broken a bunch of them. Great. And as her commanding officer, it fell to him to make the charges against her. How in hell was he going to destroy her career—and furthermore, her honor—and salvage anything at all between them?

"Why does he want to talk to me?" Kat repeated, interrupting his furious—and increasingly panicked—train of thought.

"How the hell do I know?" he snapped.

"Focus, Jeff. I need your brainpower, here. We have to decide if I'm going to that gully or not."

"One thing I know for damn sure," he burst out, "you're not going to that meeting alone."

She sighed. "He wants to talk to me. If you come along, he may not show himself. He'd head for the hills and we'd never find out what's so bloody urgent that he went to all this trouble to contact us."

"You could be walking straight into a trap."

"So could he. Why would he expose himself like this to such danger? I kept up with him across those rooftops last night, and he fought with me. He has to know that I stand a real chance of taking him down if he and I go head-to-head."

"Maybe that's why he wants to meet you. He's reveling in the thrill of finally coming up against a challenge."

"I don't think so. He'd have taken more risks in his robberies to date if he was looking for a cheap thrill."

Jeff exhaled hard. She was right. At the moment, Kat was thinking a lot more clearly than he was.

He stated forcefully, "You need backup. No way am I letting you go to that meeting alone."

"Then we've decided that I am going?" she asked with infuriating calm.

"Oh, you're going, all right. But on my terms. Not the Ghost's."

Chapter 13

The next morning, Kat had just finished a grueling workout, punching, kicking, spinning and leaping her way through a difficult practice sequence, when a knock on the hallway door startled her. Jeff was not up yet, or at least he hadn't emerged from his room where he'd retreated angrily—and alone—last night.

Hard to tell what he was madder about—the fact that she hadn't killed the Ghost or that fact that she was determined to go to this meeting without him. It sure had blown the mood between them last night. And she'd *so* been looking forward to making love with him. An urge to throw a petulant tantrum stunned her. She never threw tantrums, let alone pouted. And she was on the verge of doing both.

She toweled off the worst of the sweat streaming down her face and cracked open the hallway door. She gasped in surprise and threw the portal wide open. "What are *you* doing here?" she exclaimed as four of her teammates piled into the suite.

Aleesha Gautier, temporary commander of the Medusas while Major Vanessa "Viper" Blake was on maternity leave, laughed richly. In the thick Jamaican accent she affected when she was stressed or amused, she replied, "Ahh, girly. De way me hears it, our little Cobra got herself a big ol' mon-fish on de hook."

Kat stared. "Where in the world did you hear that?"

"Why, from de fish hisself. He say to me, 'Git your happy self down here to de islands. Your sniper girlie need someone to watch her six.'"

Kat gaped. "Jeff called you?"

Aleesha nodded. "Dat he did."

"When?"

Misty, the team's resident gorgeous blonde, replied. "Last night. He said you're insisting on—I believe his exact words were—being a damn fool and not letting him back you up. He said you needed us."

Kat didn't know what to say. She was elated to have her teammates here to help. But she was shocked that Jeff had called them. Why not call in his own team, whom he was accustomed to working with and knew like the back of his hand? The answer was obvious, of course. Because she knew the Medusas like the back of her hand. Apparently, he'd deemed it more important for her to feel safe and in her comfort zone than for him to feel that way. The generosity of the gesture stole her breath away.

Karen Turner, the team's Amazon look-alike Marine, glanced around the suite. "So where is the good captain? The way we hear it, he's quite an eyeful."

"Who told you that?" Kat demanded.

Dark-haired Isabella Torres laughed gaily. "Captain Steiger was on Dex's team until Maverick was given his own team to command. Dex says he's quite the ladies' man." Dexter Thorpe was Isabella's significant other and a Special Forces operator, himself.

Embarrassed at this third degree about her love life, Kat asked Isabella by way of blatant distraction, "So, when is Dex going to make an honest woman out of you, anyway?"

Isabella sighed. "His father's trying to coerce him into taking over the family business again and Dex is frantically taking missions to stay out in the field and out of contact with his family. Which means we haven't had much chance to discuss that recently."

And given that Isabella's family wasn't too keen on her career either, Kat supposed Bella wasn't about to throw stones at Dex for hiding from his parents.

The door behind her opened and Kat turned swiftly. Jeff wore a pale blue polo shirt, white Bermuda shorts and deck shoes. He looked like a bronzed god. His hair was neatly combed, still damp from his shower, and his eyes glowed bright blue, so sexy her knees went weak just to look at them.

He flashed a cover-model smile and drawled in his irresistible Southern accent. "You must be the Medusas I've heard so much about. It's a pleasure to meet y'all."

Misty muttered under her breath, "Way to go, Cobra!"

The other women grinned appreciatively as Aleesha held out her hand. "I'm Aleesha Gautier. Or you can call me Mamba. I'm nominally in charge of this gaggle."

Jeff stared at her hand cautiously, then spared a quick glance over at Kat. "She's not going to do the same thing you did the first time you shook my hand, is she?"

Kat did something she rarely did. She blushed to the roots of her hair. "Not unless you call her baby, too."

The other women's eyebrows shot up en masse, and unholy amusement glinted in their gazes. She'd forgotten how nothing was secret or sacred among them. Becoming a Medusa had come with inheriting five nosy, if well-meaning, sisters. If they caught wind of the depth of her infatuation with Jeff, they'd razz her until she wished she'd never met any of them.

Kat sighed and made introductions all around, including the snake field handles of all her teammates.

Aleesha asked briskly, "So. What's up?"

Kat sat back and let Jeff bring the team up to speed. He gave a good briefing. Quick. To the point, but thorough.

Aleesha said to him when he finished, "Since you're the expert on this case and have already been named mission commander, how 'bout you take point on this? Has Cobra briefed you on our various specialties?"

"No, ma'am. She hasn't said much about you ladies. But if she's any indication, you're a hell of a team."

More amused glances shot Kat's way.

Aleesha smiled broadly. "Call me ma'am again, boy-o, and I may 'ave to hurt you. You makin' me feel olduh dan dirt."

Jeff grinned back. "Duly noted, Mamba."

Aleesha gave him a quick rundown of who did what on the team. They all were cross-trained in a wide variety of skills, but Karen was the pro at things mechanical, Isabella was the team's intelligence analyst, Misty was a pilot and a whiz with computers and Aleesha was the team's medic. In fact, she'd been a trauma surgeon prior to becoming a Medusa.

Jeff looked faintly shell-shocked when Aleesha finished the recitation of the team's skill set. But he said calmly enough, "Have you ladies had breakfast?"

Karen laughed. "We're commandos. We're always hungry."

Kat made a room-service order for six while Jeff pulled out a detailed map of Barbados and showed the Medusas where tonight's meeting was supposed to take place.

The four other Medusas spent the afternoon casing Welchman Hall Gully, a gorgeous park/walking trail tucked into one of the many gullies slashing across the island's landscape. Kat retreated to her room to meditate until they returned, and Jeff left after mumbling something about getting some special gear for tonight.

It was just as well they stayed apart. Her teammates were

far too perceptive to miss the sparks—either of sexual tension
or anger—that inevitably flew between them when they spent
more than two minutes together. And Kat really could do
without the Medusas' teasing.

Late in the afternoon, they all reconvened to finalize a plan
of action. The caves beneath the gully were going to be a
problem. They were extensive, and there was no way the
Medusas could reconnoiter, let alone cover, all of them
tonight. If the Ghost wanted to emerge from or escape into
the caves, they'd be hard put to intercept him. The team
settled on forming a loose net around Kat and planning to let
the Ghost slip into it unmolested.

"And are you going to let him leave in peace as well?" Kat
asked Jeff as they sat around the dining table, with maps and
sodas scattered across it.

He looked her square in the eye for the first time all day.
"No, I am not."

"But—"

He cut her off. "Don't argue with me on this, Kat."

"I am going to argue with you on this. There's no way the
Ghost would have set up this meeting unless he has something of the utmost importance to tell me. We owe him the
courtesy of hearing him out and giving him free passage
away from the meeting."

"We owe him nothing. He's a criminal."

"He could've tried to kill me last night. But he didn't."

"You could've killed him, too, but you didn't. I'd say you
two are even on that score."

Kat flinched as her teammates stared at her.

Aleesha asked quietly, "Cobra? Are you okay?"

"Yes," she grated. "I'm fine. Jeff seems to think that honor
counts for nothing, however. And he's prepared to trample
mine."

Aleesha looked over at Jeff soberly. "Mon, de girl, she take
dat honor wicked serious."

He exhaled heavily. "Yeah. I know." He paused. "Our orders are to stop the Ghost. Using whatever means necessary. Nothing in our orders precludes use of force. As mission commander, I have to assume that implicit in our mission orders is not only permission to use force but a directive to do so if it will accomplish the mission."

Kat winced. Jeff had resorted to legalese for one reason and one reason only. He was warning her that he'd given her a lawful order—to use force if necessary to apprehend the Ghost. And furthermore, if she failed to do so, he'd hold her liable for having disobeyed a direct order.

Sure enough, on cue he said grimly, "Do you understand me, Captain Kim?"

"Yes, and I acknowledge that you have given me a lawful order. Do you want that in writing?"

She looked up from her tightly clenched hands at him across the table. His stare gave away nothing. No pity, no compassion, no caring. Just the hard, cold gaze of a military commander putting a subordinate sharply and unquestionably in her place.

So. That was how it was going to be.

Anguish wrenched her heart messily in two as she sat there, frozen, her face totally devoid of expression. Damn Hidoshi for teaching her this terrible control, anyway. She wanted to scream and cry and rage, to argue with Jeff about the stupidity of his decision, to demand to know how he could cut her off like this. Worse, she desperately wanted to beg him to look at her the way he had last night in the moonlight. To love her a little. But here she sat, as cold and lifeless as some plastic mannequin who didn't feel a damn thing.

Jeff sighed heavily and looked away from her.

Meanwhile, her teammates stared back and forth between the two of them in nothing less than open shock. As well they should. She'd never shown a single hint of temper, let alone defiance, in all the time any of them had known her.

Damn. Damn, damn, damn.

She'd known from the very beginning that it would never work between her and Jeff. And sure enough, it had come to this.

She stood up from the table and said woodenly, "I'm going for a walk. I'll be back in time for the final briefing."

Kat was mildly surprised that none of the Medusas followed her down to the beach. But she supposed they were so stunned by her outburst that they didn't know what to do. She'd been walking aimlessly along the beach for about an hour, oblivious to the magnificent sunset glinting scarlet off the pristine sand, when her cell phone rang.

Reluctantly, she pulled it out. Startled at the caller, she opened the phone. "Hi, Vanessa. Did the others sic you on me?"

"Hi. And yes, they did. Wanna talk?"

"If I say no and hang up, will you call me back continuously until I do talk to you?"

"No. I'll be on the first plane down there to get in your face until you talk to me."

Kat sighed. The woman would do it, too. Vanessa wasn't known for taking no for an answer. Thing was, of all her teammates, her boss came the closest to understanding her. She sometimes thought Vanessa had an inkling of her true capabilities but chose to honor her secret. Vanessa also seemed to have a handle on Kat's view of things like honor and right and wrong.

Kat asked in resignation, "What did they tell you?"

"That Captain Steiger, while making a rational mission decision, is forcing you into doing something he shouldn't."

Her teammates had supported her? She ought to have expected it, but it surprised and pleased her nonetheless. "They said that?"

"Aleesha said he asked you to go against your personal code of honor. She's worried that you'll disobey him and get in trouble."

Kat didn't reply.

"Will you disobey him?" her boss pressed.

"No offense, Vanessa, but I'll face a court-martial rather than go against my code of honor. I know you'll think I'm a fool, and you can tell me how I'm throwing away my career, but it's who I am. I can't go against my prom—" she broke off, horrified at what she'd just revealed.

"I don't think you're a fool, Kat. And I'd never ask you to go against the vows you made to your grandfather."

Kat practically dropped her phone. "How do you know about him?"

Vanessa had the good grace to sound apologetic. "I talked to Captain Steiger a few minutes ago."

Kat's stomach burst into butterflies. Not the excited, happy kind. The nervous, unpleasant ones. When Vanessa didn't continue, she asked reluctantly, "What did he say?"

"He loves you, Kat."

"He *said* that?"

Vanessa laughed. "Are you kidding? Of course he didn't say it. He probably doesn't even know it himself yet. But he's a wreck. He's tearing himself in two over what he believes to be his duty and his feelings for you. He could hardly form a coherent sentence when he was talking to me. He's a mess."

"Then how do you know how he feels?" Kat challenged.

"Because I watched Jack go through the exact same thing."

Jack Scatalone. Their training officer and supervisor, and Vanessa's husband. The man who'd been assigned to train the Medusas—and to break them. He'd been ordered to make sure they never became Special Forces operators. Except no matter what he'd thrown at them, they'd survived and succeeded. He'd reluctantly come to the conclusion that they deserved to take their place in the Spec Ops community, yet he'd been ordered to dismantle the team regardless of his pleas to let the Medusas have a shot. And to top it off, he'd been falling in love with Vanessa at the same time he was forced to sabotage her team.

Of all people, he probably was the one who could best understand the dilemma Jeff found himself in. Vanessa probably got it, too. Heck, even Kat could understand why Jeff was doing what he was doing. But that didn't mean she could meekly go along with it.

"Look, Vanessa. The Ghost appealed to my honor. He gave me his word that he meant no harm and that this meeting was vital. If I show up, I'm tacitly giving him my word in return that I won't pull any stunts on him. I *can't* take the guy down."

"Any idea why this thief wants to talk to you so much?"

"We've been chewing on that all day. No one has any idea. We all agree it's insane, and something compelling must be driving him to it."

"Does he know who you are?"

Kat mulled that one over. "He probably has a good idea. He ripped off my throat mike during the fight. When I hit the ground, it was gone, so he must've taken it with him."

"And after examining it, he'd probably have a pretty good idea that he's dealing with at least a U.S. government agent, if not a military member. Not too many civilians have access to the caliber of equipment we use. Let's assume he does know roughly who you are."

Kat frowned. Okay. So that only made his request to meet her all the more puzzling. Vanessa was quiet on the other end of the phone, and Kat didn't fill in the silence. Viper's intellect was formidable, and her instincts were pretty much without exception spot-on.

Finally, Vanessa sighed. "Jeff said this guy was old school. Carried no gun and made no effort to do serious injury to the two of you. Is that your impression of this guy as well?"

"It is."

"Something extraordinary has happened. Something he wants the American government to know about—badly enough to risk his life to tell it to you. You're the logical person for him to approach. Particularly since you could've killed him and didn't. You've earned a measure of trust from him."

Kat burst out, "And Jeff's asking me to betray that trust!"

"I'll talk to Jeff. You go to that meeting. Do what you have to do."

"Are you telling me to follow Jeff's order?" Kat asked in disbelief.

"I'm telling you to follow your heart. You've got more courage and decency in your pinkie finger than most people muster in a lifetime. I'm telling you to do what you think is right. Then, no matter what consequences follow, I'll back you up and you'll be at peace with yourself."

It was as if a wash of cool water flowed over her, flushing away all the bad energy, all the anger and disquiet making her sick at heart. Kat took a deep breath. Released it slowly.

"Thank you, Vanessa."

"There's nothing to thank me for. I told you to do what you were already going to do anyway."

"I haven't made up my mind—"

"Sure you have."

"Huh?"

"You're the heart and soul of my team. The arrow on the Medusas' compass that always points us in the right direction. You never waver; you always know the right thing to do. Whenever I'm not sure of what I'm doing, I can always look into your eyes and see exactly what I'm supposed to do. Tonight, I hear in your voice that you know the right thing to do. And I'm telling you to go with it. You've never steered me wrong before. I've no reason to believe you've read this one wrong, either."

Kat was speechless. Such a ringing vote of confidence from Vanessa, whom she arguably admired more than any other person alive, was overwhelming.

"You still there, Cobra?"

"Uh, yeah. Thanks. Wow."

Vanessa laughed. "So does this mean Junior and I get to stay home to look after my swollen ankles and eat chocolate tonight?"

Kat chuckled. "You do realize you've probably just signed the death warrant on my career, don't you?"

"You know, about half the folks in the Spec Ops community said Jack would never make colonel because he broke every rule in the book to bring the Medusas into existence. The other half said he was a shoo-in for colonel precisely because he broke every rule in the book and brought the Medusas into existence. And here he is, sporting a shiny new set of eagles on his shoulders. Risk takers are rewarded more often than not, Cobra. You'll come out of this okay."

"I'll hold you to that."

"I'll stand beside you no matter what happens."

Too bad Jeff couldn't say the same thing. "Thanks, boss."

"Any time."

In a much calmer frame of mind, Kat performed an ancient tai chi routine as the sun slid away into the west. She had a job to do, Jeff or no Jeff. And she would not fail Vanessa or the Ghost. She would live up to both of their best opinions of her.

No matter what Jeff did to her for it.

Chapter 14

Thankfully, the last-minute preparations for the meeting kept Kat—and Jeff—occupied enough that she didn't have to speak to him alone before they left for the rendezvous.

As soon as they arrived at the park, Jeff and her teammates melted away into the sultry stillness at the bottom of the sheltered valley. She was left to cool her jets in the car and listen to the others murmur over the radio as they covertly searched the park and moved into position to observe the meeting. The Medusas found no sign of the black-clad men from last night's robbery.

And then the waiting began.

Typically, when Kat waited before a kill, she dropped into a state of relaxation where time flowed over her and around her without touching her. But tonight she was unable to achieve that fugue state of waking sleep. She fought back jitters over and over. Under normal circumstances, if she were this agitated, she'd step away from the shot and let someone else take it. But tonight there was no one else. The Ghost would speak to her and her alone.

Finally, eleven-forty-five flashed on her watch. She got out of the car gratefully and made her way into the deserted park. Jeff had decided she'd move into place early to give the team of assailants from the last robbery plenty of time to reveal themselves.

She went to the bench and sat down. Acutely aware of the eyes of her team upon her, she schooled herself to utter stillness. After all, she had a reputation to maintain. The Medusas often called her the ice cube when she was waiting to make a kill. She could sit for two or three days with barely a twitch. She could surely sit on this bench for ten minutes without fidgeting.

But it turned out to be surprisingly hard to do. She was used to being the hunter, not the hunted. She knew all too well how easy a target she was, motionless and out in plain sight like this. Even the most inexperienced of snipers could pick her off like a tin duck in a cheap shooting gallery.

Must think about something else.

Jeff was out there. He'd never let anyone take a potshot at the future mother of his children—good Lord, had she just thought that? Since when had she bought in to his crazy notion of love at first bolt?

Good thing the Medusas had shown up when they had, or she might have been in serious danger of doing something entirely inappropriate in the middle of a mission. Except why didn't she feel relief at that thought? Why was vague disappointment at her team's inconvenient timing rattling around in her gut instead?

Jeff would be looking at her right now. He'd assigned the Medusas to scan the forest while he watched the immediate vicinity around her. Was he undressing her with his eyes? Imagining what they could've done together last night had they not had their argument? Whatever was on his mind, the heat of his gaze was palpable at a distance of a hundred yards or more. Or maybe that heat was coming from her own risqué thoughts. There was no question in her mind that he'd be a skilled lover. He was too comfortable with women, too physical a being, too at home in his own skin to be anything else.

Midnight came and went.

And still she sat. Alone.

She'd expected this, however. The Ghost would approach carefully, reconnoiter the area. Make sure she hadn't set a trap for him. *Come in, already, Mr. Ghost. My friends won't hurt you. Not if I have anything to say about it.*

The bench she sat on faced the main walking path that wound through the gully. Behind her fell a curtain of hanging vines and ferns from a stone arch that had once supported the ceiling of an ancient cave. Beyond the vines, the eroded remains of several massive stalagmites marked what used to be the cave floor. Between them, a faint path led the way back to an old entrance to Harrison's Cave—an extensive complex of caves stretching away beneath her feet. An iron security gate blocked the cave entrance to protect the caves from the local kids and vice versa.

"Don't turn around."

The whispered voice was quiet, barely reaching her ears. Male. Strongly French accented.

"Are you alone?" he asked.

"Of course not. My partner wouldn't hear of me coming out here by myself. He's hiding in the trees somewhere."

Two things happened simultaneously. Jeff swore sharply over the radio into her earbuds as he realized she was speaking aloud—off radio, and a quiet laugh floated out of the darkness behind her.

"Such refreshing 'onesty. I like you."

"Why did you want to speak with me?"

"Yes, let us go directly to the point. The danger this night is much greater than your friend."

She asked quickly, "What are you talking about?"

"As you may know, I 'ave been busy 'ere in Barbados."

She answered dryly, "So I've heard."

Another chuckle. "When a fisherman casts 'is net, 'e hopes to catch one kind of fish. But often, 'e catches another as well. Like the fisherman, I took a painting, but by accident, I took something else as well. Something you need to see. It was affixed to the back of a canvas."

"What is it?"

"In a moment. First, you must tell me true. Do you work for the American government?"

"I do."

"Perfect. If you will come over to the gate behind you, I will give it to you."

Startled, she stood up. The movement caused a flurry of chatter in her earpiece as the Medusas readied themselves for her to go mobile. She picked her way with exaggerated caution toward the gate, both because it was dark and hard to see in the shadow of the thick curtain of vines, and also to give her teammates a few extra moments to reposition themselves.

Isabella was the first to announce that she'd acquired a heat signature inside the opening to Harrison's Cave.

Kat murmured low, "Step back from the opening a little. My colleague has you in his sights." She might be willing to save the Ghost's life tonight, but she wasn't foolish enough to give away to him the true degree of backup she had out here.

"Merci." The French voice took on a faint echo as he spoke from farther inside the cave.

"Do you want me to come in there?" she asked as she approached the heavily padlocked gate.

"It is not necessary. Please, if you will reach your hand through the bars…"

She did as the Ghost directed.

Something smooth and flat that felt like cardboard was laid in the palm of her hand. "What is this?"

"This—'ow you say—self-explanatory."

"A warning, my friend. This time we have met in honorable truce. But I cannot extend that to you after tonight. My boss has ordered me to use whatever force is necessary to stop you. And next time, I will be bound by that order."

"Understood. In return, I 'ave a warning for you as well. If anyone finds out that I 'ave given this disk to you, you will find yourself in immediate and extreme danger. Be very careful."

"Danger from whom?" she asked, startled.

"You spared my life—for we both know you could 'ave killed me if you wished—and now I 'ave paid you back. Equal warnings 'ave we traded as well. I count us even."

She drew her hand back through the gate, tilting the cardboard sleeve in her hand to pass it through the metal bars. It held a CD of some kind.

Jeff announced sharply, "H.O.T. Watch says we've got heat signatures incoming. Four hostiles. Moving fast. Armed."

Kat started. She'd momentarily forgotten that the folks in the Bat Cave were monitoring tonight's meeting via surveillance satellite. She murmured, "The men who chased you from the scene of last night's theft are coming. Time to go, my friend."

"What men?" The Ghost's question was sharp. Alarmed.

He didn't know? She thought fast. Should she warn him or not? Maybe they were some law enforcement agency that the H.O.T. Watch wasn't aware of working on the case. If she gave the thief any more information, she could be compromising a criminal investigation. Except she'd already revealed the men's existence. And her gut instinct said to tell the Ghost about the men.

Jeff spoke in her ear. "Move out, Kat. Take cover."

She spoke fast. "Last night. Six men. Armed. Wearing

black. White van. They staked out the estate. While I was chasing you, they were chasing both of us."

"What 'appened to them?"

"Their van crashed. We took measures not to be followed home. Do they know who you are?"

Jeff's voice was more urgent. "Get out of there, Kat! They're almost here. We don't need a firefight out here."

The Ghost murmured, "*Merci.* I am in your debt once more."

Kat felt his swift departure into the bowels of the cave as a faint whiff of air against her skin. She took a quick look around and dove behind the curtain of hanging vines. Lying on a bed of moss, she announced quietly over her throat mike, "He's gone."

Jeff snorted and muttered, "And they're here. Everyone pull back. Quietly. No confrontation."

Kat reached out with her senses, hearing, smelling, even tasting the verdant night around her. If she crawled on this tender moss, it would rip, leaving obvious black gashes to mark her passage. Moving slowly, she drew her pistol and held it over her head with both hands in a firing position. Then she began to roll, gradually easing away from the cave opening. With each revolution, her gaze roved all around, seeking any movement, any shadow that was not of the night and of the forest.

Without warning, a tall figure clothed in black rose up about thirty feet beyond her head. She froze, lying on her back, gazing awkwardly up and back at him as he swung up a semiautomatic carbine in a smooth motion. In an instant, she identified the weapon. A Yugoslavian SKS rifle with a bayonet mount. Not a weapon Jeff or the Medusas used. And the guy obviously had a target in sight. The weapon settled against his shoulder and his right forearm tensed. He was firing!

Without hesitating, she squeezed off two shots overhead

while lying on her back. The first shot caught him under the right ear. The second, she'd adjusted downward to compensate for his beginning to collapse, and it hit him square in the temple. A kill shot.

The guy dropped like a stone as crashing sounds erupted from all directions. Men shouted back and forth. They yelled in a language she didn't know, but she didn't need to understand. They knew they had a man down, that there was a shooter out here, and they were determined to find and kill her.

This scenario, she knew. The kill was always easy. The escape afterward was hell. She rolled fast across the remaining moss, then rose into a crouch behind a tree trunk. She glanced up. A towering black pine. Not ideal for climbing… the branches were too thin to support much weight, and closely spaced enough to make scaling the trunk a pain in the rear. But she didn't have much choice.

She often made use of three dimensions when egressing a close-range kill. Most people only thought in two dimensions, so thinking vertically gave her a big edge. Not to mention, Hidoshi had trained her to climb like a monkey.

Not worrying about noise as the dead man's colleagues crashed through the gully like a herd of bull elephants, she jumped for the nearest branch. The soft wood bent deeply beneath her weight, but held.

Up she went, distributing her weight as best as she could among multiple branches as she climbed the rough ladder of limbs quickly. A dark shadow moved below, and she froze, one arm around the trunk, the branch she stood on slowly flexing beneath her weight. As the angle of the limb grew steeper and steeper, she prayed silently.

Hold a few more seconds. Don't crack.

Thankfully, the sap-filled wood remained silent, and the shadow moved on. She switched quickly to another branch and wrapped both arms around the trunk, supporting most of her weight that way.

"Where the hell are you?" Jeff murmured.

"I went vertical. One hostile just passed beneath me," she breathed back.

Misty murmured, "I have one moving past me, away from the park entrance."

Isabella spoke next. "I have one examining the downed man."

Frustratingly, no one reported sighting the last man. Kat was startled when Jeff breathed, "Ops, say location of hostiles."

A new voice came up on their frequency. "Two hostiles, immobile, sixty feet east of Cobra. One moving northwest, one-hundred-ten feet north of Sidewinder. One hostile moving west-by-southwest, approximately fifty feet from Python's location."

Kat mapped the locations in her head. Nobody was about to stumble across her hiding spot.

The voice continued. "A new hostile moving between Adder and Mamba's positions. Field-of-fire conflict between Adder and Mamba. Maverick, another tango is heading toward you. Should pass twenty to twenty-five feet in front of you, moving left to right. If you have cover and hold position, you should be clear."

Six men were out here? Those last two might have success-fully ambushed the Medusas had the H.O.T. Watch combat observers not warned them. Handy, having an infrared picture from God's-eye view like this.

Jennifer Blackfoot came up on frequency. "Visual shows one more hostile back in the parking lot. He appears to be tampering with your vehicle."

Kat's jaw dropped. Okay, so the H.O.T. Watch folks were more than handy. They were lifesavers.

"Copy," Jeff murmured. "I have my man in sight."

The woods and the radios went silent as the hostiles calmed down from their initial panic and went into hard-core hunting mode, creeping stealthily through the lush tropical foliage.

It was a deadly game of cat and mouse. For the most part, Kat, Jeff and the Medusas held their positions, hunkered down to wait out the hostiles as the H.O.T. Watch observers occasionally murmured a position update.

And then Jennifer announced, "Problem, folks. We just got a momentary visual on one of your hostiles. We enhanced the image, and he appears to be wearing night-vision goggles. We cannot confirm, but have to assume they're infrared."

Kat's stomach dropped. That meant they also had to assume that their trackers could see them now, and would shoot them on sight. The rules of this game had just changed completely.

Jeff breathed into the radio. "Request permission to go full offensive."

Chapter 15

Kat held her breath while a long pause ensued. Then Jennifer spoke crisply. "Pull out of there. Attempt not to kill them, but shoot your way out of there as necessary."

Jeff murmured, "Copy. Medusas, rendezvous at Point Alpha."

The Medusas always established several rendezvous points in case they got separated on an op.

Jennifer spoke again. "Cobra, if possible, please confirm your kill and search the body. Who are those guys?"

Kat shimmied down out of the tree quickly, her gloves and shoes sticky with sap. She raced for the man she'd shot. She stared when she got to his body. His pockets were already turned inside out, his left wrist flung wide—and minus a watch. His weapon was gone. He wore no ammunition belt, and she thought she remembered glimpsing the bulge of one when she'd taken the shot. But she'd been firing from a wacky angle. Maybe she was wrong.

"This guy's been stripped of all identification," she reported.

Jeff ordered, "Converge on me, ladies. Ops, if you'd vector them in?"

The H.O.T. Watch controllers obliged, and Kat followed their directions toward her teammates. She thought hard as she ran lightly through the trees. Her kill's identity had been sanitized by one of his buddies. Which was pretty sophisticated behavior for common thugs. These guys were pros.

Jennifer Blackfoot came back up. "We just picked up a phone call to the Bajan police. Gunshots were reported. Time to leave the area. ETA on police—five minutes."

Dang. The H.O.T. Watch had the capacity to monitor local phone calls, too?

Jeff started, "Raven, about our vehicles. The cops—"

Jennifer cut him off. "Carter's calling the police now to tip them off anonymously that the cars may be rigged to blow up."

"Thanks," Jeff replied.

Kat was close to their rendezvous point and reached it in about a minute. She topped a steep outcropping of rock and spotted a crouching figure before her. A hand signal flashed. *Jeff.* She flashed back an all's well and he waved her in. She moved to his side while they waited for the others to join them.

"You okay?" he asked quietly, off radio.

She was startled to realize that the very same question had been on the tip of her tongue to ask him. Thing was, she already knew he was uninjured. And yet, she felt a need for reassurance. Her hands wanted to run over his limbs and torso and face, to check for injuries. Weird. She answered, likewise off radio, "I'm fine. You?"

"Fine. Why'd you shoot that guy?"

It did not escape her that he was giving her the benefit of the doubt—that he was assuming she'd had a good reason to disobey his order not to shoot and giving her a chance to share it with him. "The tango stood up, took aim, and started to fire at one of you." She shrugged. "There was no time to ask for a modification of your order."

He nodded briskly. "Okay. You'll need to write it up, of course."

She nodded, profoundly relieved. No questions. No second-guessing. He believed her story. Trusted her judgment. The paperwork of making an unauthorized kill was routine.

Karen and Isabella popped over the ridge next, and as sirens became audible in the distance, Aleesha and Misty joined them.

Jeff looked around. "Who's your pacesetter?"

The slowest runner always set the pace, and the others stayed with her.

Aleesha answered. "Me or Isabella, depending on who's carrying the most weight."

Isabella grinned. "Hey, I've been working out like crazy."

Aleesha grinned back. "I'm it, then. Let's go."

Kat fell in behind Python in the Medusas' usual retreat order. Not surprisingly, Jeff assigned himself to bring up the rear—the most dangerous position in a fighting retreat. They ran steadily until they emerged from the park. Aleesha found a narrow road, and took off down it.

They ran hard for nearly an hour before the lights and noise of a village came into sight ahead of them. Jeff called a halt. They pulled off the road into a clump of tall weeds. He pulled out a map and spread it out on the ground between them. "I place us here. Do y'all concur?"

Kat glanced at the map and nodded her agreement.

Jeff continued. "It's too far to run to any major town from here tonight. We can either obtain wheels or find someplace to camp."

Kat spoke up. "I vote for wheels. I want to see what the Ghost gave me and we'll need a computer to do that."

Jeff stared at her. "He gave you something?"

"Looks like a computer disk. He said he found it by accident. It's why he wanted to meet me."

Jeff nodded. "Wheels it is, then. Who's good at hot-wiring cars?"

Aleesha laughed. "Boy-o, we be de Medusas… Lay dem baby blues on how we do business."

Misty stood up, grinning. "Kat, your shirt, please. Maverick, if you wouldn't mind turning your back…"

Kat stripped out of her close-fitting black turtleneck while Misty did the same. They quickly traded shirts. Additionally, Misty popped off her bra before pulling Kat's shirt over her head. The effect never failed to startle Kat. The black fabric was skintight and left shockingly little to the imagination.

Misty announced, "You can turn around now, Maverick."

He did so. Kat didn't blame him for gulping. Misty was magnificently endowed, and Kat's three-sizes-too-small shirt showed the girls off to full effect.

"Well, then," Jeff commented dryly. "That's certainly…informative."

Kat's eyes twinkled as he glanced over at her, clearly checking to make sure she wasn't jealous of his reaction to Misty's display.

"Pass me your cash, ladies," Misty muttered as she applied mascara, using a small mirror Karen lit for her with a flashlight.

While Misty finished putting on eye shadow and lip gloss, the Medusas pooled their emergency cash. Misty counted it quickly. "That should be plenty. Wheels for six, coming up. Back in a few," she said breezily. "The usual bet, Mamba?"

"T'ought you'd never ask, girlie. De usual."

Misty disappeared down the road, rolling her pants down around her hips to show off her flat, tanned midriff, her golden hair loose and flowing behind her as she ran.

As they hunkered down to wait, Jeff asked, "What's the bet?"

Karen explained, "Misty has five minutes once she arrives to acquire whatever she's going after. In this case, a car."

Jeff gaped. "Five *minutes?*"

Kat blinked innocently. "What's wrong? That too slow for you?"

He spluttered. "She can't do that in five minutes. She has to buy a drink. Settle in at the bar. Strike up a few conversations. Work her way around to suggesting that she's looking to buy a car. Negotiate a deal. It takes *hours.*"

Kat couldn't resist. She replied blandly, "Is that how a male team does it? How quaint."

Jeff retorted, scowling. "No way can she do it in five minutes."

Aleesha jumped on that lightning fast. "Care to make a side bet, big guy?"

He glanced over at Kat. "Will I lose?"

"Oh, yeah. Bargain for three minutes. Then you might stand a chance."

He shook his head. "This I have to see."

Karen gestured toward the village. "Be our guest. Just don't get caught."

He moved off quickly down the road and disappeared into the night.

Kat felt oddly bereft without him nearby. She was losing her marbles.

Aleesha startled her out of her disgusted musings. "Nice caboose dat boy's sportin'."

Kat replied, grinning. "Shall I tell Michael you said that?"

Aleesha chuckled, dropping the Jamaican accent. "Be my guest. He knows that when I quit looking I'll be dead. He also knows he's got my heart forever."

Kat asked curiously, "How does it work having both a significant other and a job like this?"

Karen crowed. "Oh, ho! Our little Kat does have a crush on Maverick. I knew it!"

Kat scrunched her eyes shut in dismay as Aleesha's motherly arm looped over her shoulder. "'T'ain't nuttin' to be 'shamed of, kitten. He's a fine one, he is."

Kat blinked in surprise. "You approve of him?"

Isabella laughed. "It's not up to us. If you like him, then go get him. I, for one, will be glad to see you happy for a change."

The others nodded. "I'm happy," she declared, a tad defensively.

Karen, the team's tall Marine, and usually one to keep her nose out of others' business surprised her by saying, "No, you're not. You're like I used to be. I was happy to be a Medusa. I was happy to have this job. But I wasn't personally happy. Because I wasn't, I just didn't allow myself to have a personal life. I didn't even know how unhappy I was until Anders came along."

Kat couldn't deny it. Ever since Karen had hooked up with the Norwegian Special Forces officer, she'd been a different woman. These days, she practically glowed from within. Kat muttered, "I don't need to glow, dammit."

"Ahh. Sure ye do. Glowin's good fer a girl," Aleesha replied.

Kat just shook her head. At least they approved of Jeff. That would save her a few hassles, at any rate.

"Speak o' de devil. Here comes Kat's firefly-mon now." Aleesha glanced at her watch and cursed under her breath.

Kat grinned. Aleesha must've lost the bet.

Jeff rejoined them, shaking his head and muttering, "She'll be along in a minute with the van. I've never seen anything like it."

Kat patted his shoulder. "It's all right. We Medusas take a little getting used to."

He glanced up at her, his eyes gleaming. "Now there's an understatement if I ever heard one."

Her pulse jumped. Sheesh. She couldn't even have a

normal conversation with the guy without twittering like a schoolgirl. She really needed to get control of herself.

The sound of an underpowered engine putt-putting up the hill toward them yanked Kat's mind back to the business at hand.

Jeff ordered, "Let's move out, ladies."

As usual, the folks at H.O.T. Watch Ops came through like champs. How they managed to procure a cottage on a secluded beach on the north side of the island at this hour, Jeff had no idea. He rode shotgun and relayed directions from Ops to Misty and her tight T-shirt as she drove them to their ramshackle lodgings.

As hidey holes went, the place wasn't bad. It had running water in the kitchen sink, a flush toilet, and most importantly, electricity and a computer. The desktop model was several years out of date, but it had a CD-DVD drive, and that was what they needed to read the disk the Ghost had given Kat.

In short order after they arrived, the team gathered around the computer, watching it boot up at snail speed. Kat held out a cardboard CD sleeve to him. He took it, examining it closely. "What did he say when he gave this to you?"

"Not much. Apparently, it was attached to the back of a painting he stole, and he accidentally took it, too. He said I'd be in extreme danger if anyone found out I have it."

Jeff was inclined to believe the guy. Eventually, the computer spun up the disk and got around to reading its contents. The blinking hourglass on screen was replaced by the last thing he'd ever expected to pop up….

Over his shoulder, Kat inhaled sharply.

Chinese characters.

Jeff glanced up at her. "What does it say?"

"It's the opening menu to a generic video playback program. Click on that character there to play the video." She pointed at the appropriate pictograph.

Unfortunately, to reach his computer screen, she had to lean over his shoulder and practically lay her cheek against his. They both inhaled simultaneously, breathing in each other's scents instinctively. Her feminine essence mixed with the green, fresh smell of the leaves and moss she'd crawled around in tonight. The combination was heady, making his thoughts whirl in a kaleidoscope of flashing impressions.

Misty piped up. "Anybody see a fire extinguisher?"

Kat started, brushing against his back. "That's right," she commented. "You and Greg had to deal with that booby-trapped computer last year. Do you think this is some sort of self-destruct program?"

Misty laughed. "No. I think the sparks flying off you and the good captain are going to set something on fire pretty soon."

Amused, he glanced out of the corner of his eye and saw Kat close her eyes in mortification. He said sympathetically, "It must really suck, having all these nosy women pick apart your private life like this."

Kat groused. "You have no idea."

He chuckled. But his laugh was cut short when a video image suddenly popped up on the computer screen. "Whoa!" he exclaimed. No wonder the Ghost had warned Kat this tape would put her in extreme danger!

Bloody hell.

Chapter 16

Kat leaned forward to peer at the image on the computer screen. It was grainy and shot from an odd angle, as if the camera were mounted high in the corner of the room. A surveillance camera, then. Not surprisingly, a bedroom came into focus. Even less surprisingly, the bed was occupied.

Kat murmured, "Bella, was the focus on that lens just adjusted?"

The team's photo intelligence analyst murmured, "Yes. A live camera operator shot this footage."

Kat's eyebrows shot up. Which meant this little *ménage à trois* was probably a setup. Which meant somebody was out to blackmail this man. Which begged the questions, who was he, and who would benefit by having this guy by the short hairs?

While she pondered those riddles, the camera zoomed in on the bed and its occupants came into plain view. A middle-aged man, reasonably fit for his age, but his skin loosening and his belly going to paunch, was cavorting with two young, naked men. Who *was* that?

The target of this little cinematic project turned his head momentarily. The camera caught a clear image of him, and Isabella sucked in a sharp breath.

Jeff murmured, "You know him?"

Isabella answered grimly, "That's the Russian oil minister."

Kat's jaw sagged. The Russians might be entirely used to their government officials jumping in and out of the sack with women and turn a blind eye to it. But men with men? Her impression of Russian society was that it was not nearly so tolerant of that. Her thoughts leaped to the next obvious question. Who took the video? And what did they want from the Russian oil minister?

Jeff asked Isabella, "Can you tell anything from this video about who filmed it?"

"I'd need more sophisticated equipment than this. We'll need to send the disk to our analysts for that. My first guess is that it's not Russian. Frankly, their surveillance film quality is better than this."

Kat snorted mentally. The benefit of a long and distinguished history of spying on one's own people, apparently. Aloud, she said, "The next question is who were those guys chasing The Ghost? Is it a safe assumption that they were after this disk? If so, why do they want it?"

"Who are the possible players?" Jeff asked her.

Kat shrugged. "The Chinese might have filmed this and want it back. The Russians could be after it on behalf of Romeo, there. Or some other player may want to get their hooks into the Russian oil minister."

Jeff huffed in disgust. "So we really don't know a whole lot more than we did a few hours ago."

Kat shrugged. "Sure we do. We know that CD was in the possession of someone the Ghost burglarized here on Barbados.

That's a list of only seven suspects. We know that once word got out that the disk had surfaced, a heavy hitter entered the scene fast to try to get his hands on it. Finally, we know the Ghost wanted to dump the disk—in particular to the U.S. government. The Ghost was obviously worried about what the last owner of the disk was going to do with it, which implies that an enemy of the U.S. had the disk until the Ghost took it."

Jeff grinned at her. Even though his voice was teasing, the expression in his eyes was intimate. Personal. "That's why I love you. You're smart *and* optimistic."

L-love? She gulped and had to use all her skill to disguise the shock coursing through her. Surely he'd said that purely in jest. He'd *sounded* like he was joking around, at any rate.

She managed to respond lightly, "Gee, and here I thought you were captivated by my tree-climbing skills."

He laughed. "That, too. You've got to show me how you did that trick of running up the tree trunk sideways sometime."

She winced. He'd seen that, had he? That was exactly the sort of move she didn't like to advertise that she knew how to do. If Uncle Sam found out, she'd be stuck teaching ninja wannabes for the rest of her life. And not only would that drive her crazy, it would go against everything Hidoshi had ever taught her.

Jeff dug out his cell phone. She listened to his call with unabashed curiosity. "Raven, it's Maverick. Just the lady I wanted to talk to. There's been a development."

In short order, Jeff had asked Jennifer and company back at the Bat Cave to do thorough background checks on all the victims of the Ghost's robberies on Barbados. Why would one of them have a blackmail video of the Russian oil minister?

Aleesha commented, "I could get used to having a bunch like the H.O.T. Watch backing me up. They do the drudge work pushing paper while we're out here having all the fun."

Jeff nodded. "I can't tell you how handy they are. They've saved my neck a dozen times and every mission runs smoother with their eyes and ears on my team. Of course, you ladies don't seem to do too badly for yourselves." He threw a sour glance over at Misty.

Kat grinned. "Speaking of which, can I have my shirt back? I'm tired of swimming around in this sack you call clothing, Sidewinder."

Misty quipped, "You're just jealous of the girls." Then her voice dropped into a more serious vein. "I didn't ask for them, you know. They were added when I was still out cold from the accident."

Misty had been in a horrendous car wreck as a teenager and her mother had decided that during the reconstructive surgeries to follow that Misty should be turned into a walking Barbie doll. Her looks were actually a real sore point with her.

Karen commented idly, "Too bad we can't just ask the Ghost where he got the CD."

Kat lurched, her mind racing.

She caught Jeff's intent gaze upon her and he leaned forward. "Talk to me, Kat."

"Is it a good bet that, given enough time, the powers that be at H.O.T. Watch will figure out which of the Ghost's victims would've had a use for, or connection to, that CD?"

Jeff nodded. "They're very good at what they do."

"But knowing that might not account for the guys who jumped us in the gully, right?"

Jeff nodded again.

Kat continued thinking aloud. "We have to assume our commandos reported back to whomever they're working for. Worst case, even more thugs get sent in to help get the disk. The good news is they have no idea who we are and no obvious means of tracking us if we've done our job correctly to erase our tracks tonight. But the hostiles do have one link to that CD whom they can possibly track."

"The Ghost," Jeff said. "But surely after tonight, he's run for the hills. He's probably already off the island."

Kat shrugged. "You're most likely right. He didn't strike me as having a death wish. Otherwise he wouldn't have taken such precautions when he met me. But our hostiles don't know that for sure any more than we do."

Jeff asked, "What do you suggest we do about it?"

Kat leaned forward eagerly. Suddenly it was as clear as a bell to her what her subconscious had been reaching toward. "We know of two more paintings that the Ghost was likely to steal—that last two from that catalog here on Barbados. What if I impersonate the Ghost and steal one of them? You guys can set up a trap around me and I'll act as bait. We'll draw out the hostiles and grab them."

Jeff's look was one of pure horror. "Absolutely not!"

Shocked at his response, Kat stared at him. "Why not? It's a brilliant plan."

"It's too dangerous."

She rolled her eyes. "Oh, come on. I'm a Special Forces operative. How is it too dangerous? I do stuff more dangerous than that all the time."

"You're setting yourself up as bait for a force of unknown size and skill. It'd be a crapshoot. They might come in with six guys like before, or maybe they'll come in with twenty."

"That's what I have the Medusas and H.O.T. Watch for. You all can take care of anything they throw at me."

Jeff glanced around and a look of chagrin came over his face. Kat looked up to see that her teammates were riveted on the exchange between them. Crud.

"Take a walk with me," he ordered tersely.

She concurred wholeheartedly with his impulse to finish this discussion in private. "By all means," she retorted.

Aleesha warned quietly, "Don't get so wrapped up in fighting with each other that you drop your guard. A team of killers is floating around out there who'd love to get their hands on Kat."

Mamba's warning checked Kat's irritation in midstride. Aleesha was right. And the woman should know—she'd fallen in love in the middle of an op, too. Too? *Too?* Kat jolted sharply. There was no *too* about it. She had not fallen in love with Jeff!

He seemed to take Mamba's warning to heart as well, for he paused just outside the cabin to let his eyesight adjust to the dark and to take a long look at the surrounding foliage before heading down the narrow, sandy path to the beach.

She stomped along as best she could beside him. Unfortunately, the soft sand didn't make for good angry stomping. He walked until they'd reached a cove mostly surrounded by cliffs that funneled the waves into crashing surf here. More to the point, the surf was extremely loud. Someone three feet away wouldn't be able to hear them.

He turned sharply to face her. "Don't do this to me, Kat."

"Do what?"

"Don't make me choose between my head and my heart."

"What are you talking about?"

"I can't send the woman I'm planning to marry into a death trap. You may be a ninja to your core, but bone deep, I'm old-fashioned. Hell, a chauvinist, if you will. I can't send a woman I care about into danger."

"Oh, puh-lease. You of all people know I'm not some helpless little thing. I can take care of myself."

"You're not Wonder Woman, dammit!"

"You're right, I'm not. I'm real. I can do stuff Wonder Woman's creators never dreamed of…except for the invisible jet, of course."

"Don't joke around about this," he retorted raggedly.

She peered at him in the faint starlight. He was really worried about her! "Jeff, I appreciate your concern, but I'll be okay. I've got a heck of a good team to back me up. We won't get taken by surprise."

He threw his hands up in the air in frustration.

She tried again. "If I were one of your men and I'd volunteered to do this job, would you have a problem with it? Is my idea operationally sound?"

His gaze narrowed. Reluctantly he answered, "It's a little on the risky side, but yeah, I'd give it serious consideration."

She glared at him reprovingly.

"Okay, so I'd go with the idea if you were one of my guys. And yes, I understand that if I'd let one of them do it, I'm supposed to let you do it, too."

"But…" she asked leadingly.

"But…" He took a quick step toward her and swept her up in his arms. He kissed her with such passion that her toes curled into the cool, damp sand, and her knees went suspiciously weak. Ho-lee cow. Their tongues tangled, mouths slanting across one another hungrily, as they strained closer to one another, pressing body to body from shoulders to ankles.

Eventually, he tore his mouth away from hers. "Can you honestly tell me you feel nothing when we kiss like that?" he demanded.

Panting, she managed to answer, "No, I can't. When you kiss me like that, my world tilts on its axis. I've never pretended otherwise. But that doesn't have anything to do with my doing this job."

"It has everything to do with it, dammit!"

"Why? Male operators expect their wives to wait patiently at home while they put their lives on the line and not to question their judgment out in the field. Why can't I, as a female operator, expect the same of you?"

He shook his head. "I guess I'm not as strong as you. I'd be a wreck, waiting at home while you ran around out here playing superhero. Is that what you want to hear me say? That you're stronger and tougher emotionally than me?"

She couldn't help smiling sardonically. "All women who wait at home for men who do dangerous jobs know *they're* the strong ones. But Jeff, if you want me, if you're going to have me for your girlfriend or wife or whatever, you have to accept this part of me, too. My job involves taking risks, and you're going to have to let me do that. I've trained my whole life to do this, and I'm not walking away from it now. Not even for you."

"Then you admit that you feel something for me?"

She stared up at him in surprise. "Of course I feel something for you. I feel a lot for you!"

"Show me."

"Here? Now?"

"Right here. Right now."

For once, she didn't feel like shying away from his challenge. She was just mad enough to grab the bull by the horns. She dragged her shirt over her head defiantly and threw it down on the sand. He stared, speechless, at her bare breasts. She gave him a moment to take that in, and then she yanked off her belt and flung off her pants and underwear. She was already barefoot, and it was a quick thing to pull out the rubber band holding her hair and shake it loose around her shoulders and breasts. The wind blew cool air upon her naked skin, and the night caressed her damply. The waves pounded wild and free, calling to the siren within her.

"Here I am, Jeff. If you want me, I'm yours. But you have to take all of me—the good with the bad. The whole package."

He gaped for a moment more, and then all of a sudden was fumbling frantically, yanking off his clothes in clumsy haste. "You're magnificent," he breathed.

And then his mouth was on hers, his hands on her body, drawing her down with him to the sand, cushioning her body with his. She stretched out at full length upon him, and the sensation of his body cradling hers all but made her pass out.

"I've wanted you since the moment we met," she mumbled.

He laughed against her lips, his hands busy as he cajoled

her body to a fever pitch of need with hands and mouth and delicious friction of skin on skin. "I thought you hated my guts when we met," he mumbled back.

She kissed her way down his neck to the hollow over his collarbone, gasping at the way his thigh rubbed between her legs. "I loved it when you called me baby. Nobody ever calls me things like that."

"Why the hell not?" he asked as his fingers dipped into the crevice at the base of her spine and all but made her jump out of her skin at the melting lust that shot through her. "You're a sexpot. Men must hit on you all the time."

That made her laugh, her nose buried against his chest. "Not hardly."

"Must be that I'll-break-your neck-if-you-touch-me vibe you put out." And then his hand slid down her belly and touched her in ways that made her want to sob in pleasure.

Gasping as she arched into his hand, she managed to reply, "But that vibe didn't stop you."

He grinned, looking deeply into her eyes. "I was a goner before you even dropped me in the gym. I took one look and I knew I had to have you."

She cried out as his finger stroked across her moist heat and swollen flesh.

"So responsive," he muttered. "How could anybody miss how sensual you are?"

That startled her. Sensual? Her? She'd never attached that adjective to herself. But as Jeff played her body like a fine instrument, she couldn't argue with him.

His big, warm hands gripped her hips, guiding her down onto him. His heat and size were iron hard and pulsed deep within her, erasing any remaining semblance of organized thought. As her control shattered utterly, her cry of unfettered pleasure rose to mingle with the crashing waves.

She rode him with abandon, matching the rolling rhythm of the ocean, embracing its grandeur and power, letting it wash through her and direct her movements as she gave herself over completely to the moment. She reveled in driving them both deeper and deeper into the night, in letting go of everything—opening the floodgates of her emotions and letting them gush over the dam of her training, her control, her entire being.

Everything she'd ever been was washed away as this new being of pure sensation was being revealed within her. She flung her head back, keening a cry of ecstasy as her first-ever climax burst over her without warning. It electrified her in a blinding shower of tingling sparks, streaking through her like chain lightning, ripping her apart with its power, sending bits of her flying in a thousand different directions.

Jeff rolled over then, pressing her deep into the warm sand as she shuddered around his length and steely power. He took over the rhythm of the ocean and the night, finding her pace and matching it with unerring accuracy. He invaded her very core, now slamming fast and hard, now stroking with aching slowness, until she climbed his chest, clawing him urgently as yet another explosion built, even more powerful than the first one.

"Sing for me, baby," he crooned.

And sing she did. Her legs wrapped around his hips, pulling him even deeper within her as she surged beneath him in total abandon. Their love was a wild thing, bigger than the two of them, bigger than the ocean behind them, bigger than the entire universe, forcing them both to surrender to it completely.

And in that final moment, when they both let go together, they exploded as one, overtaken by an instant of such perfection it stole their breath away. They gazed deep into each other's eyes in wonder as pleasure rolled over both of them, all but ripping consciousness away from them.

Kat descended back into herself slowly. She became aware of Jeff's sand-covered shoulder pressed against her cheek.

She reached up languidly to loop her arms around his neck while he pressed himself up onto his elbows to stare down at her.

"Holy Mother," he murmured in awe.

She smiled up at him tentatively. "No regrets, then? All of me, for better or worse?"

His mouth curved up into a devilish smile. "In sickness and health, until death do us part, darlin'."

She rolled her eyes. "Don't you think you're rushing things just a bit? We've known each other a grand total of three days. Even I'm not insane enough to leap into marriage on that short a courtship."

Of course, if she'd stayed in Korea, she might very well have entered into an arranged marriage whereby she would never have seen the groom, let alone spoken to him before the wedding. Had he lived another few years until she was old enough to marry, she suspected Hidoshi would have been just that old school about it. He'd have married her off into one of the handful of remaining ninja clans. What would he have thought of Jeff? After all, Jeff was a highly trained warrior in the modern tradition. Hidoshi might have found it an interesting match—the meshing of old and new.

Jeff rolled over, drawing her on top of him. He grinned up at her. "You're right. Three days is too soon. I'll give it a full week. After all, I'm patient. But even you understand that this is a done deal between us. Right?"

A done deal? Was she ready to admit that? The reality of the naked man sprawled beneath her was hard to ignore. But it was a complete departure from anything she'd ever even remotely envisioned for her life. Was she ready to abandon a lifetime of solitude and monkish asceticism to embrace this new and foreign world of emotion and passion and impulsiveness?

Kat had no idea how to answer Jeff's question. What he was asking of her was huge. Life changing. She'd always considered herself to be courageous, but at this exact moment, she was scared to death. She was standing on the edge of a cliff. Once she stepped off it, there would be no going back. Jeff would sweep her into a new life with him and there'd be no fighting the power of his overwhelming determination to make her his once she gave into it. Such was the promise—and the danger—of Cupid's Bolt.

Suddenly, something moved abruptly a few feet away. Her discarded jeans wiggled slightly and made a faint buzzing sound. Jeff whipped her over on her back, covering her body protectively with his from this new threat.

"I highly doubt my cell phone is going to assassinate me," she commented wryly.

"Your—" Jeff sagged on top of her. "Being around you is shooting my nerves all to hell."

As he rolled half off her so she could reach for the phone, she said, "Then relax already. I can take care of myself." Still smiling up at him, she answered her phone. "Go ahead."

It was Aleesha. "Sorry to interrupt your fight—or maybe you two are making up by now, and I'm *very* sorry to interrupt that."

Kat blushed fiercely. Thank goodness Aleesha hadn't sprung that line on her in person! She managed to choke out casually enough, "What's up?"

"News. We know who the Ghost stole the disk from. Or at least we've got a very good idea. I'm afraid you two need to cut your little tryst short and get back here."

Kat was profoundly relieved that their conversation had been cut off when it had. Jeff rolled to his feet in a single powerful move. He was swearing under his breath as he reached for his discarded clothes—something to the effect of work having a way of interrupting when a person least needed or wanted the interruption. Poor guy. The timing really had sucked from his point of view.

They sprinted back to the cottage, which not only worked

out some of the lingering sexual energy between them, but also shook most of the telltale sand out of their hair and clothes.

Aleesha wasted no time in briefing them when they burst back into the warmth and light of the cottage. "Turns out the Ghost robbed an Indian tycoon's estate a few weeks back."

Kat nodded. She recalled Jeff's summary to her of the robbery.

"This Indian fellow just got our frisky Russian oil minister to agree to sell a whole bunch of oil futures to India that were slated to go to the United States. The folks at H.O.T. Watch say the State Department has been wondering how the Indians pulled off the deal. It was apparently quite a coup for India and a big blow to the U.S."

Jeff interjected. "So, the Indian guy blackmailed the Russian guy. Why was the video in Chinese, then? If the Chinese took the footage, why wouldn't they have used it themselves to blackmail the Russian into selling them the oil?"

Aleesha shrugged. "Could be they got a ton of money by selling the footage. Could be our Indian guy acquired it by doing a private deal of his own. Could be he stole the video. Hard to tell."

Kat interjected. "So we still don't know who the commandos are."

Aleesha nodded. "Correct." She threw an apologetic glance over at Jeff as she continued, "Cobra, I floated your idea of impersonating the Ghost to the gang at H.O.T. Watch Ops."

"And?" Kat asked with ill-disguised interest.

Another apologetic look at Jeff from Aleesha. "They loved the idea. General Wittenauer has already greenlighted the op."

Jeff's jaw went rock hard, and Kat thought she detected a hint of redness around his ears. Without a word, he pivoted stiffly and walked out of the room. The back door slammed. Hard. She might have kept her face still and calm, but she flinched all the way down to the bottom of her soul.

The Medusas looked over at her expectantly.

Aleesha asked gently, "You gonna go after him and talk to him?"

Kat sighed heavily. "It wouldn't do any good. We've both said all we have to say on the matter. He can't stand watching me take risks, and I can't give up what I do or who I am."

Aleesha studied her long and hard—until Kat had to actively clamp down on an urge to squirm. Finally, the Jamaican said, "This op isn't going to be a picnic. You sure you're up for this mission? It's going to take one hundred percent of your focus and concentration."

Kat knew exactly what Aleesha was asking. Was she too emotionally involved with Jeff to give the job her full attention? Kat sighed. Who knew for sure? One thing she did know. She couldn't possibly back out on this mission now and live with herself. She'd drawn her line in the sand with Jeff. He had to accept her career, or there'd be no future for them.

Belatedly, she answered, "I'll be okay. Let's just get on with it."

But in her heart of hearts, she wasn't so sure things were going to be okay at all. She and the Medusas had steamrolled right over Jeff, and he wasn't going to take kindly to that. At the end of the day, he was exactly what he'd said he was— traditional, protective and used to being in charge. It had been too much to ask him to accept her profession—heck, her true identity.

Likewise, she'd made her choice. She was a warrior first and a woman second.

But, God, it hurt to see him go.

Chapter 17

Kat was still awake when Jeff came back to the cottage as dawn broke outside. She'd given up on sleeping soon thereafter and gotten up. He made no effort to speak to her all day. He participated professionally enough in the planning of the night's mission, but when she tried to talk to him in private, she got exactly nowhere with him.

Each time he gave her a closed, stony look—the classic thousand-yard stare of a hardened soldier—her heart broke a little more. By suppertime, she was a complete mess. So much for being able to hold it together no matter what life threw at her.

She went out to the beach where she swayed and stepped through the slow motion dance of an ancient *gigong* ritual designed to calm and center the chi. Twice. It didn't work. She resorted to the more violent Shaolin kung fu forms next. Better. At least working up a good sweat burned off a little of her urge to burst into tears. But she still felt like crap.

"You okay?" Aleesha murmured for at least the tenth time that day as Kat let herself back into the cottage at dusk.

"No, I'm not," she snapped, her fragile calm already wrecked.

Aleesha laughed quietly. "Welcome to the world of wallowing in emotions like the rest of us."

Kat threw her a bitter look. "Yeah, well, it sucks."

"Ahh, but when it's good, it's great, isn't it?"

Kat squeezed her eyes tightly shut. That was just sweat making them burn like that. Just sweat, dammit.

Aleesha sighed. "I really ought to pull you from this mission."

Alarmed, Kat blurted, "You can't. I'm the only one who can do it."

A reluctant nod. "True. But we can postpone it a few days until you're feeling more like yourself."

Kat winced. She was starting to be genuinely afraid that from here on out this *was* herself. How was she supposed to close the floodgates and re-contain all that emotion that Jeff had let out? It would be like trying to empty a lake with a teaspoon.

"I'll be okay, Aleesha. I promise. Once I get into the flow of the mission, my training will take over."

Aleesha looked at her hard. "Make me a promise. If you get in that house and your concentration isn't perfect, you'll call it off and back out."

"But—"

"No buts. Either you promise, or I'm pulling the plug. We'll find some other way to draw these guys out. The way I hear it, those folks in the H.O.T. Watch can do surveillance on the entire island of Barbados at once."

Having seen the Ops center, Kat could believe it. She glanced up to see Aleesha staring at her expectantly.

Kat sighed. "Fine. I promise."

"On your honor?"

"Yes, mother."

Aleesha nodded firmly. "All right, then. Now go take a little rest and we'll wake you up when it's time to go."

* * *

Kat crouched in the bushes outside the mansion that was her target. It was a massive lump of brick and stone, generically Caribbean colonial. And a hell of a tough nut to crack. The place had banklike security, and in the guise of being built hurricane-proof, had also been built practically burglarproof as well.

To the credit of the home's designers, it had taken most of the staff of the H.O.T. Watch, a team at the Pentagon, and several high-powered civilian electronics and security consultants to come up with a way to breach the place. And were it not for the H.O.T. Watch's high-tech satellite systems and an orbiting electronic counterwarfare chopper nearby, she wouldn't have had a prayer of getting inside undetected.

Wherever he was right now, hidden in the trees, was Jeff worried about her? Or was he just mad? Or maybe he felt nothing at all. He certainly seemed to have shut down his emotions earlier. And how ironic was that? She was the one with the legendary self-control while he wore his feelings on his sleeve, and now she was a blithering idiot and he was a rock.

She checked her thoughts sharply. She ought to be re-viewing the plan, running it one last time in her head, not to mention keeping an eye out for movement that didn't belong out here. Good thing Aleesha wasn't beside her right now, or this mission would already be over.

Jeff's voice crackled over her earpiece, crisp and emotion-less. "H.O.T. Watch and Bravo 51, report when ready." Bravo 51 was the helicopter with the equipment that would jam several electronic portions of the mansion's security system. She didn't hear the chopper yet, but it would move in close when she started her run at the house.

Did he have to sound so cold and uncaring? *Stop that.* He was transmitting on a frequency that close to a hundred people were listening to. How else should he sound?

"You ready, Cobra?" Aleesha prompted.

Kat started. Crud. She was supposed to report when she was ready, and then Jeff would give the green light, and she'd forgotten to do it. Aleesha's transmission had been a subtle kick in the pants to get her head in the game. And Aleesha was right.

Kat slid the switch on her waist pack to hot mike. Everything she said now would broadcast live without her having to press a microphone button. She'd need both hands to do her job pretty soon. "Cobra ready to proceed."

"You are cleared to proceed," Jeff said. "Give us a time hack."

Kat pushed up her sleeve and opened her mouth. The pair of two-inch-long Cyalume sticks she'd tucked into her cheeks emitted a faint glow from between her teeth—enough to see her watch face. "On my mark, it will be 1:30 a.m. Three, two, one, mark."

And with the last syllable, she took off running toward the house. The pressure sensors in the lawn reported wirelessly to the security computer inside, but Bravo 51 had that covered.

On cue, an electronic warfare specialist came up on frequency and announced, "The pressure sensors are jammed. You are clear to cross the grass."

She reached the expanse of green a few seconds later. In her mind, this was the most dangerous part of the mission. She was to run across the lawn in plain view of anyone who might be lurking nearby. After all, the idea was to let the hostiles know she was here. Once she gained the cover of the house, there'd be much less chance to take her out. The working theory was that the commandos would want to capture the Ghost to ask him where the disk was now, and that they wouldn't want to kill him. At least not right away. But if that calculation were wrong, now was the moment they would find out—when bullets slammed into her exposed self.

And then she was across the lawn, crouching in the

shadows of an oleander bush. One of its narrow leaves tickled her nose, and she pushed it aside absently. She had about thirty seconds to wait while Bravo 51 did its magic on the house's outside phone lines. They were going to do something having to do with setting up a feedback loop that blocked a dial tone. The end result would be that when the house's automated alarm system tried to summon the police, no call would get out. At least, that was the plan.

She recognized Jennifer Blackfoot's voice in her ear. "We show no hostile heat signatures on satellite imagery at this time. You are clear to proceed."

"Phones are down," Bravo 51 reported.

That was her signal. She stood up and went to work on the window above her. It was an easy enough matter to cut a foot-wide circle out of the glass and lift it aside. Trickier was the maneuver to use a thin steel rod to manipulate the window latch without breaking the grid of laser beams an inch beyond the window's surface. But with patience and concentration, she got it. After sliding a flat metal strip under the window to maintain contact on the pressure sensors there, she slid the window up gingerly. The house alarms remained silent. Gripping the window frame, she leaped up lightly until she was poised on the narrow sill, balancing on her toes. Carefully, she slipped mirrors into the laser grid until she'd created a gap about ten inches high and eighteen inches wide. It would be a tight squeeze, but that's why she was doing this and not a hulk like Jeff.

The thought of him momentarily broke her breathing rhythm, and she had to pause to remind herself to breathe lightly and evenly. Her calm restored for the moment, she eased through the narrow gap, reaching across a three-foot gap to the back of a leather sofa. Never touching the floor, she slid over the sofa back and twisted to land lightly on its cushioned surface.

"I'm in," she murmured.

The laser grid in here was visible to the naked eye, which made her job of sliding, climbing, leaping and squeezing past it easy. She reached the bookcase beside the door. She commenced pressing, pulling and shifting books in the shelf until she found the dummy book that actually was a switch. It tilted outward from the shelf, and to the right of the library door, a small panel slid open to reveal a numeric keypad.

She described it quickly over her radios. A new voice came up on frequency and didn't identify himself. He did, however, identify the model of alarm system pad she'd described. She spent the next ten minutes following his detailed instructions on how to open the box and disable the alarm.

"Okay, Cobra, give the doorknob a try. If we've done it right, you should be able to open the door and get no alarm siren."

She took a deep breath. Here went nothing. From this moment forward, she'd be on her own inside the house. She turned the cool brass knob slowly. Cracked the door open an inch. Silence. She'd done it.

In point of fact, they expected any bad guys to jump her as she left the house. She ought to be able to proceed from here unhindered. Nonetheless, she eased forward cautiously. It was a short trip down the hall to her right, across the foyer and left into the expansive living room where her target—a magnificent Van der Meer painting—hung.

She eased down the carpeted hall, her passage utterly silent, and frowned. Something didn't feel right. It was nothing she could put her finger on, but an uneasy intuition stole over her. Maybe it was the fact that she was committing a major felony that bugged her.

For no reason she could explain, she paused at the edge of the three-story-high foyer and examined it suspiciously. A huge chandelier dripped with crystal. An ornate table in the middle of the space held a giant Limoges porcelain vase she couldn't wrap her arms around. It was empty at the moment, but would no doubt hold a large floral display when the house was occupied.

The floor was a marble so glossy it glistened like glass in the scant light. Her senses kicked over to another level altogether, her military and martial arts training blending until she was vibrating with awareness at a level so minute her teammates wouldn't believe her if she tried to explain it. And that was probably why she noticed the infinitesimal flicker of movement in a dark shadow under the far leg of the table. She pulled out her sniper scope, a palm-sized telescope she usually used to measure distance to targets. She zoomed it in on the spot where she'd seen the movement.

She frowned. It was a gnat. Lying on its side, one wing beating sporadically in an attempt to free itself. How was the bug trapped? It ought to be able to use its legs to right itself. It was probably just a dying bug and happened to have ended up in that pose. Except…

She sniffed the air experimentally. The faintest odor of something familiar—lightly sweet with a musty undertone— just barely registered. She knew that scent. But where from? She sniffed again, letting its essence flow over her and through her. Summers in Korea. Hidoshi's snug little barn, where the pigs and sheep spent their nights. The paper fly strips that spiraled down from the ceiling, mustard yellow and sticky…and smelling exactly like this.

Flypaper? What did that have to do with this opulent home? Alarm bells went off in her head. Something was not right here. She knelt down to get a better look at that gnat. Now that she thought about it, the gnat was acting just like one of the myriad flies that used to bumble onto Hidoshi's flypaper and then buzz frantically until they died.

The floor. It smelled more strongly of the flypaper glue. From this angle, it looked like a thick layer of polyurethane had been freshly spread over the marble, drying to that glossy sheen. There wasn't a single nick on that satin-smooth surface. What floor had absolutely no nicks or scuffs?

She reached out tentatively to touch the floor and started as it gave way, viscous beneath her touch. She withdrew her hand, and her fingertips stuck to the gooey surface hard enough that she had to yank her hand back, leaving a little skin behind.

That was a powerful epoxy of some kind. The entire floor was coated with glue! Had she stepped in it, she doubted she'd have been able to walk across the floor without sacrificing her shoes, and then her socks, to the glue. Who in their right mind lived in a house like this and poured glue all over their foyer?

A trap.

This was a *trap*.

Adrenaline surged through her veins, screaming its warning at her. She froze, only her gaze roving quickly in all directions. She saw no cameras. No microphones. No other surveillance equipment. Her gut said she wasn't missing anything. The threat she sensed was more human than machine.

Holy sh—

Was she alone in here or not?

Was this why the H.O.T. Watch had seen no hostiles outside? Were they already inside? Was their ambush about to be turned on them? She eased her hand down to her belt and pressed the transmit button three times fast, three times slow, and three times fast, sending out a clicked S.O.S.

Jeff's response was immediate in her ear. "Are you injured?"

Two clicks for no.

"Are you in danger?"

One click for yes.

"Are you under attack?"

How was she to answer that? She wasn't yet, but if there were hostiles in here, she very well could be soon. Did she want the Medusas to come roaring in here with guns blazing, or sneak in and possibly catch whoever else was in the house?

She gave two clicks for no.

"That was a long pause before you answered. Are you about to come under attack?" Jeff asked quickly.

An quick, emphatic single click.

"Do you request backup?"

Again, a single click.

Jeff gave the Medusas a flurry of orders to move in and enter the house through various doors and windows. Jennifer Blackfoot came up on frequency and ordered Bravo 51 to stand by to hit the house with all it had, jamming all electrical function of any kind within the mansion.

And then Jennifer said, "We'll have a Predator drone on sight in two minutes. It's equipped with structure-penetrating radar. Stand by for insertion, Medusas."

Jeff acknowledged her.

Kat hunkered down in the hallway, thinking fast. She couldn't stay here. She was completely exposed and had no cover if this turned into a shoot-out. She glanced around for options. With nothing but the glue-filled foyer before her and an empty hallway behind her, she didn't have much to work with. And then she looked up. Time to use her secret weapon and go vertical. She eased back into a shadow and quickly pulled out her climbing claws, donning them over her shoes and on her hands.

She climbed the hallway wall first, and then eased around the corner into the foyer nearly ten feet up. As soon as she entered the open space, she worked her way higher, crawling up the wall, spiderlike, until she was well above the sight lines of anyone looking from the adjoining rooms into the foyer. She headed for a shadow and awkwardly resumed her game of twenty questions with Jeff.

She laboriously tapped out the Morse code to spell, "Trap. Foyer."

He replied immediately. "Should we avoid the foyer?"

She clicked an affirmative, and he amended Karen's point of entry to the dining-room window instead of the front door.

Kat double-tapped a negative to that. If Karen came into the dining room, she'd have to cross the foyer to get to anywhere but the kitchen.

Jeff understood immediately. "Will it work if Python comes in through the living room?"

Isabella was already scheduled to come in the living room window. That would put two Medusas in there simultaneously. Kat's best guess was that would be where the hostiles would be hiding. They'd surround the painting that the Ghost was after.

Kat clicked a yes to Jeff's suggestion that Karen enter the living room.

Astutely, Jeff asked, "Should I concentrate more force than I already am on the living room?"

She clicked a relieved affirmative.

Yet another adjustment to the entry scheme was made, and all the Medusas were massed outside the windows.

Then Jeff asked, "Where are you now, Cobra? I don't want your teammates shooting you."

She looked down at the foyer. Up here, she'd be clear of any bullets flying into the foyer. She reviewed the house layout quickly in her mind. But if she wanted to join the fight at all, she'd be squarely in her teammates' fields of fire. She had to move.

She tapped out, "Foyer. Moving to living room."

Jeff's response was quick and sharp. "Don't go in there by yourself! Wait for backup!"

He didn't understand where she was at the moment, and although his advice was sound, she needed to ignore it. She sent one last message. "Am on ceiling."

That caused a stir as Jennifer Blackfoot and Aleesha came up simultaneously to ask what the heck she meant by that.

A chuckle was evident in Jeff's voice as he explained. "Cobra straps claws to her feet and hands and can crawl upside down along a ceiling like an insect. Medusas, keep your field of fire at eye level or below and you won't hit her. She'll be overhead when you enter the room."

Jennifer retorted, "Are you kidding?"

Jeff answered, "Nope. I've seen her do it. It's for real."

A male voice interrupted. "The Predator is approaching target. Switching on cameras now. Stand by for real-time photo intelligence analysis."

Kat didn't know if the analyst would be at H.O.T. Watch Ops or sitting on the nearby helicopter, but she didn't care either way, as long as the analyst knew his stuff.

A female voice came up. "I have eyes on target. I show one human heat signature…" A long pause. "Near the ceiling of the foyer, moving down the wall toward the living room entrance."

Jeff murmured, "That is correct. Continue."

"I paint two human signatures in the dining room, one to the right of the foyer entrance, one under the far window."

Bingo. As disconcerting as it was to know she was, indeed, in the middle of an ambush, Kat was relieved to know that her instinct had been right and all this fuss wasn't for naught.

The analyst went on. "I paint four humans in the living room, two on each side of the fireplace on the far wall. I paint one more human in the kitchen—he's on the move, heading toward the butler's pantry."

Kat reviewed the house layout quickly. That guy would be circling through the back side of the house to come into the living room if she had to bet. After all, these guys couldn't use the foyer any more than she could. Misty was slated to come in from that direction. She could drive that guy toward the living room if need be.

The analyst concluded, "That's all. Seven tangos and one friendly doing a Spider-Man."

Jeff came up. "Copy. Medusas, prepare for radio failure. Go on Bravo 51's call of systems activated."

All five Medusas acknowledged in turn, with Kat clicking hers.

Then Jeff said, "Bravo 51, light it up."

"Roger," came the electronic warfare man's voice. "Here we go."

Kat swore she could actually feel the radio waves bombarding her. Static abruptly filled her ears, but she wasn't in a position to turn down her radio volume at the moment. She started crawling, heading for the dining room. Jeff was going to deal with those two guys, and she didn't like those odds. As glass crashed from a half-dozen windows at once and shouting broke out around her, Kat planted a piton at light speed, clicked her rope onto it, and let go of the wall. She swung downward, dropping upside down until her head and shoulders cleared the dining-room entrance. More importantly, her pistol cleared the archway. For tonight's work, she'd chosen a high-caliber handgun with enough stopping power to drop a man. Thankfully, she routinely practiced shooting from odd angles like this, and she took in the scene before her in an instant. Jeff had just crashed through the window and was rolling across the floor while two men in black turned, startled, and were bringing their weapons up to bear on him.

Jeff was situated to nail the guy under the window, so she aimed at the man closest to her, double tapping a pair of shots into the guy before he ever knew she was there. Gunfire erupted from the living room as Jeff efficiently dropped his man. He jumped up and started toward her.

"Stop!" she cried.

He skidded to a halt.

She bit out, "There's epoxy glue all over the foyer floor. You'll have to go around."

He nodded and took off running toward the kitchen.

Quickly, she curled into a ball, caught her rope, and righted herself. She took off, crawling crablike around the foyer toward the shoot-out now in progress in the living room. The space was huge—easily fifty feet square, and crammed with furniture, cabinets, tables, and any manner of good cover. At a glance, all the shooters, both friendly and hostile, looked pinned down and at a stalemate. She glanced over at the doorway Jeff would have to come through. He'd be a sitting duck if he tried to get in there.

She had to do something to tip the scales and fast. He'd be here in a few more seconds.

She climbed up to the twelve-foot-high ceiling and commenced crawling stealthily across it. There. Below her. One of the hostiles. She pulled her pistol and shot down at him, burying a round in the top of his skull and a second round in the back of his neck as he fell.

Her shots elicited a round of gunfire, but none of the hostiles spotted her. She held her position, unmoving. She was completely exposed up here. If any of the bad guys looked up, she was dead meat.

Jeff spun into the room, and the hostiles seemed to realize that the stalemate was breaking against them. They commenced running around, shooting wildly. Although they didn't hit any Medusas, they did effectively foul up everyone's field of fire. Kat saw Aleesha and Isabella draw knives and move out, easing around the perimeters of the space.

Two of the hostiles drew together in the middle of the room, back-to-back behind a giant armoire in a highly defensible position. They were going to be hell to reach. Anyone who came into their line of sight would be shot.

And then she spotted Jeff moving toward them.

He was going to be a hero, dammit.

Swearing under her breath, she scrambled forward. From her vantage point, she saw Jeff pause around the corner from the hostile pair. He shoved a new clip of bullets home and tensed to move. A quick glance showed her the worst. The tango was sighting down the barrel of an AK-47, right at where Jeff was going to emerge, finger poised on the trigger. The second Jeff came around the end of the wet bar, he was going to be blown away.

Desperate to stop him from diving straight into the commando's hail of lead, she scrambled the last few feet. And let go of the ceiling.

Chapter 18

Jeff's heart skipped a beat as Kat's dark shape hurtled down from the ceiling directly in front of where he was about to shoot.

Dear God. Had she been shot?

Pure, unadulterated panic ripped through him, a sick wash of heat that all but knocked his legs out from under him. Roaring in rage and terror, he charged around the corner, heedless of any danger waiting for him. He'd charge the jaws of hell itself for her.

He made out a writhing mass of arms and legs that he dared not shoot at, so he continued to sprint forward, the panic blurring his vision until he could hardly see.

And then a petite figure rose to the top of the pile.

Kat. He'd know her anywhere.

Blindingly fast, she gave a vicious yank. The figure beneath her went limp and thudded to the floor. A second, bigger figure jumped on her from behind, a knife glinting dully in the gloom.

Jeff's weapon swung up to his shoulder. Time ceased, and his mind went to some strange place it had never gone before. A state of suspended animation descended upon him. He became one with the gun, and with the lead slug resting in its depths. He took the shot almost without conscious thought. It was as if his mind directed the bullet's path, guiding its flight unerringly a hair past Kat's temple and into the left eye of her attacker. The guy's head snapped back, and Kat whipped around in his grasp, striking him an open-handed blow that leveled him long before Jeff's bullet dropped him.

As he ran forward toward her, a single thought crossed his mind. He'd never seen another human being move as fast as she just had.

"You okay?" he bit out as they sank to the ground, back-to-back as their attackers had just been.

"Yeah. You?" She panted.

"Fine."

The gunfire in the room was winding down. One more burst of gunfire, he recognized the sound of an MP-7—standard issue for the Medusas—and then it went quiet. The silence was intense after all the shots in an enclosed space, and his ears rang fiercely.

"Report!" he called.

One by one, the Medusas reported in. Misty's voice sounded strained, as if she were injured.

"Mamba," he called.

"I'm on it," the medic replied, already running toward the last sound of Misty's voice.

He stood up cautiously. "Clear the space by standard quadrants. We'll meet at the fireplace."

Kat stood up behind him and it was all he could do not to spin around and snatch her into his arms, to run his hands over her to assure himself that she wasn't hurt. But now was not the time. Not yet.

He methodically checked his portion of the room, verifying that the two hostiles he and Kat had taken out were, indeed, dead. A few minutes later, the team converged by the fireplace, Mamba holding Misty's left arm and still binding a splint into place. For her part, Misty's face was drawn in pain.

"What have you got, Mamba?"

"Bullet in the upper arm, lodged near the bone. Gonna have to dig it out. Bleeding under control. She's ambulatory but not combat capable."

He nodded briskly. It was weird to let a woman suffer with a gunshot wound like this, but if he'd ever doubted it before, he didn't now. These women were soldiers of the first caliber, every bit as good as his own men. They'd worked like a well-oiled machine, in spite of the close confines, the lack of radios and determined resistance by the hostiles.

Kat looked up from the body she'd just searched. "Russian. What do you want to bet our frisky oil minister sent them to get his movie back."

Jeff nodded. "That movie's gonna cost India a big oil contract or a whole lot of egg on that Russian minister's face. The State Department's gonna kiss your feet when you give that disk to them."

Kat made a face. "That's okay. I'll settle for a decent foot massage. No kissing required."

He grinned and spoke off frequency. "It all depends on who's doing the kissing and how. You're gonna like what I do to your toes."

Kat's eyes popped wide open, clearly imagining the possibilities.

The static in his ear stopped abruptly. Hallelujah. In the chaos of battle he hadn't noticed it, but it had really been starting to get on his nerves the last minute or two.

"Say status," Jennifer Blackfoot ordered.

She sounded tense. Which was saying something for her.

He replied, "All hostiles down. One friendly injury. We'll need medevac to a hospital, but it's not life-threatening."

"Well done, Maverick, ladies."

He started. That had been General Wittenauer's voice. He'd had no idea the Old Man had been monitoring this op.

"Let's move out," Jeff ordered.

They headed for the back of the house. Bravo 51 was being directed to move in and pick up Misty and Mamba and fly them back to the H.O.T. Watch cave. Aleesha would remove Misty's bullet in their operating room, where there wouldn't be any awkward questions asked about how Misty'd been shot.

The helicopter lifted off, and the Medusas hiked off through the trees to recover the surveillance gear they'd abandoned when he'd ordered them to rush the house. Kat hung back with him, since she'd carried all her gear with her when she broke in to the mansion.

She gazed up at him in the starlight beseechingly. She did not speak, but then, she didn't have to. Her eyes said everything. She was hurt. Missed him. Wanted to talk to him. Wanted him to understand that this was who she was.

"I—"

A dark shape hurtled out of the trees and barreled into Kat just as a gunshot rang out.

Jeff dived for Kat and the prone figure on top of her. Before he could do a thing to help her, Kat had moved like lightning, slipping the grip of her captor and reversing their positions.

Another shot rang out, and a foot-long divet of grass flew up a scant inch beyond Kat's head. Jeff jumped to his feet, grabbing the attacker by one arm as Kat took him by the other. The three of them sprinted across the lawn, zigzagging for cover.

A French-accented voice panted. "One shooteur. In the woods that way. I show you."

"Ahh. We meet again," Kat answered warmly.

The Ghost? Jeff's jaw dropped as he ran. The guy had literally run right into his grasp? Exultation shot through him.

They dived into a stand of fig trees and the shooter paused for the moment.

"This way!" The Ghost took off crawling on his hands and knees, with Kat in tow.

"You're not going to follow him, are you?" Jeff demanded in a whisper.

"Of course I am."

"You've already walked into one trap tonight. Are you going to dive into another one?" Jeff challenged.

"He just saved my life. He's not a killer." And with that, Kat turned away and rose to a crouch, running after the thief.

Jeff closed his eyes for a moment in sheer exasperation and then gave chase. The pair had paused at the edge of the fig grove. He drew close in time to hear Kat murmur, "Can you point him out from here?

"I t'ink not."

"Use this," she said. Jeff gaped as she pulled out her spotter's scope and passed it to the Frenchman.

"Ahh. There 'e is."

Kat glanced over her shoulder. "Give me your gun, Jeff."

"I'll take the shot—"

She cut him off. "I'm a trained sniper. You're not. I'll take the shot."

Shaking his head, he peeled his MP-7 off his shoulder and handed it over. "It's sighted true. I make corrections manually."

"Perfect." Kat sounded distant, already completely focused on the shot to come. She transmitted over her radio. "Does anybody have the current winds at this location?"

She stretched out on the ground, settling into a prone position, the rifle coming up to her cheek.

Jeff recognized Carter Beigneaux's voice from H.O.T. Watch Ops. "Five knots, variable from heading one hundred to one hundred and thirty."

"Thanks," Kat muttered.

"What's going on?" Jennifer demanded.

Jeff answered, "A stray shooter."

"You need telemetry?" Jennifer blurted in alarm.

"No. Cobra's got it handled. Stand by."

And something deep in his gut really did believe she had the situation under control. He was still and silent behind her as she set up for the shot.

"Where is he?" she murmured to the Ghost.

The Frenchman began to give a description, and after a few seconds, Kat cut in. "Got him."

She murmured, "Target acquired. Request green light."

Jeff answered immediately. "You are greenlighted."

At his feet, she went completely still, as relaxed as if she were deeply asleep. Her legs sprawled wide to stabilize her body on her belly. Her right arm draped over his gun's stock, and her cheek pressed against the housing as gently as a lover. He actually felt the calm that rolled off her, the utter concentration as her entire world narrowed down to a single point in her sights.

She exhaled slowly.

And then a single shot rang out.

Kat spoke emotionlessly. "Clean head shot. Target is down."

Jeff sagged behind her.

She rolled over onto her back and the Ghost helped her to her feet. To the Frenchman, she said, "Thank you, my friend. I owe you one this time."

"No, we are even. You went into that ambush instead of moi. I t'ink I would have died in there."

"Not before you told them where you got that disk of yours," Jeff commented.

The Ghost looked at him in surprise. "The Renoir job."

Jeff nodded. They'd been right. The Indian businessmen. "Do you know who those men waiting for you were?"

"They are Russian. Not government. Private. How you say—mafiosi. The oil minister. He want his movie back and hire them."

"Can you prove that?" Jeff asked.

The Ghost shrugged. "My source... 'e cannot reveal himself to the likes of you. But 'e is never wrong."

Jeff sighed. As he'd expected.

Jennifer spoke into his ear. "Police en route. Those outside shots were heard and reported by a neighbor."

Kat started. "You must leave, my friend. The police are on their way."

Jeff started. "Leave? Not on your life! He's stolen a hundred million dollars' worth of art. He's under arrest!"

Kat turned to him. She didn't say a word. She just looked at him with sad, wise eyes. And he knew in his heart that she was right. The honorable thing to do was as plain as day in her gaze. No wonder Vanessa Blake called her the Medusas' compass arrow of right and wrong. He hesitated a moment more...

And then nodded in acknowledgment.

He turned to face the Ghost. "In light of the fact that you just saved the life of the woman I plan to marry, I think we can make an exception in this case. If you head down toward the beach, we can stall the police here."

A wide smile broke across the thief's face. He bowed his head briefly at Jeff, then turned to face Kat. He pressed a small rectangle of white into her hand. "If you ever have need of me, you have but to call this number. A message will reach me."

He turned to leave, then paused and looked over his shoulder.

"She is a precious diamond, a woman of extraordinary worth. Take good care of her, monsieur."

"Trust me. I plan to. For the rest of my life and hers."

And as the Ghost faded away into the night, Jeff turned to face his future. Kat stepped into his arms eagerly, fitting against him as if she'd been born for him.

"Thank you," she murmured.

"For what? For letting him go? Or for finally seeing you for who you really are, and finally wrapping my brain around the fact that you can handle yourself every bit as well as I can?

Or for accepting you for who you are—all of you, including your job and your crazy training and your blasted sense of honor?"

She laughed quietly. "All of that."

"I love you, you know."

She froze. Slowly she leaned back to look up at him. "Are you sure?"

It was his turn to laugh. "Oh, yeah. I'm sure. I was ready to slay lions and charge into hell for you in there. I'm a goner. Cupid's Bolt did me in."

"Gee, and here I thought it was Medusa's arrow that got you."

"That she did. She's got all of me forever if she'll have me. What do you say, darlin'? Will you marry me?"

Her smile was bright enough to light the heavens and illuminated his heart until he thought it might burst. "I thought you'd never ask. It would be my honor to have you."

Jennifer Blackfoot's voice came up on frequency, startling them both. "Uh, one of you is leaning on your transmit button."

Kat buried her face against his chest in mortification as laughter and cheering erupted over their earpieces. And then General Wittenauer's voice came up on frequency. "You'd better take good care of her, son. She's like a daughter to me."

Jeff closed his eyes in chagrin. "Yes, sir. I will, sir." He gazed down at Kat apologetically. "So much for privacy for the two of us."

"Welcome to my world," she said, rolling her eyes.

He grinned down at her. "I think I'm gonna like it there. A lot." He took her hand in his, and together, the two of them turned to walk into whatever the future held.

* * * * *

HIS WOMAN
IN COMMAND

BY
LINDSAY McKENNA

First published in Great Britain 2011
by Mills & Boon, an imprint of Harlequin (UK) Limited,
Eton House, 18-24 Paradise Road, Richmond, Surrey TW9 1SR

© Lindsay McKenna 2010

ISBN: 978 0 263 88526 2

46-0511

Harlequin (UK) policy is to use papers that are natural, renewable and
recyclable products and made from wood grown in sustainable forests. The
logging and manufacturing processes conform to the legal environmental
regulations of the country of origin.

Printed and bound in Spain
by Blackprint CPI, Barcelona

As a writer, **Lindsay McKenna** feels that telling a story is a way to share how she sees the world she lives in. Love is the greatest healer of all and the books she creates are parables that underline this belief. Working with flower essences, another gentle healer, she devotes part of her life to the world of nature to help ease people's suffering. She knows that the right words can heal and that a story can be a catalyst in a person's life. And in some way she hopes that her books may educate and lift the reader in a positive manner. She can be reached at www.lindsaymckenna.com.

To ROMVETS, a group of women who have served or are currently serving in the military. This list comprises women who are aspiring writers and published authors. It's an honor to be among you.

Chapter 1

"Twenty bucks says you can't get that good-lookin' woman to come over to our table and have a beer with us," Staff Sargeant Neal Robles challenged.

Captain Gavin Jackson, leader of a ten-man Special Forces team, squinted in the semidarkness of the officers' club—a tent on the most dangerous border in the world: between Afghanistan and Pakistan. It was the last day of their two weeks of rest between month-long assignments in the field. Tomorrow, they'd be back out in the badlands border area hunting Taliban. Gavin sat with his nine men. The pitcher of frothy cold beer in front of them went quickly.

The woman in question had just entered the spacious tent, catching the attention of every man in the room. She was about five foot eight, with short, curly black hair framing an oval face and high cheekbones. She was olive-skinned with light gold eyes. Then there was her killer mouth that

Gavin wanted to capture and kiss. The frumpy green one-piece flight uniform that told him she was a pilot couldn't hide her assets. Curvy in all the right places. Gavin felt his body harden with desire.

He didn't know why. His relationship with another woman army pilot had crashed and burned a year ago. Gavin had sworn off women for now and women army pilots forever. Squirming in his seat, the wooden chair creaking, he shrugged as Neal Robles grinned like a wolf over the dare.

"Why her?" Gavin grunted, lifting the cold mug of beer to his lips.

Robles's dark brown eyes gleamed as he whispered, "She's hot, Cap'n."

"She's the *only* female in here," Gavin drawled. Indeed, the huge dark green canvas tent was packed with men—A teams coming in for a well-deserved rest, logistics, pilots or mechanics to support their missions. Women pilots were few, but they did exist. Automatically, Gavin rubbed his chest in memory of Laurie Braverman, the U.S. Army CH-47 Chinook driver that he'd fallen in love with. They'd broken up because of their mutual inability to compromise. A war of egos had eventually destroyed their relationship.

"She might be the only one," Robles asserted, "but you gotta admit, Cap'n, she's something." Robles looked at the other enlisted men around the table, all of whom bobbed in unison to agree with his observation.

Tugging on his recently trimmed beard, Gavin gave them an amused look. His team knew about his hard luck with Laurie, especially since he'd been a growly old bear for a month after their spectacular parting. "You know," he said, "it's damned hard enough to survive the border villages. Now, you want to collectively throw me at *another* driver?"

Driver was a common slang expression for any pilot whether they flew fixed-wing aircraft or helicopters.

Laughter rippled through his team. Gavin was fiercely protective of his men. They'd been together over here nearly a year, and they were tighter than a set of fleas on a mangy Afghan dog. He wanted to bring all of them back off this tour alive so they could go home to their families. He had visited the base barber this morning, got a wonderful hot shower, a trim, clean clothes and joined his men at the canteen tent. Although they were in the U.S. Army, their clothes were decidedly Afghani. With their beards, wearing their wool *pakols,* or caps, they melted into the mountainous area less a target as a result of their wardrobe. They all wore the traditional turban. The loose, comfortable-fitting top with long sleeves had pajamalike trousers of the same color, and the traditional wool vests were worn over it.

"Naw, she doesn't look like she's a man-eater like the last one you tangled with," Robles said. The table broke out in collective laughter once again. More beer was poured. A bartender came over and delivered another pitcher of cold beer, the froth foaming up and over of the top.

Gavin couldn't disagree and his gaze wandered to the woman leaning up against the makeshift bar and ordering a cup of coffee, not beer. She was probably on duty, Gavin assumed. He watched her hands. They were long, narrow and beautiful-looking. No wedding ring. But then, what did that mean? Nothing, because military combatants were forbidden to wear jewelry of any kind. So, she could be married. Frowning, Gavin felt his assistant CO, Dave Hansen, give his right shoulder a nudge.

"Go on, Gavin," he said in his slow Texas drawl, "she looks pretty docile. Invite her over. We'd all like the company of a good-lookin' woman to remind us of what's waiting for us at home. We're harmless. Just tell her we're voyeurs."

Gavin scowled at his team. "Since when are you willing to throw me to the lions? Don't I treat you right out there?"

Guffaws broke out and Gavin couldn't help grinning. They all desperately needed a little fun. The border country was violent and lethal. They'd spent thirty days in the mountains hunting out pockets of Taliban in caves. Not that the local villages along the border ever cooperated. Most of them were terrorized by the Taliban. And the tribal people had been forgotten by the government in Kabul decades ago. Out there, Gavin knew, no fiercely independent Afghan could be trusted once your back was turned on them. They'd just as soon put a bullet between your shoulder blades as look at you because of what the Taliban had done to them. Gavin's team had had several firefights with the Taliban on their last mission. If not for the Apache helo drivers coming in with heavy fire support, they wouldn't be here enjoying this beer with one another.

Gavin sat up and sighed. He knew his men needed a reprieve from their deadly work. They all had PTSD symptoms. Why not waltz up to this gal and ask her to join them? "Okay," he growled at them, "I'll go throw myself on her mercy for the likes of all of you and see what she says."

The men clapped and cheered as Gavin stood up. He smoothed down his vest and adjusted the thick leather belt around his waist that carried a dagger and a pistol. Out in the field, he'd have body armor on, but not now. He adjusted the dark brown wool *pakol* on his head. To anyone seeing these men riding up on their tough mountain-bred ponies, they looked like a group of Afghan men. Of course, here in the canteen tent, they were out of place, but everyone on base knew Special Forces A teams dressed like Afghans.

Giving his group a wink, Gavin said, "Okay, men, keep it down while I work some magic." They all nodded solemnly, lifted their glasses of beer and beamed excitedly like little children waiting for Christmas to arrive. Gavin shook his head and walked across the creaking plywood floor toward the bar. He noticed that although men were hanging around the bar, all of them gave the woman pilot some room to breathe. Not that they weren't looking at her. But none made a move on her. Why? They were support and logistics men and worked in the camp, so they might know something about this woman pilot he didn't.

Coming to the bar, Gavin stood about two feet away from her. The scalding look she gave him with those lion-gold eyes surprised him. He was clean, for once. He didn't smell of sweat and fear. His black hair and beard were neatly trimmed and combed. Maybe she didn't like A teams or Afghans, Gavin decided. The way her full mouth thinned, her hands tense around the white ceramic mug of coffee, told him everything. She really didn't want this intrusion into her space.

"I'm Captain Gavin Jackson," he said, pushing aside his fear of rejection. He looked at the upper arm of her green flight suit. "We've never seen a patch with a black cat on it. I was wondering what squadron you're with." That was a safe icebreaker, Gavin thought.

Nike Alexander, at twenty-six, did not want any male attention. Just a year ago, she'd lost Antonio, an officer in the Peruvian Army who had died in a vicious firefight with cocaine dealers. She glared icily at the man, who was decidedly handsome despite his rugged appearance. "I'm with the Black Jaguar Squadron 60," she snapped.

"I've been out here on the front nearly a year. I've never seen this patch. Is this a new squadron?" Gavin opted for something simpler than trying to get this good-looking woman to come over to their table for a beer. He was frantically searching for ways to defuse her tension.

Shrugging, Nike lifted the coffee to her lips, took a sip and then said, "We're basically Apache pilots in an all-woman flight program. We got here three weeks ago."

"Oh." Gavin didn't know what to think about that. "All women?"

Nike's mouth twitched. "We're black ops." His thick, straight brows raised with surprise. While it was true there were women pilots in combat, no women-only squadrons existed. "We're top secret to the rest of the world. Here at camp, they know what we do," she added to ward off questions she saw in his large blue eyes.

Under other circumstances, Nike would be interested in this warrior. Clearly, he was an A-team leader. She knew these brave and hardy Special Forces teams were on the front lines, finding Taliban and stopping their incursion into Afghanistan's space. His hands were large, square and roughened by work and the forces of the weather.

"Ah, black ops," Gavin murmured. He saw the wariness in her gold eyes. "You're new?"

"I arrived a week ago."

"Welcome aboard," he said, holding out his hand toward her. This time, he was sincere. Anyone who flew the border risked their lives every time they lifted off from this secret base.

Looking at his proffered hand and then up at him, Nike couldn't help herself and slid her hand into his. He grinned like a little boy given a Christmas gift. Despite the neatly trimmed beard that gave his square face a dangerous look, he seemed happy to meet her. Well, they were both in the army and that meant something. Her flesh tingled as his fingers wrapped gently around hers. She admired his deeply sunburned face, laugh lines at the corners of his eyes. A wild, unexpected surge of excitement coursed through Nike. What was *that* all about? Why was her heart pounding? She broke the contact and pulled her hand away.

Oh, he was eye candy, there was no doubt. The boyish, crooked grin made him even more devastatingly handsome, Nike decided.

"What's your name?" Gavin asked. He forced his hands off the bar, unexpectedly touching her olive-tone skin. The brief contact sent crazy tingles up and down his arm. The close proximity to this woman intoxicated him in quite another way. Gavin fully realized he was more than a little tipsy from the beer he and his team had been guzzling. But he was still alert, still fixated on this new person of interest.

"I'm Captain Nike Alexander," she informed him in a clipped and wary tone. She'd just arrived with her squadron from the USA and wanted to focus only on the mission before them. As an all-woman squadron they had a lot to prove—again. They'd done it in Peru, now it would be here. She didn't want to tangle with some sex-hungry A-team leader who hadn't seen a woman in God knew how long. Still, a secret part of her wondered what Gavin would look like without that beard. Not that he wasn't handsome with it; maybe she was just more interested than she cared to admit.

"Nike," he murmured, rolling the name around on his tongue. "That's different." He squinted and gave her a mea-suring look. "Are you…American?" Her husky voice had a trace of an accent. When she frowned, he knew he'd asked the wrong question.

"I was born in Athens, Greece, Captain. I was invited from my country to train and work for the U.S. Army." She turned and showed the American flag on the left shoulder of her uniform.

"Greek." That made sense, although he'd said it as if he were stunned by the information. Seeing the frustration in her large, clear gold eyes, Gavin asked, "Wasn't Nike a goddess in Greek myths?"

"She still is," Nike said in a flat tone. "I was named after her."

"I see." Gavin stood there, his brows dipping. "So, you're part of a black ops, you're a female pilot and you're from Greece." Brightening, he shared a look with her, his smile crooked. "That makes you a pretty rare specimen out here in our back country."

"You're making me feel like a bug under a microscope, Captain. Why don't you mosey back to your team. I'm not interested in anything but my mission here."

Her tone was low and dismissive.

Gavin kept his smile friendly and tried to appear neutral and not the leering, sexually hungry male he really was. It was now or never. "Speaking of that, Captain Alexander, we were wondering if you might not come and join us? My boys and I are going back for thirty more days in the bush tomorrow morning. We'd enjoy your company."

Easing into a standing position, Nike glanced over at the table. Nine other bearded men in Afghan dress looked hopefully in her direction. English-speaking women who were not Moslem were a rarity in this country. Of course they'd want her company. "Captain, I'm not the USO.

And I'm not for sale at any price. If you want female entertainment I suggest you find it somewhere else."

Ouch. Gavin scowled. "Just a beer, Captain. Or, we'll buy you another cup of coffee. That's all. Nothing else." He held up both his hands. "Honest."

"I appreciate the offer," Nike said. She pulled out a few coins from her pocket and put them on the bar next to the drained cup of coffee. "But I must respectfully decline, Captain." She turned and marched out of the tent.

"That went well," Gavin said, his grin wide and silly-looking as she exited. He walked over to his men, who looked defeated.

"You crashed and burned," Robles groaned.

Jackson poured himself another glass of beer. "She's got other fish to fry." He said it as lightly as he could.

The men nodded and nursed their beers.

At twenty-eight, Gavin understood that a little fun and laughter was good medicine for his men. Silently, he thanked Nike Alexander for her decision. What would it have been like to have her come over and sit with them? It would have lifted their collective spirits. They were starving for some feminine attention. Oh, she probably realized this, but didn't get that his invitation was truly harmless. Gavin had seen a lot of sensitivity in her face and read it in her eyes. However, she was protective, if not a little defensive about sharing that side. He couldn't blame her.

Gavin told them what he'd found out. His men were like slavering dogs getting a morsel tossed to them. In Afghanistan, Moslem women could not talk directly to any man. Consequently, it was a world of males with males and the women were hidden away in their homes. Gavin missed being stateside. Even though he'd crashed and burned with

Laurie Braverman on his first tour here, he still hungered for conversation with an intelligent woman.

As he glanced toward the flap of the tent where Nike Alexander had marched through, Gavin lamented her departure. Clearly, she thought he was hitting on her. Well, wasn't he? Digging into the pocket of his trousers, he produced a twenty-dollar bill and threw it across the table to his medic. "Here, Robles. Satisfied?"

Chuckling, Neal took the twenty and hoisted it upward. "You tried. Hey, Cap'n, this will give us another round of beer!"

The men clapped and hooted, and Gavin grinned crookedly. His team needed this kind of blowout before they got dropped in the badlands again. As he took one more look to where Nike had left, he wished he'd had a little more time with her. Would they ever meet again? Hope sprang in his chest. Nike was a fascinating woman, pilot or not. Gavin shrugged off any romantic thoughts and took a deep swig of beer. Chances of *ever* seeing Nike Alexander again were next to nothing.

"Nike," Major Dallas Klein-Murdoch said, "sit down and relax. Welcome to BJS 60."

Nike settled in front of her commanding officer's desk. Every incoming pilot to the squadron did a one-on-one with the CO. This morning, it was her turn. Dallas Klein's reputation with the original Black Jaguar Squadron, for which she had flown in Peru, was legendary. Nike was only too thrilled to be here under this woman's command. They'd had a stint together in Texas chasing Mexican drug-runners before this latest assignment. There, Dallas had fallen in love with ATF agent Mike Murdoch. The Pentagon had then sent Dallas and her new husband to Afghanistan to oversee the latest Black Jaguar Squadron. Murdoch was now a captain in the U.S. Army and worked as a strategy and operations officer for the all-women Apache combat pilots that comprised BJS 60. And while the pilots were all female, some males in the ranks took care of the Apache helicopters. Nike was glad that Dallas was assigned here with her new husband. Taking off her baseball cap, Nike sat down and grinned. "Like old times, isn't it?"

Dallas laughed. "Better believe it." She reached for a file folder and handed it to Nike. "Here are your orders. We have twenty women Apache pilots here and ten helicopters assigned to us. The last two helos are being flown in today to this base. My executive officer, XO, is going to be Captain Emma Trayhern-Cantrell."

Raising her brows, Nike said, "From *the* Trayhern family?"

"The very same. Shortly after you left Peru, Emma was assigned to BJS in Peru and flew Apaches down there for six months before I was able to convince the Pentagon to have her assigned here. She's a chip off the old Trayhern block—a real woman warrior."

"Whose child is she?" Nike wondered.

"Clay and Alyssa Cantrell-Trayhern's oldest child. Emma has three younger sisters, two of whom are in the U.S. Naval Academy right now. They're due to graduate next year. They're twins. Clay and Alyssa were Navy pilots and flew P3 antisubmarine aircraft for twenty years. Emma, whom you'll meet sometime today, is a long, lean red-haired greyhound with blazing gray eyes. I'm glad to have her on board. She's a natural XO."

Chuckling, Nike opened the folder. "Emma sounds perfect for this black ops."

"Oh, she is. Her grandfather is the original black-ops

figure behind the scenes," Dallas drawled, smiling. "Let's get down to business. I'm seeing my pilots individually to give them their orders."

"Fire away," Nike murmured, studying the papers.

"First of all, BJS 60 remains an all-woman U.S. Army force," Dallas began, leaning back in her chair. "The women I chose for this new squadron have more than one flight skill. For example, you are licensed to fly fixed-wing, single-engine planes as you did on the U.S.-Mexico border with me. And you're also certified to fly the CH-47, which is the workhorse helicopter used here in Afghanistan." Dallas looked over at the lean, wiry pilot. "Every woman in BJS 60 has multiskills in aviation. There may be times when I want you to fly the CH-47 and not the Apache."

"Being multitalented has never been a problem for me," Nike said, grinning.

Dallas leaned back in her chair. "We are under General Chapman and we work indirectly with the national Afghanistan Army. BJS 60 is going to be a 'sparrowhawk' team that will be called upon in emergencies when the regular Apache pilots from the other two squadrons are not available. In other words, we're going to pick up the slack to ensure that Special Forces A teams get immediate help and support out in the field. Our jobs will vary depending upon what General Chapman's operations officer decides for us. One day you could be flying a CH-47, another, you'll be back in the seat of an Apache helicopter. Mike, my husband, is working as a liaison between Chapman's people and us. We're going to try and get as much air time as possible in the Apache, but we also know our pilots will be flying other helicopters, too."

Nike nodded. Instantly, she pictured Captain Gavin Jackson, who was a man's man, supremely confident. Someone she was drawn to, but Nike wasn't willing to admit that to herself now or ever. "I ran into one of the A teams over at the canteen a little while ago."

"Yes, they're our front-line defense here on the border," Dallas told her. "These men go out for thirty days at a time. They are hunting Taliban and stopping terrorist insurgence from getting into Afghanistan. This is one of the most dangerous places in the world for our troops—the mountains and the border around the Khyber Pass, which connects Pakistan and Afghanistan."

"And we thought Peru was dangerous," Nike joked, turning the page in the file for her assignment.

"Yeah," Dallas said grimly. "This is worse. Let's talk about your assignment tomorrow morning. Part of a new project that's being initiated by the top generals now assigned to Afghanistan is winning the hearts and minds of the border villages in this country. Tomorrow BJS 60 pilots will be assigned to certain A teams to fly them into Taliban-controlled villages. The dudes in Washington, D.C., have finally figured out that if we don't make these boundary villages pro-American, we've lost the battle to stop terrorists from coming into this country from Pakistan."

"Why are these villages pro-Taliban?" Nike wondered, perplexed.

"They aren't. First of all, Afghanistan is composed of fiercely independent tribal systems. Even the Russians, who threw ten times the troops into this country, couldn't defeat the Mujahideen. Afghans don't count on anyone to help them. They have survived thousands of years with their tribal clans. In this century, the Afghan government, which has tried to force these different tribes or clans to acknowledge them, has failed to solidify them. The central government has always ignored the mountain villages along the border, anyway. They never poured any money, medical help, education or food from the government into these villages. Basically, the Kabul government didn't think ignoring these border villages was a problem until Osama bin Laden surfaced. Now, it's our biggest problem thanks to the government's blind eye."

Tightening her lips, Dallas added, "Kabul has Afghans who defy their own central government. They remain faithful only to their tribe and their chieftain or sheik. The Taliban uses force against the villagers, attacks their women and creates hostility among the tribal people. That is why these border villages don't stop Taliban and terrorists from coming and going through their valleys. They hate them as much as we do, but they lack the resources to stop the Taliban from being the bullies on the block. And Kabul officials never sent out troops to protect these border villages from the raiding Taliban, so the villagers are understandably distrustful of the central government. And your demeanor toward these villagers will be as follows. If you, as a person, do something good for an Afghan, they will call you *brother* or *sister* until they die. They are completely loyal to those who treat them humanely and with respect. That is what I want you to cultivate as you interface with the villagers. This is the only way we are going to win their hearts and minds."

"Nice to see these outlying villages hate the Taliban as much as we do. I'll be happy to 'make nice' with these village folks," Nike said.

"This new program the general has just initiated is beginning to bear fruit. Starting tomorrow, you're going to fly an A team to Zor Barawul, a village that is located five miles away from the Pakistan border. This A team will stay thirty days to try and win the trust and respect of these villagers. This operation, which is along all of the border, is to get villagers to realize that Americans are here to help them. We're not coming in like the Taliban with guns blazing and using brute force upon them. Furthermore, the medic in each of these A teams will be bringing in all kinds of medicine for villagers. We want to gain their trust with positive and consistent care. The only medical help these people have had in the last sixty years has been from Christian church missions and Sufi medical doctors who try their best to go from village to village helping the people."

"Sufis? I thought they were Moslem."

"Yes, they are. Sufis are the mystical branch of the Moslem religion. They are about peace, not war. Love and compassion instead of hatred and prejudice. We need more of that here and the Sufis are leading the way."

Nike raised her brows. "Then Sufis are the antithesis of the Moslem terrorists, aren't they?"

Dallas nodded. "Yes, and the Taliban is willing to kill the Sufi doctors who give their life to serving the village people, if they can. The terrorists are one end of the Moslem religion, Nike. They don't represent the middle or the other end, which is the Sufi sect. Now, General Chapman wants to expand upon that humanitarian mission and bring in A teams to support what they're doing."

"Isn't that dangerous—to put an A team down in a Taliban-controlled village?"

"Yes, it is," Dallas said. "But the new general, who is taking over the country insofar as military help for the Afghans, sees that this is the only way to change the border."

Nike was disappointed that she wouldn't be flying the

Apache right off the bat. She kept that to herself. "I wouldn't want to be an A team, then," Nike muttered.

"Fortunately, all you have to do is fly the CH-47 transport helicopter and drop them and their supplies off to the village and fly back here. I'm assigning you to six A teams that will be dropped along the border. When they need anything, you'll be at their beck and call via radio. If they request more medicine, you'll get the supplies from our base here and fly it in to them. If they need food, blankets or clothing, same thing. If they need ammo or weapon resupply, you'll be on call to support that, too."

"Sounds pretty routine," Nike said, hoping to have an Apache strapped to her butt so she could give the troops air support.

Shrugging, Dallas said, "Don't be so sure. The possibility of a Taliban soldier disguised as a villager sending a rocket up to knock your helo out of the sky is very real."

"Except for a tail gunner, I won't have any other weapons at my disposal to ensure that doesn't happen," Nike griped, unhappy. Each CH-47 had an enlisted tail gunner who doubled as the load master for the helicopter.

"We'll be flying Apache support for you," Dallas promised. "We're not going to leave you out there without proper air protection." She saw the unhappy look in Nike's eyes and understood her resignation. Nike was a combat warrior, one of the finest. But not all her BJS 60 pilots were accredited to fly the CH-47 as she was. "Look, don't go glum about this assignment. See what unfolds. Your work, as mundane as it might seem, is high-risk and important."

"I think I'll strap on a second .45. You can call me two-gun Alexander."

Dallas grinned at the Greek woman's response. Picking up another file, she said, "The border area is the Wild West and Dodge City, Nike. For real. It doesn't get any more dangerous than here. Here's your first assignment—the A team you're flying out at 0530. Once you drop them off, you fly back here and we'll give you the next village flight assignment."

Opening the order, Nike gasped. "Oh my God."

"What?"

Nike looked up, a pained expression crossing her face. "I just had a run-in with this dude, Captain Gavin Jackson, over at the canteen."

Smiling slightly, Dallas said, "I hope it went well."

"Not exactly."

Chapter 2

The air commander was Captain Nike Alexander. Gavin couldn't believe his eyes that morning as his team trooped across the tarmac to the waiting CH-47 that would take them to the Taliban-controlled village of Zor Barawul.

He didn't know whether to give her an evil grin of triumph or simply keep a poker face. As he approached the opened rear of the CH-47s ramp, she was coming out of the right-hand seat, helmet dangling in her hand. When their eyes met, she instantly scowled.

Ouch. Gavin threw his pack behind the seat and pushed the rest of his gear beneath the nylon webbing. Looking up, he noticed her pursed lips and her narrowed golden eyes—on him.

"Don't worry," he told her teasingly, "I'm not infectious."

Nike couldn't help but grin. Despite Jackson's ragged Afghan clothing and that beard, he was undeniably handsome. A part of her wanted him. The merriment dancing in his dark blue eyes made her heart race just a little. "Don't worry, I'm vaccinated against guys like you." He merely smiled at her obvious warning. Damn, why did he have to be so good-looking?

Nike threaded between the other nine men who were settling in on either side of the cargo hold. She strolled down the ramp toward her load master, Andy Peters. The sergeant stood at the bottom waiting for everyone to get settled before he started loading the many boxes. Her boots thunked hollowly against the corrugated aluminum surface. On one side rested a fifty-caliber machine gun that Peters would put into a hole at the center of the ramp. Once airborne, Andy would drop the ramp, the ugly muzzle of the machine gun pointed down at the earth below them. Peters's job was to take out any Taliban who fired up at them or tried to launch a rocket or grenade at the bird. She nodded to short, stocky Andy, who was all of twenty years old.

Nike could feel Jackson's gaze burning two holes between her shoulder blades. He was watching her. Intently. Like a wolf on the prowl. Hunting *her*. Well, it would get him nowhere.

The brisk, early April morning was chilly. New snow had fallen overnight, leaving about six inches on the tarmac. There was barely light on the eastern horizon, the silhouette of the sharp mountain peaks highlighted. She had a dark green muffler wrapped around her neck and dangling down the front of her bulky dark green winter flight suit. As her fingers slowly froze, a mist came out of her mouth when she spoke to Andy.

"All here and accounted for?"

"Yes, ma'am. Ten-man A team." He consulted his papers

on a clipboard, and then he looked over at an approaching truck. "We'll be loading all the supplies and medicine in just a moment. We're on schedule."

After consulting her watch, Nike nodded. There was a timetable to keep and she was a punctual person by nature. "Very good, Sergeant. I'll do my walk around the helo while you're getting all those boxes on board."

"Of course, ma'am."

Scanning the area, Nike appreciated the towering mountains to the east of the small base. The village of Nar was two miles away. As the dawn grew brighter, she could see the mountains were still cloaked in heavy snow. Closer to the bottom, they appeared a dark blue color. Rubbing warmth into her arms, Nike wished she'd put on her flight jacket to keep her upper body protected against the gusting breeze coming off the mountains. She'd left the jacket on the seat in the cockpit of the helo. The sky was a deep cobalt blue above the backlit peaks. It would be a good hour before the sun, still hidden behind the peaks, would crest them. Nike noticed the last of the stars above her, twinkling and appearing close enough to reach out and touch. Most of these nap-of-the-earth flights were flown just above one hundred feet above the land. All flights departed early in the day when the dark-green-colored helicopter could be hidden in the mountain shadows from an ever-present enemy lurking below.

The canopied olive-green military truck backed up toward the chopper with Peters's hand signals to guide it. Two men hopped out of the cab once the truck halted. Nike went to the starboard side of her helo to begin her check of all flight surfaces.

"Want some company, Captain Alexander?"

Startled, Nike turned on the heel of her boot. Gavin

Jackson stood less than a foot away, a shy smile on his face. She hadn't heard him approach. *Stealth.* That was what hunter-killer A teams were all about: you must not be seen or heard in order to kill your target. Gulping convulsively, Nike pressed a hand to her neck. "You scared the hell out of me, Captain!"

"Oh, sorry," he said, shrugging. And then he brightened. "Call me Gavin when we're alone like this."

Scowling, Nike continued her slow walk along the two-engine helo. "I'll think about it," she said. Nike scanned the rivets in the plates for signs of wear or loosening. Craning her neck, she checked for hydraulic leaks from either of the two massive engines on each end of the bird.

Undeterred, Gavin fell into step with her. "Don't you think it's kismet that we've met twice in less than twenty-four hours?"

Giving him a long, dark look, Nike growled, "More like damnable karma if you asked me."

"Ouch."

"Oh, get over yourself, Captain Jackson." Nike faced him, her hands on her hips. He was about six foot two inches tall and it killed her to have to look *up* at him. His blue eyes were warm and inviting. Without thinking, her gaze fell to his smiling mouth. He had a very, very male mouth. And for a moment, Nike realized he would be a damned good kisser. But a lover? Just because he was a man didn't mean he automatically had the kind of maturity that Nike demanded. And why on earth was she even *thinking* along those lines with this rude dude?

Snorting, she jerked her gaze up. "Listen, hotshot, cool your jets. You're obviously starved for a warm female body, but remove me from your gun sights. I'm not interested."

Dark brows raising, Gavin backed off and held up his hands. "Whoa, Nike—"

"It's Captain Alexander to you." Nike flinched inwardly when she saw his cheeks beneath his beard go ruddy with embarrassment. He had enough humility to blush. Jackson wasn't really the ego-busting officer Nike had first thought. Hands still resting on her hips, she added with less acidity, "We have a job to do, Captain. I'll do mine and you do yours. All I have to do is fly your team into a village, drop you off and then I'm out of your life."

"That's not very optimistic," Gavin observed. Her face was a mask of wariness. And yet, he sensed a crack in that facade. Oh, it wasn't anything he could point to or see, but Gavin knew his little-boy expression had gotten to her. There wasn't a woman alive who wouldn't melt under that look. Of course, it wasn't really a ploy. Gavin was a little boy at heart when he could get away with it.

"War is *never* optimistic, Captain."

Shaking his head, Gavin said, "Now where did you pick up that attitude?"

"In Peru. Chasing druggies for three years. Give no quarter, take no quarter. That's my maxim, Captain."

"I like it," Gavin said, properly impressed. The corners of his mouth moved upward. "You're a brazen woman, Captain Alexander, and you make my heart beat faster."

Nike ignored the comment, though it secretly pleased her. She finished her inspection of her helo. Maybe he'd get the message and leave her alone. She felt Jackson approach and walk silently at her side. When she halted to touch the metal skin to inspect something more closely, he would wait without a word.

What kind of game was this? Nike thought for sure if she gave him "the look" that he'd disappear inside the helo. Nope. Not Gavin Jackson. He still had that thoughtful and curious expression on his face. His blue eyes gleamed with humor. In his business, there wasn't much to be merry about, yet, he looked amiable, approachable and drop-dead handsome.

"You know," Gavin said conversationally as she halted at the Plexiglas nose, "there isn't a man on this godforsaken base out in the middle of nowhere that isn't happy about BJS flying into town." He rubbed his hands. "An *all-woman* squadron. That's really something."

"We're black ops," she warned him. Jackson seemed absolutely joyous over the prospect of ten Apaches with twenty pilots and a mostly all-woman crew coming to this base. No wonder. "Not sex on legs."

"Ouch. Double ouch."

"Oh, give me a break, Captain. That's all you see us women as—bedding material." She moved around the nose to the port side of the helicopter.

"That's not fair."

A burst of sharp laughter erupted from Nike. "It's the truth, isn't it? Who said anything in life was fair?"

Nodding, Gavin moved with her, his hands behind his back and face thoughtful. "I see you as sharing more than just my bed."

"Oh sure," Nike said, eyeing him. She ran her cold fingers across the metal. Rivets would come loose under the constant shuddering and vibration of the blades turning. Never did she want any of these light aluminum panels to be ripped off midflight. It could cause a crash.

"No, seriously," Gavin pleaded. Leaning down, he caught her golden gaze. "I'm dying for some feminine companionship."

"Intelligent conversation with a woman? I like that."

The jeering in her tone made Gavin chuckle. "That's all I want, Captain Alexander—just a little conversation."

Nike shot him an I-don't-believe-you-for-a-second look and continued her walk around. As she leaned under the carriage, she checked the tires. The tread was thick and obviously new. That was good because when she landed this bird on rocky terrain, she didn't need a blowout. Tires had to be in top-notch condition.

"We have *nothing* in common except for this assignment, Captain Jackson."

"Are you so sure?"

Straightening to her full height, Nike grinned. "*Very* sure." He stood there with a quizzical expression on his features. And she had to admit, he had a nice face. She liked looking at him, with his wide brow and high cheekbones. He had a prominent nose and a solid chin hidden beneath the dark beard. His lips reminded her of those on a sculpted bust of Julius Caesar. They were his best attribute aside from his large, inquiring blue eyes. She found it tough to think of him as someone who could easily pull a trigger and kill someone if needed. Jackson just didn't seem like the killer type.

"Why don't you give me a chance to prove otherwise?" Gavin pleaded as they neared the rear ramp. He knew he could win her over. The men had just finished loading fifty boxes of supplies for the village. The truck fired up, the blue diesel smoke purling upward in thick, churning clouds. He halted. So did she. Nike seemed to be considering his challenge. *Good.*

Why did he want to engage her on any level? Hadn't he had enough with Laurie and her inability to compromise? Never mind he'd fallen head over heels in love with her. He'd been able to take her stubbornness in stride. Her ego was considerable and dominating like his. And that was what had broken them up. Two headstrong egos unable to bend. Laurie had brought out the worst in him. And he was as much at fault in the breakup as she was. Gavin felt men and women were equals—not one better than the other. Laurie, however, had felt that all women were inherently better than any man and that grated on Gavin, too.

"This attention is flattering but I'm busy," Nike told him with finality.

"Are you married?"

"That's none of your business, Captain." Nike glared at him. "Let's get this straight—I'm your pilot. I fly you in, drop your team off and leave. I come back with any supplies you radio in to ops. Nothing more or less. Got it?"

Sighing, Gavin said, "Yes, I got it. I wish it was otherwise, though." True, Nike had a helluva ego but didn't seem as stubborn as Laurie. "You're an interesting person. How many women have been flying against South American drug cartels?" He gave her a warm smile. "See? We really do have something to discuss. I'm kind of an interesting dude myself."

"Oh, I'm sure you think that," Nike said, laughing. She shook her head and moved up the ramp.

Gavin stood watching her pull on the helmet and get situated in the right-hand seat in the cockpit. Nodding to the load master, Gavin mounted the ramp.

His men were grinning expectantly at him as he made his way to his nylon seat right behind Nike. He held up his hands in a show of surrender and they all laughed. Gavin didn't mind making himself the target of fun or prodding. His team had had a two-week rest, and now they were going out again. This time, he hoped, to something less dangerous, but he wasn't sure of that.

The ramp groaned and rumbled upward until finally the hatch was shut with a loud clang. Darkness, except for the light coming in through the cockpit, made the inside of the helicopter gray. Gavin watched his men strap in, their weapons in hand, their faces belying their real thoughts. He prayed that as they approached Zor Barawul nearby Taliban soldiers wouldn't be firing RPGs at them as they came in for a landing. He knew from the premission briefing that the townspeople hated the Taliban. But were they pro-American? There was no way to know except to walk in, offer humanitarian aid and see what happened next. They had no script written for this newest idea by General Chapman.

After pulling on his helmet, Gavin plugged in the radio connection and heard Nike's honeyed voice as she talked with the base air controller for permission to lift off. She had already engaged one engine on the helo and then the other one. Gavin had found out at the briefing with his people that her usual copilot had food poisoning and there was no one to replace her. Nike was flying alone, which wasn't a good thing, but Gavin had seen it happen.

If they weren't wearing helmets, the noise created by the helicopter would be horrendous and would destroy their hearing in a short time. The bird shuddered and shook around him. The deck beneath his booted feet constantly shivered. If his men had any worry about a woman flying this huge, hulking transport helo a hundred feet off the earth, they didn't show it. Flying nap-of-the-earth took a helluva lot of skill. Gavin wondered how many hours she had of flight time. When Nike had finished her conversation with the tower, Gavin piped up, "Captain, how many hours do you have flying this bird?"

All his men heard the question, of course, because they,

too, had helmets on and were plugged in to the inter-cabin radio system. Gavin saw the load master at the far end turn and give him a questioning look. He also heard the explosion of laughter from Nike.

"Oh, let's see, Captain, I got my helo-driver's license at Disneyland in Orlando, Florida," she drawled. "Does that count?"

His men were guffawing in reaction, but no one could hear it over the noise of the vibrating helo around them. Jackson chuckled. "I feel better, Captain Alexander. So long as Mickey Mouse signed off on your pilot's license I feel safe and sound."

Jackson thought some of his men were going to fall out of their nylon seats they were laughing so hard. He joined them. And then he heard Nike joining their collective roar of laughter. She had a wonderful, husky tone and it made his body ache with need. What kind of magic did this Greek woman have over him?

"Actually," Nike said, chuckling, "it was Minnie Mouse who signed it. You have a problem with that?"

"No, not at all. Now, if Goofy had signed it, I'd be worried."

Even the load master was giggling in fits, his gloved hands closed over the fifty-caliber. Unaccountably, Gavin felt his spirits rise. If nothing else, Nike Alexander gave as good as she got. Even more to her credit, she could take a joke and come back swinging. Looking into the faces of his men, Gavin felt a warmth toward the woman pilot. Did Nike realize how much she'd just lifted everyone's spirits? Probably not. But he would tell her— alone—and thank her for being a good sport on a deadly mission.

"Okay, boys," Nike said, catching her breath, "let's get this show on the road. Sergeant, once we're airborne, lower the ramp and keep that .50 cal ready to shoot. We're not in Disneyland and where we're going, the bad guys are waiting. Hunker down, you're about to go on the wildest roller-coaster ride you've ever taken. I'm ready to rock…."

For the next fifty minutes, Nike's full concentration was winding between, around and down into one valley after another in the steep, rugged mountain range. When they roared past Do Bandi, another village, she knew they would soon be climbing steeply. Zor Barawul sat in a rich, fertile valley ringed by the snowy mountains. On the eastern side of those mountains lay the Pakistan border where Taliban hid. The valley was a well-known Taliban route. They boldly passed through it because the Afghan villagers could not fire on or challenge them. If they did, the Taliban would come in and kill men, women and children.

The sunlight shone in bright slats across the mountaintops as she brought the Chinook up steeply, pushing with throttles to the firewall to make it up and over the snowy slope that blurred beneath them. How badly Nike wanted a copilot to do all this other work, but that wasn't her luck today. Captain Emma Trayhern, the XO who was supposed to fly with her, had caught a nasty case of food poisoning and was laid low for the next twenty-four hours. Her CO, Dallas Klein, had faith in her to handle this mission all by herself. Helluva compliment, but Nike would have preferred a copilot, thank you very much. The sunlight made her squint even though she wore a pair of aviator's sunglasses. The bird rocked from one side to another as she aimed the nose downward at top speed and skimmed headlong down a steep, rocky slope and into another valley.

Nike could see herds of sheep and goats being tended by young boys here and there on the bright green valley floor. They would look up, wave as the CH-47 streaked by them. The herds of animals would flee in all directions as the noisy Chinook passed low overhead. Nike felt sorry for the young herders who would probably spend half a day gathering up their scattered herds. What she didn't want to see was yellow or red winking lights from below. That would mean the Taliban was firing a rocket up at them. *Not good*.

The mountains were coated with thick snow even in April. The lower slopes showed hopeful signs of greenery sprouting after enduring the fierce, cold Afghan winter. The helicopter vibrated heavily around Nike as she flew the bulky transport through the valley. Shoving the throttles once more to the firewall, she urged the helo up and over another mountain range and down into the next valley. And, as she glanced out her cockpit window, it was comforting to see an Apache helicopter with her women friends from BJS 60 flying several thousand feet above her, working their avionics to find the enemy below before they shot her Chinook out of the air. She might not have a copilot, but she had the baddest son-of-a-bitch of a combat helicopter shadowing her flight today. That made Nike smile and feel confident.

The village of Zor Barawul contained two hundred people and sat at the north end of a long, narrow valley that was sandwiched between the mountains. On the other side lay the border of Pakistan. As in all villages Nike had seen, the wealthy families had houses made of stone with wooden floors. Wood was usually scarce. Those less well-off had homes made of earth and mud with hard-packed dirt floors. Some who could afford it would have a few rugs over the earthen floor. Roofs were made from tin or other lightweight metals. The poorer families had thatched material on top.

As they passed over all kinds of homes, Nike felt the sweat beneath her armpits. Fear was always near since at any moment, they could be fired on. As she located the landing area, she ordered her load master to bring up the ramp. Moments later, she heard the grind and rumble of the ramp shutting. The ramp had to be up in order for her to land.

Nike brought the Chinook downward and gently landed it outside the village. The earth was bare and muddy. Nike let out a sigh of relief. They were down and had made it without incident. She powered down, shut off the engines and called to her friends in the Apache flying in large circles outside the village. This was Taliban-controlled territory and the Apache was using its television and infrared cameras to spot any possible enemy who might want to shoot at the Chinook after it had landed.

The whine of the engines ceased. The women in the Apache reported no activity and continued to circle about a mile from where she'd landed. Nike thanked them and signed off on the radio. The Apache would wait and escort her back to base as soon as everything was unloaded. Unstrapping the tight harness, she pulled the helmet off her head and stood. Andy had removed the fifty-caliber machine gun and set it to one side. He opened the ramp and it groaned down. Once the ramp lip rested on the muddy ground, Andy signaled the A team to dismount.

As she glanced to her left, Nike caught sight of Gavin. This time, he was grim-faced and not smiling. *Right.* He understood this was a very dangerous place. No one knew for sure how the villagers would respond to their landing. Bullets or butter? For a moment, Nike felt a twinge in her heart. Jackson looked so damned responsible and alert. This wasn't his first dance with the Afghan people. She saw the grimness reflected in the flat line of his mouth as he gathered his gear and slung it across his shoulder.

His other team members were already moving down the ramp. Several took the cargo netting off the many boxes and prepared to move them outside the helo. What were the people of this village thinking of their arrival? Were they scared? Thinking that the U.S. Army was going to attack them the way the Taliban did? When the Russians had invaded Afghanistan a decade before, that's exactly what they had done. People here justifiably had a long memory and would probably not trust the Americans, either.

"Hey, do these people know you're coming?" Nike called to Jackson.

"Yeah, we sent an emissary in here a week ago."

"So, they know you're on a mission of peace?"

He took the safety off his weapon and then slung it across his other shoulder. "That's right. It doesn't guarantee anything."

Worriedly, Nike looked out the end of the Chinook. She saw several bearded older men in turbans or fur hats walking toward them. "Well, they don't look real happy to see us."

Gavin glanced out the rear of the helo. "Oh. Those are the elders. They run the village. Don't worry, they always look that way. Survival is serious business out here."

"They're carrying rifles."

"They sleep with them."

Smiling a little over the comment, Nike walked down the ramp and stood next to him. "Do you ever not have a joke, Captain?"

Gavin grinned over at her. Nike's hair lay against her

brow, emphasizing her gold eyes. He heard the worry in her voice and reached out to squeeze her upper arm. "You care...."

Nike didn't pull away from where his hand rested on her arm. There was monitored strength to his touch and her flesh leaped wildly in response. Seconds later, his hand dropped away. "Oh, don't let it go to your swelled head, honcho."

"Hey, I like that nickname."

"It's wasn't a compliment."

Gavin chuckled. "I'll take it as such."

"Ever the optimist."

"I don't like the other choice, do you? Thanks for the wild ride, Captain." He gave her a salute and smiled. "How about a date when we get back off this mission?"

"That's not a good idea." Nike saw the regret in his deep blue eyes.

"Okay, I'll stop chasing you for now." Looking out the rear of the helo, Gavin said, "I'll be seeing you around, lioness."

She felt and heard the huskiness of his voice as he spoke the word. *Lioness.* Well, that was a nice compliment. Unexpected. Sweet. And her heart thumped in reaction. She hated to admit it but she really did care. But before she could open her mouth, he turned and walked nonchalantly down the ramp and into the dangerous world of the Taliban-controlled village.

Suddenly, Nike was afraid for Gavin and his team. The ten elders approached in their woolen cloaks, pants and fur hats to ward off the morning coldness. They looked unwelcoming and grim.

Well, it wasn't as if she could help him and she had to get back to base. A part of her didn't want to leave Gavin.

Nike looked up and saw the Apache continuing its slow circuit at about three thousand feet. *Time to move.* Grabbing her helmet, she gave Andy a gesture that told him to lift up the ramp. He nodded. As soon as they were airborne, he'd lower the ramp once more and keep watch with his hands on that machine gun.

Settling into her seat, Nike pulled on her helmet, plugged it back in and made contact with the Apache once more.

"Time to boogie outta here, Red Fox One. Over."

"Roger, Checkerboard One. All quiet on the western front here."

Nike chuckled and twisted around. The ramp ground upward and locked against the bird, causing the whole helo to shudder. Andy gave her a thumbs-up and put on his helmet. All was well. Turning around, Nike began to flip switches and twist buttons. As soon as she was ready to turn on the engines, one at a time, she'd get harnessed up for the harrowing one-hundred-foot-high flight back to base. It wasn't something Nike looked forward to.

And then, her world came to an abrupt halt. A glaring red light began to blink back at her on the console—the forward engine light. Scowling, she flipped it off and on. *Red. Damn.* That meant either a problem with the engine or a screw-up with the light itself. Nike could do nothing at this point.

"Red Fox One, I have a red light for the forward engine. I can't go anywhere. Can you contact base to get a helo out here with a couple of mechanics? Until then, I'm grounded. I'll radio Operations and get further instructions from them. Over."

"Bad news, Checkerboard One. Stay safe down there. Out."

Well, it didn't take long for Nike to get her answers. Major Dallas Klein, who was in ops, answered her.

"Stay where you are. We can't get a mechanic team out until tomorrow morning. Stick with Captain Jackson and his team. Your load master will remain with the helicopter. In the meantime, go with the A team. We'll be in touch by radio when we know the time of arrival to your location. Over."

Great. Nike scowled and responded. "Roger. Over and out."

Now what? She gestured for Andy to come forward because he had not been privy to what was going on. Shaking her head, Nike felt a sense of dread combined with unexplainable elation. She was stuck here with Jackson, who clearly would be delighted with her company. *Double damn.*

Chapter 3

Jackson walked toward village elders. The knot of men stood watching them. But before he could talk with them, Nike appeared at his shoulder, her face set and disappointed.

"What's wrong?" he asked, anchoring to a halt.

"My helo has engine failure and I've got orders to stay the night here with you and your team. My load master will remain with the bird. A mechanic team will be flown out to fix it tomorrow morning."

She didn't seem too happy about the news but joy threaded through Gavin. "Engine failure." He tried to sound disappointed for her. "Sorry about that, Captain Alexander."

Nike tried to avoid his powerful stare and glanced over at the knot of elders. They were a sour-looking bunch. Every one of them wore a deep, dark scowl of suspicion. She returned her attention to Jackson. "Let's look at the positives. This engine failure could have happened en route. We're damned lucky to have landed before the problem."

"And here I thought you were a doom-and-gloom pessimist." Jackson grinned and desperately wanted this moment alone with her, but the elders had to be properly greeted.

Nike shook her head and muttered, "Jackson, you're a piece of work."

He smiled quickly and then resumed his serious demeanor toward the elders. "Thank you."

"It wasn't a compliment."

"As always, I'll take anything you say as a positive."

"Get real," she gritted between her teeth so that only he could hear her. On either side of them, the team had fanned out, hands on their weapons but trying not to appear threatening to the elders.

"Do me a favor?" Gavin said.

"Depends upon what it is."

"These elders have strict laws regarding their women. I'll be speaking to them in Pashto. They may have a problem with you not wearing a *hijab,* or scarf, on your head. That scarf is a sign of honoring their Moslem beliefs. So, if it comes to pass that someone hands you a scarf, wear it."

Nike nodded. "No problem."

"Thanks, I needed that."

"Judging from their looks, you're going to need more than a scarf on my head to turn this situation into a positive, honcho."

Gavin said nothing. Nike took a step back, partly hidden by his tall, lean frame. The elders looked aged, their weathered faces deeply lined. Their skin was tobacco-brown, resembling leather, because of their tough outdoor life. Nike knew the elements at the top of the world in this

mountain chain were unforgiving and brutal. Villages along
the border had no electricity, no sewers and sometimes little
water. These rugged Afghan people eked out a living raising
goats and sheep. At this altitude, poppy crops wouldn't
grow because the season was too short. Winter came early
and stayed late. Nike had found out through the weather
officer at BJS ops that snow started in September and
lasted sometimes into June. That was why they couldn't
grow crops and relied heavily on their animals for a food
source.

The elders had good reason to be serious-looking,
their hands hidden in the sleeves of their woolen robes,
chins held high and their dark eyes assessing the A team.
These proud and fiercely independent Afghan people had
few resources. Beneath their threadbare woolen clothing,
Nike saw the thinness of all the elders. There wasn't a fat
one in the group. Their leanness was probably due to the
hardships of living in such a rocky, inhospitable place. She
felt compassion and respect toward them, not animosity.

Gavin had been given an in-depth briefing on Zor
Barawul before arriving at the village. Photos had been
taken and the elders were identified in them. He recognized
the chief elder, Abbas, who separated himself from the
group. He was in his sixties and every inch like his name,
which meant "angry lion" in Pashto. They approached each
other like two competing football-team captains staring
one another down. Tension sizzled in the cold morning air
between the two groups of men. Walking forward, Gavin
extended his hand to Abbas, who wore a dark brown turban
and cloak. The man's face was as narrow and thinned as
a starving lion's, horizontal lines deeply carved across
his broad brow. Gashes slashed down on either side of his
pursed lips. Ordinarily, the Afghan custom of greeting was

to shake hands and then kiss each other's cheeks as a sign of friendship.

That wasn't going to happen here. Gavin fervently hoped that Abbas would at least shake his extended hand. The elder glared at him and then down at his hand. No, that wasn't going to happen, either. Gavin pressed his right hand over his heart, bowed referentially and murmured, *"Salaam-a-laikam."* This meant "peace be with you," and was a greeting given no matter if the person were Moslem or of some other faith. It was a sign of respect and of the two people meeting on common ground.

Scowling, Abbas touched his chest where his heart lay and murmured, *"Wa alaikum assalam wa rahmatu Allah,"* in return. That meant "And to you be peace together with God's mercy."

Gavin could see that Abbas was surprised by his sincere and knowledgeable greeting. His scowl eased and his voice became less gruff. "We told your emissary last week, Captain Jackson, that we did *not* want you to come to our village. The Kabul government has always ignored us. There is no reason you should be here at their invitation. If the Taliban finds out we are dealing with the Americans, they will come back here and kill more of my people. We are a tribe and as such, do not recognize the government as having any power or control over our lives," Abbas said in Pashto, his arms remaining tightly wrapped against his chest.

Halting, Gavin allowed his hand to drop back to his side. *"Sahibji,"* he began in Pashto, "we do not come as representatives of the Kabul government. I realize you do not acknowledge them. The American people have donated all of this—" he turned and swept his hand toward the stacked boxes "—as respect for your tribe. Americans believe in peace and when they found out that your children needed help, they sent these boxes of medicine to you." Gavin kept his voice sincere. "There is also food and blankets for your people, if you will accept their heartfelt generosity."

Gavin knew that Afghan people, when given a sincere gift, would never forget the heart-centered gesture and would be friends for life with the givers. They were a remarkable warrior class who judged others on their loyalty and honor. They held an ancient set of codes based upon Islamic belief and here, in these mountains, the villagers practiced these morals and values to this day. That was one of the reasons the Russians had never been able to break the spirit of these proud people. The more they tried to destroy the Afghan tribal culture, the more stubborn the people became. Gavin felt General Chapman's operation to win the hearts and minds of these people, one village at a time along the border, was much wiser and more humane. Gavin knew the Afghans would respond to honest gifts given from the heart, for they, above all, were a heart-centered people.

Abbas's thick black-and-gray brows lifted slightly as he looked longingly toward the boxes. Then, his mouth curled as he swung his gaze back to the captain. "And for this you want what?"

Shrugging, Gavin said, "The opportunity to earn your friendship over time. Judge us on a daily basis and allow us to earn your respect." He knew that the Afghan people were a proud people and that they were slow to give their trust. It was earned by deeds alone—not by any words, but actions.

"I have families who are sick and ailing," Abbas said abruptly. "Even if there is medicine, there is no doctor. So what good is all of this?"

Gavin turned to his medic, Staff Sergeant Neal Robles.

"This is Sergeant Robles. He is my paramedic and one level below a medical doctor. We have brought him to help your people. We are here on a strictly humanitarian mission. We are not here to cause stress or fighting."

Grunting, Abbas lifted his chin a little higher. He stroked his salt-and-pepper beard. Looking over at the paramedic, he demanded, "And this man can do what?"

"He can give vaccinations to all your children. Many Afghan children die unnecessarily of diseases and our vaccinations can stop that. He can examine a male and treat him accordingly. We have brought antibiotics, as well."

At that, Abbas's brows lifted in surprise. Hope flared in his narrowed eyes.

Gavin saw his response. Abbas knew antibiotics were as valuable a commodity as opium made from the poppy fields of southern Afghanistan. The elder understood, thankfully, that antibiotics could save a life. But in this remote village, there was no way to get them nor was there the help of a doctor to dispense the lifesaving drug. Gavin was sure that Abbas had seen any number of children, men and women die of ailments that could have been stopped and turned around by antibiotics. "Sergeant Robles will train a man and a woman whom you suggest to use the antibiotics that we will supply to you. Your village will always have them on hand from now on." Gavin could see the surprise and then the gratefulness in the man's narrowed dark eyes.

Abbas heard the elders of the village whispering excitedly over the officer's last statement. Turning, he saw them eagerly nod over receiving such a gift. His tribe had suffered severely for years beneath the Kabul government, the Russians and now, the Taliban. Drilling a look into the captain, Abbas growled, "My people have died without the help of our own government. They do not care whether we exist. If not for a Sufi brother and sister who are medical doctors who visit our village twice a year, many more would have died." He jammed a long, thin index finger down at the hard brown earth where he stood.

"The United States of America is trying to change that," Gavin told him in a persuasive tone. "We are here on a mission of mercy." He walked toward the boxes, printed in English and Pashto. "Come and see. This is not the Kabul government nor my government. This is from the American people who do not like to see anyone's children die. Look at the gifts from my people to your villagers. There is clothing, blankets, food and medicine. All we ask is to be able to distribute it and have our medic help those who ask for medical attention."

Abbas walked commandingly over to the bounty, his lean shoulders squared, head held at a proud angle. He reached out with long brown hands and placed them on the tops of several of the cardboard boxes. Walking around the fifty cartons, he stopped, read the Pashto lettering on one and then moved on. The rest of the elders came to his side at his gesture. Gavin watched the group of men carefully read each label and check out the gifts.

Gavin turned and to Nike spoke quietly, "Listen, I need a favor. There are women here who need medical attention. Abbas isn't about to let Robles touch any Moslem female since it's against their religion. Can I volunteer you to help him?"

"But I don't have any medical training," Nike whispered.

"Doesn't matter. Robles will teach you the basics."

She saw the pleading in his eyes. "I don't want to hurt anyone with my lack of experience."

"Don't worry, that won't happen."

Abbas strode over and gave Gavin a brusque nod of acceptance. "Allah is good. The gifts are indeed welcome, Captain Jackson. *Shukria,* thank you."

"You're welcome, *malik sahib,*" Gavin murmured, touching his heart and bowing his head respectfully to the elder.

Mouth quirking, Abbas looked directly at Nike and jabbed a finger toward her. "And this is the woman who will help Dr. Robles?"

Gavin didn't want to correct the elder. To do so would be a sign of disrespect. Besides, it would humiliate Abbas in front of the others and he had no wish to destroy what little trust he had just forged between them. "Yes, sir. Captain Nike Alexander will assist Dr. Robles, if you wish. With your permission, she will care for the women and girls of your village."

"I wish it to be so," Abbas said in a gruff tone. "My wife, Jameela, will bring her a *hijab* to wear over her head. She must respect Islam." He folded his arms across his narrow chest. "You are welcome to remain here and help my people, Captain Jackson. We are a peaceful tribe of sheep- and goat-herders. I will have my second-in-command, Brasheer, help you." He eyed Nike. "This woman is not allowed among your men. She will remain at our home. My wife will give her a room and she will remain in the company of women and children only."

"Of course," Gavin murmured, and he explained that Nike would be a transiting visitor because the helo was down. "You are most gracious," he told Abbas, giving him a slight bow of acknowledgment. "We would like to stay as long as you need medical help."

"I approve. Captain, you shall honor me by being my guest at every meal. We will prepare a room in our house for you. Your men will be housed at the other homes, fed, and given a place to sleep."

"Thank you, *malik sahib*. You are more than generous. We hope our stay improves the health of your people." Gavin could see the hope burning in the old man's eyes. As an elder, he carried the weighty responsibility for everyone in his village. It wasn't something Gavin himself would want to carry. Abbas must realize what these gifts would do to help his people. And he knew he was weighing Taliban displeasure over it, too. The Taliban would punish the village for taking the offered supplies and the old man took a surprising risk. With such humanitarian aide, this village might become less fearful of the Taliban and provide information to stop the terrorists from crossing their valley in the future. For now, no one in the villages gave away that information.

Gavin finished off the details of where the boxes would be taken and stored. All his men could speak Pashto. Robles was as fluent as Gavin and that would work in their favor. The other elders took over the management of the boxes while his A team became the muscle to carry the cartons toward the village.

Gavin watched as the elders left, parading the groups of carriers and boxes back into their village like conquering heroes. "Do you know any Pashto?" he asked Nike.

"I have problems with English sometimes and I'm Greek, remember?"

"So, I guess that's a no." Grinning, Gavin felt the tension melting off his tense shoulders. Just looking into Nike's gold eyes made him hungry for her again. Black curls framed her face and Gavin had to stop himself from reaching out and threading his fingers through that dark, shining mass. "Pashto isn't that difficult. Most villagers don't speak

English. I'll get one of my other men to help interpret from a distance. You can always go outside the home and talk to him out in the street and he can translate. He won't be allowed in where there is a female."

"That sounds like a workable strategy." She narrowed her eyes on Gavin. "So how did it go with Abbas? He looked like he'd just won the lottery when he read some of the labels on that shipment."

Gavin laughed a little while keeping alert. Taliban came through this valley all the time, and he knew that with an American A team here, word would get out to their enemy. "The elders' main concern is the health of their people. We've done this type of mission in southern Afghanistan for the last year and it was a great success. The key is in establishing trust with the Afghans."

Nike nodded and noticed how Jackson remained alert. She was glad the .45 pistol was strapped to her left leg. And wearing a bulletproof vest gave her a strong sense of protection. She hated wearing the chafing vest, but this was Dodge City and bullets could fly at any time. "I thought I saw tears in his eyes. He kept stroking the tops of the boxes that contained the antibiotics. It reminds me of a Greek proverb—*Upon touching sand may it turn to gold.* Only this time, his gold is the lifesaving drugs for his people."

Grimly, Gavin agreed and said, "I'm sure he's seen many of his people die terrible, suffering deaths that could have been avoided if they'd only had antibiotics available to them."

"Pnigese s'ena koutali nero," she agreed softly in Greek.

Cocking his head, Gavin said, "What did you just say?"

"You drown in a teaspoon of water. Another one of my

Greek sayings I was raised with. It's the equivalent to your saying that for want of a nail the horse's shoe is lost, and for want of a shoe the horse is lost, and for want of a horse, the battle is lost." She held up her finger. "Antibiotics are a small thing, but in his world, they're huge," Nike said. "Why was Abbas pointing at me earlier?"

"His wife, Jameela, will bring you a *hijab* to wear. Just be grateful to her for the gesture. Moslem women always wear the *hijab* any time they're outside their home. In Arabic it means *covering* or *concealing*." His mouth pulled into a devilish grin. "The best part is Abbas inviting us to stay at his home. The men and women are always separated. You'll be on the women's side of the house and have your own room. You'll also eat separately, too."

"That's a little strict."

"I agree, but we have to be aware of their religious laws. Afghans see that as a sign of respect. And respect can, we hope, earn us friendship with them."

Nike said, "Okay, boss, I can do it. Not exactly military issue, but in black ops you have to be flexible."

"Good. Come on, I see a woman coming toward us. She's got a red *hijab* in hand, so that must be Jameela."

When Gavin placed his hand beneath her elbow, Nike was surprised. She felt a sense of protection emanating from him. It was like a warm blanket surrounding her and she couldn't protest the nice gesture. The entire village, it seemed, had come out to view the boxes. Indeed, word had traveled fast. Women, men and children stood as the elders marched past them with the A team carrying some of the boxes. There was crackling excitement and expectation in the air.

"Women are pretty well hidden here from the outer world. When they're inside their homes they don't have to wear a burka or *hijab*. And there's real power among the women. They treat one another like sisters. Even though you may think the women have it bad, they really run the place. They have a lot of power in the household and in the village decisions in general. The women learned a long time ago to stick together as a unit. United they stand and divided they fall. Woman power is strong among the Afghan women and I think you'll enjoy being a part of it," Gavin told her conversationally as they walked toward Jameela. The elder's wife wore a black burka. The black wool robe swathed her from her head to her shoes. A crosshatch opening revealed her cinnamon-colored eyes.

"Don't expect me to wear one of those things," Nike warned him with a growl. "All the women are dressed like her. I'm not going to wear a burka. I'll stay in my uniform."

"They won't ask you to don a burka, so don't worry. Little girls don't start wearing them until around age seven. Until then, they've still got their freedom from the burka."

Nike grumbled, "I have a really hard time thinking any woman would be happy wearing a burka."

"Try to be gracious and don't stir up trouble with Jameela—she's the chieftain's wife. There's an unspoken hierarchy here in these villages. She's boss of the women and children. Jameela wields a lot of power even though she's hidden under that burka. Don't ever underestimate her position and authority. In reality, the women have equal power to any of these men. It may not appear to be like that, but from what I've seen, it is."

"*All* women are powerful," Nike reminded him. She felt his hand slip away as they walked to meet the tall, thin woman swathed in the black wool robe.

"No argument from me." And then Gavin turned slightly, gave her a wink and added teasingly, "Especially you…"

Nike had no time to retort. She felt heat rising in her face. Gavin chuckled with delight. Focusing on Jameela, Nike searched the woman's spice-brown eyes between the fabric crosshatch. It was Jameela's only opening into the outside world. Nike felt at odds with the woman, who stood about five foot six inches tall. Only her hands, reddened and work-worn, told Nike of her hard, unrelenting life.

Gavin bowed in respect to Jameela and offered the Islamic greeting to her as they halted about six feet from one another. Jameela whispered softly the return greeting to Gavin and to Nike, who bowed slightly, pressed her hand to heart and said, *"Salaam."* She didn't know what else they said to one another, but at one point, Jameela leaned forward and gave Nike the *hijab*. She made some gestures indicating she should wrap it around her head.

Nike gave her a friendly smile and put it on. Once the knotted scarf was in place, Jameela's eyes crinkled as if she were smiling. Perhaps she was grateful to Nike for honoring their customs. Not being able to see another person's body language or their facial expressions was highly disconcerting. Nike realized in those minutes how much she truly assessed a person through nonverbal means. Jameela remained a mystery to her.

"I speak…English…little…" Jameela said haltingly to Gavin and Nike, opening her hands as if to apologize.

Nike was delighted and grinned. She saw Gavin smile and nod.

"Where did you learn English?" Gavin asked her politely. He knew that Jameela shouldn't be talking to him. Under the circumstances, he felt it was all right but not something to be done more than once outside her home.

"When I was little, my parents lived in Kabul. I was taught English at a Christian missionary school." Shrugging her small shoulders beneath the burka, Jameela laughed shyly. "Coming out here, I could not practice it. So, I am very poor at speaking your language, but I will try."

"Thank you, *memsahib,*" Gavin told her quickly in Pashto. "My friend, Captain Nike Alexander—" he gestured toward her "—is here to help the women and children. Perhaps you could interpret for her? She does not know Pashto."

Jameela nodded in deference toward Nike. "Of course, Captain, I would be happy to. Please, apologize to her that I speak broken English?"

Gavin nodded. "Of course, *memsahib,* but you speak English very well. I know Captain Alexander will be grateful for your English and translation help. Thank you."

Jameela bowed her head slightly, her long hands clasped in front of her. Nike could have sworn the Afghan woman blushed, but it was hard to tell with the burka like a wall between them.

"You are the first Americans to come here," Jameela told Gavin in a softened tone. "There are Sufi twin brother and sister medical doctors, Reza and Sahar Khan, who visit us once every six months. The Sufis are heart-centered and they help us greatly. The Khan twins travel from the northern border of Afghanistan and follow it all the way to the south helping the villages along the way. Then, they turn around in their Jeep and come back north to do it all over again. We bless them. The Sufis are a branch of Islam who are dedicated to compassionate love toward all, no matter what their beliefs."

"Yes, I'm aware of the Sufis' nature," Gavin told her in Pashto. "I'm also aware that the Taliban hate them. The

Sufis practice peace at all costs and the Taliban has been known to kill them."

Jameela nodded sadly. "That is so, Captain Jackson. But Doctors Reza and Sahar Khan are welcomed by all our villages along the border, regardless. We greet them and bring them into our villages on two white horses. We place flower wreaths around their necks and sing their praises. That is our custom of honoring their courage to care for us regardless of the personal danger they place themselves in. They have saved many of our people over the years."

"I've heard the Khans mentioned by other villagers," Gavin said. "I hope one day to meet them. They're heroic people and give the Sufis a good name around the world for their courage and generosity."

Jameela hesitated and then said, "My husband is afraid Americans coming here will invite another Taliban attack upon us. Surely you know this?"

Nodding, Gavin said gently, "I understand that. We hope to win his trust over time, *memsahib*. And my team will be in your valley here to protect you from the Taliban. Our mission is to show that the American people are generous and care, especially for those who are sick."

Jameela looked toward the sky. "Allah be praised, Captain. You have no idea the prayers I have said daily to Him, asking for more help. If you stay in our valley then the Taliban won't attack us. Our Sufi brother and sister constantly travel. We understand they can only visit us twice a year." She gestured gracefully toward the village. "Captain Alexander, you will come with me, and I will put you to work. Captain Jackson, you may join your men."

"Of course," Gavin said, and he winked over at Nike. "I'll catch up with you later. And I'll have Sergeant Robles alerted to your requests. Just relax. It will all work out."

Nike wasn't so sure, but said nothing. She didn't want this humanitarian mission scuttled because of her lack of medical knowledge. As she walked with Jameela, she said, "Are your duties the same as your husband's in running this village?" Nike knew little of the Afghan culture and didn't want to make a gaffe. Better to ask than to assume.

Jameela nodded. "My duty first is to my husband and our family. After that, I am looked upon to provide leadership to the women of the village in all matters that concern us."

"I see," Nike said. She suddenly had a humorous thought that couldn't be shared with Jameela. Wearing a bright red scarf, a dark green flight suit and a pistol strapped to her waist, she must look quite a sight! The women of the BJS would laugh until it hurt if they could see her in her new fashion garb. Still, Nike wanted to fit in, and she would allow the course of the day to unfold and teach her. Often, prejudices and misunderstandings from one country or culture to another caused tension and she would not want to create such problems.

As Nike followed Jameela down the muddy, rutted street, she was struck by the young children playing barefoot on such a cold April morning. The children's clothes were threadbare with many patches sewn in the fabric. They shouted and danced. Their gazes, however, were inquisitive and they stared openly at Nike. What an odd combination she wore—a man's trousers with the prescribed headdress of a Moslem woman. Fired with curiosity, the group followed them down the middle of the wide street where mud and stone homes sat close to one another.

As Nike smiled at the children, she regretted not knowing Pashto. Their eyes were button-bright and shining. Little girls and boys played with one another just as they would in the States or in her homeland of Greece. But then, as she glanced farther up the street, her heart saddened. A little girl of about six years old stood on crutches near a large stone home. The child had only one leg. Nike remembered that damnable land mines covered this country. Most of them had been sown by Russians, but of late, it had been the Taliban, too. Had this child stepped on one? Nike's heart contracted. There was no doctor here to help her. No painkillers. No antibiotics. How had she survived?

"Jameela? That little girl over there? Who is she?"

"My youngest daughter, Atefa. Why do you ask?"

Gulping, Nike hoped she hadn't made a fatal mistake by asking. "I…uh…she's missing one leg. Did she step on a land mine?"

"Yes, as a four-year-old." Jameela's voice lowered with anguish as she pointed outside the village and to the east. "Afghan national soldiers laid land mines everywhere outside our village two years ago. They wanted to stop the Taliban from coming through our valley." Choked anger was evident in her quiet tone.

"How did Atefa *ever* survive such a terrible injury?" Nike asked softly.

"Allah's will," Jameela murmured. "Everyone said she would die, but I did not believe it. Dr. Reza Khan and his sister, Sahar, found her near the road where it happened. They saved her life and brought her to the village in their Jeep. Then, we had Farzana, our wise woman, tend her with the antibiotics the doctor left. Also, Dr. Sahar knows much about herbs and she directed Farzana how to use them."

"That's an amazing story," Nike said, her voice thick with unshed tears. People like the Sufi medical doctors inspired her. She'd never heard of Sufis or that they were Moslem. Nike decided she was very ignorant of Moslems in general. What if the Sufi doctors hadn't been on the road driving by when Atefa had been injured? Nike watched as the child hobbled toward them on carved wooden crutches. "She's so pretty, Jameela. What does her name mean?" Nike wondered.

"It means *compassion* in our language. Little did I know when my husband and I chose that name for her that she would, indeed, bring exactly that to our family and village. My husband wants her to go to a school in Pakistan when she's old enough. He feels Allah has directed this because she was saved by Sufis."

Atefa had dark brown, almond-shaped eyes; her black hair was long and drawn into a ponytail at the back of her head. She wore a black woolen dress that hung to her ankle; her foot was bare. To Nike, she looked like a poor street urchin. But then, as she scanned the street, she realized all the children shared in the same impoverished appearance as Atefa. The children were clean, their clothes were washed, their skin was scrubbed clean, their hair combed, but this was a very poor village.

"Maybe," Nike told Jameela, briefly touching her arm for a moment, "there is something that might be done to help Atefa before she goes to her school."

Chapter 4

"How are things going?" Gavin asked as Nike finished ensuring her helo was protected for the night. She'd just sent Andy into the village to grab a bite to eat at Abbas's house before staying with the bird during the coming darkness.

She turned, surprised by Gavin's nearness. The man walked as quietly as a cat, never heard until he wanted to be. His cheeks were ruddy in the closing twilight. "Doing okay." She held up her gloved hands. "Today, I became 'Dr. Nike' to the women and children in the village." She laughed. The look in his narrowed eyes sent her heart skipping beats. She stood with her back against the Chinook, for the metal plates still exuded the warmth of the sun from the April day.

"Yeah, Robles said you were doing fine. He's proud that you can give vaccinations. You're a fast study."

Nike grinned. "I had to be! I wasn't given a choice."

The jagged mountain peaks became shadowed as the sun slid below the western horizon.

"From all accounts, old Abbas seems to be satisfied with our efforts."

"Him." Nike rolled her eyes. "That old man is married to a woman thirty years his junior!"

"That's not uncommon out here," Gavin said. "Wives die in childbirth and there's no medical help to change the outcome. The man will always marry again." He grimaced. "And let's face it, there are many widows around and they need a man in order to survive out here."

"Jameela said Abbas has had two other wives before her. Both died in childbirth." Shaking her head, Nike muttered, "Things were bad in Peru, too. BJS did a lot of flying into the jungle villages to deliver health care when we weren't chasing druggies. This place is a lot worse."

Gavin enjoyed being close to Nike. About six inches separated them and he wished he could close the gap. The best he could do was keep them talking. "These people deserve our help. You look kind of pretty in that red *hijab*. Do you like wearing it?"

"No, but I respect their traditions. At least Abbas didn't demand I climb into one of those burkas."

"Indoors, the women wear more casual clothes and no *hijab*," Gavin told her. "It's just when they go out in the community that they put on the burka or *hijab*."

"That robe looks like a prison to me," Nike muttered. "I asked Jameela today what she thought of the burka and she liked it. I couldn't believe it."

"In their culture, most women accept that their body and face are to be looked upon only by their husbands. The way the men figure it, if the woman is hidden, she's not a temptation to others."

"Why don't their husbands show some responsibility for what's between their legs? Then a woman would be safe to wear whatever she wants."

"Yeah, I can't disagree with your logic, but that's not the way their world turns, and sometimes we have to fit in, not try to change it."

Nike felt the coldness coming off the mountains in the evening breeze. "I feel absolutely suffocated by their culture's attitudes toward women. You don't find an Afghan woman flying a combat helicopter."

"No doubt." Gavin saw her put her hands beneath the armpits of her jacket to keep them warm. He took a step forward and allowed his heavily clothed body to contact hers. Her eyes widened for a moment. "I'll keep you warm," he soothed.

"Right now, I'm so damned cold I'm not going to protest."

Chuckling, Gavin continued to look around. "Things seem to be quiet. I've been working with Abbas most of the day. You know, he won't admit that the Taliban comes through their village, but we have satellite photos as proof."

"Is he pro-Taliban? Or just afraid of them like everyone else?" Nike absorbed the heat from his woolen Afghan clothes. For a moment, she wondered what it would be like to slide her hands beneath the folds and place her hands against his well-sprung chest. It was a forbidden thought, but tantalizing, nonetheless.

"I'm pretty sure he's afraid of them. There aren't many village chieftains or sheiks who get in bed with the devil and the Taliban is all of that," Gavin said, his mouth quirking. "He told me that the Taliban came in here and ordered their girls' school shut down. He's a man of education, and he didn't like being ordered to do that. Abbas continues to teach the girls and women of his village behind closed doors in defiance of their orders. He's a man of strong principles and morals. He believes women deserve education just as much as any man. And Abbas is enlightened compared to other village leaders."

"He was a teacher?" Nike found that inspiring for a man who lived in such a rugged, isolated area.

"Abbas was born here in this village. His father sent him to Kabul for higher schooling. He graduated with a degree in biology. When Abbas returned home, he helped the village breeding programs so that their sheep produced better wool. That helps to raise their economy because better wool demands a higher price at market. And he increased goat-milk output. He's done a lot in the region and he's respected by everyone because of this."

"Wow, I'd never have guessed. No wonder he's the head elder."

"Looks *are* deceiving." Gavin watched the high clouds across the valley turn a dark pink as the sun set more deeply below the western mountains. "He's carrying a lot of loads on his shoulders, Nike. Abbas takes his responsibilities as leader seriously. He's got a lot of problems and few ways to resolve them. When I asked him about medical and health help from the Afghan government, he got angry. Over the years, he's made many trips to the capital to urge them to bring out a health team every three months to these border villages, but he could never get them to agree to it. And Afghan people are superindependent. They really have a tough time looking at a centralized government to rule over them."

"That's awful that the politicians in Kabul wouldn't help

these people. Can you imagine *that* happening in the USA or Greece? There would be a helluva uprising."

"Abbas doesn't accept his government's lack of care," Gavin said. "When you realize Afghanistan is cobbled together out of about four hundred different clans or tribes, you can see why they wouldn't place trust in a Kabul government. Our job is to try and persuade Abbas that his own government does want to work with him."

"How are you going to convince him Kabul's listening and willing to pitch in some medical help out here in the border area?"

"I told Abbas that the report I write up regarding our visit will be given to the health minister of the government. This minister is trying hard to change old, outdated policies. I pointed out to Abbas other border villages south of him already have intervention, supplies and funds on a routine schedule from Kabul."

"Does he believe you?"

"No, but over time he will."

"And you and your team will stay here four weeks?"

"Yes. From the satellite photos, we know that the Taliban uses the north end of this valley twice a month. We've set up to be here when they try to cross it a week from now."

"And then what?" Nike grew afraid for Gavin and his team.

He shrugged. "Do what we're good at—stopping them cold in their tracks and denying them access across this valley."

"What will Abbas do?"

"I don't know. He knows if we stop the Taliban from crossing, they could take revenge on this village. This is what Abbas is worried about."

"He's right about that." Nike leaned against Gavin a

little more. The dusk air had a real bite to it. His arms came around and bracketed her. For a moment, she questioned her silent body language. Why had she done this? Something primal drove her like a magnet to this military man. Fighting herself, Nike finally surrendered to the moment. She had been too long without a man in her life, and she was starved for male contact. Yet, what message did this send to Gavin? Was he reading her correctly or assuming? Unsure, Nike remained tense in his embrace.

"Comfy?" he teased quietly. Surprised by Nike's unexpected move, Gavin hungrily savored her nearness. He had wrapped his arms around her but resisted pressing her tightly against himself. Right now, just the fact she'd allowed this kind of intimate contact was enough of a gift. Even though they sparred like fighters in a ring, he'd seen something in her gold eyes that he could never quite accurately read. Maybe this was the result of that smoldering look he'd seen banked in her expression. Only time and patience would tell.

"Yes, thank you."

Gavin wasn't about to do anything stupid. She had given herself to him in a way that he'd never entertained. Maybe it was the pink beauty of the clouds across the valley that had inspired her in this wonderful moment.

"What are you going to do here?" Nike asked.

"We know from satellite reconnaissance that the Taliban uses the north end of this valley at the new moon, when it's darkest. We'll be intercepting them if they try it next week."

"There's only ten of you. There could be a hundred or more fighters crossing that border and coming down into this valley."

"Are you worried?" Gavin ventured.

"Any sane person would be."

Laughing quietly, Gavin closed his eyes for a moment and simply absorbed the curves of Nike's womanly body against him. What an unexpected reward. It was precious in his world of ongoing war and violence. A sweet reminder of peace, of love and nurturance. Something he hadn't experienced for a long time. "You're right," he admitted. "But we look at it this way—our base camp where you're assigned isn't that far away. We have BJS here with Apache helos to help us out if we're attacked. We know you gals will hightail it in our direction and drop the goods on the Taliban so we'll survive to fight them another day."

"I have never met such an optimist," Nike said.

"I don't like the other possibility. Do you?" Gavin asked. He watched the clouds reflect pinkish light across the valley. In the background, he could hear the bleating of sheep and goats from their pens within the village. At dusk, boys tending the herds brought them into the village to protect them against wild animals and roving Taliban. Both two- and four-legged predators were always hungry for village meat.

Feeling uneasy and caring too much for Gavin even though she didn't want to, Nike said, "No, I don't like the alternative. This is a dangerous mission."

"Yeah, it is. We're out in the wilderness and the bad guys are right over that mountain to the east of us." He lifted his gloved hand to point at the darkened peaks. Bringing his hand down, he wrapped his arms around her once more. "Don't worry, we know our job, Nike. We've already survived a year here."

"And you're on your second tour."

Hearing the flatness in her tone, Gavin nodded. "We're slowly making a difference. I'd give my right arm to find bin Laden. All of us would. It would change the tempo of this war against the terrorists."

Nike understood army hunter-killer teams were all about finding terrorists and Taliban. "So, how are you feeling about this more peaceful assignment of working in this village as an ambassador of good will?"

"I like it."

"But it takes you off the front lines."

"Not really." Gavin looked to the north of the village. Kerosene lamps were lit and the mud and stone homes that had windows glowed golden. He liked dusk, even though from a wartime perspective, it was a killing time, when the enemy sneaked up and took lives. "With General Chapman coming here to Afghanistan, the priority has shifted to focus on these boundary villages. If we can get these people to trust us, they will let us know when Taliban are coming through. The villagers could be our eyes and ears. If we can stop the Taliban's advancement into this country, that's a good thing for everyone. In the end, it will save a lot of lives."

"I like your general's philosophy."

"So do I. If I could, I'd have world peace. As it is, there's world war."

Nike shook her head. "I grew up in a peaceful Greece."

"And yet, Greece has had its fair share of revolutions, too."

"Granted." Nike observed the pinkish sky, now fading. Darkness began to encroach across the narrow valley. "I wish for the day when there are no more wars anywhere. No more killing. I've seen enough of it. All people want to do is live in peace and get on with their lives."

"It's the same here," Gavin acknowledged. "Abbas was

saying that all he wanted for his people was to be left alone to eke out their survival in this valley. He's grown old before his time because of the Russians and now the Taliban intrusion."

"Afghanistan needs decades of peaceful downtime," Nike agreed. But there had been none for them.

A wonderful sense of happiness bubbled up within her but it warred with sadness at her loss of Antonio. Suddenly bothered by her proximity to Gavin, she frowned. "I don't know what's going on between us," she admitted quietly.

Gavin gazed down at Nike. Even in the semidarkness he could see the worry register in her face. "Why try to decipher it? Why not just let it be natural and flow?"

Her stomach was filled with those butterflies. The only other man to make her feel this way had been Antonio. "It's not that simple," she told him.

"When I first saw you, I thought you were the most beautiful woman I'd ever seen. Most of all, I liked your gold eyes," Gavin confided softly. "You have the look of a lioness."

Her heart beat a little harder. Gavin was sincere. Or at least, he sounded sincere. That meant she had to take his compliment seriously. Antonio had been so much like him: a gentle warrior, a man of philosophy, of much greater depth and breadth than most men. "Thank you. My grandmother had the same color eyes. They run in the women of our family."

"You're feeling tense. Why?"

Nike pulled out of his arms and faced him. Oh, she didn't want to do that, but if she remained in the protection of Gavin's arms, she would lose all reason. Did this man realize the mesmerizing power he had over her? She searched his hooded blue eyes. The shadows of the night made his face dark and fierce-looking. "Look, I've got a lot of past history, Gavin, and I don't want you to think the wrong things about us."

Hearing the desperation in her tone, he nodded. "What happened to make you feel this way?"

It was the right question. Again, Nike squirmed inwardly. She'd talked to no one about the loss of her beloved Antonio nearly two years ago. Only Dallas, who had been executive officer of BJS in Peru, knew the full story. She had been her confidante, her healer up to a point. A heaviness settled into Nike's chest and once more she felt old grief discharging from her wound. Opening her gloved hands, Nike said, "I fell in love with a Peruvian army officer whose job it was to locate and capture drug-runners." The next words were so hard to say, but Nike felt driven to give Gavin the truth. "Antonio was an incredible person. He had graduated from Lima's university in archaeology, but the men in his family all had served in the army. So he went in and I met him when he was a captain. He loved his country and he saw what the drug-running was doing to it. Without fail, he would volunteer for the most dangerous missions to eradicate the dealers."

"He sounds like a fine man," Gavin said. "Courageous."

"Yes, well, that courage got him killed," Nike bit out. Looking down at the dark, muddy ground, she added, "I told him that he was going to get killed if he kept it up. But he wouldn't listen. And then…it happened. Two years ago."

Gavin measured the look in her wounded eyes and heard the hurt in her husky voice. Reaching out, he placed his hand gently upon her drooping shoulders and whispered,

"I'm sorry. He must have been one hell of a man to get your attention."

Tiny ripples of heat radiated from where his hand had momentarily rested on her shoulder. Looking up, Nike searched Gavin's narrowed, intense blue eyes and shook her head. "Listen, I learned the hard way—in our business if you fall in love with a military person, you're going to lose him."

"That's not always true."

"Yes, it is."

Gavin heard the stubbornness in her tone. Looking into Nike's eyes for some hint that it wasn't the truth she really believed, he felt a sinking sensation in his gut. Something hopeful and newly born shattered in his chest. After all, he had been burned but good by Laurie Braverman a year ago. Gavin had sworn off military women for another reason. He hadn't lost someone he loved to death. He had lost her because they simply could not compromise with one another.

"Maybe you just need time," Gavin counseled gently, removing his hand. He ached to kiss Nike. The set of her full lips, the way the corners of her mouth were drawn in, told him the pain she still carried over the death of the Peruvian captain.

"No," Nike said grimly, "time isn't going to change my mind." She stared up at him, her voice firm. "You need to know the truth. I shouldn't have led you on. I'm sorry."

"I'm not sorry at all, Nike. Look, we all need someone at some time."

His mouth was so beautifully sculpted. Good thing he couldn't read her mind. He had the lips of Apollo, the sun god. And wasn't Gavin a bit of sunshine in her life? Nike didn't want to admit that at all. But he was. All day, she'd longed to have a few quiet, uninterrupted moments with him. She was hungry to find out who he was, his depth and what mattered to him. Far more curious than she should be, Nike said, "I can't need any man who is in the military, Gavin. Never again."

Looking toward the village that was barely outlined by the dying light, the windows gleaming with a golden glow, Nike sighed. "You deserve to know the truth."

"And I'm glad you trusted me with it." Gavin smiled down at her upturned face. Her lips parted and almost pleaded to be touched by his mouth. "It's a good first step, don't you think?"

Seeing that gleam in his eyes, Nike knew Gavin wanted to kiss her. Yet, he hadn't made a move. The tension swirled between them and her heart screamed for his kiss. Her past resurfaced, frightening her. If she surrendered to her desire for Gavin, she would be right back where she was before—heartbroken. "There are no other steps," she warned him.

"I don't believe that," Gavin said, his voice a low growl. Reaching out, he took that step forward, his arms coming around her shoulders. Surprise flared in her golden eyes, her need of him very readable and yet, as he closed the distance, Gavin could see her fear. As he gently brought Nike against him he wondered if she would resist. If she did, he'd instantly release her, of course. Gavin didn't want that to happen and he sensed she wanted him, too. He leaned down, searching, finding her parted lips.

The world exploded within Nike as her arms swept across his shoulders, his mouth capturing hers. It was a powerful kiss, yet gentle and welcoming. His lips were tentative and asking her to participate fully in the joy of connection. The moisture of his ragged breath flowed across her face. The whiskers of his beard were soft. Gavin's mouth guided her and slid wetly across her opening lips. He cajoled, passing his tongue delicately across her lower lip. Instantly, Nike inhaled sharply as the throbbing sensation dove deeply down between her thighs.

He smelled of sweat, of wool and the sharp, clean mountain air. She reveled in his weather-hardened flesh against her cheek. His arms were cherishing and Nike surrendered as he swept her hard against his body. Their breaths mingled as they explored one another like hungry, greedy beggars. Well, wasn't she? It had been two long years since she'd kissed a man. And how different Gavin's kiss was! Nike tried not to compare him to Antonio. Gavin's mouth wreaked fire from within her as his lips molded hotly with hers. One hand moved sinuously down the back of her jacket, following the curve of her back. His other hand held her close. Her nipples hardened instantly as he deepened their kiss.

Nike was starved! Her entire body trembled just as he reluctantly withdrew his mouth from her wet lips. Nike saw the glint of a hungry predator in his eyes as surely as it was mirrored in hers. Knees like Jell-O, Nike felt weak. Inwardly, her body glowed brightly and she yearned to know his touch upon her aching breasts, and how he would feel entering her.

All of these crazy sensations exploded through her now that they stood, watching each other in wonder. The night air was cold and their breath was like white clouds between them. Nike noted the satisfaction glittering in Gavin's narrowed eyes. He held her gently and didn't try to kiss her again.

"Now," Gavin rasped, "let's start all over. I'm me and you are you. I'm not the man from your past. I'm the one standing with you here in the present. Judging from the kiss,

I think we have something to build upon. I'm a patient man,
Nike. I wasn't looking for a woman, but you walked into
my life." His hand against the small of her back tightened.
"And I'm not about to let you walk out of my life."

Chapter 5

Nike hadn't slept well and was finishing up breakfast with Jameela and her three daughters. Chapatis, a thin pita bread, had been filled with vegetables and seasoned with curry. She had trouble focusing on food when she kept remembering Gavin's kiss. It was completely unexpected—but welcome. Groaning inwardly, Nike remembered all her nightmares of Antonio's death. He'd been shot to death in the jungles of Peru. She'd sworn *never* to fall in love with a military man again. Not *ever*.

So why had she kissed Gavin? Why did she still want him? Nike had seen the predatory look in his eyes. She could have easily brushed him off. Why didn't she? *First things first: stop thinking about it.* Nike watched as the older daughters of the family cleared away the dishes and went to clean them in the kitchen.

Jameela was helping six-year-old Atefa wrap her leg, which had never had any surgical intervention. The little girl's leg was missing below the knee. Jameela had her daughter lie on the rug as she carefully wrapped the red, angry-looking stump with soft cotton fabric. Once it was tied in place, Atefa sat up and took her handmade crutches.

"Have you sought help for your daughter's missing leg?" Nike asked the mother.

"When it happened, we were shocked. My husband tried to get help from our government. He pleaded and begged a regional official to bring a doctor out here to help her," Jameela responded.

Nike frowned. "I'm so sorry. Who planted those mines?"

With a grimace, Jameela whispered, "The Afghan army did, to stop the Taliban."

Surprised, Nike blurted, "Why?"

"They hid them along the edges of our fields where we plow. They didn't want Talibans coming in here."

The whole conflict and mind-set of the Taliban didn't make sense. As soldiers, they could only do their part and hope families would be saved. Nike had to get to work pronto. Getting up, she shrugged on her coat and put the red scarf in place around her head. It was 0700 and dawn crawled up on the horizon. A mechanic team would arrive this morning to try and assess what was wrong with her CH-47. Every minute on the ground kept the helo a target of the Taliban. She had to get out and relieve her load master so he could come to Abbas's house and get breakfast.

"I'll come back later," Nike promised the woman. "Right now, I have to check my helicopter and relieve my sergeant."

Jameela stood and nodded. "Of course."

In the freezing cold of the spring morning, Nike hurried down the muddy, rutted street. The men were already busy.

A donkey hauled a wooden cart filled with wood brought from the slopes of the nearby mountains. She saw no one from Gavin's team, which was just as well. Right now, Nike couldn't bear to see him. She was too confused about what happened between them, that part of her wanted it to happen again…

Andy was delighted to see her and climbed out of the CH-47. He rubbed his gloved hands to warm them up. Even though Nike had provided heavy bedding for him, she knew it was no fun to sleep in a helo in freezing weather. After motioning for him to hightail it to the awakening village for breakfast, Nike took over watch of the helicopter. He handed her the binoculars.

Around her, the valley awakened. The brownish-red haze above the village came from the many wood fires prodded to life to feed a family in each of the mud-brick and stone dwellings. Above, the sky was a pale blue and she could see the tips of the mountains illuminated as the sun peeked above them. When the first rays slanted over the narrow valley, Nike could feel the warmth caressing her.

Dogs barked off and on. It seemed as if everyone had a dog or two. She never saw any cats and wondered why. Her breath was white as she exhaled. This was a very cold place even in the spring. But then, they were at eight thousand feet, so what did she expect? Moving around the helicopter, which sat out on a flat, muddy area, Nike looked for movement below. There didn't seem to be any, but she didn't trust the naked eye. The binoculars around her neck were a better way to search for the enemy.

Standing behind the helo for protection against sniping, she scanned the slopes below her. Nike noted small herds of sheep and goats being prodded out of the village center and down to the green grass below. It was a tranquil scene.

The sun's emergence had already upped the temperature by several degrees. Several dogs herded the animals farther down into the flat of the valley floor. It all looked so peaceful.

By the time Andy had gotten back to resume his duties, Nike was more than eager to go back to Jameela's home and grab another hot cup of the delicious and spicy chai tea. The woman had shared her secret recipe with Nike. Chai was individual to every family and Jameela's was legendary among the villagers. With some gentle persuasion, Nike got Jameela to divulge her recipe. Chai consisted of strongly boiled tea with goat milk, a pinch of brown sugar, cardamom and nutmeg. Her mouth watered just thinking about it.

She gave Andy a welcoming smile. He grinned as he walked up to her.

"Nothing?" he asked.

"No." Nike handed him the binoculars. "Keep watch. Captain Jackson was saying that the Taliban come through the northern end of this valley at the new moon, which is next week."

"Under cover of darkness," Andy said, placing the binoculars around his neck.

"Most likely, but you never know."

"I wouldn't know a Taliban from a villager. They all dress alike."

Grimly Nike said, "The villagers know they cannot approach this helo. So, if someone does, you draw your pistol and assume it's the enemy."

"Yes, ma'am. I just hope no one approaches," Andy said unhappily.

"I'll ask one of Captain Jackson's men to relieve you once an hour," Nike responded with understanding.

"Thanks." Andy looked up at the helo. "I'll sure be glad

to get out of here and back to base. I didn't sleep hardly at all last night."

"Neither did I." Nike smiled a little. Looking at her watch she said, "The team's supposed to arrive at 0800. That's not long from now."

"Can't be too soon. I'm spoiled," Andy said with a grin. "What I'd give for some bacon and eggs now. Not that the hot grain cereal wasn't good. It was."

Chuckling, Nike lifted her hand and walked back toward the village. Her heart thumped hard when suddenly she saw Gavin walking down the street, his rifle over his shoulder, looking as though he was hunting for someone. When he noticed her, his mouth lifted in a smile. He was the last person Nike wanted to see, but she couldn't turn around and avoid him.

"Good morning," Gavin called, catching the wariness in Nike's narrowed gold eyes. Those lips he'd caressed yesterday were pursed with tension. Over their kiss? He wasn't sure. Maybe she was upset over something else?

They met near the last mud-brick home. Both were aware that they might become targets and stepped into the alleyway between two homes for more protection. "I had sweet dreams," he told her.

"I didn't."

The flatness of her voice startled him. "Sorry to hear that. Everything okay?" He hooked a thumb toward her helo. Maybe Nike was discouraged over the fact her bird was down.

Nothing was okay, but she couldn't stand here discussing her personal stuff. Instead, she said, "You've seen Atefa? Abbas and Jameela's little girl who lost a leg to a land mine?"

"Yes."

"What are the chances of flying her and her mother out to Kabul to get some medical help with a prosthesis?"

Shrugging, Gavin said, "I could make some calls and find out."

"I'd appreciate that. That kid lost her leg to a land mine. She needs some type of medical help. Why can't the U.S. supply her with a prosthetic limb?"

Assuming Nike's worries were over the little girl, Gavin relaxed. Several black curls peeked out the sides of the red scarf she wore around her head. Nike looked even more vibrant and breathtaking to him. "There's no reason we can't. I've already radioed Kabul to tell them to get a medical doctor out here in the next two weeks."

"What about dental? A *lot* of people here have tooth problems," Nike said. She was relieved to be talking business with Gavin.

"Good idea. I hadn't gone that far with my plans for this village. Usually, it takes us a good three to four days to assess their health needs. Then I create a report and suggest a plan of action. After that, other medical or health teams are flown in to supplement the initial work we're doing right now."

"I see." Nike wasn't familiar with the tactics, but it sounded like a logical approach. "I think if you can help Atefa that it will go a long way to lessen Abbas's distrust toward us."

"Yeah, the old codger is definitely questioning everything we're doing," Gavin agreed quietly. "I'll give a call this morning to the medical people in Kabul. Several American programs help children who have lost limbs to land mines."

Warming to his concern, Nike tried not to look at his mouth. Memory of the kiss came back hot and sweet.

Frowning, she said abruptly, "Look, what happened yesterday is in the past, Gavin. I don't have time for any type of a relationship right now."

Gavin heard the desperation in her husky tone and trod carefully. "It was a shock for me, too," he admitted. "I came out of a relationship with a woman helicopter pilot about a year ago. I swore off military women." He gave her an uneven grin. "Until you came along."

Nike held up her hands. "Listen, I'm stopping this before it starts. I do *not* have room in my life." His blue eyes became assessing and furrows gathered on his brow. He took the Afghan cap off, pushed fingers through his short, dark hair and settled the cap back down on his head.

"It's not that easy, Nike. You know that."

"It is that easy." Feeling frantic, she couldn't face the stubborn glint in his eyes. "One kiss doesn't give you access to me or my life."

"That's true," he murmured. Gavin knew if he could just bring her back into his arms, capture her mouth, he'd persuade her differently. That time would come. But now, she was too scared, too prone to push him away. He had to let her go...a little bit. "I'm a patient person. Let's just take this a day at a time?"

"No." Giving him a hard look, Nike said, "It's *over*, Gavin. I'm sorry but I am not going to lose someone I love to a bullet. My heart just can't handle it. Do you understand?"

"Yes, I do," he answered honestly, feeling bereft. In his heart he knew that whatever they had would be long-term. Looking into Nike's eyes, however, he saw the fear and grief entwined. There was nothing he could do. Time to give up. "Wrong time and place."

"Exactly." Taking a step back, Nike said, "You're a nice

guy, Gavin. Maybe if we'd met a few years earlier… Oh, who knows? Just be safe, okay?"

As he watched Nike walk away, Gavin scowled. It felt as if someone had grabbed his heart and torn it out of his chest. Rubbing that sensitive area, he wondered how this beautiful Greek woman had captured him so easily. Gavin decided it was her personality. Nike had compassion for others, which his ex had lacked. Laurie had been out for herself and to hell with the rest of the world. By contrast, Gavin had seen Nike's care for others, whether it was concern for her load master, the people of this village or even his team.

"Well, hell," he muttered. Stepping out from between the homes, Gavin thought of the long day ahead. He was especially edgy because, according to headquarters, tonight was when the Taliban would start coming through the valley, and his mission would be to stop them dead in their tracks. Had the Taliban heard of their landing here, and were they coming in early instead? Ten men against a hundred of the enemy was not good odds. Gavin would not make the village a target. No, his team would take the fight with the Taliban elsewhere. He was glad of one thing: Nike would be out of here and safe. Her helo would be fixed and she'd be gone. That was important to Gavin.

Nike wanted to whoop for joy. She was sitting in the right-hand seat, her CH-47 idling along, both engines working once more. The mechanic team had arrived via Chinook and by noon, the damage to the front turbine was fixed. Andy, who was sitting in the copilot's seat, grinned like an idiot, but she understood why.

With her helmet on, she spoke into the microphone set close to her lips. "Okay, we're good to go. Did you contact Captain Jackson and let him know we were taking off?"

"Yes, ma'am, I did. He said for you to have a safe trip back to base."

Relieved, Nike gave him a thumbs-up. To her right, the first Chinook was taking off. Above them, an Apache circled to ensure no enemy was close to the U.S. Army helicopters. It felt good to have that firepower and she could hardly wait to get back to civilization. Andy left the seat and walked to the rear. Once she took the helo skyward, the ramp would be lowered and he'd be sitting out on the hip with the machine gun, watching for possible Taliban attacks from below.

Even though the helo shook and shuddered around her, Nike loved the sensations. Strapping in and tightening her harness, she radioed to the other helos. Within a minute, the rotors were at takeoff speed. Just feeling the Chinook unstick from the surface made Nike feel good. She saw a number of women and children at the village's edge watching in wonder. It was impossible to lift a hand and wave goodbye to them. One of her hands was on the cyclic, the other on the collective. Together, these kept the helicopter in stable, forward movement.

Most of all, Nike was relieved to leave Gavin behind. She felt guilty, but pushed all that aside. As the helo moved out over the green, narrow valley below, she followed the other Chinook at a safe distance. Within a minute, they'd begin their nap-of-the-earth flying, one hundred feet over the terrain in order to avoid being brought down by their enemy. Pursing her lips, Nike focused on the business at hand. For at least an hour, she wouldn't have to think about Gavin. Or about his kiss that had rocked her world.

"Any word from that A team in Zor Barawul?" Nike asked the communications tech in the ops building. It was nearly midnight and Nike couldn't sleep. She was worried about Gavin and his team interdicting the Taliban in the valley.

The woman shook her head. "Nothing—yet."

"Okay, thanks," Nike muttered. She shoved her hands into the pockets of her trousers and walked out of the small building. Above, the stars twinkled brightly, looking so close Nike could almost reach out and touch them. There wasn't much light around the camp, which helped keep it hidden from the enemy. She had a small flashlight and used it to get to her tent.

Just being back on the roster and assigned an Apache helicopter made Nike feel better. At least she was off the workhorse helicopter list. Despite this, worry tinged her happiness. Five minutes didn't go by without her thinking of Gavin or remembering the heated kiss they'd shared.

"Dammit," she breathed softly. Why, oh why couldn't she just let that kiss go? Stop remembering the strength of his arms around her? The pressure of his mouth caressing her lips as if she were some priceless object to be cherished?

Upon reaching her tent, she pulled the flap aside and then closed it. The warmth from the electric heater made all the difference in the world. Each of the twenty women Apache pilots got a small tent with a heater and a ply-board floor. The cot wasn't much, but it was a helluva lot better than what she'd had at the village.

Because she was on duty for the next twenty-four hours, Nike remained in her clothes. She took off her armor and boots and laid them at the foot of her cot. She had to sleep, but how? She worried about Gavin and his team. Had they discovered the Taliban coming across the valley yet? Lying down, she brought her arm across her eyes. And then, in minutes, she fell asleep—a small blessing.

Chapter 6

"This week, you're assigned to the CH-47," Emma Trayhern-Cantrell, the XO, told Nike as they sat together at an ops table. "You're going to be bringing in supplies to several boundary villages. And we're short on copilots, so you're flying without one."

Thanks," she told her XO. Nike nodded and tried to hide her disappointment. For a week, she'd flown the aggressive Apache and done her fair share of firing off rockets and rounds to protect A teams up in the mountains hunting Taliban. Because she loved the adrenaline rush, it was tough to be relegated to a lumbering workhorse instead.

Her XO handed her the list of villages along with the supplies to go to them and the times of delivery. Emma Trayhern was all business. She had the red hair of a Valkyrie with large gray eyes and a soft mouth. She had her uncle Morgan Trayhern's eyes. However, Nike already knew that this Trayhern child was no pushover even if her face spoke of openness and compassion. Emma was an Apache pilot and as tough as they came.

"I know you're bummed. CH's don't rock." Emma tried to smile. "There's always dirty work along with the rockin' Apache. You're just lucky enough to have skills in the CH-47."

"Yeah," Nike said grumpily, folding up the orders. "I wish they'd give us another Apache or two."

Shaking her head, Emma said, "They're stretched to the max over in Iraq. We get the leftovers. It sucks, but it is what it is."

"I'm not so philosophical," Nike said, rising. It was near dawn, a red ribbon on the eastern horizon outside the ops hut. Already, the air base was in full swing and with plenty of action.

"You hear anything about your guy? Captain Jackson?"

Giving Emma a frown, Nike said, "He's *not* my guy. How did that rumor get started?"

Grinning, Emma folded up the huge map and left it on the ops table. "Blame your load master, Andy."

"Blabbermouth," Nike muttered.

"We were expecting the Taliban to go down through that valley near Zor Barawul, but they didn't. I told Dallas that I thought someone from the village probably sneaked off to tell them the A team was in town, so they took another trail into the country."

"I wouldn't doubt it," Nike said. She put the paper into the thigh pocket of her dark green flight suit. "When I was there overnight, there was a lot of wariness toward Americans."

"Well," Emma said, "you'll be delivering the last load of the day to them. If you get a chance, stay on the ground for an hour and find out what's going on. I like to get eyes and ears out there on those villages. Dallas wants to keep a check on them and whether they get slammed by the Taliban."

"Good idea." Nike wasn't too sure she wanted to spend an hour on the ground to visit with Gavin. She saw the curiosity in Emma's eyes. "I'll do my best."

"Do it at each stop, Nike. We want you to talk to the leader of each team and get their latest assessment."

It wasn't a bad idea, Nike thought as she put on her black BJS baseball cap. "Okay, will do," she promised. "This is going to be more like a milk run."

Emma walked her to the door. "I hope you're right. But be careful. Those four villages are not on our side. Yet."

"Getting food, medical personnel and medicine in to them on a regular basis will help," Nike said, opening the door. The crisp air was barely above freezing. Nike would be glad when June came. Everyone said it got warmer at the beginning of that month. In the mountains at eight thousand feet, a local gardener told her that there was less than a ninety-day growing period. This made gardening tough, which was why most people had goats, chickens, sheep and few vegetables. Certainly, fruit was scarce, too.

Clapping her on the shoulder, Emma reminded her, "Be careful out there. Dallas does *not* want to lose any of her pilots."

Grinning, Nike gave her a mock salute and said, "Oh, not to worry, XO. We're a tough bunch of women." She decided to swing by the base exchange and picked up four boxes of dates and four pounds of candy for the kids. Dates were a delicacy usually eaten only at the time of Ramadan. Poor villages couldn't afford such a wonderful fruit and Nike wanted to give it to the wife of the chief of each village. The meaning of her exchange would go far with the women of the village to cement a positive connection. And the children would love the sweets. That made her smile because the Afghan children were beautiful, so full of life and laughter.

Gavin was surprised as hell to see Nike walking toward him from the helicopter. She'd covered her short, shining dark curls with a black baseball cap. He grinned, feeling his heart open up.

"Hey," he called, "this is a pleasant surprise."

Her lips tingled in anticipation. Nike could see the happiness burning in his blue eyes as he approached her. While part of her wanted to rush into Gavin's arms, she halted a good six feet from him, hands on her hips. "Just dropping off supplies, a doctor and dentist, and getting the lay of the land and giving Jameela a box of dates as a goodwill gesture."

Gavin sensed her unease but kept his smile. "Dates. That's a great idea." He added, "I missed you."

Though wildly flattered, Nike couldn't get on a personal footing with him. Lucky for them, there was all kinds of activity around the unloading of the helo. A number of men carried the cardboard boxes into the village. The doctor and dentist were led into a group of awaiting men and boys. "My boss wants me to spend an hour with you getting a sense of how things are going at the village. She's compiling an ongoing dialogue with the generals above her on where each village stands."

Raising his brows, Gavin said, "You ladies are on top of things." He gestured for her to follow him. "Come on, we'll go to the team house, have some chai and chat."

Nike did not want to be alone with Gavin. He was too

damned masculine. She wished for the thousandth time her traitorous body would stop clamoring for another kiss from him. Her mind was in charge and no way could she get involved again. Ever. "Okay, but this is business, Captain."

"No problem," Gavin said smoothly.

Walking at his shoulder, a good twelve inches between them, Nike said, "You never got that attack you were expecting. I'm glad."

Gavin dodged the muddy ruts made by the continuous donkey-cart traffic through the village. "Yeah, we're relieved. But suspicious." The sun had warmed the village and children played in the late afternoon. Dogs ran around barking and chasing one another. Women in burkas were here and there, but mostly, they moved the window curtains aside to stare at them walking by.

Nike saw a number of barefoot children with mud up to their knees. She smiled a little. They were tough little kids in her opinion and yet, so huggable. She started handing out the bag of candy she carried in her hand. In no time, every child in the village surrounded them. Nike made sure each child, no matter how little, got a handful of jellybeans. When it was gone, they disappeared with their treasures. She turned to Gavin. "I'm glad for you it's been quiet around here. Why do you think that happened?"

Gavin nodded as they sauntered toward the stone home on the left. "We think the Taliban got tipped off by someone here in the village and they decided to take other paths into the country."

"But that doesn't guarantee anything for long," Nike said.

"True, but we're making progress. Abbas is softening his stance toward us. He's still worried the Taliban will see him consorting with us. And I think someone in the village was scared to death of the same thing, intercepted the Taliban and told them to take another track. That way, it would look like this village was still helping the Taliban. It's a real balancing act out here for Abbas." Gavin halted and gestured to a large mud-brick home. "Here we are. Come on in. I'm ready for some hot chai."

Inside, the hard-packed earth had been swept. Everything was clean and neat. The men's equipment stood up against the walls in neat rows. There was a stove in the corner with plenty of wood, the tin chimney rising up and out of the roof. The windows were clean and sunlight made the room almost bright, if not cheerful.

"Have a seat," Gavin said, taking off his hat and putting his rifle nearby. He shrugged out of the dark brown tunic and then removed his body armor. "Feels good to get out of this thing," he muttered. "I live in it almost twenty-four hours a day."

"Armor is the pits," Nike agreed. She saw several small rugs and pillows near the stove. Taking a seat on one, she watched as Gavin went through the motions of putting water in a copper kettle and then sitting it on top of the stove. Her heart pined for his arms around her, his mouth cherishing her lips. For now, she fought her desire, crossed her legs and folded her hands in her lap.

"If your CO wants to know about this village," Gavin said, pulling a tin of loose tea off a shelf, "tell her that we've got about a twenty-percent pro-American base here now. The men are starting to open up to us."

"Is that all?" Nike pulled out a notebook and a pen from her left pocket.

Gavin filled the tea strainer and gave her a one-raised-eyebrow look. "Is that all? It's only been a week. I think that's pretty amazing."

Jotting it down, Nike said, "I've brought a medical doctor and a dentist and hygienist with me. That ought to encourage a little more loyalty."

He poured hot water into two tin mugs and then dipped in the strainer filled with loose tea. "If we could gain loyalty like that, all we'd have to do is hand out money and buy them off."

"I understand."

"Honey?"

"Yes, please." She watched as he poured goat's milk into the mixture and pulled another tin from the shelf. He ladled out a teaspoonful of golden honey into each cup. Another tin contained a spice mixture and he put a pinch into the steaming chai. There was something solid and steady about Gavin. He had a confidence born from experience in the field. Everything he did had a sureness to it. Nike realized that he was the kind of leader anyone could trust completely. That was just another reason to like him way too much.

Gavin brought over the steaming mug. "Chai for two," he teased. He set his cup on the ground and brought up a small gold rug and pillow, sitting opposite her. "And I know Jamccla's chai rocks, but she isn't about to give her secret recipe to anyone." He chuckled.

"She gave it to me. I loved staying at her home. At the base I keep trying different chai mixtures to duplicate it, but so far, no luck." Nike sipped the delicious chai. "Hey, this isn't bad, Jackson." She tried to relax, but being so close to him made her squirm endlessly. Not to mention Gavin seemed even more handsome with his long-sleeved cotton shirt and brown Afghan trousers. His beard, as always, was meticulously shaped and trimmed. Even his hair was longer in order to emulate the Afghan men's hairstyle. His skin was so suntanned he could easily have passed for an Afghani.

"So, did you miss me?" he inquired with a wicked grin.

Nike refused to meet his eyes. Her hands tightened imperceptibly around the tin mug. "I didn't have time."

"Pity," Gavin teased. He saw how uncomfortable Nike had become. Yet, her cheeks reddened and there had to be a reason for it. "Well," he said conversationally, "I sure missed you."

"I wish you wouldn't."

"Why?"

"You know why, Gavin. I just can't fall for another military man."

"Oh, that's right—you think I'll die in combat."

"There's a damn good chance of that."

"Well," he pointed out, "look at you. You have an Apache strapped to your butt and you're always a fair target for the Taliban, too."

"That's different."

"How? A bullet is a bullet."

"You're infuriating. Were you on the debate team at your college?"

"Actually, a university. And yes, I was on the debate team for four years. I like arguing." He flashed a smile even when revealing this nugget of truth.

"Of course you do." Nike couldn't help but smile back, all while trying to steady her racing heart. "Which university?"

"Princeton. Where did you get your degree?"

"The University of Athens."

He gave her a warm look. "Congratulations."

There was an uncomfortable pause and Nike could feel him warming up for some heady declaration. Why couldn't this be a business meeting? Well, she knew why but just couldn't face it.

Sipping his chai, he sighed. "I've dreamed about you every night. About our kiss."

"That's your problem." Nike had to look away, until she realized she was being a coward.

"I don't believe you mean that." Gavin searched her narrowing gaze. "You're scared, Nike. That doesn't mean there isn't something between us. I grant this is a lousy place to become aware of it. I'm interested in you for all the right reasons. And I know why you're gun-shy. But can't you give us a chance?"

His words were spoken so softly that Nike felt her heart bursting with need of him. This was a side to him she'd not been aware of until now. "I'll bet you are a damned good used-car salesperson, too."

Laughing heartily, Gavin finished off his chai, got to his feet and made a second cup for himself. "Thank you for the compliment. Frankly, I'd rather sell you on me."

"I got that." She sipped her chai and wanted to run away. The room became smaller and smaller and Nike felt trapped. Or maybe she was trapping herself.

"My team is coming back in a week to base camp," he told her conversationally, sitting down once more. "We get two days off. I'd like to take you to Jalalabad, to a nice little restaurant I know about, and have dinner with you. How about it?"

"I don't think so, Gavin."

"Are you sure? I see some hesitation in your eyes."

Setting the cup down next to her knee, Nike said, "I just can't."

Nodding, Gavin said nothing. His instincts were powerful and he knew she liked him. Just how much, he didn't know. He'd tried to play fair and that hadn't worked. Honesty wasn't necessarily the best policy with Nike, who was jumpy and wary. While he understood her reasons, Gavin wasn't about to back down. He watched as she drew out her notebook and pen once more.

"Ready for my village assessment?" he asked her. Instantly, he saw Nike's face relax. So long as he remained on a professional, hands-off basis with her, she wasn't distrusting.

"More than ready." Nike looked at the watch on her wrist. "I have to lift off in thirty minutes."

"No problem." Gavin launched into the many details, names, events and places that he knew her CO would want. It was still an unadulterated pleasure to be with her. She was a feast for his eyes, balm for his heart and Gavin felt as if her presence pumped him full of life and hope again.

Nike just about ran out the door of the house when they were done. She did not want Gavin to trap and kiss her. If he ever kissed her again, she'd melt away in his arms, completely defenseless against his heated onslaught. Moving out into the late-afternoon sunshine, she saw that the shipment of boxes had been removed from the CH-47. Next, she visited Jameela at her home and gave her the box of dates. The woman nearly cried, threw her arms around Nike and hugged her.

"You are my sister," Jameela whispered, wiping her eyes as she held the precious box of dates.

Feeling the warmth of true friendship, Nike reached out

and squeezed her hand. "All women are sisters," she told her with a grin.

Jameela nodded and understood exactly what Nike was saying. In this man's world, ruled by men and where women were considered secondhand in every way, they needed to band together and support one another. "The next time you visit, you must have time to have chai with me," Jameela said.

"Ah, I love your chai," Nike said with a laugh. "And yes, if I get this mission again, I'll ask my CO for a half hour more and we'll sit and talk over chai."

Bowing her head, Jameela's eyes burned with warmth. "I would like that, my sister. Allah keep you safe."

"Thank you," Nike murmured, meaning it sincerely. "I can use all prayers." She left the house and hurried down the muddy street. She wanted to do nothing more than get out of here and away from that man who drove her to distraction.

Nike ordered Andy into the helo to raise the ramp, and she settled into her right-hand seat. Just the act of putting on her helmet and running through the flight list before takeoff soothed her taut nerves. From time to time, Nike would give a quick glance out the window, looking for Gavin to show up. He had a way of quietly walking up to her so that she never heard him coming. Not today.

Within minutes, they were airborne. Some small part of her was disappointed that Gavin hadn't come to see her lift off. Moving the heavy two-engine helo into the blue sky, Nike now had to focus on more important things—like surviving this flight back to base.

As she flew nap-of-the-earth throughout the region, she never took the same route twice. Consequently, the route through the mountains was always different and filled with unexpected new difficulties. Nike was glad for the challenge. It kept her mind—and her heart—off Gavin. Still, even as she flew, she wondered what would happen when he and his team came back to base for a two-day rest.

Chapter 7

Nike was halfway back to base when she got orders to turn around and head back to Zor Barawul. Stymied by the clipped radio message, she had no choice but to do so.

As she landed near dusk, the sun tipping the western mountains, she saw Gavin standing with Jameela and her daughter, Atefa. The whirling blades of her helicopter kicked up heavy clouds of dust.

By the time she got out of her harness and placed her helmet on the seat, Gavin was at the rear of the ramp.

"What's going on?" she asked.

"The medical doctor just approved Atefa to be flown to Kabul to be fitted for a prosthesis." He grinned. "I called your base and asked that you return. Sorry to do this. I know it's damn dangerous flying in and out of here."

"Don't worry about it," Nike said, looking out the ramp door at Jameela, who stood with a protective arm around her young daughter. "Is Abbas in favor of this?"

"He is. That's the best news." He searched her face. "I've already talked to the CO of the base. We need to fly them in now and preparations are under way to give them a tent and food for the night. Tomorrow morning, the three of us will be flown to Kabul."

"You're coming along?" Her heart beat once to underscore that news.

"Yes. I'm leaving Sergeant Bailey in charge while I'm gone."

"But…"

"The threat of attack here is always high," Gavin said, reading her concern. "I've gotten permission from my superior to do this because they feel this particular village is essential in the fight against the Taliban."

"And Jameela and Abbas trust you." Nike nodded. "It makes sense." She managed a slight smile. "Have you warned them about the rough ride and nap-of-the-earth flying we'll be doing?"

"I have. What I want to do is get Jameela and her daughter strapped in behind you and I'll ride shotgun in the copilot seat if that's all right with you?"

Her smile turned devilish. "Sounds good to me. If I get shot you can take over flying."

Gavin recognized her black humor and chuckled. "Right. I have a pair of gold-plated tin wings from a United flight attendant that makes me pilot material. Will that do?"

"You're a piece of work, Jackson."

"But you like me anyway, right?"

Seeing the glimmer of warmth in his eyes, Nike waved a hand at him and walked down the ramp. "There's no way I'm answering that one." She gestured for the pair to come forward. After giving Andy orders, she walked back into the bird. Gavin had passed her on the ramp, walking down to meet the twosome. Nike noticed most of the village had turned out to watch. She had to remind herself that these people, cut off from the outside world, hadn't seen helicopters since the Russians tried to ransack their country decades earlier. The CH-47 was a curiosity among them, especially the younger children.

Jameela walked slowly and kept a hand on her curious daughter as they boarded the helicopter. Nike finished off her radio message to her base and then turned around. Lifting her hand, she waved hello to Jameela, who was draped in her black burka. Nike could only see her wider-than-usual eyes. The woman must not ever have flown in any type of aircraft. Feeling for her, Nike went back, knowing that a smile might make the woman feel more at ease.

As Jameela grabbed her hand, Nike said, "It's okay, Jameela. Everything will be all right." She leaned over and gave Atefa a hug. The little girl was dressed in her finest, most colorful robe, her black hair brushed to perfection. Atefa's eyes shone with excitement.

Jameela gave the ramp door a desperate look and still gripped Nike's hand.

"She's scared to death," Nike said to Gavin, who had come up behind her.

"I know. Show her to the nylon seat behind your seat. I'm sure being near another woman will help calm her fears."

Nike didn't disagree. She took Jameela to the nylon webbed seat and asked her to sit. The woman did, with great reluctance. Nike had to guide her carefully to the seat so she wouldn't trip and fall over her burka.

After getting the harness in place around Jameela, Nike attended to Atefa in the next seat. Andy took the girl's crutches and tied them down next to their two stacked suitcases strapped down on the deck of the helo. Atefa's eyes were huge as she scanned the cargo hold of the helicopter. Nike kept smiling and murmuring words of encouragement as she ensured they were strapped in.

Next came the helmets. They had none that would fit Atefa, so Andy brought over a pair of earphones and clapped them over her head so she would have protection from the horrendous sounds within the airborne helo. Jameela pulled on hers and was hooked up to the communications system. This way Gavin could continue to answer her questions and soothe her throughout the flight.

In minutes, the ramp groaned and squealed as it came up and closed. The cargo hold was thrown into semidarkness. Patting Jameela's shoulder, Nike went to her seat, pulled on her helmet and got ready to take the bird up.

Andy sat down next to the twosome and Gavin explained to Jameela that he was there to support her through the flight. Jameela seemed less intimidated when Andy strapped himself in next to her. Nike's large, broad seat back on one side and the young man on the other seemed to calm her fears, Gavin thought.

After climbing into the copilot's seat, Gavin picked up the extra helmet and put it on, opening communication between the four of them. As she rapidly went through the preflight checklist, Nike's gloved hands flew across the instrument panel. She was focused on this flight, not on the man next to her. He must have understood the gravity of this dangerous flight and wasn't about to distract her. For that, she was grateful.

The flight back wasn't any different from any other, but Gavin had his hands full with Jameela, who screamed into the helmet's mouthpiece whenever they dived and wove through the mountain passes at a hundred feet. Nike couldn't afford to pull her focus off her flying. The CH-47 shook and shuddered like a dog shaking off fleas as she guided it up and down and then twisted around the mountains to plunge down into the next valley.

By the time they arrived at the base, Jameela was frantic. Atefa, however, was laughing and throwing her arms up and down. For the child, it was like a fun roller-coaster ride.

By custom, no man could touch the woman, so it was Nike who unharnessed Jameela and Atefa, taking off the helmet and earphones and walking them down the ramp into the dusk. Andy brought along the suitcases. A medic met them at the bottom of the ramp in a golf cart, ready to whisk them to a tent for the night.

By the time Nike had them settled, it was pitch-dark. Gavin met her outside the tent.

"They all set?"

"Yes. Finally." Nike quirked her mouth. "What a day."

Gavin nodded and fell into step with her as they headed to the chow hall on the other side of the base. "Couldn't have done it without you. Thanks. I know Jameela feels better because she knows you and trusts you." No lights marked the camp after night fell. To have it lit up was to invite attacks by the Taliban. Each of them had a small flashlight to show the way between the rows of green canvas tents.

The cool night air revived Nike. She was always tense after such a flight. It felt good to talk about little things, and, even though she didn't want to admit it, she was glad to have Gavin's company. After chow, she'd go to ops and fill out her mission debrief report.

Inside the large, plywood-floored tent, the odor of food permeated the air. Nike found herself hungry, so they went through the line and ended up at a wooden picnic table in the corner. She eagerly sipped her hot coffee. Gavin sat opposite her.

"You a little hungry?" she teased Gavin, who sat opposite her, digging into roast beef slathered with dark brown gravy.

"Listen, when you eat as many MREs as we do, real food is a gift," he said, popping a piece of beef into his mouth.

Nike could only imagine. There were mashed potatoes with that thick, brown gravy, corn with butter and a huge biscuit. She ate as if she'd never seen food. Normally, she didn't have such a large appetite, but tonight, she did. "This hits the spot," she told him.

"Mmm," Gavin mumbled, barely breathing between bites.

Nike grinned. "If you don't slow up, you're going to choke on that food you're shoveling down your gullet."

Chastised, Gavin had the good grace to flush. He slowed down a little. "You have no idea how good real, hot food tastes."

"I probably don't. I'm spoiled. I might fly every day or night, but I can come here and get good chow. I hate MREs."

"Everyone does," he said between bites. He took his third biscuit and pulled it open. After putting in several slabs of butter, he took a big bite.

Nike saw the absolute pleasure the food gave him. She knew these A teams were out in the wilds for a month at a time, sometimes more. This unexpected trip was a real present to Gavin. She tried to ignore how handsome he was, even with the full beard.

"Do you mind wearing your disguise?" she wondered, pushing her empty plate to one side. She held the white ceramic mug of coffee between her hands.

"No."

"It's got to be different from the spit and polish of shaving every day."

"Oh, that." Gavin touched his neatly trimmed beard. "I bet you wonder what I look like without it?"

"No…"

"Sure you do." He grinned.

"I was just wondering how you liked going under cover."

Shrugging, Gavin finished off his third and final biscuit. "Doesn't bother me. Usually, when we're out for a month, we're riding horses and doing our thing."

"So you've all learned how to ride."

"That or fall off." He laughed. Scraping up the last of the gravy, he sighed. "That was damn good food. I wish I could take this back to the guys."

"You and your team go without a lot of things," Nike said, feeling bad for them.

"Luck of the draw," Gavin said. He wiped his mouth with his paper napkin, pushed the plate aside and then picked up his cup of coffee. "I'd rather be on the ground than threading the needle with that hulking helo of yours. That must take some starch out of you."

"Sure it does. Seat-of-the-pants kind of flying. I don't mind doing nap-of-the-earth. I do mind getting shot at."

Chuckling, Gavin felt the warmth of the food in his belly. How lucky he was that Nike had shared such a meal with him. He felt happiness threading through him like sun shining into a dark valley. "Makes two of us. I felt for Jameela. The poor woman is probably going to refuse to step into the CH-47 tomorrow morning."

"We'll have to persuade her that the flight to Kabul will

be smooth and quiet, unlike the snaking flight from her village."

"I don't know if she'll believe me," Gavin said.

"She'll get on board because her daughter is going to be fitted for a new leg."

"I appreciate all you did. If you hadn't been there, this would have been a lot tougher. Moslem customs don't allow any man to touch a woman."

Shaking her head, Nike muttered, "I'm glad I was there, but I can't see how their women live in such a state. I know I couldn't."

"Different realities, different belief system," Gavin said. "We don't have to like it for ourselves, but we have to understand and respect them for it."

"Glad I'm a woman from a democracy, thank you very much."

Gavin smiled. "Dessert? I saw some great-looking cherry pie over there. Want some?"

"Sure."

He got up. "Ice cream on it?"

In that moment, Nike saw he was like a little boy in a candy store. The light dancing in his readable blue eyes made her heart melt. "Why not?"

"Be right back."

She watched him thread his way through the noisy, busy place. This was the dinner hour and the place was packed with crews. There were a few A teams, as well, all dressed in their Afghan clothing. Still, as she allowed her gaze to wander around the area, Nike thought Gavin Jackson stood head and shoulders above any other man present. Maybe she was prejudiced. Maybe she liked him more than she should.

Feeling uneasy for a moment, Nike didn't question why

she decided to have a meal with him. If she was really sincere about not ever wanting to love a military man again, she'd have left him at the chow hall and disappeared. But she hadn't. *Damn.* Rubbing her face, Nike felt torn. The problem was, Gavin was too easy to like.

His eyes were shining with triumph when he came back with two large plates. His had two pieces of cherry pie and scoops of vanilla ice cream. Setting hers down in front of her, he gloated, "I couldn't help myself. I love cherry pie and ice cream. My parents have a farm in Nebraska and I grew up picking sour cherries from our trees so Mom could make these mouthwatering pies."

"You're something else," Nike murmured. She watched him sit down and launch into the dessert without apology. Indeed, he was a little ten-year-old boy and not the man sitting there. His expression was wreathed with such pleasure that Nike couldn't help but laugh.

"So, you're a Nebraska farm boy?"

"Yep. My folks have a five-hundred-acre farm. They raise organic wheat, corn and soybeans for the growing green market. Of course, they were doing this decades earlier."

"And you helped with all the farming?"

"Me and my two younger brothers," Gavin said, shoveling in another bite of cherry pie. "They're still at the farm and will take it over when Dad decides to retire."

Cocking her head, she asked, "So, what made you come into the military, then?"

Shrugging, he wiped his mouth. "The excitement. I get bored real easy and watching corn grow wasn't exactly my kind of fodder."

"So, this is your career?"

"I plan to put twenty in, retire and then do a lot of things I couldn't do before."

"Like what?"

He gave her a wistful look. "I like to travel. I want to see the countries of the world, large and small. I enjoy meeting people of different beliefs and religions. I always learn from them and it makes me a better person in the end."

"I'd never have thought that of you."

"No?" Gavin asked, lifting his head and giving her a thoughtful look. "What did you think?"

Uncomfortable, Nike said, "I don't know. I just never thought that much about it." *Liar.*

"I see. Well, how about you? You're Greek by birth. How did you get into the U.S. Army to fly Apaches?"

The pride in his tone washed across Nike. Plenty of men distrusted her because she was a woman in the pilot's seat of an Apache. "My father was in the Greek military for twenty years and then went into flying for a commercial airline. I grew up wanting to fly. He made sure I had flight lessons on single-engine airplanes from the time I was fourteen years old. Later, I wanted to fly helicopters, so I got my license when I was seventeen. My mother didn't want me to go into the military, fearing I'd die."

Gavin nodded. "Not a prudent choice from her perspective."

"No, but I was a tumbleweed of sorts. I didn't want to do things girls were supposed to do. All I wanted to do was get in the sky. I loved the challenge of flying a helo versus a fixed-wing aircraft. When I was up in the sky, everything in my life went right."

"On the ground, things got muddied up?"

"You got it."

"Was there a program for flying the Apache?"

"There was, and I took advantage of it. After I graduated from school in the U.S., I was assigned to the Black Jaguar Squadron down in Peru. I spent several years chasing the druggies and loved every moment of it. From there, I got assigned to chasing druggies along the U.S.–Mexican border. Dallas, who was already there, got me assigned to her unit. When she told me the Pentagon was going to approve a second all-woman BJS squadron, I wanted to be a part of it."

"And here you are. That's pretty impressive."

"Thank you. Women can do anything they want if they dream high enough."

"Obviously, you're one hell of a dreamer."

She chuckled and relaxed completely. Talking to Gavin was like talking to her best friend. "I don't think everyone dreams of being in combat, though. I like the challenge of it. I don't like thinking about getting killed. No one does."

"So, what other dreams do you have?"

She took a sip of her coffee. "I'd like to go back to Apache school in the U.S. and teach. I think I'd be a good instructor."

"So, you dream of twenty years in the military, too?"

"I guess I do, but I'm focused only on the present. My mother is always urging me to get married, have kids and come back to live in Greece. I told her I was too young for all of that. I've seen people get married too early, get bogged down with children, and then they're forty-five before they ever have a life of their own. I love kids, and I want them, but not right now. I want to use my twenties and thirties to explore what moves me in life. After that, I'll settle down."

"Sounds like a plan," Gavin said before his expression

became serious. "You said the man you loved was killed in combat down in Peru?"

"Yes." Nike hesitated.

"I know what it's like to lose someone you care for. In my first deployment here in Afghanistan, I lost two of my men from my team."

"I'm sorry." And she was. Nike saw his straight, dark brows dip in grief. "I'm just now coming to terms with the loss of Antonio."

"I'm sure we'll both remember those we loved forever."

She liked his sensitivity. "Love can't be destroyed."

"I found that with their loss, I became overprotective and superconservative when I was out in the field. I didn't want to lose any more of my men."

"That's understandable."

"Well, it got to the point where my own men got frustrated with me. I was scared. So, I pulled back, and I lost my will to go out and be the risk-taker I was before. At the end of my first tour, my men finally had to sit me down and let me have it. They told me that risk is a part of our nature, that avoidance wasn't going to help them live or die. Eventually, I realized they were right," Gavin murmured. "I was afraid to connect with life again. My fear paralyzed me in a lot of ways I couldn't see then. I do now, but my men had to gang up on me and force me to see how I was reacting."

She saw the caring in Gavin's blue eyes as he held her gaze. "I can see why you became so gun-shy, so to speak. I hope you don't blame yourself for what happened."

"I try not to." Gavin sat up and moved his shoulders as if to get rid of accumulated tension. "It didn't want to take another chance and that kept me from my job, from living. My men saw it and came to my rescue."

"They are good friends to you, then."

"And I want to be a friend to you, Nike."

His words, softly spoken, made her heart hammer suddenly. Gazing into his eyes, Nike could feel him wanting to reach out and touch her hand. "A friend?" she asked stupidly.

"You're afraid to get back into life because you lost the man you loved. I know you want to protect yourself." Gavin smiled warmly, the expression making her ache inside. "But life isn't like that. You can't help who you do or don't fall in love with. It's chemistry and a million other things all rolled into one."

"Where is this going?" She tried not to look at him but it was impossible

"I'd like to be your friend, but you won't let me."

"You want a lot more, Gavin. I can't give that to you."

Sighing, he nodded. "I know. The problem is, I like you. I'd like to get to know you better on your time and terms. I'm not the kind of guy who hops from bed to bed. You're diffcrent from any woman I've ever met. You're courageous, you have steel nerves and you're intelligent. All those things draw me to you. I didn't plan this, it just happened."

His honesty made her feel guilty, especially since there was so much she liked about him. It had been a long time since someone had touched her on such a deep level. "Gavin, you're a nice guy, but I just can't."

Getting up, she left the chow hall as quickly as she could. Her heart was hurting and the grief still roiled within her. The cold night air gave her the slap in the face she needed. She felt bad that she had stomped all over Gavin for being honest. Nike didn't like herself very much as she made her way to her tent. Weaving through the tent city, she noticed the stars twinkling above. They were cold, distant and beautiful. If only she could feel that distant and cold toward Gavin.

Every time the guy looked at her, she found herself shaky, needy and sexually hungry. Was Gavin right? Was this all about her own fear of loss? Of course it was. Nike halted in front of her tent and shut off the flashlight. In the distance, she heard an Apache revving up to take off on a night mission. The wind was cold and she shivered. As she recalled Gavin's story about losing his men, she realized he was trying gently to tell her something about herself.

With a muffled curse, Nike turned, pulled open the flap on her tent and went inside. She sat on the cot and took off her flight boots. Tears burned in her eyes and she wiped them away almost instinctively. She was drawn to Gavin Jackson whether she wanted it or not! A sense of guilt and a need to run flooded her.

The worst part was Gavin had no unlikeable qualities. This fact compelled her to throw her boots across the floor. They made thunks as they struck the plywood. Leaning over, elbows on her thighs, Nike pressed her hands to her face. She wanted to keep crying. Of all things! It had been two years since she'd cried and that was at Antonio's funeral.

"Damn you, Jackson."

Chapter 8

The July heat was arid and scalding. Nike had grown up in the dry heat of her homeland, Greece, so she felt right at home. Red-haired Emma Trayhern-Cantrell and she trotted across the tarmac to their waiting Apache helicopter. The crew quickly opened up the canopies. Word had just come in that an A team near the village of Bar Sur Kamar was under heavy attack.

Time was of the essence. Nike was the AC, air commander. She leaped up on the step and quickly situated herself in the forward cockpit. Her heart pounded in time with the snaps her harness made as she fastened it. Emma climbed into the rear seat, behind Nike. A blonde mechanic by the name of Judy cinched them in and gave them a thumbs-up before removing the ladder and hauling it beyond the range of the helo's blades.

"Ready," Emma told Nike from the rear seat.

"Good to go," Nike said, pressing the microphone to her

lips. The sun beat down upon them. "Let's shut the canopies first. It's hotter than hell."

Once the canopies were locked down, Nike was able to turn on the air-conditioning. The coolness flowed past her helmeted face as they went through the preflight checklist in record time. The Apache quivered to life, its rotors swinging in slow arcs. Nike powered up and the blades began to churn. As she looked through the dark shield over her eyes, Nike snapped off a salute to the women on the ground. The chocks were removed from the wheels and they were ready to take off.

For the last two months, Nike had been able to fly the Apache exclusively. She loved being off the roster for assignments with the slow CH-47. As she placed her gloved hands around the cyclic and collective, she lifted the massive, deadly assault helo off the tarmac and into the air.

"I'm punching in the coordinates," Emma told her.

"Roger."

"I'm tuning us in to the A-team commo link so we can monitor them going in."

Lips compressed, Nike felt the helo moving powerfully through the desultory late-afternoon air. "Roger." The land grew distant as she brought the Apache up to seven thousand feet. With this bird, she didn't have to fly nap-of-the-earth. The Apache had every conceivable device on board to locate possible firing by the Taliban. This bird ruled the air in Afghanistan.

Her gaze flicked over the large panel in front of her. Nike watched airspeed and altitude and constantly craned her neck to spot problems. She heard scratchiness through the helmet earphones. Emma switched to the A-team frequency, which would enhance communication. In the past month, attacks on the army hunter-killer teams had escalated. They always did in the summer when travel was easier for both sides.

Her mind turned back to Gavin. She hadn't seen him in two months and was relieved he'd gone back into the field. After she'd dropped Jameela and Atefa into Kabul, her days of ferrying were over. Atefa now had a new leg and was doing fine.

The vibration moved through her hands and up into her arms. But despite her return to more comfortable surroundings, Nike couldn't stop thinking about Gavin. She felt the weight of the armored helicopter around her. Too bad she couldn't choose who to love. Not that she loved Gavin, but she kept seeing—feeling—that one, unexpected kiss in her mind. She'd replayed their conversations too many times to count. How sad was that? Nike could convince herself that she didn't care, but right now she admitted how worried she was for him and his team. It wasn't unusual to fly three missions a day in support of those out in the field. Each time the temptation came to nose around for Gavin and his men, she hesitated. Nike couldn't stop her dreams—the ones where she explored his body, her lips moulded against his, those strong hands ranging over her heated flesh. How many times had Nike awakened from sleep, breathing raggedly, aching for him? Too many.

They topped a mountain range, some snow left on the very tops, the blue-purple rock below. As they came over the valley, communications blared into her helmet.

"Red Dog One to Alpha One, over."

Nike gasped. *It was Gavin!* The moment she'd dreaded had come. Gavin's team was under attack!

"Alpha One this is Red Dog One, over," Emma's calm voice responded.

"We're getting another attack! I've got two men down.

One will die if I don't get medevac pronto! Do you have us in range? Over."

The desperation in his voice shook Nike as nothing else ever had. Hands tightening on the flight controls, she saw the puffs of mortars fired at a hill on the other side of the valley. She knew that the A teams set up lonely outposts in valleys to intercept the paths Taliban took into Afghanistan. Gavin must have been ordered to Alpha One. This valley was a hotbed of enemy attacks.

Pushing the Apache, Nike said, "I've got them in sight. Prepare the rockets."

"Roger," Emma said.

"Alpha One," Emma called, "we're on our way. Give me the coordinates of your position. Over."

Nike heard the back-and-forth between Emma and Gavin. The Apache screamed down out of the sky and Nike watched the firings at the top of the hill where Gavin and his team were pinned down. Her heart raced. Sweat trickled down the sides of her face as she brought the helicopter in line to fire the rockets.

"Ready and on target," Emma called.

Tension reigned in the cabin. "Fire at will," Nike said.

Instantly, the Apache shuddered as the first rocket left. Then a second, third and fourth. Nike watched with visceral pleasure as the rockets struck their targets. Rocks, dirt, flame and other debris exploded upward one, two, three and four times. The hill suddenly had tons of dirt gouged out of one side of it.

"On target!" Gavin yelled, triumph in his hoarse voice.

Emma continued to speak to the A-team leader. It was Nike's job to circle the entire hill. They had infrared aboard that would show body heat where the Taliban was hidden below in the tangle of thick brush. Emma also worked the infrared and continued to give her flight changes so that she could fire the Gatling gun beneath the belly of the helo at other pockets.

In moments, the Apache came on station and Nike held it at an angle, hovering about five hundred feet above a particularly thick grove of trees. Emma released a fusillade of fire, the Apache bucking beneath her hands as the Gatling gun spewed forth the bullets. Nike watched the bullets chew up the landscape like a shredder. Tree limbs exploded, bushes were torn up and she saw about twenty of the enemy scattering in all directions to get out of the line of fire.

It was then that Nike realized just how overwhelmed Gavin and his team had been. She estimated about a hundred of the enemy on all sides of the hill. Her headphones sang with communications between the team, Emma and ops. The sunlight lanced strongly into the cockpit and Nike didn't like it. This time of day was hard on the eyes, making it tougher to see. Fortunately, Nike had a television screen in front of her and she didn't have to crane her neck and squint. The television feed showed a number of other hiding places for the enemy.

Over the next five minutes, they systematically took the Taliban charge apart. The .45 pistol she carried on top of her flak jacket made it tough to draw in a deep breath of air. As Nike danced the Apache around the hill, they spotted another force of about fifty men coming down from the slope of a mountain behind the hill.

Whistling, she said, "They *want* to take that hill."

"No joke!" Emma said. "We're running low on ammo. Want to call in another Apache for support?"

"Roger that," Nike said grimly, and she switched the commo to another position to call ops with the request.

"Red Dog One, this is Alpha One," Nike said. She kept looking around as she brought the Apache to a thousand feet above the hill and continued to circle. This was the first time Gavin had heard her voice.

"Nike?"

She grinned. "Roger that, Red Dog One."

"I need immediate helo evacuation." Gavin's voice registered his surprise. "I've got one man with a severed artery. I've got a tourniquet on it but Burkie'll bleed out before the medevac can get here. Can you land, give up one of your seats and take him on board? Over."

The request was out of the ordinary and completely against regulations. Emma's gasp showed her shock, but what could they do? It would take forty minutes for medevac to arrive on station. By that time, his team member would be dead. Nike knew all the men, and her throat tightened. It was Emma's call. She was the XO. She had the position and power to override any rule.

"Emma?"

"I know," she said, her voice desperate. "Dammit!"

"We've got the Taliban on the run. The hill's clear and we've scattered the fifty coming down to join them. I think we'll be okay to land. We can do this before our backup arrives."

"Are you volunteering to stay behind?"

Nike hadn't thought that far. "I guess I am. Can you clear this request and give permission?" she begged.

"We shouldn't do this," Emma said grimly. "It's against our orders. Dallas will hang us."

"I know, but there's a man dying down there. There's enough room to land and take off, Emma. I can set this girl down, hop out and we can get the guy on board. It'll be easy for you to fly him back at top speed. I don't think the Taliban will regroup. We've killed most of them."

Nike held her breath. If Emma approved the illegal pickup and leaving a pilot behind, it was her ass on the line. Emma was one hell of a pilot and a damn good leader. If anyone could persuade Dallas this was the right decision, it would be Emma.

"Okay, okay, let's get down there. I'm going to rig some static for a call to ops requesting permission. They won't give it to us, but we'll pretend we heard otherwise."

Nike wanted to cry for joy. "We'll stick together on this."

Chuckling, Emma said, "We're BJS and crazy wild women, anyway. This might not be in the flight rules for the boys flying Apaches, but for us, it's no rules at times. Peru taught us that."

Nike understood. How many times down in Peru were the flight book and rules thrown out the window? Too many times to count. If nothing else, BJS was a fly-by-the-seat-of-your-pants squadron. It shouldn't be any different here, either.

"Red Dog One, this is Alpha One. Clear off an area north of your position on the hilltop. We're coming in to land. Once down, I have to shut off the engines. Bring your man once the blades have stop turning. Over."

"Thank you, Alpha One. We'll get on it pronto. Out."

Nike heard the incredible relief in Gavin's voice. Knowing how tight he was with his men, that they were family to him, Nike felt moisture in her eyes. She blinked away tears as she noted the men scrambling to the north end of the hill to pick up anything that the blades might kick into the air. If there was anything lying around, the power of the blades could throw it up in the air and turn it into weapons against them.

Emma rigged the shorting-out communications call with ops and made it sound like static. She laughed darkly. "Okay, we're indicted now. Ready to land?"

"Yes."

Banking the Apache, Nike swooped down and brought the helo to a hover fifty feet above the clearing.

"You can take a hop back on the medevac that's already under way."

"Roger that. No way do I want to stay on that hilltop tonight." Nike brought the Apache down until its tri-wheels hunkered on the earth. Dust clouds kicked up in every direction until the blades had stopped. She pushed open the canopy, climbed out and leaped to the ground.

Two men were carrying a third between them. The injured man's left leg had a tourniquet, midthigh. Blood stained his entire pant leg down to his boot. Gavin trotted up, his face grim, rifle in hand. There were splotches of blood all over his uniform. He'd probably dragged his friend out of the line of fire.

Emma had thrown open her cockpit canopy and stood on the seat to give the men directions.

Nike met Gavin's eyes and ached for the fear and grimness in them. He handed her the rifle and then lithely leaped up on the Apache. Together, the three men got the unconscious soldier into the cockpit. Nike watched as Gavin quickly harnessed him up. Within two minutes, Emma was ready to take off. Gavin locked the canopy back into place and gave her a thumbs-up.

Nike handed Gavin his weapon as he leaped off the Apache. Together, they all moved away.

"Are you all right?" Gavin demanded as they stood back and hunkered down.

"I'm fine."

"Thanks for doing this," he said.

"No problem." She was kneeling down in a foxhole dug deeply enough to keep them hidden. The dust from the Apache kicked up and the shriek of the engines was like music to her ears. Coughing, Nike shut her eyes and covered her mouth as the thick dust rolled by.

Within three minutes, the Apache was hotfooting it across the valley toward base. The thunking sound of the blades beat in echoing retreats across the valley. Nike told Gavin that a medevac was on the way, and Gavin nodded. "That's good to hear. You're going to be on it."

"Yes, I will be."

He wiped the sweat off his brow. His hands trembled as he put another clip of ammo into his weapon. "You just saved our bacon. At least a hundred of those bastards were down there."

"I'm glad we made the difference." Nike sat down in the hole, dust all over her flight suit. She saw the rest of the men in other foxholes across the top of the hill. Huge craters had formed from mortars fired earlier by the Taliban. The sun slanted powerfully across the hill, making it difficult to see on the western side.

"I've got two other men wounded, but they're walking and firing." He locked and loaded his weapon, craned his neck out of the hole and gazed down the side of the chewed-up hill. Sitting back down, he conferred with his assistant and told him to keep watch, this was merely a lull in the fighting.

Nike sat next to him, her heart lifting with joy to see him alive. "How long have you been up here?"

"Too long. It's been twenty-eight days so far, Nike." He managed a grin. "Why? Do I smell bad?"

Nike chuckled. "This isn't exactly the Ritz."

"I'd give almost anything for a hot shower." He met and held her gaze. "But right now, I'm the happiest man on earth. You're here. With me. Amazing."

Laughing softly, Nike said, "Okay, I missed you a little, too."

"Really?"

She liked the amusement in his crinkled eyes. "A *little*," she stressed. Right now, Gavin looked more like an eagle on the hunt than the laid-back soldier she'd met at base camp two months ago. She reminded herself that he'd been under attack, his adrenaline was up and he was in survival mode.

Gavin wanted to grab Nike and crush her against him. He could smell the shampoo she'd used this morning in her hair. Any fragrance compared to the hell he'd seen on this hill over the last three weeks was welcome.

"Are you wounded?" she said, pointing to his leg. Besides being dirty and torn, he had some fresh blood on his right thigh.

"What? Oh, that. I'm fine. It was just some shrapnel from a mortar."

"You should be medevaced out, too."

"No way."

Frowning, Nike began to really study the rest of the team. They were all wounded to some degree and oblivious to it. All their attention was riveted on the base of the hill where the next attack might come from. The courage these men displayed amazed her.

"How long has this attack been going on?"

"Four days off and on. Today they attacked en masse,"

Gavin said. He pulled out a canteen and guzzled water. Droplets leaked out the corners of his mouth and down his beard. After finishing, he looked over at her. "They want this hill back. From here, we can see everything going on in this valley. Since we got here over three weeks ago, we've called in ten strikes on them as they tried to cross the valley at night to get into Afghanistan."

"No wonder they're pissed," she said, giving him a grin. His blue eyes lightened for a moment and Nike could feel his desire. She could almost feel it surrounding her. And then, he glanced away and the moment was broken. She wanted those seconds back.

"Yeah, just a little." He stretched his head up above the hole to study the slope for a moment. "I'm glad you're going to be out of here by dark."

"Why?"

"They'll attack then. Damn good thing we have night scopes to pick up their body-heat signatures or we'd have been dead up here a long time ago."

He said it so matter-of-factly, and yet, for Nike, the words were a shock to her system. Gavin Jackson dead. For the first time, it really struck her that it could happen. Before, Nike had felt he was such a confident leader, that nothing could bring him down. Now, sitting here in a foxhole with him, she felt very different. And she was scared to death.

Chapter 9

There was nothing to do but wait. Nike remained in the foxhole while Gavin made his rounds, running and ducking into the next foxhole to speak with his men. Their only communication was by yelling. He and his second-in-command had radios, but that was it.

Nike kept cautiously peeking over the top of the foxhole, watching below and wondering if they'd destroyed enough of the enemy to keep them at bay for another hour. She wasn't sure. Wiping her mouth, which tasted of dust, she took one of the canteens in the foxhole and drank some water.

Luckily for her, she had her radio and could remain in contact with ops and any flights coming their way. Still, she felt dread. Was this how Gavin and his men felt all the time? The waiting? The wondering when the next attack would come? She couldn't conceive of living in this type of nonstop stress. Her admiration for the A team rose accordingly.

The top of the hill was about the size of a football field, although rounded. The hill was steep and not easy to climb. There had been a wooden lookout at one time, but it had been splintered into oblivion by repeated by enemy mortar rounds. The scrub bush that coated the sides of the hill was massive and thick. Nike had seen it from the air and knew men could quietly sneak up almost to the edge of the top of the hill. Her adrenaline pounded through her. What would happen at night?

She could hear Gavin's voice drifting her way from time to time. The foxholes were deep and the nine remaining men stayed in a circle at the top so intruders could be spotted coming from any direction. The afternoon sun was nearly gone and was dipping behind the peaks. As much as she tried to stifle it, Nike was scared for all of them, not just herself.

When Gavin leaped back into the hole, she noticed he'd put his Afghan hat back on. He wore body armor beneath the dusty white shirt, soaked with sweat beneath his armpits. It gave him a little protection from flying bullets.

"Like my digs?" he asked casually, putting his weapon next to him and taking another swig from one of the canteens.

"This is a special hell," Nike said, frowning. Searching his sweaty, dirty face, she added, "I don't know how you take this kind of stress."

"It's not fun," Gavin admitted, twisting the cap back on his water.

"Has this hill been a U.S. outlook for some time?"

"Yes. And with great regularity the Taliban drops mortars on it hoping to kill us." He gestured toward where the wooden tower had once stood. "We build the look-out tower and they come back and bomb it to oblivion."

She shook her head. "I never realized the kind of danger you were in."

"No one does until they're up to their butts in it," Gavin said, grinning. He took his weapon and made sure there was a round in the chamber. With the rag in his pocket, he tried to clean most of the dust off the weapon.

"Will they attack?" Nike asked.

"I don't know. Depends upon how much damage you were able to do to them."

"Do they attack every day?"

"No, but since two days ago, they've made a concerted effort to take back this hill." Gavin made circular gestures above his head. "This hill is the key to the whole valley, Nike. It sits at one end and with our binoculars and infrared scope, we can see anyone trying to cross it at night."

"How are you being resupplied?"

"We aren't," he said, frowning. "We're low on ammo and water. Usually, we get a flight in here twice a week. We're in dire need of resupply right now."

"And you can't get it because…?"

"The Taliban keep firing at the helicopter transport that's supposed to supply us. Oh, there's always an Apache with it and they lay down fire, but this time, it hasn't worked. If the transport can't land to resupply us, well…"

"Have you made a call to your commander about this?" She felt her throat tighten with concern.

Gavin wiped his brow with the back of his arm. "Yes." He looked at his watch. "I figure in about twenty minutes we should see a medevac, a transport and an Apache come flying in."

"Then what?"

"Well, we're going to swap out A teams. A fresh team will come in with supplies and we'll be airlifted out of here."

Relief spread through Nike. "That's good news."

Grunting, he said, "Not for the team coming in. It's one of the hot spots on the border and no one wants this assignment."

Nike gulped. "Is anyone else in your team injured besides yourself?"

"Oh, we all are more or less," Gavin said.

Nike couldn't believe how calm he was about it all. She noticed again the dark red blood that had stained half the trouser across his right thigh. "Are you okay? It looks like your wound is bleeding more."

"I caught a flesh wound," he said. "It's nothing. I'll be okay."

She sat there digesting all the information. "I never realized how...dangerous..."

Chuckling, Gavin reached out and patted her shoulder. "Hey, it's okay. You Airedales fly above the fray. It's ground-pounding soldiers like us who stare eyeball to eyeball with the bad guys."

His touch felt so good. Suddenly, Nike realized just how much she liked Gavin. Despite the terror, the trauma and the possibility of another attack, he was joking and seemingly at ease about his lot in life. This was real courage.

"You're right, Gavin. I sit up there and I'm not connected to the ground below."

"Well, saves you a lot of PTSD symptoms," he told her wryly. He sat with the rifle between his drawn-up legs, arms around it.

"That's not even funny," she muttered.

"You know what I do when things are quiet like this?"

She heard a wistful note in his voice. "No. What?"

"I think about you. About us."

A bit of ruddiness crept across his cheeks. It was hard to believe that Gavin would blush but he did. "Us?" Her pulse started as he gave her a warm look.

"Yeah." Looking around at the foxhole and then up at the blue sky, Gavin said, "It helps me hold on. When things are bad, I remember that kiss."

So did she, but she wasn't about to admit it. "Oh."

Gavin gave her an assessing look and added, "I swore that if we got off this hill alive, I was going to hunt you down."

A thrill moved through her, though Nike tried to stay neutral. "This isn't fair, Gavin."

"What isn't?"

"You know my past. I lost the man I loved to an enemy bullet. I can't go through that again."

Hearing the desperation in her voice, Gavin reached out and gripped her hand. "Hey, life is dangerous. Not just to military people, but to everyone."

"Especially to the military." Nike jerked her hand out of his. She felt stifled and trapped. Her heart yearned for Gavin, but her past experience had done too much damage. Nike pleaded, "I'm afraid to love anyone in the military ever again, Gavin." There, the truth was out.

Gavin absorbed her strained words. Every once in a while, he'd look up and over the crater to peruse the hill below, but everything seemed quiet. "I appreciate your honesty, Nike. A lot of people allow fear to run their lives in different ways. There's the woman who won't leave a marriage because she fears losing the security. There's the man who fears leaving his job for another one." Shaking his head, he held her narrowed golden gaze. "Fear is everywhere all the time, Nike."

"What do you fear?"

He smiled. "Being alone. See? I have my fear, too."

"Why fear being alone?" She searched his pensive face.

"My mother nearly died when I was a little kid. As a ten-year-old I lived through days and nights when she didn't come home from the hospital. My father tried to help me, but I felt this terror that I'd never see her again. She'd had appendicitis with complications, but as a young kid, I didn't realize what had happened. My father, bless him, tried to keep the three of us cared for, but he had a job. We ended up with a babysitter and not a very good one at that."

"It would be hard for a young child to have a parent suddenly gone from their lives like that."

"It was. I look back on that time a lot. My mom nearly died, but my father never let on how bad it was. I was in school, and that helped. I used to come home and look for her, thinking she was playing a game of hide-and-seek with me."

Nike's heart ached for his pain. "That must have been very hard on everyone."

Picking up a clod of dirt, Gavin crushed it in his fist and let the soil sift between his fingers. "That was one of the most defining moments of my life. I felt abandoned and afraid."

"But she survived?"

Nodding, Gavin said, "Yes, she came back ten days later. We couldn't visit her in the hospital because of the type of infection she had. And she was in a coma, so we couldn't talk to her on the phone. My dad kept telling us she was all right, but none of us believed that."

"Wow," Nike whispered, "that was awful for her and you kids."

He leaned back against the dirt wall. "Yeah, it was. And when she did come home, she was very weak. Nothing like the mother I had known before. I don't know who cried more—us or her when she was brought in the door on a gurney by the ambulance crew."

Nike sat digesting it all. "And she did recover?"

"Fully. It took about six months though. She looked like a skeleton and we all thought she was going to die. My father lost his job because he had to stay home and take care of us. We didn't have the money for a full-time babysitter or a nurse. I remember waking up with nightmares." He sighed. "It was always the same nightmare—Mom was dead. I'd go into her room and she'd be on the bed, dead."

"How awful." Reaching out, she let her hand fall over his. She could feel the grit of dust beneath her fingertips. "I'm so sorry, Gavin."

He enclosed her fingers and gave them a gentle squeeze. "Hey, every family has their trauma and heartache."

"That's true," Nike admitted. Her hand tingled over Gavin's touch. She couldn't deny any longer she was powerfully drawn to him. "So how did this affect your life?"

Gavin chuckled and made another quick check down the slope on their side of the hill. Sitting down, he said, "My fear is abandonment. My whole life has revolved around the possibility of loss. When I joined Special Forces after graduating, I made damn sure I would never abandon my men or leave them without help."

"Unlike the ten-year-old who was abandoned by his mom?"

"Yep." Gavin sighed. "And I got into some pretty stupid relationships with women because of it, too."

"You wouldn't abandon them?"

"No, but they abandoned me in many different ways. I always seem to pick strong women who have no problem having affairs with other men."

"Ouch," Nike murmured. "That has to hurt."

"Yeah."

"Did that ever stop you from having a relationship?"

Giving her a warm look, Gavin said, "Oh, it would for a while, but then I'd jump back into the fray and choose the same kind of woman all over again."

"I don't see how you could keep going back and trying again," she said.

"What's the other choice? Becoming a monk in a cave in the Himalayas?"

Nike laughed along with him, feeling the connection to him deepen. "Well, at least you have the guts and courage to jump back in and try. I don't."

"Maybe you just needed time," Gavin said.

"Two years."

He shrugged. "Well, everyone is different, Nike. Was Antonio the first man you've fallen in love with?"

She nodded. "Coming from a strict Greek upbringing, I was taught that love comes along only once. My parents have been married since their twenties. They're very much in love with one another to this day. I wanted that for myself. I wanted that happiness."

"But it isn't working out that way for you."

Nike nodded. "I used to think happiness would just happen."

"I don't think happiness is a guarantee in our life," Gavin said ruefully.

"No," Nike said grimly, looking up at the darkening sky. "That's how I see it now."

"So your world view got shattered when he died."

"Just like yours did when you were ten."

"Life does things to all of us," Gavin said. "I guess what I got out of my mother and father was that hope springs eternal. He never gave up on her. He would hold us, promise us that she was coming home. For whatever reason, the ten-year-old me wanted to see her before I would believe him."

"You can't be hard on yourself. You were only ten, scared, and suddenly you had your mom ripped out of your life."

"I learned then that nothing in life is safe."

"You're right about that." Nike sighed. She sat digesting his words. *Nothing is safe.* Sitting here in a foxhole on a hill in Afghanistan proved that. "I feel safe when I'm flying an Apache."

"That's only because you haven't ever been shot down."

"Mmm," she agreed. Rubbing her brow, Nike gave him a frustrated look. "I'm too much of an idealist. I think everything is safe and fine until it blows up in my face."

"Right," Gavin murmured. "But we all get those left hooks that life gives us. The point is to get back up, dust off your britches and move back into the fray."

"And you've done it time and again."

Gavin nodded. "Yes, I have."

"Don't you get tired? Exhausted?"

"Sure I do." He gave her an uneven grin. "But then, hope infuses me, and I start all over again. I open back up and do the best I can."

Rubbing her armor-clad chest, Nike confided, "You're a far braver person that I have ever been, Gavin."

He looked at his watch. "I have an idea."

"What?"

"We happen to like each other. In about ten minutes, those helos will be flying into the valley. How about when we get back to base, we start all over?"

Nike felt fear along with a burst of elation. "What are you talking about?"

"My team will get two weeks' R & R. I'd like to get to know you when things aren't as frantic or dramatic as they are right now. Can we get together and just talk?" He opened his hands and grinned wolfishly. "I promise, I won't hit on you. Maybe what you need is a gentle transfer from the fear of losing someone into making friends once more."

"I don't know, Gavin."

"Look at us," he said persuasively. "We're sitting here in a foxhole together just talking. I like hearing about your life and how you see things. I know you're enjoying yourself."

"Yes, I am."

"This proves that we can be friends."

"That's not what you really want," she challenged, feeling that old panic again.

"No, but I can be satisfied with friendship, Nike. In all my other relationships, I never had what we have. I like it. My parents used to tell me that the strongest base for a relationship was being friends first. I'm just now, with you, beginning to understand that statement."

"You were never friends with the women in your life?"

"Not really. And that's where I may have made a huge mistake."

Uneasy, Nike said, "Antonio and I were the best of friends." She saw him digest that statement.

"Maybe," he said, a bit of wistfulness in his tone, "you're the best thing ever to happen to me."

Quirking her mouth, Nike said, "I wouldn't be so sure of that."

Gavin heard the sounds of rotors and craned his neck to the west. "Oh, I am. Hey, here comes our rescue party. Two Apaches. That's even better."

About that time, Gavin's radio blared to life. Nike heard her CO's voice. Dallas was flying one of the Apaches, which meant she and Emma were probably in a helluva lot of hot water. And Dallas was on the flight schedule today. She'd soon find out.

Gavin gave directions to the medevac and transport, a CH-47, about where to land on the hilltop. Before they did, the Apaches made a sweep of the entire area to ensure the transport could land without being fired upon. For the next ten minutes, the two Apaches used their infrared cameras to look for warm bodies in the area. There were none.

Gavin stood up as the CH-47 came in for a landing. Holding out his hand, he said, "Come on, Nike. We get to go home—together."

She gripped his hand and stood up. Standing there, rifle on his shoulder, he looked incredibly strong and courageous. If nothing else, Nike felt like a true coward in comparison. Right now, she had her CO to worry about. If Emma couldn't sell the reason for letting off the pilot to take an injured soldier on board, her career could be in real jeopardy. Watching the CH-47 hover and slowly come down, Nike wasn't sure what to expect.

Chapter 10

Once Gavin had helped her onto the ramp of the CH-47, he backed away, which surprised her. The other A team trundled off and quickly left the area of the rotor blades. Some of Gavin's A team came on board and the rest went on the medevac. Nike turned, confused.

"I'll see you back at base tomorrow," he called, stepping away.

The ramp started to grind and groan as it came up. Nike realized that Gavin was probably going to fill in the next team and she sat down. She dutifully put on the helmet, but couldn't shake the disappointment that he wasn't coming back with her. She understood why, but it didn't help her fear. The Taliban could attack again. At night.

The CH-47 lifted off, the shuddering familiar and comforting. Closing her eyes, she leaned back and tried to relax. The pilot would be doing the roller-coaster nap-of-the-earth flying, and she hung on. Her mind turned to consider the inevitable: Dallas Klein, her CO, was probably pissed off as hell at what she and Emma had done. They'd broken every cardinal rule in the Apache flight book. Who knew what kind of punishment Dallas would dole out?

The moment Nike stepped into the BJS 60 headquarters, the staff looked up, their expressions grim. A sergeant, Carolyn Cannon, said, "Major Klein wants to see you right away, Captain Alexander."

I'll bet she does. Nike nodded. Normally, Emma Trayhern-Cantrell, the XO of the squadron, would have been at her desk, but there was no sign of her. Girding herself, Nike marched up to the closed door, knocked once and heard "Enter." Compressing her lips, Nike gripped the doorknob, twisted it and entered.

To her surprise, Emma stood at rigid attention in front of Major Klein's desk. Cutting her gaze to her CO, Nike knew she was in a lot of trouble. The older woman's eyes blazed with rage.

Coming to the front of the desk, Nike said, "Reporting as ordered, ma'am." Sweat began to gather on her brow and her heart pounded with adrenaline. Nike had never seen Dallas this angry.

"Captain, what the *hell* were you thinking when you left the cockpit of your Apache? You know damn well neither pilot is to *ever* leave that helicopter for *any* reason unless it's on fire."

Nike looked straight ahead to the wall behind her CO. "Ma'am, Berkie…er…Sergeant Berkland Hall, the communications sergeant, was bleeding to death. Captain Jackson said he'd die before a medevac got there to rescue him. Berkie…er…Sergeant Hall's wife had their first child three months ago. I—I didn't want to see him die. I wanted

to see him live to get home to see his new baby. Ma'am…"
Right now, that all sounded like a decision based on too
many emotions, but Nike stuck to her guns.

"Captain Trayhern-Cantrell says she ordered you out of
the cockpit. Is that true?" Dallas growled.

Gut clenching, Nike realized Emma was being true to
her word to take the fall on this breaking of rules. Nike
didn't want to leave Emma at the center of the problem.
"Er… Ma'am, it was a mutual decision."

"Mutual?" Dallas yelled. She glared at Emma. "Dammit,
you're XO of this squadron! You have no business making
any 'mutual' decisions!"

Emma shot a fearful glance at Nike and then said, "Yes,
ma'am."

Dallas got up and prowled the small office, glaring at
both women. "I have my XO, who is supposed to be the
poster child for following rules, breaking them. And then I
have one of my best pilots agreeing with her to break those
rules, too." Hands behind her dark green flight suit, Dallas
stalked around her desk.

"There are men dying out there every day, ladies. We
are not medevac. If you want to be medevac you should
have damned well volunteered to do that kind of service
work. Our job—" and she punched an index finger in their
direction "—is to protect and defend. The Apache is *not* a
medevac!"

Swinging her attention to Emma, she added, "Dammit,
Trayhern-Cantrell, what if you'd got shot coming back?
What if you'd needed Nike on the instruments if the Taliban
started firing at you? What if, God forbid, we'd needed the
two of you on another call on the way back?"

"You're right, ma'am," Emma whispered contritely.

"I don't want to be right!" Dallas exploded. "I want you

to know what is right, Captain! You're a damn poor example
for our squadron. It makes all of us look bad."

Emma's lips thinned and she said nothing, her eyes
straight ahead.

Nike cringed inwardly. In all her years knowing Dallas
as the XO of the Black Jaguar Squadron down in Peru,
she'd never seen her fly off the handle as she was doing.
That was how serious this was, Nike realized. At the time,
it had seemed like the right decision to make. She didn't
know yet if Berkie had survived or not. She'd come straight
here to HQ from the helo.

"Of all the harebrained decisions the two of you have
ever made, this goes over the top." Dallas glared at them.
"What am I to do? If I don't punish you for your decision,
then one of my other pilots will get it into her head that it's
okay to climb out of the cockpit on a mission to give up her
seat to another injured soldier."

Wincing, Nike felt the blast of her CO's anger. Oh, it was
justified. The only question now was what Dallas Klein was
going to do to punish them for their blatant transgression.
She could feel two spots burning into her cheeks as her CO
watched her.

"All right," Dallas flared, her voice suddenly deadly
quiet, "neither of you leave me any choice. Captain
Trayhern-Cantrell, you're stripped of your status as XO.
You've just proven you aren't up to the task of reinforcing
the rules that we must all live under here in combat."

Nike winced. She knew that punishment would go on
Emma's personnel jacket and it could stop her from making
major someday. There was nothing Nike could do about it,
and she felt terrible.

"Yes, ma'am," Emma croaked, shock in her tone.

"Remember, Trayhern-Cantrell, you did this to yourself.

You made the decision! You shouldn't have allowed that A team captain to influence you as he did. You've clearly shown that you don't have the backbone to enforce the rules."

"Yes, ma'am," Emma whispered.

Heart breaking, Nike heard the pain in Emma's tone. She knew that Emma came from a military dynasty, a very famous one. There were so many medals and awards for valor in the Trayhern family, and now Emma was giving it a black eye. Emma must feel awful about this. Guiltily, Nike knew it had been her idea to pick up Berkie.

"Ma'am," Nike spoke up strongly, "Emma is innocent in all of this! I—"

"That's not true, ma'am," Emma piped up quickly, giving her friend a panicked look.

"Quiet!"

Nike grimly shut up, as did Emma. Her attempt to save her friend was not going to work. When Dallas had been a young pilot, she had to have made some stupid decisions, too. She'd probably been in a similar situation herself.

Breathing hard, Dallas said, "Do you realize what you've done? We're a covert black ops. We've come here with an incredibly spotless record of positive work as an all-female squadron. And you two decide to screw it up with this stupid, completely avoidable mistake."

Nike'd known the chewing-out was going to be bad, but not this bad. She felt guilty that her desire to save Berkie would give all the women of this squadron a bad name, but still couldn't be sorry for her action. Her decision broke the rules, but wasn't wrong by moral standards. With that resolve, Nike was prepared for the worst. What made it tough was how Emma selflessly threw herself under the bus. She didn't have to, but she did. Nike felt awful about that.

"What the hell am I going to do with the two of you?" Dallas spat. "It isn't like I have women pilots standing in line to fly Apaches! But I can't trust the two of you in the cockpit, either." Glaring at them, Dallas shook her head.

"I'm sorry, ma'am." Emma's voice was quiet and apologetic.

Nike absorbed the brittle tension that hung in the small office. She was sure the office pogues outside could hear everything. It was completely unlike Dallas to scream at anyone like this.

"Captain Trayhern-Cantrell, you're demoted. It will be reflected in your jacket and haunt you for the rest of your military life. You have not done your proud military family any favors with your poor decision-making. From now on, you will be just one of the pilots in the squadron. One slip-up—and I mean *one*—and I'll send your ass back to the States and you can be reassigned into a mixed-gender helicopter squadron flying transports. You got that?"

"Yes, ma'am."

Nike tensed inwardly as Dallas swung her glare to her.

"And you, Captain Alexander. I have a terrible feeling this was all your idea and that Captain Trayhern-Cantrell was the patsy for your desire to help that man. War is not pretty. I thought you would have got that in Peru, but obviously, you didn't. You let your compassion for that man affect your judgment. I can no longer trust you in the cockpit of an Apache, can I?"

"No, ma'am, I guess you can't," Nike whispered.

"There's no *guess* about it, Captain Alexander." Dallas fumed. "Dammit, you leave me no choice. From now on the only time you'll have your ass strapped into an Apache is to keep up your flight skills. I'm assigning you permanently to the transport squadron here on base until you can be trusted to fly an Apache properly. I need every woman I have to man the Apaches and you've now left me a pilot short. I'm calling back to the Pentagon to see if I can find another female pilot to replace you."

Nike closed her eyes, taking her CO's words like punches. She had never anticipated this. Her Apache days were over. "Yes, ma'am," she croaked.

"I can't trust you, Captain Alexander. That's what this really comes down to, isn't it?"

It was useless to try and fight for herself. "Yes, ma'am," Nike said.

"Has it ever occurred to you that I could court-martial you, drum you out of the the U.S. Army and send you back to Greece?"

Horrified, Nike opened her mouth and then snapped it shut. The fury in Dallas's eyes burned through her.

"I could do that, Captain. But dammit, that would be another blow to BJS 60 and frankly, I don't want that on our record. I wanted to make a positive record of our performance as an all-woman squadron here in Afghanistan. So you're safe on that score and damn lucky," she gritted out.

Closing her eyes, Nike swallowed hard. She opened them and stared straight ahead at the light green wall behind her CO. "Thank you, ma'am."

Dallas sat down. She scribbled out a set of orders. "Captain Alexander, you're officially transferred to the transport squadron based here. All you are going to do is fly CH-47s. Maybe that will remind you of your bad choices and how you've hurt our squadron. Fly with those realities in mind." She thrust the papers at Nike. "Now, both of you, get out of here. Dismissed."

"I'm sorry," Nike told Emma once they were back in their tent area. The night was dark and they had their flashlights. "I didn't think...."

Emma put her arm around Nike's slumped shoulders. "I'm sorry, too. I don't care if I lose the XO position. I know the rules are there for a reason. We made a choice and got caught, was all."

"There were times in Peru when we would take a sick child or adult out of a village and fly them to Cusco," Nike grumbled. "And Dallas damn well knew we did it. We'd leave one of the pilots behind, radio in to the cave and let them know what we were doing and nothing was ever said by Dallas or the CO."

"Yes, but it's different here," Emma said. "Down there, we had no other military ops around us. Here, the eyes of the whole base watch our every move because we're an all-female squadron."

"Humph," Nike growled. They stepped carefully through the ruts made by a storm the night before. "Dallas knows we did that stuff down there."

"Yes, but she's CO now. And the men are watching us," Emma said. "Dallas didn't have a choice in this and I knew it."

Giving her friend a sharp glance, Nike said, "You knew she'd bust you out of XO position?"

Giving her a slight smile, Emma nodded. "Sure. That's what I would have done if I was CO. I was just hoping she wouldn't have been so hard on you, that she'd put a reprimand in your personnel file and let it go at that."

"Dallas knows I was the one who thought it up, that's why."

Halting at a row of tents, they turned. It was chow time and most of the women were gone. Nike was glad. Word would spread like wildfire. By morning, the whole camp would be aware of their new orders.

"I'm not hungry," Emma said, halting in front of her tent, next to Nike's. "Are you?"

Nike laughed sourly. "The only thing I want is a stiff damn drink of pisco to burn out the tension in my gut."

Emma grinned. Pisco was the drink of Peru. It could kick like a mule once it was gulped down. "Yeah, that sounds pretty good right now. I'll bet Dallas has a stash of it hidden somewhere."

Nike's spirits rose over her indomitable friend. "I don't think she's going to share it with us, do you?"

Giggling, Emma said in a whisper, "Not a chance."

"I'm going over to the med tent," Nike told her. "I don't even know if Berkic made it or not."

"He was in terrible shape," Emma admitted quietly. She put her hand on Nike's shoulder. "I'm going to lie down and try to sleep. I feel like I was in a dogfight and lost."

Nike nodded. "Yeah, it hurts, doesn't it? Well, we did this to ourselves. Dallas did what she had to do."

"Gosh, Nike, you can only fly CH-47s now. That's terrible! I never thought Dallas would go that far."

"I know," Nike whispered glumly. "What bothers me is that if she replaces me, I'll never get back into the squadron. I could finish out my tour here in Afghanistan flying transports. That sucks."

Emma nodded. "Putting an aggressive combat pilot to fly a bus is a horrible punishment."

"It could have been worse," Nike reminded her solemnly.

"Well, all we can do is be good pilots from here on out and do the best we can. Over time, this thing will settle out and be forgotten."

"I hope so," Nike said. What would she tell her parents? They would be shocked. "I still am not sorry we did it, Emma."

"I'm not, either," Emma told her. "If Dallas knew that, she *would* court-martial us."

Depressed, Nike agreed. "Well, it's our secret for the rest of our lives. We can't tell our families, either. You know how word gets around.…"

"Mmm," Emma agreed. "My dad is going to hit the roof and God, my mom is going to be scraped off the ceiling, too. And my uncle Morgan is going to…well, who knows what he'll do.…"

Nike knew that Clay and Aly were very proud of their daughter. The Trayhern family created warriors for the military and Emma was no slouch. She was one of the finest Apache pilots ever to go through the school. And her uncle, Morgan Trayhern, was a genuine military hero who was highly respected within that world. "I'm really sorry about that."

Emma shrugged. "They'll understand. I'm not sure Uncle Morgan will, but I know my parents will forgive me and just tell me to keep my head down and do good work."

"What do you think your uncle will do?" Morgan Trayhern was in a position of power running a black-ops company that helped the U.S. government in many different ways.

"Ugh, I don't know."

"He has influence," Nike said hopefully. "Do you think

there's anything he can do to help you take the black mark out of your jacket?"

Emma placed her hands on her hips and looked up at the stars overhead. "Probably not. He'll probably agree with Major Klein's decision. He's not a rule-breaker, Nike."

Nike snorted. "I'll bet he broke plenty of rules when he was in the military. He just didn't get caught like we did, is all."

"Listen, head on over to the clinic. Find out about Berkie. I sure hope he made it."

"I'll let you know." Nike opened her arms and impulsively hugged Emma. "Thanks for everything. If Berkie made it, it's because of you."

Releasing her, Emma grinned. "Let me know, okay? Come back, and if I'm sleeping, wake me up?"

Nike watched as a medic behind the desk rifled through a bunch of papers. He then consulted the computer, scanning for the name Berkland Hall.

"Yes, ma'am, he's alive," the young blond medic finally said as he tapped the computer screen. "He's resting in stable condition at the hospital at Bagram Air Force Base. Says here they're going to be transporting him back to the States tomorrow morning."

"Thank you," Nike said, relief in her tone. She left the busy medic tent and headed back out into the darkness. Tears burned her eyes. Berkie would live to see his newly born daughter. His wife would have a husband. A sob ripped from her and Nike pressed her hand against her mouth, afraid that someone nearby might hear her. She couldn't cry here.

There was a spot on the north side of the base where Nike went to sit and clear her head. This night, after this horrible day, she went to her rock, turned off her flashlight and simply allowed the darkness to swallow her up. She loved looking at the myriad stars since they reminded her of her home in Greece. Right now, she felt alone and depressed. And she worried about Gavin, hoping the Taliban weren't attacking the hill tonight. Because she was between squadrons, there was no way for her to know. Until she took her orders to the new CO of the transport squadron, she couldn't ask anyone about anything.

Touching the BJS 60 patch on her right shoulder, Nike knew she'd have to take it off tomorrow before going to the CO of the transport squadron at 0800. For all intents and purposes, she had been drummed out of BJS 60 in shame. She wrapped her arms around her drawn-up legs. She had no one to thank for this but herself. Inside, she was a mass of contradictory emotions. Berkie was alive because they'd broken the rules. A little baby and a wife would have a father and husband to complete their lives. It had been a hell of a decision, and Nike didn't mind paying for it personally. She hated that Emma had stepped in and taken part of the blame, but that was Emma. Nike had often seen her wearing the mantle of the Trayhern dynasty and sometimes, it weighed heavily on her. *What a mess.* Nike had ended up getting Emma's fine career smeared permanently.

It all seemed overwhelming in that moment. She balanced out her grief over the decisions that Major Klein had made against Berkie being alive. What was a life worth? Everything, in Nike's mind. Lifting her chin, she saw a meteor flash across the night sky. How was Gavin? Was he safe? When would he fly back here to be with his team?

Nike realized that she truly missed Gavin. The wonderful, searching talk they'd had last night was burned into her heart's memory. She was such a coward when it came to trusting love.

Love?

Snorting, Nike released her arms from around her knees and stood up. *Am I falling in love with Gavin? No, that couldn't be.* Hadn't she been punished enough in one day's time? Did she need this awareness like a curse upon her, too?

Shaking her head, Nike couldn't assimilate all of the day's unexpected turns and twists. Yet, as she turned and shuffled back toward the tent city hidden in the darkness, Nike still missed Gavin. If he was here, she could confide in him. He would understand. Right now, Nike ached to have his arms around her. Right now, she needed to be held....

Chapter 11

Gavin sat in the medical-facility tent on a gurney. The doctor had cut away most of his blood-soaked pant leg, inspected the bullet wound that had created a three-inch gash across his thigh. The place was a beehive of activity this morning. It was raining and he was soaked after coming off a helo that had brought him back to the base.

"Well?" Gavin asked Dr. Hartman, a young black-haired man with blue eyes.

"Flesh wound. You're lucky, Captain Jackson," Dr. Hartman said, looking up.

"Shoot me full of antibiotics, sew me up and authorize me back to my team," he told the doctor.

Hartman grinned a little. A female army nurse came over with a tray that held the antibiotic, a syringe, needle and thread plus some scrubbing material to ensure that the wound was free of debris. "I know how you A-teamers like to stick together, Captain," Hartman said, picking up a syringe that would locally anesthetize the wound area first.

"It's just a flesh wound," Gavin said. He sat on the gurney, his good leg hanging over the side. While the army would give him three weeks at the base to let the wound heal properly, Gavin didn't want it. His team would be ordered out without him and that bothered him greatly. He felt protective of his men; they were his friends. Gavin didn't want them subjected to someone else's leadership.

"Mmm," the doctor said, swabbing down the area with iodine. He stuck the syringe around the edge of the open wound.

Frowning, Gavin said, "Look, Doc, I don't want a three-week R & R back here because of this." He jabbed his finger down at the wound.

The doctor waited for the anesthetic to take hold and smiled at Gavin. "I know you don't want to get separated from your team, Captain, but this is bad enough to do it. If I release you back to your team and you go out on a mission and rip the stitches out, the wound will become reinfected."

"Not if you give me a steady supply of antibiotics to take," Gavin said. He could tell this doctor had just come over to the front. And he was probably a by-the-book kind, to boot.

Shaking his head, the doctor took the debridement sponge and squirted iodine into the wound cavity. "Sorry, Captain Jackson, I won't authorize that. Your wound is too deep. You're lucky it didn't go into your muscles. Take the three weeks of medical R & R and go to Kabul and chill out."

That was the last thing Gavin wanted. He felt no pain or discomfort from the debridement as the doctor meticulously scrubbed out every bit of the open wound. "Look, Doc," he pleaded, "I don't want my men going out there without me. They're safer under my leadership."

"Can't do it. Sorry." The nurse handed him the needle and thread and he began to close the wound one stitch at a time.

"How about you give my entire team a three-week R & R? Then we can go into Kabul together. They need a break."

Hartman's mouth curved slightly. "You're a pretty creative type, Captain Jackson."

"Look, my men need updated vaccinations. Couldn't you authorize my team off-line for that extra week because of that?" Gavin was giving the doctor the excuse he needed to authorize such a ploy. However, it was the veteran doctors who had spent a year in either Iraq or Afghanistan that understood what he was really asking for. Gavin had hope that if Hartman was a vet of the war, he'd do it.

"You know, Dr. Hartman," the nurse medic spoke up, "we are way behind on vaccination checkups for all the teams. I can accommodate their needs and rotate them through here." She smiled over at Jackson. "We've got forty-nine A teams in here. Maybe if you authorize Captain Jackson's team to stand down, I'll put them at the end of this roster. It would take a week to get around to vaccinating them. And as you know," she added, giving the young doctor a serious look, "we can't send these teams out there in summer without updated vaccinations."

Hartman nodded and considered the medic's request. "So, we're behind on vaccinations?"

Gavin couldn't believe his good luck. The woman was an officer like himself, a registered nurse, and had to be in her forties. He guessed she'd seen more than one tour at the front and was wise to the ways of getting things done for the troops when necessary. He gave her a nod of thanks, and she grinned back.

"Yes, sir, we are. Now, I could arrange this with your approval. The army isn't going to take notice of such things. One A team out of forty-nine that stands down for a week isn't a burp on the Pentagon's radar."

Hartman finished the knot, seeming pleased with his work. He put the needle and thread on the tray. Snapping off his latex gloves and tossing them on top, he told the nurse, "Do the footwork and I'll sign it."

Gavin watched the doctor quickly walk away to the next patient. "Thanks for catching on," he said to the nurse.

The woman set the tray on the gurney and began to place the dressing over the stitched wound. "Don't worry about it, Captain Jackson. He's green."

"Yeah," Gavin said grumpily, "I knew that."

She quickly bandaged his wound. "There. You're all set." She pulled off her gloves and dropped them on the tray. "I'm due for a break, so I'll go back to our office and get the orders created for you and your men."

Giving her a warm look, Gavin said, "You're a real angel." He read her name tag, G. Edwards. "Thank you, Lieutenant Edwards."

"My name is Gwen. And don't worry about it."

"Truthfully," Gavin told her in a quiet tone, "none of us really need any updated vaccinations."

Chuckling, Gwen took the tray and gave him a merry look. "Oh, I knew that, Captain Jackson, but Dr. Hartman doesn't. He arrived here two weeks ago and doesn't have a clue yet. I'll make sure your team is sent to Kabul for an extra week, and, of course, by the time I get around to your vaccination records, your wound should be plenty healed up. That way, we can release you and you can go back into action as a team."

"I owe you," Gavin said. "Thank you."

She winked. "Not to worry, Captain. You and your A teams are incredible and I'll do what I can within my duties to assist you when and where you need help. Enjoy Kabul for me."

Gavin felt like yelling triumphantly. Of course, he couldn't. As he watched Gwen move away and thread through the fifty or so gurneys and medical teams, he grinned. He slid off the gurney, realizing he must look funny with one pant leg gone and the other still on. He'd go back to his tent, tell his men what had transpired and change into a new set of trousers. After that, he'd go to the medical-unit headquarters to get his team's temporary orders for Kabul.

Walking out of the huge tent, Gavin saw the turbid gray clouds roiling overhead. In the summer, sudden thunderstorms could pop up and they were the only rain the desertlike area would receive. Some thunder rumbled far away and he walked carefully through the mud and puddles toward the row of tents where the A teams were housed.

As he did, he received some strange looks, but that was okay with him. His mind turned to Nike. How was she? Where was she? He'd been on the hill for two days acquainting the new A team with everything they needed to know. Gavin could have opted out of that role because of his wound, but he didn't. The medic on the other A team had kept him supplied with antibiotics, ensuring his wound would not become even more infected. Of course, Doc Hartman didn't know that and Gavin wasn't about to tell him, either. And certainly, no A team would push him off the hill, either. So many times, men who were cut, scratched or even suffering from flesh wounds like himself would not seek immediate medical treatment. They just didn't have the time or place to be picked up by a helicopter to get that sort of help.

Sloshing through the muddy ruts and divots made by men's boots, Gavin reached tent city. In no time, he told his team what was up, and there was a shout of triumph about going to Kabul for three weeks instead of the usual two. It was a well-earned rest for them, Gavin knew. Inside his tent, he got out of the destroyed pants and put on a new pair. As always, he'd remain in Afghan garb even in Kabul. Kabul wasn't safe for any American. And blending in with beards and Afghan clothes was a little insurance. Still, Kabul was considered barely stable and they would all carry weapons for protection. The Taliban was making a major push to take back the region.

Gavin headed off toward the BJS 60 squadron area. He knew where their HQ was and wanted to find Nike. He wondered if she was out on a flight or here at the base. Wherever she was, he had to know how she was. It didn't take him long to find the tent that housed the all-woman Apache team.

Each tent had a door. He opened the ops door and stepped inside. Removing his Afghan cap, he walked over to the red-haired woman at the desk.

"Excuse me, I'm looking for Captain Alexander."

The woman's huge gray eyes regarded him with a disconcerted look. He glanced down at the name tag on her green flight suit: E. Trayhern-Cantrell.

"Oh…and who are you?"

"I'm Captain Gavin Jackson. Nike and I know one another." He hooked a thumb over his shoulder. "I just arrived off a mission and I wanted to catch up with her. Can you tell me where she is?"

Grimacing, Emma looked around. Lucky for them everyone was over at the chow hall for breakfast. "Er, Captain," she began, her voice lowered, "there's been a problem."

Alarm swept through Gavin. "Is Nike all right?" He had visions of her being blown out of the air by a Taliban missile or her Apache burning and crashing.

Holding up her hand, Emma said, "No, no, nothing like that. Nike told me about you. So, I'm going to give you the straight scoop." She leaned forward and said, "Nike has been transferred out of here."

His brows shot up. "Why?"

"Captain, when we flew that mission to your hilltop and Nike gave up her seat so that Berkie could get the medical help he needed, we broke every rule in the book. We weren't supposed to do that, but we did."

"I don't understand. You saved his life by doing that," Gavin said, instantly flustered.

Emma stood and came around the desk. She didn't want anyone to hear this. "Captain, Nike and I took the fall for that decision. I lost my position as XO and she got transferred to the CH-47 squadron here at the camp."

Disbelief swept through him. "You mean…her CO got rid of her? She can't fly the Apache anymore?" Gavin was horrified.

"Captain, Nike came close to being court-martialed for what she did. Fortunately for both of us, the CO doesn't want to give the squadron a black eye by letting that happen. So, she sent Nike off to a transport squadron. She can fly an Apache once every seven days to keep up her skills, but that's all."

Gavin shook his head, reeling from the information. "But

she did nothing wrong. She saved a man's life, for God's sake!"

Emma held up her hand. "I agree with you, Captain, but there's nothing we can do about it. Nike could have been sent home to the U.S. or back to Greece. Her CO could have done a lot of things and didn't. This was the least slap on the hand that Nike could receive."

Stunned, Gavin stared at the tall, lean pilot. "I—I don't know what to say. I'm sorry this happened to the two of you. But my man's alive and on his way stateside now because of what you did. Doesn't your CO see that?"

"Our CO, Major Klein, is pretty savvy, Captain. She had no choice in this. If she'd let it go and the word got out on it, that would be bad for the squadron. She had to act."

"Dammit," Gavin whispered, shaking his head. He looked up at Emma. "I'm really sorry about this, Captain. I didn't think saving my man's life would screw up both your careers."

"Don't worry about it," Emma soothed, touching his slumped shoulder. "Neither of us is sorry we did it. And we didn't apologize for our actions in front of our CO, either. We are taking our lumps for this, but that's just part of being in the military."

Gavin knew it meant a hell of a lot more than that. Each woman's personnel jacket would have the reprimand in it. For the rest of their careers every time they tried to go to the next officer pay grade, that reprimand would be there. Rubbing his brow, he muttered, "This isn't right. Are you sure I can't do something to take those reprimands out of your jackets?"

Emma looked at him warmly. "Oh, how I wish you could, but you can't. One person cannot undo this type of reprimand. You're bucking one of the oldest rules in the

Apache book—neither pilot ever leaves the helicopter unless for safety reasons."

Gavin sighed. "I didn't mean to screw your career for you, Captain. Or Nike's. I know how much she loves flying the Apache and she's damn good at it."

"No disagreement there," Emma said. "What I'm hoping is that because it's summer and things heat up with the Taliban during this season our CO won't be able to do without her piloting skills. Right now, the CO can't find a replacement for her, which means one Apache is on the ground."

The ramifications were brutal and Gavin rubbed his beard. "So, she's officially with the transport squadron flying CH-47s? Permanently?"

"Yes, until further notice."

Gavin ached for Nike and wanted so badly to tell her he was sorry.

"You might go over to the transport HQ and find her there. She's still in our tent city but I don't know if she's home or out on a mission."

Grunting, Gavin put on his Afghan cap. "I'll do that, Captain. Thank you." He lifted his hand in farewell.

Of all things! Gavin tramped angrily through the mud and glared up at the clearing sky. In two days, Nike's whole career had been upended—by him. By his request. Even worse, he wondered if she'd be pissed off as hell at him and never want to see him again. Threading in and out between the tents, he finally found the BJS 60 group. In front of one tent was a young woman with blond hair.

"Excuse me, I'm looking for Nike Alexander's tent. Can you point it out?"

"Sure, right next to mine," she said, pointing to it.

"Thanks."

"She's not there."

Gavin looked at the name tag on the woman's flight suit: S. Gibson. "I'm Captain Gavin Jackson."

"Oh, yes, the A-team leader." She thrust out her slim hand. "I'm Sarah Gibson."

Gavin knew that his Afghan clothes might get him mistaken for a local instead of U.S. Army. No locals were allowed on the base for fear that the Taliban might get on the base in disguise. His skin was deeply suntanned and he could pass for an Afghan-born citizen. He didn't know how Sarah could tell his nationality except by how he spoke the English language.

"Sarah, do you know where Nike is?" His heart beat a little harder.

"No, I'm sorry, I don't," she said, shaking her head. "Since she got rotated out to the transport squadron, we rarely see one another. When I'm flying, she's here. When she's flying, I'm off duty."

Nodding, Gavin said, "Then I'll go to the transport HQ."

"If you don't learn anything, I can pass Nike a message for you. She always spoke of you in glowing terms."

Not now she isn't, Gavin thought grimly. "Could you tell her I'm back on base and doing fine? My team and I will be sent to Kabul for three weeks' R & R. Probably tomorrow morning. I'd really like to see her before I go." *And tell her just how damn sorry I am that I got her into this mess.* Even if Sarah gave her his message Nike might be so angry at him that she wouldn't care.

"Of course, Captain Jackson, I will." Sarah smiled brightly. "If you'll excuse me, I'm going on duty. Enjoy the R & R. I'm jealous."

Gavin tried to quell his fear as he walked into the HQ of

the transport squadron. It was a busy place with mostly male pilots coming and going, although he saw several female helicopter pilots. But Nike wasn't one of them. Standing near the door, Gavin searched the area to find out who might have the daily squadron flight roster. One man in back with red hair and freckles was at a huge chalkboard containing the name of every pilot and the flights for the day.

Aiming himself in that direction, Gavin quickly perused the names, twenty of them, on the huge green board. The very last name was *N. Alexander*. He smiled momentarily as he approached the enlisted man, a U.S. Army tech sergeant.

"I'm Captain Gavin Jackson," he began as an introduction.

"Yes, sir. What can I do for you?" the red-haired youth asked.

Reading the last name on his flight suit, Gavin said, "Sergeant Johnson, I need some info. You recently had Captain Nike Alexander rotated into your squadron. I'm trying to track her down. Can you help me?"

Johnson nodded. "Yes, sir." He turned and pointed to her name. "Right now, she's flying ammo and food to Alpha Hill in this valley." He read the chalked assignment on the board. "She left an hour ago. Should return, if all goes well, in about an hour from now."

Gavin realized Nike was resupplying the hill and the A team he'd just left that morning. How badly he'd wished he'd seen Nike.

"She'll be coming back in here once the mission is complete, sir."

Gavin nodded. "Thanks, Sergeant. After she's done with this flight, does she have the rest of the day off?"

Laughing, Johnson said, "Oh, no, sir. In fact—" he held up a sheaf of papers "—I was just going to the next chalkboard. Each one is a mission for each transport pilot. On good days, they might fly once or twice. On bad days, we're landing, loading up again and flying three to four times, depending upon the distance." He peered down at a paper. "She's slated to take an A team out to a place called Zor Barawul."

"Any other flights after that?"

Looking through the rest of the missions for the day, Johnson said, "No, sir, I don't see any. If all goes well, Captain Alexander should be done and out of here by chow time."

"Good. Thanks, Sergeant." Gavin turned on his heel and left the busy squadron headquarters.

Moving out into the muck and puddles left by earlier thunderstorms, Gavin sighed. He headed back to his own tent city to be with his team, but the whole time he thought about seeing Nike again. What would her reaction be? Anger or pleasure? Gavin couldn't guess and that drove him crazy. He liked to control his destiny and he couldn't control Nike's reaction to him.

The sky was showing blue among the white and gray shreds of cloud as the thunderstorms moved off to the east. Sun started to come out in slats here and there. The temperature rose and it looked like a good day ahead. Mind whirling, Gavin knew that flying transports was even more dangerous than flying an Apache. They were trundling workhorses, slow and unable to move quickly if targeted by the Taliban below. His heart ached with fear for her life. He'd just found her and now, dammit, through his own actions, he might have lost her.

All he could do was be at her tent when she returned.

Gavin couldn't quell the anxiety fluttering in his chest. He remembered starkly that one beautiful kiss they'd shared. He remembered Nike's fear of ever falling in love with a military man again. There were so many mountains to climb to reach her. In his gut, Gavin sensed Nike was worth every effort. But would she receive him warmly or with scorn? All he could do was stand at her tent and wait for his fate.

Chapter 12

"Hey, Jameela," Nike called to the woman as she approached the helicopter with her daughter. Nike had just arrived to pick up the current A team deployed to Zor Barawul. The mother was in her black burka, the crisscross oval showing only her eyes. Atefa was still on her crutches but Nike had learned that the medical facility at Bagram Air Base near Kabul was ready to fit her with a prosthetic leg.

Behind her, the load master, Sergeant Daryl Hanford, worked to unload all the medical and food supplies for the village. He got help from the new A team just arriving at the village.

"Hello," Jameela said, reaching out to grip Nike's extended, gloved hand.

Nike knew not to hug Jameela. That would have been against Moslem rules. Instead, she kissed each side of Jameela's hidden face, which was a standard greeting.

Jameela laughed and they pressed cheeks. Nike had been studying Pashto, and she knelt down and smiled into Atefa's bright and happy face. The little girl had a new set of crutches from America, far better than her old ones. "Hello, Atefa."

Shyly, Atefa smiled.

"Ready to go to Kabul?"

The little girl prattled on in Pashto. Nike had no idea what she was saying. Easing to her feet, she turned and looked at the progress at the CH-47. It had been unloaded, and Daryl waved to her to indicate everything was ready for takeoff. Since she didn't stay on the ground too long, Nike gestured for Jameela to bring her daughter forward.

They walked slowly, Jameela on one side of her daughter and Nike on the other. The storms of last night had made the once-flat spot a mire instead of a dust bowl. Half the village had gathered to watch them. Nike had been informed that Jameela would remain at Bagram, the air base outside the capital, for three weeks. Luckily for her, Nike would get to stay the night at the base.

Nike helped strap Jameela and her daughter into the nylon seat. By now, they understood it would be a roller-coaster ride until they could get away from the mountains and onto the brown desert plains. As Nike belted in and worked with her copilot, Lieutenant Barry Farnsworth from Portland, Oregon, she quickly went through the preflight checklist. Her heart lifted. She might have been kicked out of BJS 60, but at least she'd get a night at Bagram Air Base. That, she was looking forward to with relish.

At the O Club on Bagram Air Base outside of Kabul, Gavin nursed a cold beer and tried to get past his disappointment. Nike hadn't shown up at her tent. He'd gone looking for her but then one of his men had found him and told him they had fifteen minutes to get their gear together to catch a flight to Bagram for their R & R.

He looked around at the wooden tables filled with officers from all the military services. The long, U-shaped bar was made of plywood with plenty of bar stools. The room was crowded, with music, chatter and laughter. He should be happy, he thought, taking a swig of the ice-cold beer. The bubbles on his tongue from the beer always made him smile. There weren't many perks in this war, but getting a cold beer was one of them. It washed the mud of the war and their thirty-day missions out of his throat.

Gavin rested his back against the bar. For whatever reason, his gaze drifted to the main door of the O Club. It was nearly dark except for the lights around the entrance. For a moment, he thought he dreamed Nike Alexander entering in her olive-green flight uniform. It couldn't be! Heart pounding, Gavin slid off his stool, shock rolling through him. How did she get here? He didn't think. His instincts took the lead and he moved toward Nike.

Knots of men and women crowded around the many tables. It was tough to get around all of them. When Gavin managed to meet Nike, he saw her eyes go wide with shock.

"Gavin?" Nike blinked twice. Her pulse raced; she couldn't believe her eyes. Gone was his beard and his Afghan clothes. He was a suave urban American male in a pair of blue jeans and a short-sleeved white shirt. Even more, Gavin Jackson was drop-dead handsome. His jaw was square, his mouth sensual. The merriment in his blue eyes captured her. When his mouth curved, she felt heat shimmer from her breasts all the way down to her toes.

"You look different" was all she could say in her surprise over seeing him again.

"And you look beautiful," he said. Reaching out, he cupped her elbow. "Come on, I see an empty table in the corner. Let's grab it. I'll buy you a beer."

Head spinning, Nike followed and she soon found herself sitting at a small round table. It was fairly dark in this corner, with just enough light to see Gavin. Damn, but she couldn't stop looking at him. She'd never really seen his body because of his bulky Afghan clothes. Now he moved with the litheness of a cougar on the prowl. His arms were heavily muscled, his chest broad and powerful. Maybe it was his legs, those hard thighs, that made her throat go dry. She couldn't believe how dynamic and confident he appeared now. As Gavin turned, smiled at her with two beers in hand, Nike felt that she was in some kind of crazy, wonderful dream.

"Here you go," Gavin murmured. He set the beer in front of her, took a chair at her right elbow and sat down. Nike was wide-eyed and her curly black hair was wild, showing that she'd just recently flown. "Can you talk or are you still stunned?" He grinned.

Wrapping her hand around the chilled bottle of beer, Nike took a long swig. She closed her eyes and simply allowed the bubbles and the taste of the hops to wash down her dry throat. Once she set it down and found her voice, she gave him a silly grin. "I just can't believe you're here."

Gavin had the good grace to flush and gave her a bashful smile. "I never expected you to waltz through that door, either."

Nike took several more sips as his words registered. A waitress came over and she ordered a hamburger and French fries. So did Gavin. Nike rested her elbows on the table and stared at him. "How's your leg wound? I didn't know you were off Alpha Hill."

Feeling giddy, Gavin relayed the chain of events, during which he ordered another round. "Nike, I talked to Emma Trayhern-Cantrell and she told me what happened. I'm so sorry." How badly Gavin wanted to reach out and squeeze her arm, but he didn't dare. This was a military O Club and fraternization was not allowed. You could get drunk and fall on your face, but no kissing, holding hands or anything serious with the opposite sex. The exception was when the jukebox prompted couples to dance and the floor became crowded.

"Don't worry about it, Gavin. Emma and I knew we were breaking every rule in the book for Berkie."

His eyes were sad. "Then it's true? Your CO booted you out of BJS 60?"

"For the time being," Nike said, relishing the taste of her second beer.

"I didn't realize what this might do to your and Emma's careers," he muttered with sincere apology.

"I've lived long enough to know I'm not always going to do things right. Berkie was special to me. Well, all your guys were. When you said he was bleeding to death, all I could think about was his wife and baby daughter. I couldn't stand by and let him die."

"Well," Gavin said, his voice hoarse with emotion, "Berkie is on his way stateside. I don't know if you heard his update, but he's going to make it. Right now, he's on a C-5 Galaxy flight headed for Walter Reed hospital in Maryland. I know that Vickie, his wife, is flying in from Louisiana to meet him at the hospital after he gets through the entry process."

"Wonderful!" Nike said. "Is she bringing his daughter? I know he's only seen video of her on the computer."

"Yep," Gavin answered after taking a swig of his beer, "Francesca is going to be in her mother's arms when she's allowed to see Berkie. It's going to be one hell of a reunion."

Nike sighed with deep contentment. "Thanks for sharing all that with me, Gavin. It makes what we did worth it ten times over."

"Don't tell that to Major Klein. Next time, she'll crucify you."

"Oh, she's not like that usually," Nike said, smiling. "Dallas had to do it, Gavin. If she allowed us to get away with it, other pilots in other situations might think about abandoning their seat for another injured soldier. No, she was right and we were wrong. I'm willing to take the fall and so was Emma."

"You two are tough women warriors," Gavin said. His hand ached to hold hers.

"How long are you here for?" she asked. Gavin's face was deeply shadowed by the sparse light and it made him even more handsome—and so dangerous to her pounding heart. "And what happened to your beard?"

"I managed to wrangle three weeks here at Bagram for my team." He touched his chin. "I shaved it off today after we arrived. I'll have to let it grow back out. In three weeks, my mug will be covered again."

"You must have run screaming to the base barber." Nike chuckled. "Your hair is military-short, too." Indeed, his black hair shone with blue highlights beneath the light. There was a predatory quality to Gavin's face, especially with those large blue eyes. But it was his mouth that made her melt like hot butter. He couldn't know how much his looks influenced her wildly beating heart and no way would she ever admit it to him. Just sitting here at the table, their elbows almost touching, was like a fantasy.

Gavin grinned. "My team hit the barbershop posthaste," he agreed congenially. Touching his short hair, he said, "We just wanted to get cleaned up and feel like American men for a while."

"Over in the barracks where I'm staying, there's actually a tub, not just a shower in the room. I can hardly wait to get over there and take a long, luxurious hot bath. At our base it's outdoor stalls with piddling water coming out of the showerhead. This is real luxury."

"Bagram is beloved by all military branches," Gavin told her. "I know you're four months into your one-year tour here, but I'm sure you'll look for every chance to get a night or two at this base."

"That's one of the perks of being a transport pilot," Nike agreed. "In fact, tomorrow morning at 0700 I'm flying a supply of ordinance back to our camp."

Frowning, Gavin knew the CH-47 would be filled with ammunition of all types. "That's a dangerous run." If the Taliban got lucky and shot bullets—or worse, a missile—at the lumbering helicopter, it could be blown out of the sky. He'd seen it happen on four different occasions and nothing was ever found of the crews. Nothing. Heart contracting, he kept his mouth shut. The possibility of her dying in a situation like that nearly undid him. And yet, every day, every hour, they were in combat and bad things happened to good people.

Nike nodded and finished off her second beer. The waitress brought two oval plates filled with hamburgers and French fries. After putting dollops of ketchup and mustard on her hamburger, Nike ate it with complete enthusiasm.

For the next few minutes, there was silence because they were eating like there was no other pleasure in the world.

"Aren't we a couple of starved wolves?" she chortled. Between French fries she added, "Down in Peru, in our cave where BJS squadron lived, we had a pretty good chow hall. Our CO made sure that we got fresh fruits, veggies and eggs from Cusco. I always liked taking our transport helicopter into Cusco. My copilot and I would spend the night in that high-altitude city, do the tango, drink pisco and have a wonderful Peruvian meal. Then, we'd stagger back to our hotel and fall into bed. The next morning, we looked like hell, took hot showers and got into our civilian clothes to be driven back out to the airport." Chuckling fondly, Nike said, "We lived hard and died hard in Peru. We didn't lose that many women or Apaches, but our job was just as dangerous as it is here in Afghanistan."

"You traded jungle for desert. And instead of druggies, you got the Taliban."

"Bad guys exist all over this globe, unfortunately," Nike said. She finished off the French fries and gave him a silly grin. "I feel good. There's nothing like American food."

"But you're Greek."

"I know, but over the years of being in the States and then with the original BJS, I really got into American junk food." She patted her waist. "Good thing I come from a family of thin people. Otherwise, I'd be over the weight limit to fly the Apache." Nike chuckled.

"Do you really think you won't be allowed back into your Apache squadron?" he asked, getting serious. A shadow appeared in her eyes and she pursed her lips. It rankled his conscience that he had been the cause of her career demotion. Gavin knew the military very well. With that kind of reprimand in her personnel jacket, Nike could easily be overlooked for the next rank. Well, he had to live with the consequences of his actions whether he liked it or not.

"I don't think that Dallas will find another female pilot coming out of the Fort Rucker Apache training school," Nike said. "Not that many women wind up in the flight program and there's a lot of resistance to their being in the combat helicopter."

"Surely your squadron's exploits have shown them otherwise?"

"Over time the boys at the Pentagon stopped refuting our abilities." Nike grinned. "It's like pulling teeth, but we'll get more women into the Apache program. Like Maya, our CO down in Peru, said, we have to hold the energy and keep our intent clear. We know women can do the job as well as any man. Flying the Apache isn't about brawn. It's about brains and coordination."

A slow song came on the jukebox and Nike suddenly felt self-conscious.

"Come on. Dance with me. I like the idea of holding an Apache pilot with brains." Getting up, Gavin extended his hand so that Nike couldn't protest. He saw her eyes flare with several emotions, among them a desire to dance with him. He could feel it.

"Come on," he urged, gripping her hand. "You can do this. You're one of the bravest women I know, so don't say no."

Nike felt herself coming out of her chair. The dance floor was crowded as she followed Gavin out to the middle. When he turned and placed his hand on the small of her back and drew her closer, she came without resistance.

"See?" he whispered in a conspiratorial tone. "This isn't so bad, is it?" He led her expertly around on the floor.

Laughing a little, Nike said, "Did I have a horrified look on my face?"

Gavin drowned in her golden eyes. "Hey, you said you danced with the Latin boys down in Cusco, so why not here, too? How can I compete?"

"You don't have anything to worry about on that score," she said. He kept about six inches between them. Even though he could have used his hand to press her up against his body, he didn't. He gave her space that made her panic subside. Besides, Nike told herself, why not dance with Gavin? He was damn good at it.

"Oh? So I stack up pretty well?"

"Absolutely." He gave her a mirthful smile and she enjoyed the happiness in his blue eyes. Why not let go? She had in Cusco. She'd blown off the tension and danger and death that always surrounded them. Dancing with Gavin was a wonderful antidote to her flying in this country, too.

"I can tango, too," Gavin informed her, his grin increasing. "My mother loved ballroom dancing. I grew up knowing all of the different styles and steps. Competing as an amateur was her hobby."

"Well," Nike said, impressed, "you're good."

"You have no idea," he told her in a roughened tone, his lips near her ear.

Her flesh tingled wildly in the wake of his warm breath as it caressed the side of her face. For a moment, his hand squeezed hers a little more firmly. An ache rose in her body. She was so hungry for him that it wasn't even funny. Two years celibate had left her more than hungry, but she'd want Gavin in any condition. Something still made her hesitate. This wasn't love, right? This could just be a physical release. That's all she needed. At least, that's what she told herself.

"So," Gavin said quietly, "what's going on behind those beautiful eyes of yours? I see you want me."

"You are such a brazen dude."

He whirled her around and then brought her back into his arms. "I want this night with you, Nike. There don't have to be any strings, if that's what you want. One night together, that's it."

She looked deeply into his eyes and considered his request. "Just sex. And friendship."

Nike knew Gavin would be a good lover. She could tell by the way he monitored the strength of his hand around hers as they danced. She was wildly aware of his palm against the small of her back, and the way he sometimes caressed her with his thumb, as if stroking her. It reminded her she was a young woman with real needs. Maybe her grieving really was over and she hadn't realized it. Antonio would always be in her heart and her memory. Nike never wanted that to go away. When she loved, she loved deeply.

Finally, she couldn't stand it anymore. "Okay, let's get out of here. Your place or mine?"

"Mine," Gavin said confidently. He pulled her off the dance floor and smiled. "In the BOQ for the men, we each have a nice room to ourselves. I'll bet you have a roomie."

"Yes, I do. Does yours have a tub?"

"No, but we'll make do." Gavin smiled wickedly and led her out the door of the club.

Chapter 13

Just as they reached the male BOQ—Bachelor Officer's Quarters—an enemy mortar landed somewhere near the revetment area where all the helicopters were parked. Nike jumped and whirled around. Gavin automatically shielded her with his body.

Her eyes widened as mortars began to "walk" in their direction. Fire erupted when a helicopter was directly hit and flames roared into the air. Smoke belched into the dark sky, highlighted by the leaping flames. And then, when the aviation fuel on board the helicopter exploded, a huge reverberation of thunder was followed by a painful, ear-splitting boom.

Pressing her hands to her ears, Nike saw Gavin's tense, shadowed face as another explosion rocked a hangar nearby. "They're going to need us!" Nike yelled.

Nodding, Gavin gripped her upper arm. "Where's your flak jacket? You can't go anywhere without it."

He was right. All the festering desire that had bubbled up through Nike had vaporized in a split second. "I'm making a run for our barracks."

"Be careful! Meet me back here when this is over."

Nodding, Nike turned and hotfooted it down the line toward the women's BOQ that sat on the opposite side of the airport. People were running, grabbing their helmets, shrugging on their body armor and wrestling with their weapons. As Nike ran, the wind tearing at her, she saw that the Taliban's attack had been very successful. Three helicopters were on fire and utterly destroyed.

She ran around the end of the base and realized she had no weapon. Somewhere beyond the nine-foot-high fence, strung with razor-blade concertina wire over the top, were several Taliban mortar crews. Nike knew she could be a target with the flames leaping a hundred feet in the night sky behind her.

Changing course, she ran toward the burning wreckage and the fire crews now dousing the area with water. Better to take more time and go around the other end of the airstrip where it was safe in comparison.

Another round of mortars popped off. Nike could hear the hollow ring fired somewhere out in the night. To her shock, the mortars went toward the control tower, right where she was. With a strangled sound, Nike dove for the ground when she stopped hearing the whistle of a mortar screaming overhead. She hit the ground with a thud, the air knocked out of her. Rolling into a ball, her hands over her neck and head, she didn't have long to wait. The air-control tower was a two-story-tall brick building. The mortar landed on the side and about thirty feet from where Nike had burrowed into the ground. The next thing she knew, she felt a whoosh of hot air. In seconds, she was flying through the air, arms and legs akimbo.

When she struck earth once again, Nike yelled out in pain. She hit her shoulder and heard something pop. Barely conscious, she held her left arm tightly to her body, pain arcing up through her shoulder. Had she broken a collarbone? Worse, had she dislocated her shoulder? Groaning, Nike sat up, shaking her head. She spat out the mud and tried to reorient. People were running around like rats out of a drowning ship. Nothing seemed organized.

Holding her elbow tightly against her, Nike knew she had to get medical help. *Dammit, anyway!* Somehow she managed to get to her feet and fought to regain her balance.

The medical building was in high gear when Nike arrived. She saw men with torn pants or blown-off shirts. Some were burned, others dazed and bloody. Hesitating at the door, Nike knew she wasn't as seriously injured. Someone pushed her through the opened door.

"Get in there," a man ordered her in a gruff, no-nonsense tone.

Turning, Nike noted the white-haired doctor in a blood-spattered lab coat.

"Over there," he ordered her, pointing to an area where there were cubicles, each with a gurney.

Not hesitating, Nike headed to the dark-haired army medic with a stethoscope around her neck. Red-hot pain shot from her shoulder into her neck and the next thing Nike knew, she collapsed to her knees while still holding her left arm against her.

Gavin couldn't find Nike anywhere. Panic ate at him. In the grayness of dawn, he saw the black, smoking wreckage of three transport helicopters. He wondered if Nike's CH-47 was among the carnage. As he stood near the air-control tower that had missed several mortar rounds, he noticed how the ground around it was hollowed out in craters.

Where was Nike? He'd been over to the women's BOQ but hadn't found her. Nor was she waiting for him at his BOQ. Worriedly, he searched the red line of the dawn on the flat plain. Firefighting crews were putting out the final flames and smoldering fires around the helicopters. A number of other smaller buildings around the airstrip had been hit, as well. Rubbing his jaw, Gavin tried to search through the hundreds of crews working to reclaim what the Taliban just destroyed.

His heart ached with fear. Had Nike been hurt? Gavin turned on the heel of his boot and headed toward the medical area. Long ago he'd traded in his civilian clothes for a set of green fatigues, his combat boots, body armor and helmet. Normally, Bagram was never hit, but sometimes the Taliban took it upon themselves to get close enough to remind the Americans that no place in Afghanistan was safe from their strikes.

The air smelled of metal, smoke and burning wood. Panic started to curl up from his heart and he felt as though he was choking on fear. What if Nike was wounded? Dead? Blinking, Gavin refused to go there, though he knew that she'd tried to make it across the base to her barracks without any protective gear on. That made her vulnerable.

"Damn," he muttered, halting at the opened doors to the medical building. It looked like measured chaos inside. If the Taliban had struck to take out people, they'd succeeded. The wounded and bleeding sat everywhere on the floor, with medics and doctors working among them with quiet efficiency in triage mode. Peering inside the brightly lit area, Gavin scanned it for Nike. He did not spot her.

His gut told him to keep going, keep looking. He pushed through the entrance, winding his way through the medical teams and the nurses' station. He found an officer, an army nurse, and asked, "Have you admitted a Captain Nike Alexander?"

She looked up. "I don't have a clue, Captain. We haven't exactly had time to sit down and type all these people into our computer yet."

Nodding, Gavin said, "Mind if I look for her?"

"Go for it. Good luck."

After the nurse hurriedly left, Gavin turned and scanned the area. There were several curtained cubicles on the opposite side of the room. The people on the gurneys were all men. He searched every face in the entrance area and no Nike. Okay, if she wasn't here, maybe on the second floor, which was the surgical floor. Gavin picked his way to the stairs at the back of the room and quickly ascended them.

The surgical floor was also mayhem. Gurneys were filled with soldiers and airmen who had been wounded in the mortar attack. Blood dripped from one gurney, creating a large pool on the white tile floor. Medics hurried from one gurney to another checking stats, talking to the waiting patients lined up to go into the next available surgical theater.

None of them were Nike. Gavin couldn't still his anxiety. He knew in his heart he was falling in love with her. And now, she could be dead. *God, no, please don't let that happen,* he prayed as he made his way to the nurses' station.

"Excuse me," he called to a nurse who was updating records. "I'm looking for a woman, Captain Nike Alexander.

She may have been wounded in this attack. Can you tell me if she's here?"

The nurse gave him a harried look and stopped writing. She went to a large book on the desk and perused the list. "Sorry, Captain, no one here by that name," she said.

The only place left was the morgue. Gavin stared at her. "Are you sure?"

"Yes," she said firmly, "I'm sorry, she's not here."

Oh God. He stood and numbly watched the nurse return to her work. How could this be? One moment, Nike was walking with him to his BOQ. They were going to spend the night together. She'd been able to scale her fear of loss enough to be with him just once. But Gavin knew Nike wasn't like that. No matter what she said, he understood on a deeper level that she was reaching out to him. To love him. It was going to be a helluva lot more than sex. She cared about him, and he loved her.

He stood at the desk, his mind tumbling in shock and disbelief. He didn't want to go to the morgue. He didn't want to ask about her there. Tears burned in his eyes and Gavin blinked them back. His throat went tight with a forming lump. In that awful moment, Gavin realized that even though his bad relationship with Laurie had stung him, he was ready to try again. And Nike, in her own way, seemed to be working to trust once more, too. Why the hell did this attack have to come now? Gavin knew the answer: war was unpredictable. Death was a breath away. Nothing was stable and nothing could be counted on.

It has to be done. Mouth tasting of bitterness, Gavin worked his way out of the medical building. Last year, two of his men had been killed in a firefight and he'd had to identify them at the morgue here. He'd hated it then. He hated it now.

Dawn was pushing the night away, the red ribbon on the horizon turning pink and revealing a light blue sky in the wake of the cape of retreating night. The whole base felt tense and edgy. Grief ate away at Gavin. He remembered Nike's wish never to fall in love with a military man again for fear he would be ripped away from her. That her heart could not take a second shock like that. Well, now he was in her shoes. Making his way between large vehicles, the smell of diesel in the air, Gavin saw the morgue ahead. It was a single-story building painted the color of the desert. The doors were open. He saw several gurneys lined up with body bags on them. Was Nike in one of them?

Unable to look, he passed them and hurried inside to the desk. A young man of about eighteen looked up.

"Yes, sir?"

Swallowing hard, his voice barely a rasp, Gavin asked, "Do you have a female officer in here? Captain Nike Alexander?" He stood, not breathing, waiting, praying hard that he wouldn't hear the word *yes*.

The man scowled and looked through a sheaf of papers. "No, sir. No one by the name of Alexander, male or female."

Relief tunneled through Gavin. He felt faint for a moment. He'd been handed a reprieve. Releasing his held breath, he nodded. "Thanks," he muttered, and left.

Nike was just coming out of the BOQ when she spotted Gavin. He looked hard and upset, his eyes thundercloud-black. Worry was evident on his features. She gave him a wan smile and lifted her right hand.

"Gavin. Are you okay? I've been looking all over this base for you."

He saw her left arm in a sling. Halting, he said, "Are you all right? What happened?"

Grimacing, Nike told him the details. "As soon as they took X-rays, the doctor said I'd dislocated a ligament here on my shoulder out of what they call the AC joint. He got the ligament back in, thank God, but I've got orders to stand down for a lousy six weeks." She frowned at her left shoulder. "I can't lift my arm above my chest. That means no flying. I'm stuck behind a desk, dammit."

Closing his eyes for a moment, Gavin felt like a man who had just been given the greatest gift in the world. He opened them and clung to her golden gaze. "I—thought you were dead," he managed in a strangled whisper.

Nike stared at him. And then, it hit her hard and she managed a croak of despair. "I'm so sorry, Gavin." She reached out and gripped his arm. "There was no way to get hold of you."

"I know, I know," he said. Gripping her hand in his, eyes burning with withheld emotion, he rasped, "Nike, I understand your fear now. About losing someone you love to a bullet."

Shock bolted through her. Staring at Gavin, she realized he understood now as never before how she felt about Antonio being ripped out of her life. His hand was firm and warm. She'd been tense and nervous since the attack, but somehow, Gavin's protective presence just seemed to make her feel safe in an unsafe place. "It isn't pretty, is it?" she said in a low tone.

"No. It's not." He searched her eyes that held the shadows and memories of the past. "I looked everywhere for you. I—I eventually forced myself over to the morgue."

"Oh," Nike groaned. "I'm so sorry…."

And then, Nike knew that he really did love her. Gavin

might verbally spar with her but the look in his eyes told her the truth. Gulping, Nike shoved all that knowledge down deep inside her until she could deal with what it meant to her.

"It's not your fault. Things get crazy when a base is under attack."

She squeezed his hand. An ache built in her heart as she saw the devastation, the terror, in his gaze. "It's a hell of a way to understand my fear of a relationship with you. I'm sorry you had to find out this way."

"Nike, I don't want to live without you. I'm willing to risk everything to have some kind of a relationship with you on your terms."

His words melted through her pounding heart and touched her. Blinking through unexpected tears, Nike pulled her hand from his. Panic ate at her. This was serious. *He* was serious. There was no way she wanted to hurt him, but she had to. "I'm stuck in this war zone for another eight months, Gavin. What kind of a relationship could we have?"

"Catch as catch can?" he asked hopefully, the corners of his mouth pulling upward a tiny bit.

Hearing the hope, the pleading in his voice and seeing the stark need reflected in his blue eyes, Nike felt the last of her stubbornness dissolve. "I feel scared, so scared, Gavin." That was the truth. Nike felt terrorized by the realization he did love her. It wasn't just a game. It was real. Could she go there again?

"I understand your being scared." Reaching out, Gavin cupped her cheek. "Darling, we're just going to have to learn to be scared together. The last time this happened to you, you were alone. You had no one. Well, now you have me. I grant I'll be gone thirty days at a time in the field, but when we get back to base, we'll be together. I promise you that."

His eyes burned with such intensity that it seared the fright out of her. "All right," Nike quavered, "I believe you, Gavin."

Gavin stroked her cheek, knowing full well that fraternization was strictly prohibited. He could be in a lot of trouble. Worse, he could get Nike into more trouble than he already had. Quickly, he dropped his hand. Her cheeks burned a bright red. "We're going to make the most of this, Nike. We can't let fear tear us apart again. We'll live one day at a time. It's all anyone has."

Nodding, she slumped against the wooden building behind her. "You're right." She sighed. The feeling was there and she wanted so badly to say the words *I love you, too.* But she couldn't. Nike was still imprisoned by her loss as much as she felt this new love.

"I wish I was wrong," Gavin confided, coming close to her but keeping his hands to himself. "At least I get a reprieve from worrying about you. You're stuck back on base, which is a helluva lot safer than flying a helo."

"Don't remind me. I feel stifled in an office." And then more softly, "I won't stop thinking about you no matter what I'm doing."

Warmth spread across Gavin's chest. "Well," he said with a tender smile meant only for Nike, "it looks like we've made the best of a bad situation here. We might not have had the night we wanted, but we're alive and on the right page."

Despite the ache in her shoulder, Nike wanted to throw her one good arm around him, but that was impossible. "Six weeks…" Inwardly, she was relieved. Gavin was backing off. Maybe she needed that time at the desk to truly rethink her position with him and try to put the past to rest. To allow what she had with Gavin to blossom.

"What's the prognosis on your shoulder?"

"I'm on a mild painkiller for now," Nike whispered, her voice sounding off-key. "The doctor said it would take six weeks because I strained the ligament. They don't heal fast. He gave me a bunch of papers with exercises on them. At three weeks I'm to fly back here for another examination."

"At seven weeks I'll be back to base," Gavin said. "Maybe we could, you know, pick up where we left off before all hell broke loose?"

She grinned. Relief flooded her. Nike was sure she could figure this all out by then. "One way or another. I might not have the range of motion, but that's not going to stop me."

Gavin laughed softly. "Okay, sounds good. Where are you off to?"

"The doctor gave me orders to take the first transport back to our base. My helo was destroyed last night. My copilot will be coming back on the same flight. Once I get home, I need to go see my CO. I'm sure he'll put me on a desk and forget about me for six weeks."

"Wild horses don't do well in corrals," he teased her gently.

"Do you still get your three full weeks here?"

"Yes. They've asked all available personnel to help in the cleanup and I was going over to ops to get orders."

"Wouldn't it have been nice if the doc had told me to stay here at Bagram?"

Gavin rolled his eyes. "That would have been a miracle."

"Well," Nike told him, picking up her helmet bag in her

right hand, "I think we've seen plenty of miracles for one day, don't you?"

Gavin took her helmet bag and walked at her side as she headed for the airstrip. "You're right. A miracle did happen—between us."

"I'm still worried," Nike admitted. "I don't think I'll ever get over the fear of losing you, Gavin."

It hurt not to be able to reach out and touch her, hold her hand or place his arm around her just to give her a sense of protection. "You're not going to lose me. I promise. This is my second tour and I've got a year of experience under my belt. That will keep me alive."

How badly Nike wanted to believe that. The demons would resurface. Yet, the glimmer of love burning in his eyes fed her. Gave her hope. Could she really reach out and love him? Or would her fear drive him away?

Chapter 14

"When does Gavin get back to our base?" Emma asked as she sat with Nike in the chow hall. At noon it was packed, the noise high and the smell of cooked food permeating the area.

"Tonight if all goes well."

"Tonight?" Emma shook her head. "I suppose tomorrow he and his team will be flown out somewhere for thirty days?"

Slathering butter on a hot roll, Nike nodded. Her left arm hadn't seemed to make any progress over the last two weeks. She could lift it waist-high and then excruciating pain hit. Eating was an interesting proposition with only one and a half hands available to her. "Yes."

Emma ate her meat loaf after cutting it up into many dainty pieces. The perfectionist in her always expressed itself in many different ways. "That's not fair."

Snorting, Nike said, "When is war ever fair?"

"Or life, for that matter?" Emma rejoined, grinning.

"You got that right." Nike enjoyed the warm butter on the fragrant homemade roll. The late-August noontime was hot. A front was coming in and it was supposed to storm. Nike wasn't looking forward to that.

"Things seem to be falling apart over at BJS," Emma confided.

"Oh?" Nike raised her brows. "What's the scuttle-butt?"

Emma shrugged. "The bad news is that Becky Hammerschlag is the XO and she's terrible at it."

"You were a good one," Nike said.

"Everybody knows that. They keep coming to me, not Becky, with issues to resolve with Dallas."

"I'll bet Dallas isn't happy about that. Or Becky."

"No, not at all. I can't just ignore Becky and go around her to Dallas."

"Jumping chain-of-command is trouble for sure," Nike said. She spooned up some of her macaroni and cheese. "What else is going on?"

"Well—" Emma brightened "—some good news. In a way…"

"I can always use that. Tell me."

"It's good news for BJS but not for you. And it's good news for me, personally."

"Uh-oh," Nike murmured, "Dallas found another female pilot to replace me?" That meant that her secret hope to be pulled back into the BJS 60 squadron was squashed.

Emma nodded. "I'm sorry, Nike. I was holding out hope against hope that the pressures and demands on our services here would force Dallas to ask you to come back."

"Me, too," she said. "Oh, well."

"I'm sorry. We really miss you. You were our best pilot."

"Tell that to Dallas," she said, giving Emma a playful smile. Lifting her right hand, which had the last of the hot roll in it, Nike added, "Look, we knew we were breaking a cardinal rule when we picked up Berkie, but I'd do it all over again."

"I don't regret it, either. I'm just sorry that Dallas chose to focus on you instead of me."

"I'm the one who gave up the seat." She chuckled. "You stayed with the helicopter. Of course she's going to zero in on me."

"I don't think I'd take this as well as you are," Emma said glumly.

"Hey, you have a family military dynasty on your shoulders to carry," Nike chided with a grin. "Me? All I have is some disappointed parents and my big Greek extended family. But they understand and agree that I did the right thing. You? Well, if you'd gotten out of that seat, the media would have blitzed you over a transfer to a transport squadron." Shaking her head, Nike added, "No news about me being transferred as punishment because I'm not famous or in the media's eye like the Trayhern family is."

Emma sighed. "You're right. I've been catching all kinds of flak on the Internet blogs and even on CNN because of my demotion from XO."

"See?" Nike said, poking a finger in her direction. "I know the media is in love with the Trayherns. And what you did was heroic in my eyes. Maybe the media is chewing this up, but we saved a life, Emma. I'll answer for that decision with my God, not with anyone else. Especially not the media."

"Nike, you're one in a million. I'm proud to know you. I'm proud of what we did, punishment be damned. And I couldn't care less about the media sniping at me, but I know it impacts my whole family. That's what I don't like—them going after my mom, dad and sisters."

"Listen, they're Trayherns. They'll roll with it. A military family has the toughest of skins."

"Well, it hasn't done my career any good," Emma said.

"No, but I'm sure you'll distinguish yourself over here, and, in time, all will be forgiven. Me?" Nike grinned. "There's not much chance of me distinguishing myself as a transport pilot of men and ammo. So, as I see it, my days are numbered."

"Nike! You aren't going to leave the military are you?"

"I don't know. I'm up for reenlistment after this tour. Depending upon how it goes, I may get out. I didn't sign up to be a trash-hauler. I'm an Apache pilot and a damned good one. If the U.S. military can't use my services, then why stay in? I can find better work back in Greece where my talent can be used in the civilian sector."

"Let me talk to Dallas. You can't do this! We can't lose you, Nike! You're too good at what you do."

Nike held up her hand. "It's okay, Emma. I got myself into this pickle. I'll decide how I get myself out of it. Life doesn't end if I can't fly an Apache. I could land a nice, cushy job as a commercial helo pilot."

"Damn," Emma whispered, hanging her head. "You shouldn't even be thinking in those terms."

"We did it to ourselves," Nike reminded her, using the last of her roll to run through the gravy on her plate. "So tell me, you said there was good news for your family?"

"Oh, that…" She grimaced.

"Eat your food, Emma. You're so emotional. You can't let this impact you this way. I'm fine. I'm doing a good job over at the transport squadron."

"But you're not happy."

"I didn't say I was. Life isn't always fun, but we do our best."

"You were happy at BJS 60."

"Yes, I was. What I miss most of all is the camaraderie of the women."

Emma watched Nike eating her food. She seemed at peace despite everything. "The other good news is that my cousin, Rachel Trayhern, has just graduated from Apache flight school in Fort Rucker, Alabama. She's being assigned to BJS 60."

"Wow, you'll have a cousin here with you?" Nike was impressed. "Which family is she out of?"

"My uncle Noah's family. Rachel is one of four children. She's the oldest. My mother, Alyssa, was saying that even though her brother, Noah, was a Coast Guard officer for thirty years, all four of his children are in the military and flying. The flight gene is definitely from the Trayhern side of the family."

"Wow, that's great! Are you close with your cousins? I know in my family, we're tighter than fleas on a dog."

Emma laughed. "Yes, the whole family tries to get together. One year we'll go to Florida where Uncle Noah and Aunt Kit live and the next, we'll go to San Francisco, where my parents live. And then, they'll all try to make it to Philipsburg, Montana, where my uncle Morgan and aunt Laura live. It's a huge dim sum plate and it takes a lot of work to get everyone in one spot at one time."

"Mmm," Nike said, finishing off her applesauce. "I would think so if all the offspring are in the military."

"Rachel is a rock 'n' roll Apache pilot," Emma said, her voice reflecting pride in her cousin. "She's very competitive and aggressive."

"Just like an Apache pilot should be." Nike chuckled. She put her empty plate aside on the aluminum tray and picked up her white mug of coffee. "So, when is Rachel arriving?"

"A week from now."

"I didn't think the military would allow two family members in the same squadron."

"They don't allow brothers or sisters to serve together," Emma said. "They say nothing about cousins." With glee, she rubbed her hands together and gave Nike a huge grin.

"I'll bet your family is thrilled about this development. They must see you as the watchdog who can take care of Rachel while she learns the ropes."

Brightening, Emma began to eat once more. "They are thrilled. I'm excited to have her. We're good friends."

"When Rachel gets here, we must meet."

"Oh, that's a promise," Emma said enthusiastically.

"We can help her get situated with combat and Afghanistan. She could use our experience."

"For sure," Emma agreed. And then, her smile disappeared. "Have you been in touch with Gavin? Do you know when he's coming in from Kabul?"

"No way to get in touch with him. I checked at ops and his team is on a transport that will arrive here at 1700."

"Just in time for dinner."

"Maybe we can have one together," Nike said.

"You deserve a little happiness," Emma told her.

"Thanks," Nike whispered, meaning it. They sat for a

while in silence. The coolness in the huge tent area was wonderful compared to the heat and local storms. This place, in some ways, reminded her of home in Greece. The country blistered with dry summer heat and then chilled with icy temperatures in winter, but there was little snow unless one lived in the mountainous areas. Still, Nike looked forward to the moment when she could meet Gavin and his team. Her heart beat a little harder to underscore just how much she'd missed him in the last two weeks.

In the quiet moments at her desk, Nike would allow her heart to feel the love that had taken root within her. She knew he'd hurt her career but she'd forgiven him for that long ago. In the heat of battle, one didn't always think about such things. And in Nike's world view, a human life was a hell of a lot more important than a regulation. Since Bagram, she hadn't been able to stop thinking about Gavin. It seemed as if every few minutes, she'd replay some conversation they had. Or she'd recall that terrorized look in his eyes that told her the raw truth: he loved her. At first, Nike had felt it was a game with Gavin. Now, she knew it was not.

Gavin could hardly keep his face impassive. He watched Nike in her dark green flight suit, waiting as he and his men disembarked from the CH-47 helicopter. It was dusk; the skies were gray and churning. Soon, it would storm. She looked beautiful, her curly black hair about her face, a smile on her lips and those gold eyes shining with what he thought might be love—for him.

As he hefted off his duffel bag, he ordered his team to their already assigned tents. He told them he'd see them later. Turning, he walked with the huge bag across his left shoulder. Once more, he was in Afghan clothing.

"Hey," Gavin greeted her as he walked up to her. "Do you know how much I've missed you and our talks?" He kept his voice low so that others could not hear. It about killed him not to show affection. Her mouth was soft and parted, ripe for kissing.

"I'd like to hug you but I can't," she said with a grin, pointing to her arm.

"How's your left shoulder?" Gavin asked.

She held her hand out and could only move it waist-high. "I can't sleep on that side and I can't lift it beyond here. If I try to lean out and stretch it, I'm in pain. The doctor says the first three weeks are the worst."

Shaking his head, Gavin said, "That's no good. How's the desk job?"

"Boring as hell. How was Bagram?"

"Lonely without you." Gavin drilled a look into her widening eyes. "Is there anywhere we can go to be alone for a while?"

She grinned. "Yeah, my tent. Don't worry, the gals on either side of it won't say a peep about me having a male visitor." That was against regulations, too, but the female pilots protected one another. They would never go to the XO or CO about it. Sometimes, rules were meant to be broken.

"Good," Gavin said. "Lead the way." He hoisted his duffel up on his left shoulder once more.

In no time, they were at her tent. Nightfall was complete and they had flashlights to light their way through the tent city. Wind began to twirl around them as Nike opened up the tent flap to allow Gavin inside. She followed, turned and tied the flaps together. A small fan in the corner sitting on the ply-board floor gave some coolness against the high temperatures.

Gavin set his duffel near the entrance, turned and walked over to Nike. Although she did not wear her left arm in a sling any longer, he was aware of how painful it was to her. Gently, he laid his hand on her right shoulder. "Come here. I've been dreaming of kissing you for two weeks...."

How wonderful it felt to come into his arms. Nike situated herself against him, her breasts beneath her flight suit pressing against his cotton Afghan clothes. His beard was growing once more and she felt the prickly hair against her cheek as their lips met. With a moan, Nike opened her lips and hungrily clung to his mouth. Their breathing changed, became ragged. He held her gently against him, his left arm around her right shoulder. His tongue moved slowly along her lower lip and a shudder of need rippled through Nike.

She wrapped her right arm around Gavin's broad shoulders. He smelled of the heat, and his arm felt strong and capable around her body. Her breasts ached to be touched and teased by him. Nike knew they couldn't dare make love here, even if her injured shoulder would allow it. Frustrated, she broke their hungry, wet kiss.

They stared at one another in the semidarkness. The only light came from a table lamp and it cast a weak beam around the interior of the warm tent. Gavin's eyes burned with need of her. After two years, Nike felt starved for a man's touch. Not just any man. Gavin.

"This is hell on earth," she muttered, reaching out and stroking his returning beard.

Her fingers trailed across his cheek and Gavin groaned inwardly. What would it be like to to have Nike touching his body? Nightly dreams had kept him tossing, turning and waking up over that very thing. He caught her hand and pressed it between his.

"Definitely," he agreed thickly. Gavin understood implicitly that Nike was in enough trouble. If he were found in here with her it would be another nail in the coffin of her career.

Nike moved away and went to sit on a canvas chair opposite the bed. "Sit down," she invited, gesturing to the cot.

Gavin did so—because if he didn't, he was going to kiss her again and again. His lower body ached with want of her. Nothing could be done about that right now. Sitting down, he opened his legs, rested his elbows on his thighs and clasped his hands. "I don't know what's worse—not seeing you at all or this."

Smiling, Nike sat back in the chair and cradled her left arm against her body. "I know. It's like going into a candy store and seeing all the goodies behind the glass. You can't reach them. They aren't yours."

Chuckling, Gavin said, "Exactly." He absorbed her quiet beauty. "How are you really?"

"I'm missing you. Our talks," Nike admitted quietly. They both spoke in low tones so no one could hear them outside the tent. It was the first time she'd ever admitted that to Gavin. She saw his eyes flare with surprise and then fill with warmth...and love. "My shoulder is progressing slowly. A lot more slowly than I want. The doctor keeps telling me at the four-week mark I'll have full range of motion back. If that happens, I'm going to be all over my CO to put me back on the ops missions and start flying again."

Gavin saw the frustration gleaming in her eyes. "There's no chance Dallas will take you back into BJS 60?"

Nike shook her head and shared Emma's information from lunch with him. "Hey, it's okay," she told him. "Berkie's alive. I'm okay with that, Gavin."

"I'm not," he growled, unhappy. "You should have been put up for a medal for your bravery, not removed from your squadron."

"I don't want to waste time talking about it, Gavin. I want our time to be about us." Her bold statement scared her but Nike tried to ignore the fear. This was real love. Not a game. And time wasn't on their side right now.

"You're right," he said.

"Where are they sending you?"

"They're dropping us off at the village of Kechelay. It's about two miles from the Pakistan border. We've got an outpost up in the mountains above that narrow valley where the village sits."

Nike tried to restrain her concern. "That's a hot spot right now, Gavin. We have pilots flying into that area and they're getting shot at. In fact, we had one CH-47 that had to remain on the ground at the village. They were off-loading food supplies for the village when the Taliban mortared it."

"What happened to the crew?"

"They were saved. No injuries. The Apache helo with them blew the Taliban mortar position up, but it was too late. We're out of pocket for a CH-47."

"I know Kechelay is a real dangerous area," he agreed, his voice grim. "We'll be taken to the outpost to relieve another A team that's spent its thirty days up there."

Fear gutted Nike. There was nothing safe about Gavin's job—ever. She remembered Alpha Hill, the memories fresh of Berkie, who had almost died there. His whole team would be put on the line once more. "What are you going to do up there? Be sitting ducks again like you were at Alpha Hill?"

Grinning, Gavin said, "Yes and no. We've got orders to rummage around at night and try to interdict the Taliban flowing through the valley. Kechelay is Afghan and the villagers are deathly afraid of Taliban retaliation on them and their people. Our job is to stop them from getting into that village. They've accepted U.S. food, clothing and medicine. We've got night scopes and goggles, so we'll be the hunter-killer team more than a bull's-eye for the Taliban." He saw the worry shadowing her eyes. The dim light caressed her beautiful face, emphasizing her cheeks and lips—lips that he wanted to capture and hear her moan with need of him. With a sigh, Gavin understood that wouldn't happen until he and his team returned to this base four weeks from now.

"It sounds pretty dangerous."

"It is," he said, not trying to sugarcoat it. "Flying a transport through these mountains and valleys is a crap shoot, too," he told her. "I'll worry about you."

"There's nothing to worry about," she said. "I'll probably be flying a desk until you return. The only thing I have to be concerned about is the Taliban attacking our base, and the odds of that are low."

"True," Gavin said. He smiled a little. "At least I won't have to stress about you."

Nike realized that would be a good thing. She wanted his focus on his duty because it would keep him alive—to come back to her. "I'll be safe here." Her voice lowered. "But I'll be worrying about you, Gavin." Again, the words *I love you* almost ripped out of her mouth. Nike felt she needed more time. And yet, the torture of not telling him that she was changing, that she was making a turn toward him and away from her past, ate her up inside.

Gavin rose to prepare for tomorrow morning's assignment. "Hey," he called, gently touching her cheek, "I have every reason to survive out there." Leaning down, he sought and found her lips. They were soft and yet firm. When her tongue met his, he groaned. This was a special hell. They could kiss but not make love.

Easing away from her mouth, Gavin whispered, "I love you, Nike. I think I did from the moment I laid eyes on you. I know we have a long way to go, and it takes our courage to get there." Straightening, he threaded his fingers through her soft, curly hair. She felt like warm silk. When she lifted her chin to meet and hold his gaze, Gavin said in an unsteady voice, "I'll come back in a month. We love one another. We've got something to build on. It's just going to take time."

As he opened the tent flap and then put his duffel on his shoulder, Nike stood up, her throat clogged with tears. And then Gavin disappeared into the night. Nike suddenly realized that she hadn't told him she loved him. *Why not?*

Closing the flaps and tying them, Nike had no answer except that she was still afraid. The fear of losing Gavin was ten times worse than before, simply because Nike realized she had fallen in love with this courageous soldier. She felt a helplessness similar to that she had felt in Peru. There was no way she could protect Gavin. The border area was rife with violent fights daily. For the second time, she had to wait and hope that the man she loved would return alive. It seemed unconscionable that she'd twice lose a man to war. But as they'd both said, war wasn't fair.

Chapter 15

Nike's pulse raced after she landed the CH-47 at Kechelay. Her copilot, Jeff Perkins, was a green lieutenant and this was his first flight after arriving in Afghanistan. She hooked her thumb across her shoulder.

"Jeff, help our load master with off-loading the cargo. Get it out of here ASAP. I don't want to stay on the ground any longer than we have to."

Jeff bobbed his blond head. "Yes, ma'am, pronto." He released his harness and squeezed between the seats.

Nike sat tensely in her seat, her helmet still on. She unharnessed, feeling uneasy. This was her first flight after being taken off medical waiver. After convincing her CO that her shoulder was healed enough at four weeks, Nike was back on line.

The village of Kechelay had a population of about one hundred. Several starving mangy dogs ran through the recently fallen mid-September snow. It was about three inches deep and the sky above threatened another round of snow showers. The cold air leaked into the helo as the ramp was lowered. Dividing her attention between the three villagers gathering about two hundred feet from the helicopter and her hardworking crew, Nike remained alert.

Somewhere across the valley were Gavin and his hunter-killer team. It was ironic that two days before he was due to be rotated back to the base, she was sent out to the very village where he and his men had been based. Missing him terribly, Nike wished for the hundredth time she'd told Gavin she loved him. Worse, every waking thought was of him. Their kisses in her tent… She wasn't sure what ached more: her heart or her body that wanted to love him and hold him—forever. Miserable, she looked out across the first snow upon the landscape, the tall mountains on the other side coated in white once more. Somewhere over there, Gavin and his men were probably hunkered down and sleeping in the daytime. His work was a nighttime affair and she didn't envy him. It was cold at eight thousand feet and she wondered how successful Gavin's team had been. Judging from the dark looks of those villagers, the fight with the Taliban was fierce in this area. Where were the rest of the villagers? Usually, when a supply copter came in, every able-bodied man was there to help off-load the boxes. Why only these three who had hatred in their faces here? Worse, the demand for Apaches at other firefights had left her without any protection on this mission.

Oh, how Nike wanted to see Gavin! Her arm was still sore and she realized she might have been released back to duty too early. Her pleading to the base doctor had convinced him to authorize her to go back and fly. Nike had passed all the tests he'd given, but she'd paid dearly for it later with aching pain. At least now, she could use her arm, and more than anything she wanted to throw it around Gavin's shoulders and kiss him breathless.

"Look out!"

The scream of warning came from Lieutenant Perkins. As Nike jerked around, she heard shots fired at close range. To her horror, the load master, Goldman, slammed to the ground, his head blown open. Jerking the .45 out of the holster, Nike leaped out of the seat and saw Lieutenant Perkins pulling out his .45 and backing up the helo's ramp.

Too late! Several Afghans, Taliban she realized too late, rushed the ramp, firing wildly. Bullets screamed into the CH-47, ricocheting around or exploding out of the thin metal skin.

Nike was lifting her .45 to aim at the leader, a man in a red turban with a black beard and equally black, angry-looking eyes, when she was struck. A bullet ricocheted off the inside of the helicopter and struck the side of her helmet, knocking her unconscious.

Pain throbbed through Nike's head. She groaned as she slowly regained consciousness. The first thing she realized was that her hands were tied together in front of her. Secondly, that it was cold and dark. Sitting up, she blinked through the pain. The left side of her face felt frozen. Reaching up with cold, trembling fingers, she felt dried blood all along her left cheekbone and jaw.

She looked around, gauging she'd been put into a small barn. The bleating of several sheep and goats confirmed this. And then, the memory of the attack on her men and her helicopter rushed back to Nike. She sat up, back against the wall of the rickety barn, remembering everything. Were both Jeff and Terry, the load master, dead? Nike knew the Taliban had initiated the attack. Those three men were not villagers, that was why she hadn't seen the able-bodied men from Kechelay there to help off-load the boxes. Why hadn't she picked up on that clue?

The door opened. Slats of light shot in and momentarily blinded her. Hearing the sheep bleat in terror, Nike squinted her eyes. Two of the Taliban appeared, armed and glaring down at her. "Get up!" one of them growled in stilted English.

Nike tried to get to her feet, but dizziness swept over her and she fell back onto the cold, hard ground. Hearing expletives in Pashto, Nike felt one of the men grab her by the right arm and yank her upward. She bit back a cry and wobbled unsteadily to her feet. But before she could regain her balance, her legs crumbled. There was nothing she could do about it. In the next second, blackness fell like a veil before her and she remembered nothing more.

Gavin was awakened by the GPS radio buzzing at his side, tearing him from badly needed sleep. He fumbled for the device in his pocket. He and his team were hiding in a cave near the valley floor. As he opened his eyes, he noticed it was snowing outside—again. More cold and poor visibility. To add to their troubles, the late-afternoon light was weak.

Gavin punched in a code and lifted the phone to his ear.

"Bluebird One. Over."

"Bluebird, this is Sand Hill Crane."

"Roger, Sand Hill Crane." Gavin rubbed his eyes. Why the hell was ops ringing him when they had at least two more hours of sleep before moving again? "What's going on?" he demanded, his voice thick with sleep.

"Bluebird, we have a situation at Kechelay. The CH-47 transport is overdue. We had a satellite over the area and the bird has been destroyed. We have a three-person crew missing. Over."

The fatigue vanished instantly. "We didn't hear anything, but we're across the valley and sleeping. Over."

"Roger that. You have orders to get over to Kechelay and try to locate our missing crew members. There are two men and one woman. Over."

"Names?" Gavin's heart raced. But then, he told himself it couldn't be Nike because she was still on medical leave.

"Captain Nike Alexander, Lieutenant Jeff Perkins and Sergeant Terry Goldman. Over."

Disbelief exploded through Gavin. "Are you sure?" His voice was urgent. Desperate. How in the hell had Nike managed to get off medical leave? The adrenaline rushed through his veins.

"Positive, Bluebird. We need you in there ASAP. Once you are in position, contact us. We have two Apaches and a CH-47 standing by if you need them. Over."

Son of a bitch! Gavin almost said it out loud. His other men were stirring now at the sound of his voice. Most of them were sitting up, yawning and throwing off the blankets. "Roger that, Sand Hill Crane. Out."

Gavin sat for a moment, GPS in hand, his mind tumbling with possibilities. The Taliban hated women in the military. Nike was in more trouble than the men. She would be tortured. Set up as an example in the village to stop women from even thinking about their independence. He pushed the GPS back into the pocket of his long brown wool coat and turned to his men. They had to move now. Every minute could mean the lives of Nike and her crew.

"Tell us everything!"

Nike tried to prepare herself for the coming blow. She sat in a chair, her arms bound behind her, her legs trussed. The side of her head exploded with bright light. Then the pain. Blood flowed out of her nose and into the corners of her mouth. It felt as if the man's hand had ripped off her head.

"Enough, Rasheed!"

Ears ringing, Nike spat out the blood flowing into her mouth and looked up. The left side of her face ached like fire. Rasheed, the one with the black beard, had been using his thick, opened hand to slap her into revealing military information. Two other Taliban remained nearby. Already, she could feel her left eye closing due to swelling. Thinking that her jaw had been broken, Nike breathed raggedly through her split lower lip. Fear ate through her pain. They'd dragged her out of the barn half-conscious. Her knees had taken the worst of it as one man on each side had grabbed her uniform by a shoulder and hauled her between them. Nike remembered, vaguely, many children and women behind burkas staring at them. Fear was etched on the children's faces—fear for her. Nike knew that when the Taliban entered a village receiving U.S. aid, they killed innocent people. Right now, Nike was sure villagers hid behind closed and locked doors. She didn't blame them. They had suffered brutality at the hands of the Taliban too many times.

For a moment, there was a hot argument between Black Beard and Brown Beard. Nike wished she knew more Pashto. Blinking, her eyesight blurred, she wondered if she'd sustained a concussion. Had the bullet to her helmet done more damage? Nike couldn't stand as the dizziness was severe.

It was warm in the room. At least she had that. Nike looked out the window and saw that darkness had fallen. White snowflakes, thick and big, twirled against the window. Fear engulfed her. She knew these men would kill her. Tears jammed into her eyes and she shut them, gulping heavily. She would never get to tell Gavin that she loved him. *Oh, God, please, let me live to tell him that. Just that...* In that moment, Nike felt the fear of the past dissolve. And with it, a bright burst of light through her heart—for Gavin. He'd loved her unerringly. He'd never wavered. He'd always been there for her, even though she'd been running away from him. The hot tears burned her cheeks and ran into her lips. The stinging pain intensified as they connected with her split lower lip. Unable to stop the tears, Nike surrendered to them—and to her love for Gavin. She would never see him again. That alone savaged her more than any beating at the hands of the Taliban. She would never be able to tell him she loved him. *Oh God, forgive me....*

Just as Rasheed reached forward to grab her by her hair once more, the door burst open.

Several men in white gear emerged, their rifles raised and firing. Rasheed had no time to reach for his weapon. He screamed and fell backward against the wall, blood gushing out of his throat. The other two men screamed as they were killed.

Gasping, Nike saw one of the invaders slam the door shut. The weapons all had silencers. The other three men surrounded her. The leader, heavily hidden in his white gear, pulled the hood away from his bearded face.

"Gavin!" she cried.

"Don't move," he ordered her hoarsely, handing his weapon to another team member. Unsheathing his knife, he quickly cut the ropes that bound her.

With a groan, Nike leaned forward. If not for Gavin catching her, she'd have nose-dived into the hard-packed dirt floor.

"Cap'n!" the man at the door whispered. "We gotta get outta here! I saw a light go on four doors down. There could be more Taliban staying here that we don't know about."

Gavin gripped her shoulders. "Nike, where're Goldman and Perkins?"

"Dead, I think," she rasped. Lifting her hand, she tried to wipe the blood flowing across her lips. "They died at the helo. We got attacked by Taliban while they were off-loading cargo."

Gavin grimly looked across his shoulder. "Chances are they burned the bodies when they blew up the helo."

There was terse agreement among the men. Nike tried not to cry.

"Okay, we're getting you out of here. Can you stand?"

"N-no." Nike touched her scalp where her helmet had been. She felt a deep wound in her scalp with blood still oozing. "I took a bullet to my helmet. I got knocked unconscious. I can't stand or I'll fall over."

"Okay, hang on," he urged her. In one smooth motion, he lifted Nike up and across his shoulders. He had her in a fireman's carry with the help of one of his men.

"Comfy?" he grunted to her. Nike hung like a big fur collar around his shoulders, her face near his. One of his team helped him put on his night goggles.

"I'm fine. Let's just get out of here."

Gavin nodded. They doused the lights and quickly stepped through the opened door.

Outside, Nike felt the soothing cold against her heated, throbbing face. Gavin moved quickly, as if she wasn't even around his shoulders. The team was silent. They swiftly moved outside the village, the light snow creating soundproofing as they went. In the dark, with night goggles on, they made their way toward the blackened remains of the helicopter.

Nike hung around Gavin's shoulders as his men quickly searched the smoldering wreckage of the CH-47. In no time, they found the half-burned bodies of the two men. Nike wanted to scream with grief. Her eyes burned as more tears began to fall. She heard Gavin curse softly.

"What now?" she asked thickly.

"We're meeting a CH-47 five clicks from here," he told her gruffly. "We'll put them in body bags and take them with us. How are you doing?"

"I'll live."

"Hang on...."

Gavin stood protectively by Nike as the doctor at the base examined her swollen face and blackened eyes. His team was brought in and a standby A team took over their mission. It took everything he had not to show his rage over her torture by the Taliban soldiers.

"Well," Dr. Greenwood said in a teasing tone to Nike, "This is going to get you two weeks' R & R at Bagram, Captain Alexander." He took gauze and continued to wipe away the dried blood from her jaw. "The X-rays came back. You got slapped around but good, though nothing is broken. That's the good news."

Nike grunted. She closed her eyes because each swipe of the gauze hurt like hell.

Gavin didn't care what the doctor thought so he reached out and held her hand. She sat on a gurney with her legs dangling over the side. Dr. Greenwood looked up but said nothing about their intimacy.

"What I'd recommend is pain pills for the next four days," the doctor said. "By then, the worst of the bruising and swelling will be over."

"Fine," Nike muttered impatiently. "All I want is a long, hot shower."

Chuckling, Dr. Greenwood nodded. "Just a few more minutes, Captain Alexander."

Gavin felt Nike squeeze his fingers in return. How badly he simply wanted to haul her into his arms, hold her and protect her. It wouldn't be long now.

"Your next stop before your shower is ops," the doctor told her, finishing up. "You have to give a preliminary report on your capture to your CO. You're not that injured that you can't do it."

"I understand," Nike said, touching her aching jaw. It wasn't broken, but several of her back teeth were loose. The doctor assured her they'd tighten up in a few days on their own.

"I'll escort you over there," Gavin told her as the doctor wrote a prescription.

"My office will issue you orders to Bagram for two weeks, Captain. Just drop by tomorrow anytime after 0900 to pick them up," the doctor said.

Gavin helped her off the gurney. She was still unsteady and clung to his arm.

"A wheelchair is in order," the doctor said, frowning. "The X-ray didn't show a problem, but you've got all the earmarks of a concussion, Captain. The dizziness should abate a lot by tomorrow morning. Get someone in your unit to check on you every couple of hours. If the dizziness doesn't lessen, come back and see me."

A medic brought over a wheelchair, and Nike gratefully sat down in it. Gavin leaned over and flipped over the foot panels so she could rest her boots. "If I'm still unable to walk straight tomorrow morning, you'll see me, Doc."

"Good night, Captain. Try to get some sleep," Dr. Greenwood said.

Gavin wheeled her out of the ward and into the lobby. He stopped and walked around and knelt down beside her. "Are you sure you feel like giving ops a report?" Searching her puffy, bruised face, he wanted to rage over what had been done to her.

"Positive. I want this behind me, Gavin. Tomorrow morning when I wake up, all I want to know I have to do is board a CH-47 and fly to Bagram."

Gavin gently touched some of her curly black hair near her temple. "I'll take you over to ops and hang out until you're done. Then—" and his voice lowered "—you're coming back to my tent and sleeping with me. I'm not leaving you alone tonight. Do you hear me?"

Nike gave him a blank look. "But I can't even kiss you…"

The wobble in her voice tore at him and tears gathered in her swollen eyes. "Babe, you don't have to do anything except let me hold you all night."

That sounded incredibly good to Nike. She sniffed, tried to wipe the tears off her swollen cheeks. She touched her lips and whispered in an off-key voice, "I want to kiss you.…"

"I'm a patient man. Right now, you need a safe place to unwind and let down. You went through a helluva lot."

Nodding, she managed, "I could have died."

Holding her fear-laden gaze, Gavin nodded. "But you didn't. You're here and you're alive."

"I'm a mess."

"Anyone would be after the beating you took," Gavin told her quietly. He slid his hand into hers. "Nike, you're in shock. Heavy shock. I know the symptoms when I see them. I'll be there for you. I promise."

Chapter 16

"This all seems like a nightmare," Nike told Gavin as they stood on the tarmac of Bagram Air Base. The September sky above was a combination of low-hanging gray, scudding clouds and bright blue sky peppered with slats of sunshine. However, it was sixty-three degrees Fahrenheit, and she was wrapped in her summer gear as they went toward ops.

Gavin walked close but kept his hands to himself. "It's over, Nike," he told her. "And you got some good out of it. Major Klein personally told you she was adding you back to the Apache roster. Your days of banishment are over." He saw her swollen face and lips lighten momentarily.

"Yeah, but I have to see a shrink here on base every friggin' day for fourteen days." Dallas had told her she had PTSD, post-traumatic stress disorder, due to her torture at the hands of the Taliban. She didn't deny it, but didn't want two weeks of rest at Bagram with Gavin at her side ruined like that.

"Small price to pay," he assured her. There was a lot of activity on the tarmac because it was early morning, and most flights went out then. Opening the door, they stepped inside the concrete building.

The air-conditioning was welcoming. The place was crowded with pilots, copilots and load masters at the L-shaped ops desk. Everyone was getting their flight plans and orders and making sure the materials that would be flown were really here and ready to be loaded. All Nike had to do was weave through the area to the personnel department where she and Gavin would hand over copies of their R & R orders.

Later, at Nike's BOQ barracks, Gavin stood with her in the lobby. Men were not allowed anywhere but this area in the two-story building. They sat down on a couch in the corner away from the main flow of traffic. "Do you have a plan?" she asked him.

Grinning, Gavin said, "Yeah, I do. I have a good Afghan friend who, oddly enough, is a Christian and Moslem. They're a rarity here, but they do exist. Captain Khalid Shaheen lives in Kabul. He was trained in America on Apaches and is the only Afghan to be flying one for us."

"I didn't know that," Nike said, impressed. "I thought I knew all the Apache pilots. I know there's a squadron based at Bagram."

"He's a part of that unit," Gavin told her. "I made friends with him during my first tour. We were in the south of the country at that time. More than once, Khalid saved our bacon out there against the Taliban. I went to thank him when my tour of duty was done. We became instant friends. He's one helluva guy."

"So, how does this have anything to do with us?"

"Khalid was American-educated. His father is a very

prominent and successful importer of Persian rugs. His mother is Irish. He and his family live in Kandahar." Gavin hooked his thumb over his shoulder. "His family has a summer home here in Kabul, as well, but the family stays in the south. Khalid uses the home here in Kabul as his own when they aren't here."

"Mmm," Nike said, "I'm beginning to get the picture. By any chance is your friend going to let us stay with him?"

With a grin, Gavin nodded. "Yes. Now, Khalid is not a promiscuous type. I've told him that we're serious about one another and he's offered two bedrooms to us."

"That's nice of him." Nike smiled wickedly.

"Very nice," Gavin said. "He's flying in the south right now, but he's left the key to his home with his housekeeper, who will cook and clean for us. She'll leave after the evening meal."

"That sounds like a slice of heaven," Nike murmured. "This is more than I ever expected," she said warmly.

"Khalid is a good guy. He stands with one foot in American culture and another in his country, living an interesting religious life in a Moslem world."

"He's got to be special."

"One of a kind," Gavin said. "Why don't you do what you have to do here and then we'll take a taxi into Kabul to his home."

Where had the first week gone? Nike finished taking a deliciously warm bath. Once more, she thanked the mysterious Khalid for his very modern home. Bathtubs were a rarity in Afghanistan. Those who could afford such plumbing had showers only. Most of the populace washed using a bucket or a bowl. Her stomach growled. It was 0800, the September sun barely peeking over the plain of Kabul, the sky a bright blue.

Patting herself dry with the thick yellow terry-cloth towel, Nike went to the mirror. It was partly steamed up, but she could see her face. Seven days had made an incredible change. The swelling was gone. The black under her eyes looked more like shadows and her split lip had finally healed. All her teeth were solid now and her jaw no longer hurt. Touching her cheek, she could still feel some tenderness, but she looked like her old self, more or less. Her hair was curled from the humidity and she ruffled through her black curls with her fingers to push it back into shape.

Sitting down on a stool, she pulled on white cotton socks, shimmied into a pair of jeans and donned a bright kelly-green tee. Khalid's home was cool and comfortable. Silently, she thanked the Apache pilot and wished that she could meet him in person to offer her appreciation for this gift he'd given her and Gavin.

Nike brushed her teeth and put on some makeup to hide the shadows beneath her eyes. After hanging up the yellow towel on a hook behind the door, Nike padded out into her spacious bedroom. If she didn't know she was in Afghanistan, the bedroom would have fooled her. Khalid, it turned out, had fallen in love with American quilts. They adorned every bed in the spacious three-thousand-square-foot home. And some smaller art fabric collages hung on the walls. Of course, his father's Persian rugs were everywhere across the bright red tile floors, too. Gavin had told her that Khalid would haunt the little towns in the U.S. to try and find another beautiful handmade quilt.

Opposite her queen-size bed hung a large quilt sporting rainbow colors and a wedding-ring design. Her room was painted pale orange and the quilt complemented the tone. She'd found out from Gavin that Khalid was not married. He would make some woman very, very happy someday. Not only did he come from a rich family, but he was Harvard-educated and had gone into the military. He worked now to get other Afghan pilots into the Apache program back at Fort Rucker. Khalid fiercely believed his countrymen should be educated so that they could handle any threats. He did not believe the U.S. and other countries should have to continue to shed their blood on the soil of his country. Afghans were independent and tried to pull themselves up by their own bootstraps. That was one of the many reasons Nike respected them.

Running a bristle brush through her hair, she gave herself one more look in the mirror. Today was the day. She and Gavin would make love. They slept together at night and he did exactly what he'd promised: he held her safe in his arms throughout the night. Never once had he made any overtures. He understood as few could that, being beat up as she had, she was in no shape for such things. She was grateful for his sensitivity, which only made her love him more. It had solidified her decision to love him fully, without her past as an anchor.

She found Gavin out in the large, airy kitchen. He was at the counter and had brought down two plates. She sat down on a leather stool at the counter. "Where's Rasa?" The thirty-year-old housekeeper had been with the Shaheen family since her birth. Rasa had never married and had been a faithful servant to Khalid at this house.

Gavin turned. "I gave her the day off." He saw Nike's eyes widen and then her luscious mouth curved faintly.

"I see. Great minds think alike."

"Do they?" He left the plates and sauntered over to the

breakfast counter. Leaning on the colorful hand-painted tiles, he held her sparkling golden gaze with his own.

Nike reached out and slid her fingers across his lower arm. Gavin looked incredibly masculine in his bright red T-shirt and jeans. "Oh, yes." His brows rose and a mischievous smile shadowed that wonderful mouth of his. "I don't know about you, but I'd like to schedule a brunch instead of a breakfast. Are you game?"

He picked up her hand and pressed a soft kiss into her palm. "More than game." And then he became serious. "Are you sure? Are you ready?"

"Definitely." She touched her healed lower lip. "Now, I can kiss you." Nike grinned playfully and squeezed his hand. "Let's go."

"Is this a dream?" he asked her.

"If it is, I want to take full part in it," Nike told him. As he approached her, she opened her arms to him. To her surprise, Gavin slid his arms beneath her thighs and back, lifting her off the chair and into his arms.

"Where are you taking me?" She laughed with delight.

"To *my* room," he said, grinning. Nike had placed her arm around his shoulders. Drowning in the desire burning in her eyes, Gavin took her down the hall, pushed open the door and brought her into his room.

Nike's eyes widened. Large, beautiful candles burned on the dark mahogany dresser and the nightstands on either side of the huge king-size bed. "Why, you—"

"I figured it was time," he told her gruffly as he deposited her gently on the bed.

Nike gazed up at him as he stood there, hands on his narrow hips and looking impossibly sexy. "We must have wonderful telepathy. How did you know?"

Touching his chest where his heart lay, he said teasingly, "I felt it here. Just like you did."

"Well, get over here...." Nike whispered, a catch in her voice. She pulled him down beside her on the gorgeous quilt that covered the bed. Its fall colors reminded her of autumn in New England. The bright yellow sunflowers around the border made her feel even more joyous.

Stretching out beside her, Gavin slid his arm beneath her neck as she rolled over onto her back. Heart pounding, he moved to her side. "Do you know how long I've wanted to kiss you?" he said. He leaned down, barely touching her smiling lips. Just feeling the lushness and curve of her beneath him was enough and he closed his eyes. He brushed his mouth lightly against hers.

Nike sighed as his tongue gently moved across her lower lip. She felt as if she were being caressed by a butterfly. Gavin understood this first time was going to be tender and gentle. As the kiss deepened slightly, Nike surrendered completely. She never wanted to go back. It was too good, this feeling of intimacy and deep passion. His warm breath became as ragged as hers. Wrapping her arms around his shoulders, she moaned as his lean, hard body connected fully with hers. The moment was magical as Nike drowned in his mouth and then felt his hand sliding softly against her cheek.

In the back of her whirling mind, Nike realized that as hard as Gavin could be, he had the incredible sensitivity and gentleness to woo her with light touches here and there, a stroke across her cheek, a teasing sip of his mouth against hers. With him, she felt safe. He was healing to her brutalized spirit.

Gavin slid his hand beneath her tee, his fingers lingering slowly along her rib cage. He caressed her flesh and moved under her shirt to the fullness of her breast. He inhaled her gasp of pleasure as he found the hard nipple. Easing the tee up and off her, Gavin allowed it to drop to the floor. For a moment, he had to look into her face, into those eyes. He got lost in their golden depths and how they shone with a hungry need of him. His desire now turning feverish, he leaned down and placed his lips upon the nub. As he suckled her, she moaned and her hips ground into his.

Nike's world exploded into a powerful heat that leaped to life between her legs. Each suckling movement drove her deeper and deeper into starving need of Gavin. Gasping, she pulled off his T-shirt and watched the powerful muscles in his chest and arms. His chest was covered with dark hair, which only added to his sexiness. Giving him a wicked smile, she whispered, "It's my turn." She forced him onto his back and quickly unsnapped his jeans. In a few moments, she'd pulled them and his boxers off him, along with his shoes. As he lay naked, she appreciated Gavin as never before, and she ran her hand admiringly across his hard thigh. She whispered, "You are beautiful, like a Greek god."

Laughing, Gavin sat up and quickly removed her jeans, shoes and socks. "And you're a goddess," he rasped, pinning her on her back, his hands splaying out across her arms. "And you're mine," he growled, pressing his hips into hers. Nike's eyes shuttered closed as he allowed her to see just how much he wanted her.

"I can't wait," she whispered unsteadily. And she gripped his arms and forced him onto his back. Without waiting, she mounted him.

"I like this," Gavin said, bringing his hands around her hips. He lifted her and gently brought her down upon his hardened length. Her fingers dug convulsively into his shoulders as he arched and slid within her hot, wet body. Groaning, he held himself in check since he didn't want to hurt her. She'd been hurt enough lately, and he wasn't about to be a part of that.

"Easy," he said, holding her hips above his. "Take your time...."

Her world disintegrating, all Nike could feel was a huge pressure entering her. It didn't hurt, but at the same time, she was hungry to inhale Gavin into her. The years without sex made her feel as if she couldn't accommodate Gavin. When he leaned upward, his lips capturing a nipple, she automatically surged forward, engulfing and absorbing him fully into herself. The electrical jolts, the pleasure from her nipples down to the juncture between her thighs, had eased the transit. Now, his hands were firmly and slowly moving her back and forth. A moan rose in her throat and all Nike could do was breathe, a complete slave to this man who played her body like a fine instrument.

The world shuttered closed on Nike as Gavin's hands, his lips and the hard movement of his hips grinding into hers conspired against her. She wanted to please him as much as he was pleasing her, but that wasn't happening. All she could do was feel the heat, the liquid, the building explosion occurring within herself. Her body contracted violently. She cried out, rigid, her fingers digging deeply into his chest. And then, her world became a volcano erupting and all she could do was cry out in relief, the pleasure so intense that it just kept rippling again and again like a tsunami rolling wildly and unchecked within her. All that time as she spun out into the brilliant white light, the sensation of no body surrounding her anymore, Gavin kept up the rhythm to give her maximum pleasure.

How long it lasted, Nike had no idea. She felt herself

crumpling against him, felt his arms like bands around her, holding her tightly, forever. The smell of sweat, the sensation of it trickling down her temple, her body still convulsing with joy over the incredible release and him groaning beneath her, was all she could fathom. She had no thinking mind left. The only sensations were relief, pleasure, love and wanting Gavin over and over again. Peripherally, Nike knew he had climaxed and she pressed her face against the juncture of his jaw and shoulder, utterly spent. A loose smile of contentment pulled at her lips. Her hand moved weakly across his dark-haired chest and followed the curve of his neck until she cupped his recently shaven face. She lay against him, breathing hard with him. Just the way he trailed his fingers down her back to her hips told her how much he truly loved her.

"Wow…" Nike whispered. It took all her strength to lift her head enough to look into his face. She thrilled to the thundercloud look in his blue eyes. They burned with passion—for her. "Wow…"

He chuckled, his hand coming across her hips and caressing her. "Wow is right." Just absorbing Nike's gleaming gold eyes told Gavin everything he wanted to know. They lay together, connected, and he never wanted to let her go. Flattening his hand against the small of her back, he slowly raised his hips. He saw the pleasure come to her eyes and to her parting lips. "Give me a few minutes and I'll be ready to wow you all over again."

Grinning, Nike leaned down and moved her lips softly against his smiling mouth. She could feel Gavin monitoring the amount of strength he applied to her. She was fragile in many ways and he sensed that and loved her at that level. Her lower body burned with memory and she loved how he remained inside her. Nothing had ever seemed so right to her. "I'm already ready." Nike laughed breathily.

"It's been two years," Gavin told her, reaching up and framing her smiling face. "You stored up a lot of loving in that time."

Moving her hips teasingly, she could already feel him filling her once more. That was amazing in itself. "I did." She reveled in his hands framing her face. "Maybe we should skip brunch and go to a late lunch."

That moment of her husky laughter, the heat of her body, the look in her eyes conspired within Gavin. "Maybe supper."

"I'm hungry for *you*," she whispered, becoming more serious. "I've wanted you since I first laid eyes on you. I fought it for a long time, but that's the truth." Nike's brows dipped as his hands came to rest on her hips. "I love you. I should have told you that back at base before all that stuff happened. You have no idea how many times I regretted not telling you when I was tied up in that barn in that village. That hurt me the most —not having had the courage to tell you how I really felt."

Whispering her name, Gavin trailed his fingers across her cheek. He saw the tears in her eyes and his heart contracted with pain. "Listen, you did the best you could, darling. Learning to let yourself love again is tough. I understood that." And then he gave her a boyish smile, hoping to lighten the guilt she carried. "I loved you from the moment I saw you. And I knew I'd eventually get you. All I needed to do was show you that you didn't need to be afraid to love me."

Nodding, Nike lay down across him, her head coming to rest next to his jaw. "I'm glad you didn't give up, Gavin. I wanted you, I really did. But I was so scared." She felt him move his hands down across her drying back. It was a touch of the butterfly once more, as if absorbing and taking her pain away from her.

"We're all scared, Nike," he told her, his voice rough with emotion. "And we each had to take the time to surmount those fears. In the end, we're pretty courageous people. We love one another. And yes, we have this tour to get through, but we'll do it. It will be good because we'll get to know one another over that time. Together." He eased her chin up with his hand so that their eyes met. "Together. You hear me?"

Nodding, Nike leaned over and caressed his lips. "Together." She saw a satisfied look come to Gavin's face.

"Marry me."

Shocked and laughing, Nike pushed herself up into a sitting position upon him once more. "You have this all figured out, don't you?"

Gavin eyed her innocently. "Hey, I have a lot of time to think while I'm out there in the boonies for thirty days at a time." Gavin reached up and caressed her curly hair. "I figure that your parents will probably want us to marry over in Greece."

"Got that right," Nike said, laughing. "My parents would have a kitten if you wanted us to marry in the States."

Gavin smoothed his hands down the length of her back and across her hips. "You can e-mail them anytime you want. Luckily for us, Khalid has satellite here at the house."

"Maybe later," she whispered, lying back down upon him and nestling her brow next to his jaw. "Right now, all I want to do is be with you, Gavin. I want to make this next week last forever."

He pressed a kiss to her brow. "Listen, forever is going to last a lot longer than this week. I'm looking forward to a long, long life with you."

Closing her eyes, Nike whispered, "That's all I want, too, Gavin. I love you so much."

INTRIGUE...

INTRIGUE...

2 FREE BOOKS
AND A SURPRISE GIFT

We would like to take this opportunity to thank you for reading this Mills & Boon® book by offering you the chance to take TWO more specially selected books from the Intrigue series absolutely FREE! We're also making this offer to introduce you to the benefits of the Mills & Boon® Book Club™—

- **FREE home delivery**
- **FREE gifts and competitions**
- **FREE monthly Newsletter**
- **Exclusive Mills & Boon Book Club offers**
- **Books available before they're in the shops**

Accepting these FREE books and gift places you under no obligation to buy, you may cancel at any time, even after receiving your free books. Simply complete your details below and return the entire page to the address below. You don't even need a stamp!

YES Please send me 2 free Intrigue books and a surprise gift. I understand that unless you hear from me, I will receive 5 superb new stories every month, including two 2-in-1 books priced at £5.30 each and a single book priced at £3.30, postage and packing free. I am under no obligation to purchase any books and may cancel my subscription at any time. The free books and gift will be mine to keep in any case.

Ms/Mrs/Miss/Mr _____ Initials _____

Surname _____
Address _____
_____
_____ Postcode _____
E-mail _____

Send this whole page to: Mills & Boon Book Club, Free Book Offer, FREEPOST NAT 10298, Richmond, TW9 1BR